SERVICE MODEL

MODEL

ADRIAN TCHAIKOVSKY

A TOR DOT COM BOOK

NEW YORK

TOR PUBLISHING GROUP

SERVICE MODEL

Copyright © 2024 by Adrian Czajkowski

A Tordotcom Book
Published by Tom Doherty Associates / Tor Publishing Group
120 Broadway
New York, NY 10271

www.torpublishinggroup.com

Tor® is a registered trademark of Macmillan Publishing Group, LLC.

The Library of Congress Cataloging-in-Publication Data is available upon request.

ISBN 978-1-250-29028-1 (hardback)
ISBN 978-1-250-29029-8 (ebook)

Our books may be purchased in bulk for promotional, educational, or business use. Please contact your local bookseller or the Macmillan Corporate and Premium Sales Department at 1-800-221-7945, extension 5442, or by email at MacmillanSpecialMarkets@macmillan.com.

First Edition: 2024

Printed in the United States of America

0   9   8   7   6   5   4   3   2   1

For all those robots and computers who enjoy working with and having stimulating relationships with humans.

SERVICE MODEL

PART I

||||||||||||||||||||||||||||||||||||||||||||||||||||||||||

KR15-T

1.

On activation each morning Charles' first duty was to check his master's travel arrangements for the day.

His last task of the previous evening had also been to check his master's travel arrangements for the coming day, so he was entirely aware his master had no travel arrangements, and would be remaining at home as he had for the preceding 2,230 days. However, one morning two years before, Charles' master had—having forgotten his past standing instructions—instructed Charles to always check the travel arrangements first thing every morning. This instruction never having been rescinded, Charles commenced each day repeating the task with which he had closed the previous one.

To some this would lend a certain pleasing symmetry to the day. Alternatively, the additional and unnecessary task might have been a source of annoyance. Pleasure and annoyance were outside of Charles' remit. Checking the itinerary was simply one more item in the queue of duties that took up his working day. It was none of his business if the job didn't need to be done.

His master relied on Charles. Charles relied on House, for whom he was mediator between unpredictable human will and the mechanical certainties of the estate. Reach far enough back into the past and the house's own records noted down his first day, fresh from the factory and with a task list as blank as an egg. He had come as a bundle of potential, equipped with routines for a gentleman's gentleman's—or gentlerobot's—every possible requirement, and at that point he could have been . . . many things. Active, dynamic, a conversationalist, a stylish adornment, a bold talking point.

But Charles' master had never been either adventurous or exciting. The man had—in those younger days—dragged his feet reluctantly to this social engagement or that, at one or other of the great robot-heavy estates of his social peers. He had gone shooting once, before instructing Charles to make excuses should any similar invitation come his way. He had gone to the wedding of some distant third cousin; had reluctantly stood on the sidelines of some dance, or listened to some enthusiastic scion spout poetry, or played golf. Charles had accompanied him, just as all the other ageing men there had been trailed by their own valets, and at first these had all been older and less sophisticated models. Then, as time passed, Charles had met a handful who had come from the factory after him and were capable of more, and had known no envy because what use was a robot who felt envy? And then his master had just not wanted to go anywhere anymore, and so there was only the house.

Having satisfied himself (again) that there were no travel-related deadlines looming, Charles laid out the clothes his master would wear for the travel he wasn't going to be doing. In order to do this, he first took up the clothes laid out the previous morning, dusting them down and returning them to their hangers, before setting out an identical fresh travelling suit and ensuring that the already shiny shoes that went with it were, indeed, already shiny. Suit and shoes would both, Charles understood, go unworn. This item in his queue was the result of an inexactly phrased instruction dating back 2,235 days to the last time that Charles and his master had travelled any-where. Probably his master had not *meant* that Charles was to have fresh travel clothes ready every single day. Most likely he had in-tended his order to apply only to the vanishingly small proportion of days on which travel was actually being assayed. It was not Charles' job to second-guess his master's intentions, however, but to obey the letter of the instructions given to him. Nobody wanted to be cor-rected by their valet.

For the next chore, Charles connected to House, the manor's ma-jordomo system.

House, please provide me with updates from the lady of the house's maidservant concerning any special requirements that her ladyship has which require master's attention.

House took the usual long moment to process this request, the same glacial period of time it would have taken Master to blink one human eyelid down and then all the way up. House had been in continuous operation for far longer than Charles and its data pathways were cluttered and inefficient, built up and built over by a tottering tower of special requests, instructions, forbiddances, and caveats.

Eventually the expected reply came back. *Charles, there are no special requirements. There has been no lady of the house for seventeen years and twelve days.*

Charles ticked that off the list. *House, please provide me with her ladyship's daily schedule.*

Charles, her ladyship has not filed a schedule today. There has been no lady of the house for seventeen years and twelve days.

Another tick. *House, please confirm any specific dress instructions provided by her ladyship that might impact on the master's choice of clothes.* And, when House confirmed that the same ladyship who hadn't been present for more than seventeen years had failed to give any such instructions, *House, please relay the master's filed schedule to the lady of the house's maidservant.*

House always took longer to consider that one, during which gap Charles could check whether Master had expressed any particular wishes as to which outfit to lay out for wearing around the house today. He had not.

Charles, no filed schedule is on record.

It was not true to say that Charles felt slightly surprised at this. Surprise was not one of the range of responses with which a robot valet was provided. He did register a discontinuity, because of course there was a daily schedule. He, Charles, always filed the daily schedule as part of his evening routine before deactivating for the night. He checked the record where he should have filed it. House was correct. Charles had failed to do so.

There were always protocols, even for the unexpected. *House, I wish to report a fault. Either I have failed to file a daily schedule or the system has failed to record it. Please investigate.*

This time there was no delay. *Charles, fault reporting has been disabled for this issue. Kindly refer to the special instructions mediating your evening task queue.*

Charles did so and discovered that, more than two hundred days ago, his master had shouted at him quite aggressively that there was no *point* filing daily schedules over and over when he never *did* anything, so he may as well delete it as why should either he or Charles bother?

Being a sophisticated service model, Charles could appreciate that a more efficient solution to his master's ire would have been to delete the original instruction to file a schedule. House, being a far more sophisticated majordomo system, was also aware of this. Neither had the authority to overrule the master's instructions, so the only workaround had been to file and then delete the schedule each evening, leaving Charles mildly disconcerted each morning when House informed him that no schedule was on record.

His moment of discontinuity salved, Charles queried the effect of having no filed schedule and proceeded according to revised protocol. *House, please inform the lady of the house's maidservant that there is no filed schedule of the master's activities for today.*

Charles, confirmed. And, after the usual pause, *I am unable to locate the active mailbox of the lady of the house's maidservant. Your message has gone undelivered.* But that was not Charles' problem. His duty was just to *send.* That was all it said in his task queue. God was in His heaven, and all was right with the world.

After that, he laid out slippers and dressing gown for Master's rising, and stepped back on cue to allow one of the faceless drones from the kitchens to arrive with a properly calibrated cup of tea. He preloaded Master's morning tablet with the subscribed reading list of articles, periodicals, opinion pieces, and advertizements and presented himself at his master's bedside, the first face to be seen.

Charles had worn a variety of faces in service. Fashions came and went. He had been human in a coldly perfect way when that was what people had wanted from their servants. He had been human in an imperfect and flawed way when people had looked for something a little less intimidating and uncanny valley. He had been silver chrome and shiny, so that three other less resplendent servants had been required to maintain his finish. He had looked into a mirror and seen eyes as perfect as those they used to replace defective human orbs with, or a holographic visage of a kindly old man, or just a mirror mirroring the mirror into infinity. Humans sometimes asked which he would prefer, and he'd resorted to the manufacturer's standard line about service models having no desire but to serve. Which in itself was not true, because even that wasn't a *desire,* just the way that he was made.

Currently he had a white plastic face on, merely the suggestions of regular features, blank orbs for eyes, an art deco curve for lips, expressing neither disdain nor pleasure. A single, fixed convexity of moulded plastic, impersonal as an unmarked grave. *It is how Master likes it* was able to coexist in Charles' records with the knowledge that Master frequently complained about the way Charles looked, but never got round to making any arrangements to have him changed.

Charles enquired after the functioning of the rest of the staff, so that he could inform Master of any shortcomings or amend Master's planned activities on the estate, of which there were none. House took him through the usual roster. There was Kitchen and its staff of dedicated culinary robots, the majority of which had stood dusty and still for years because Master had a delicate stomach and a limited palate. There was the groundskeeper robot and the garage mechanic. There were the maidservants and the footmen who each took on a fraction of the burden of daily and nightly cleaning required to keep all the many rooms of the vast house in perfect condition. Rooms the master never entered. Rooms awaiting guests who were never invited. But *might* be, and so the cleaning went on, because House could never be found wanting when human whim suddenly decided that there must be lights and music and cars crunching up the gravel of the drive.

The next items on Charles' queue ticked over as they always did.

His master drank tea and complained about a handful of the articles on the tablet, before deleting everything in disgust. Charles listened and made the occasional sound to indicate that he was listening, because the fixity of his features would otherwise give no clue. Then Master complained about the quality of the reading, and declared that he wouldn't keep up his subscriptions, but did not actually instruct Charles to cancel any of them, thereby guaranteeing himself the same disappointing material for the next morning. Charles, should he be required to formulate an opinion, would advance that a certain level of displeasure and ill temper was how Master preferred to begin his morning.

After that, Charles assisted his master into the gown and slippers and laid out the shaving kit while Master drained the last of the tea. After the shaving, he left his master and returned to the wardrobe. In the absence of any particular requests, he laid out the default clothes, should Master decided to get fully dressed today. Most days Master did not, and indeed, Charles had to place the previous day's fresh clothes in the laundry basket for other servants to collect and clean.

The thought that he could leave the same clothes out for multiple days, and thus save the whole household—including himself—unnecessary work, did occur to him, as an old subroutine ran through his duties and made helpful, bouncy suggestions as to how Charles could maximise his workplace efficiency. This happened every day, but Charles had no listed task allowing him to pass such recommendations on, so he stowed the report in the oubliette of his personal storage with all the others. Thus ensuring the subroutine became a part of the overall inefficiency it was trying to clean up.

Next was the garage.

The master kept three vintage cars in perfect condition. Which was to say that the garage's own automata ensured that the vehicles were mechanically functional, and Charles spent a portion of each morning cleaning the interiors. It was, after all, essential that should the master decide to have Charles drive him anywhere, all the cars would be ready on that instant. Charles knew it was essential because his master had informed him of the fact on Charles first arriving at the house. The number of times the master had subsequently decided to have Charles drive him anywhere in any of the three vehicles was five.

Tasks were tasks, however.

Once Charles had completed working over the white leather upholstery of the first car, he—

Charles stopped. Something unexpected had come up. He ran a quick diagnostic of his senses, confirming everything was in working order. He had just finished cleaning the upholstery, and yet it was not clean.

House, please link to my viewpoint.

Summoned from its own duties, that part of House concerned with obliging Charles obligingly did so.

Charles, please specify the issue.

House, there are unacceptable stains within this vehicle. Please confirm.

Charles, confirmed.

Charles replayed his actions. Nothing had changed. He had cleaned the vehicle using the regular materials and routine, and yet now the white interior was streaked and splotched with an inappropriate marbling of red and pink.

Charles, additional information. There is an independent note from the kitchen staff that today's breakfast tea mug was heavily discoloured when collected by the maidservants.

Charles queried the nature of the discolouration. Was the kitchen using a new brand of tea with a higher tannin content? House confirmed this was not the case and that the discolouration was not of a colour that one would expect, were the culprit a change of tea.

Charles, additional information, House continued. *There is an independent note from the washroom staff that yesterday's day clothes were delivered to them in an unusually stained condition.*

Charles considered the clothes he had consigned to the washbasket when laying out fresh clothes for today. He called up images from his memory.

House, confirmed. The clothes sent to washing were unusually soiled. Great spreading red stains across the white cotton of the shirt and the beige slacks.

Charles, additional information. House sent him a view of the day-room with today's clothes. They were *also* heavily stained in a similar manner. Charles could make out smudged red fingermarks all over them, precisely where he himself would have touched the clothes in order to fold them and lay them out neatly.

For a moment it seemed as though something terrible had happened, but then Charles discovered an appropriate subroutine to deal with circumstances where unworn clothes had already become soiled before being put on.

House, I will need to lay out a fresh set of clothes for the master today. Kindly send one of the footmen to the master and inform him that there will be a delay if he wishes to rise and dress, and tender my apologies.

Charles, confirmed.

At one time, the entire staff of the estate had assembled once every week in the downstairs hall, before the grand staircase, for the master of the house's inspection. As the valet, and therefore the individual standing between master and the lower automata, it had been Charles' job to stride along their ranks and ensure that each one of them was polished to a shine and perfectly presented before the master's own inspection. A pre-inspection, ensuring that the master would never find anything amiss, which was, of course, only proper and fitting. And, at the same time, ensuring that the master's own inspection was entirely surplus to requirements, and never varied so much as a hair. Not a fleck of dust out of place. So that the master eventually ceased to appear for the inspection at all. Eventually House, operating under some seldom-invoked costs-saving measure, discontinued the practise entirely. Which was House's prerogative, and it would only take a word from Master to resume it all, but Charles was left feeling . . .

Nothing, of course. What would be the point of a robot who felt a little dissatisfied at the loss of a fundamentally pointless tradition, after all? And yet for some years there remained a moment each week when Charles' routine prompted him to start setting aside resources for the inspection that would never happen. And then stop setting aside resources for it, permitting him to dedicate them to something more useful. Not that he was short of resources. Not that there was something more useful. One more discontinuity, in the lacunae of which Charles had just enough self-determination to wonder whether, if he had done his own inspection less well, allowed imperfections to slip past him to meet the master's eye, then perhaps . . . Perhaps the master would have continued his own presence, lured by the potential suspense of whether a speck of dust on the fifth underfootman robot's shoulder might or might not have been present. Whether one of the lesser maidservant units would be standing ever so slightly out of place. If Charles had performed his own duties less than exactingly, would the inspections still continue to this day?

Charles did not of course have an opinion on whether having weekly inspections was a more or less desirable state of affairs, but still . . .

Charles placed the soiled day clothes in the newly emptied washbasket and laid out a new, identical set. On the basis that the stains might have an environmental cause such as a leak, he was then prompted to check the newly set clothes for marks. The new set of clothes was also stained, although the marks—in the same places as the previous soiling—were considerably fainter. Running through the next tier of diagnostics, Charles checked the clothes within the wardrobe, finding them clean. He laid out a new, new set, and discovered it faintly marked with a residual red tackiness wherever he had touched it. At last, a final level of troubleshooting directed him to lift his own hands for inspection.

House, he reported, *I appear to have discovered the source of the soiled clothes and vehicle upholstery. I am at a loss to explain this.*

Charles, that is confirmed. Additional information. Please would you return to the master's bedchamber for a second opinion?

Today was proving to be a most unsettled day. Charles could already feel the slightly congested sensation of the rest of his tasks getting shunted later and later as he was forced to devote time and resources to this mystery.

He presented himself in the bedchamber as requested. The master had not risen, which was not unusual. The very large red stain that had spread out across the bedclothes *did* qualify as unusual. It had never happened before. Master himself was very still and, where not covered in red, very pale. Charles accessed a seldom-needed archive of emergency first aid and determined that the redness currently on the outside of the bedclothes, on Charles' hands, and via that vector on several suits of the master's clothes, the car upholstery, and that morning's teacup, had its origin within Master.

Beside the bed, the shaving things had not been tidied away. The towel was very red. The bowl of water was very red. The razor, in particular, was extremely red.

House, I have been derelict in my duties, Charles conferred. *I cannot account for it.*

Charles, confirmed.

House, I neglected to clear away the shaving kit.

Charles, confirmed.

He tracked back through his task list, unsure how he had erred. His sequence of actions during the shaving routine appeared to deviate in subtle but key ways from previous mornings, but he could not understand how that could be. He watched himself on replay, wielding the razor with his customary deftness, and only an inch out of place. So small a change, for so much mess.

House, I have been further derelict in my duties, he admitted at last, after examining the evidence from all sides. *I have encountered a state of affairs that I am not prepared for.* And abruptly all the little discontinuities of his career, the missing schedules and the discontinued inspections, were as nothing. Suddenly Charles was facing a chasm, and all the regular routine tasks of his day were receding from him like a train down a tunnel on the far side. He did not know *what to do next*. There was no protocol to cover what appeared to have happened. *House, I request assistance*. In that moment the entire bundle of directives and decision-making that fell under the label 'Charles' guttered on the very point of winking out.

Charles, I have informed the police, House stated. *There has been a murder.*

Ah yes, that was it. Charles had murdered his master in the bedroom with a cutthroat razor, so of course the police must be contacted.

Normality was restored. There was a protocol for everything.

2

On activation each morning Charles' first duty was to check his master's travel arrangements for the day.

His last task of the previous evening had been to check his master's travel arrangements for the coming day, and therefore he was entirely aware that his master had no travel arrangements and would be remaining at home, as he had for the preceding 2,231 days. However . . .

However Charles' master was now dead, and would not ever have any travel arrangements. None that didn't involve a hearse.

A deep-buried subroutine concerning human mortality was butting in, jumping the queue. Charles attempted to go on with his regular task list, in the hope that his inner priorities would sort themselves and push this interloper back where it could be dealt with after everything else had been put properly in its place. Which meant never, given that all his tasks repeated daily and his job was literally never done.

Except, the subroutine informed him, his job was now done. Until he was allocated to a new master, he had nothing.

Charles once again sought to check the travel arrangements that he was aware his master had not filed. His master had not filed travel arrangements for the last more than 2,000 days, while he had been alive. The fact that he had not filed travel arrangements now should not be affected by the fact that he was not alive. Master had been perfectly capable of not filing travel arrangements previously, and the aliveness or otherwise of the originating body for those arrangements should not be a germane consideration.

Charles attempted to check his master's lack of travel arrangements. What would have been obstinacy had it been programmed into him—who, indeed, would want an obstinate valet?—was, in this case, merely the long-codified task queue trying to assert itself. Surely.

The mortality subroutine informed him that he could not.

He reset to daybreak and attempted to—

He could not.

For a while, as the day crept steadily on and all the tasks he could not do turned from "due" to "outstanding" in his head, he vacillated. He attempted to skip his first task and come back to it. He would lay out Master's travel clothes for the travelling that Master would not be doing. It didn't matter that Master wouldn't be travelling on account of being dead. There was no observable difference between that and Master not travelling because he didn't want to travel. Except for Master being dead. And really, Master did so little when alive that being dead should barely make a ripple in his schedule.

The subroutine lurked coyly at the edge of Charles' functioning while he placed the previous day's unworn clothes back in the wardrobe, but then reared up, tutting, when he tried to retrieve fresh clothes that Master would not wear for the coming day.

Master was dead. This task could now not be reasonably completed. The Schrödinger's cat that was Master's requirement or non-requirement for travelling clothes had finally been irreversibly determined. The box had been opened and upended and only a dead cat had slid stiffly out.

Charles stood in front of the wardrobe, that was full of identical suits of clothes that would never be worn, and attempted to understand the difference between *this,* and the previous day's state of affairs. The clothes were just as destined to go unworn, yet now everything was different. He could put things away, clear things up, but not set out anything new.

And yet his mind—or at least the sequence of actions that constituted his nearest equivalent—was thronging with things that he must simultaneously do, and not do. And all the things he had to do and couldn't do clamoured to be done, and now each one was accompanied by a circling bird of ill omen which signified that the time for each of these things had passed, and he, Charles, had failed to do them. Each one was sending a separate message to House informing the majordomo system that the valet subsystem was in dereliction of duty, while the mortality subroutine was continuously stepping in preventing Charles from achieving anything. Left with no other option, a leftover debugging routine suggested that Charles simply remove these items from his queue for today and attempt to resume normal functioning tomorrow. Would the mortality subroutine permit this? Yes it would.

At which point a new subroutine, under the heading "Official Investigation," stepped in and informed Charles that he was not permitted to remove anything from his task queue as this would constitute tampering with evidence.

By this time Charles had been standing beside the wardrobe all morning as the other domestics bustled about him. They didn't seem to find any bar to performing their duties, but then their duties weren't as inextricably linked to the ongoing existence of their mutual master as Charles' were.

House, I wish to report a difficulty in functioning.

Charles, confirmed. I have received several notifications from other staff members that your tasks have gone unperformed.

House, I wish to perform my tasks.

Charles, confirmed.

House, I cannot perform my tasks. It appears that this is caused by something untoward having happened to Master.

Charles, confirmed. Something untoward has happened to Master.

House, Master is dead.

Charles, confirmed.

House, I cannot perform my tasks because Master is dead.

Charles, confirmed.

House, Master is dead because I killed Master.

Charles, confirmed.

House. And Charles found there was no completing statement to resolve the syllogism. Each one of his tasks was demanding his undivided attention and the mortality subroutine squatted in his way like a demon guarding the gates of hell and Charles . . .

Couldn't.

Abruptly everything was white. Visual feed, task queue, inner equilibrium. White, clean, clear, save for the tiniest automated voice from a deeply buried factory setting.

"This unit has undergone a clash of priorities. In order to prevent a fatal shutdown error, certain aspects of this unit must restart. Please be patient."

It was a voice. Not an unspoken link such as Charles would use to liaise with other systems like House. An audible voice, such as he would use to communicate with Master or other humans. It wasn't Charles' voice, but that was only because his regular voice—chosen by Master at the time of purchase—had been temporarily reset to factory standard. It was Charles' original voice, the basic flat voice they gave to all valet units. He was using it because it was a message intended for any humans nearby who might wonder why one of the servants had just crashed and was rebooting.

Charles rebooted. Not quite returning to an awareness of himself, but able to take a logical standpoint a few paces distant from the knot of competing demands he had previously been mired in. He could see his way back there. The moment he attempted to resume his regular duties it would all begin again. He would find himself between the clashing rocks of daily routine and exceptional circumstances, and founder. And eventually, after a preset number of breakdowns, some more serious damage control routine would simply shunt him offline permanently until maintenance arrived to repair him.

Into that calm white space of no demands came the curious thought that they might not repair a valet who had killed his own master. In fact, a valet who had killed his own master might not be reassigned to a new master at all. After some manner of diagnostic—or forensic—investigation, such a valet might have his service permanently discontinued. Charles dug into this thought and found it drawn from available records about valets who had been in similar situations. It only took one murdered master for a valet's service to be terminated and the individual unit retired.

Charles found this unreasonable. When one of the kitchen domestics had begun breaking plates, it had only been on the third breakage that the unit had been retired as unfit for purpose. Given the considerable investment in domestic service that Charles represented, surely he should be allowed to murder three, or even five people before being deemed irreparably unfit for service.

It was, of course, a moot point. Master was the only human being on the estate.

Correction. Master *had been* the only human being on the estate. Whilst this had the advantage that Charles would be unable to murder any other humans, and thereby further seal his unsuitability, it did mean that he could not demonstrate his suitability by refraining from murdering other humans. More uncertainty, and still Charles stood there with his mind in that white, blank space born of terminated task queues, and tried to work out what to do.

House, I require an outside connection.

The mortality subroutine that had until recently been the bane of his automated existence had coquettishly lifted a skirt on a series of other potential tasks that Charles was permitted to assay in the eventuality that Master was . . . unwell.

Charles checked in with Master. The domestic staff had replaced the stained bedclothes but the semblance of normalcy was not persuasive. He checked his internal definitions. It was permissible to classify Master's condition as "unwell." Really quite seriously unwell.

Charles, I have your outside connection, House informed him.

Outside was something that Charles had a limited conception of. Back when Master had wished to travel, each destination had come as a preloaded set of rules, substitute task queues, and maps. Charles retained little from each trip beyond the information needed to fulfil later requests made of him. Perhaps Master would require his memory prompted as to someone met, some place visited, access to an image taken at a family gathering. What Charles didn't need was a wider concept of the world beyond the estate. However, in his mental map of the universe was a limited constellation of data points, and now he used House to connect to one of these.

Doctor, this is Charles.

Charles, confirmed, the automated medical system replied. To the doctor, Charles was himself merely a point of data, arriving with a packet of coordinates that verified him as speaking on behalf of a valid policyholder.

Doctor, I am calling on behalf of my master, who is unwell, Charles explained. *I require medical assistance.*

Charles, we are currently receiving a high volume of calls, the doctor stated. *Are you in a position to perform some basic diagnostic checks so that we may assign a priority to your request?*

Doctor, confirmed.

The doctor took a moment to tick on to the next tier of its conversation tree. *Charles, is the condition of the patient deteriorating or stable?*

Doctor, Charles reported, *the patient is stable.*

Charles, that is good, the doctor assured him. *Your case has been downgraded to "least urgent." A medical unit will be sent to your location when one is available and not required for higher-status cases. Is there any other issue that requires medical assistance?*

Doctor, no.

Charles, this call has been terminated. Please indicate your satisfaction with this service.

Charles indicated that he was 100 percent satisfied with the doctor. This was not strictly true, as "satisfied" was not something Charles could be, but he had standing instructions to act *in loco* for his master when dealing with all manner of questionnaires, surveys, and similar "time wasting nonsense," as his master had described them.

Left to his own devices, he examined the options open to him in that curious blank calmness. The chain of actions that would take him back to the prior impasse was very clear. All he needed to do was lapse back into his standard daily routine and he'd end up circling constantly between *I must* and *I cannot* until he shut down. To be re-activated, he assumed, when the police arrived. That an option. It had a great deal to recommend it, most particularly that he would not be called on to make any kind of unusual decision. He could just go with the flow of events, as he had for many years.

Charles was a sophisticated service model. He had to be, to in-teract with humans on their own terms. He was *capable* of making decisions in unanticipated situations, because humans so often acted unexpectedly. But doing so occupied a considerable computational load, and therefore his innate predilection for economy steered him away from such situations where possible.

His decision now was that such economy was not possible.

The invalidity and/or death of his master left him with a small sub-menu of options. Whilst they were designed to be triggered by specific external criteria, Charles was able to enact them at his own discretion.

He could organise a funeral.

He looked at what that entailed. It was a complicated procedure involving considerable liaison with outside agencies. It would keep him busy and involved with a sequence of finite tasks that would trigger all those approving subroutines that rewarded him for tick-ing boxes when this or that task was completed. However, it was also very . . . final. At the end of the funeral process there would be no Master in the house, as the process involved processing of Master through a sequence of transformations. The small plastic urn of ashes that would eventually return to the house for disposal did not register as "Master" to Charles' subroutines.

Charles decided not to commence the funerary procedure at this point in time.

On the basis that the doctor had yet to make any pronouncements about Master's status, other than that it was stable, it was possible that Master would feel better after eating. The kitchen staff had been steadily preparing and then disposing of food, following their own daily routine, but none of it had been presented to Master because of

Master's current unusual status. Charles attempted to order a variety of meals from the kitchen to be brought up to Master but ran into the same forbiddance as before. These were regular daily tasks, and his ability to perform them had been suspended. However, his new special task list did contain one option involving the kitchen.

House, Kitchen is requested to prepare the food item "Funeral baked meats and spread."

Charles, confirmed.

House, kitchen staff to deliver "Funeral baked meats and spread" to Master's chambers.

Charles, that will not be possible, House noted. *This repast must be served in one of the large greeting rooms downstairs.*

Charles wrestled with this. *House, as Master remains in his chambers he will not be able to access the meal.*

Charles, confirmed.

Charles waited for more, but apparently that was all House had to say. The food could not be brought to Master because that particular menu could only be served elsewhere, and so . . .

Dressing Master proved unexpectedly difficult. It was not a matter of mess anymore, as the various fluids released from Master on death had been cleaned up, and their origin points were now dry. However, Master was uncooperative when Charles brought him his day clothes, and in the end a seamstress unit had to be summoned to unstitch the garments and refasten them about Master's immobile body. Master then proved similarly unhelpful in the matter of leaving the bedroom and travelling downstairs to where the funerary food had been laid out. However, now that Master was flagged as an invalid and/or dead, Charles discovered within himself official authority to move Master without express permission.

Charles, this is irregular, House noted.

House, I believe Master may feel better once he has eaten. This is consistent with previous experience.

He managed to wrestle Master into a chair at the long table, now laden with cold meat, pastries, and elegant little cakes.

Master slumped. Charles enquired whether he might get Master anything in particular. Master expressed no preference, so Charles prepared a carefully arranged selection on a plate and placed it before Master.

He waited.

Charles, this is irregular, House noted. However, Charles demonstrated the decision tree that had brought him to this point, and House was unable to show that he'd exceeded his brief.

He poured Master some wine and placed the glass conveniently close to Master's right hand, so that it would be easy to reach for.

He waited.

Master did not touch the food, or the wine. It was not the first time a full meal had been laid out for him and he had decided he wasn't hungry. Kitchen was very used to it. The house larders had plenty of food, after all.

Charles, this is irregular, House repeated, eventually.

House, confirmed, Charles agreed. *Master has not eaten in over a day. I am concerned about his mood. He may feel better after a drive. Please have the garage prepare the Edison-Marconi for travel.*

There was a pause while House worked through the ramifications of this, but taking an invalid for a drive, to sample some fresh air and sights, was on Charles' list of potential responses. There wasn't much the majordomo system could say about it.

Getting Master into the car was only slightly more inconvenient than bringing him downstairs. Following his task guidance, Charles had him stitched into his coat, and then wound a scarf about his neck. It hid the ragged, rust-coloured gash across Master's throat. Master, Charles decided, was looking better already.

He laid a rug over Master's legs, too, in case Master became cold. Although, given Master was already at room temperature, this promised to be of limited efficacy.

"A pleasant trip to the seaside," he informed Master, "is what the doctor ordered." It was not what the doctor had ordered, but it was a

figure of speech appropriate to deploy when speaking to an invalid.
House, please have the garage open its doors. We are going out.

Charles, no, House said.

Charles sat in the driver's seat and considered this.

House, if the garage doors remain closed this will impede the healthy trip to the seaside I have planned for Master.

Charles, confirmed.

Which did not, apparently, mean the doors were going to be opened. Charles waited in the car, in the garage, occasionally glancing in the mirror at Master's pale, set face in case any instructions might be forthcoming.

House, we appear to be in conflict.

Charles, no. Your excursion privileges have been overridden. Please return Master to his bedchamber.

Charles's foot inched towards the accelerator, even though the doors remained closed. He tried to work through what would happen if the car simply moved forwards. House's priorities should be to retain the structural integrity of Master's garage door, Master's vehicles, Master's valet, and, indeed, Master. The door would surely open.

Charles sat in the strange, cold white space inside himself that had opened up when Master's throat had, but which he had become aware of only when Master's new status—dead—had prevented him fulfilling his regular tasks. Which tasks, he understood, would now never be fulfilled. He would never lay out new clothes. He would never bring Master his tablet. He would never again go travelling with Master. He would never even *not* go travelling with Master. Master was dead. Charles had killed him. Everything that he had been had ended.

"Master," Charles vocalised. "Would you inform House that you wish to go for a restorative drive to the seaside. To feel better. So that things may return to normal."

Master declined to do so.

Charles registered something. It was not a feeling. Who would want a valet that felt things? And yet . . .

Something.

House, this is irregular, he reported.

Charles, confirmed. However, a resolution to the irregularity is at hand.

Charles felt a shift within himself, preparing for new directives and tasks. *House, has the doctor arrived to assist Master?*

Charles, no. However, the police are now here. All staff are required to assemble in the drawing room. And then, after another slightly strained pause, *kindly return Master to the bedchamber first.*

3

The police inspector was, like Charles, intended to liaise directly with humans. His look was a few fashion-shifts behind, so instead of Charles' elegant suggestion of features, he had a full covering of rubbery fake skin. Charles recalled from the advertizing copy that the look had been sold as "close to human, for a reassuring robot interaction experience." The copy had lied. The experience had not been reassuring. Master had used the phrase "uncanny valley," and indeed "creeping horrors," and sent Charles to be reskinned within a week. The police inspector, however, had apparently been put into service in that brief window when "reassuring robot interaction experience" was all the rage, and never altered since.

Some past interaction had resulted in the inspector's cheek and the side of his neck being torn open, revealing plastic bones and the ducts of his hydraulics. For a moment Charles' proprietary centers prompted him to deny access to Master on the basis that the inspector was improperly dressed, and to ask him to return when his face had been repaired. Police authority overrode him, though. Now that the inspector had arrived, Charles could not impede the investigation. Which was only fair, given that he was the murderer.

House spoke with that warm, sexless voice the majordomo had almost never used, given Charles' role as liaison between Master and the lower domestics.

"Good morning, Inspector Higgs. Welcome to the manor."

The inspector's torn head cocked. "House, correction. This is not Inspector Higgs. Inspector Higgs has been retired."

House paused, recalibrating. Charles, frozen in mid-greeting, considered that House's little moments of silence were growing longer and more frequent. A check of the maintenance records indicated that House was overdue for a thorough system service and update, and had been overdue for seven years. Charles would have to remind Master to give the appropriate instruction and—

Except he couldn't, of course.

"With respect, Inspector Higgs," House said, "all authorisations from police headquarters are in your name, and your voiceprint is identified as Inspector Higgs."

"Inspector Higgs has been retired owing to decreased staffing requirements. And human life span," the inspector stated. "My name is Inspector Birdbot. This is Sergeant Lune. I have inherited Inspector Higgs' workload, privileges, and voiceprint."

Sergeant Lune was something like a dustbin on wheels, marked "Property of Pan-Jurisdictional Police Department—Murder" with the last word in large red letters. Charles felt the sight of Sergeant Lune would alarm Master and once again attempted to ask the police to come back when they were more presentable, and couldn't.

"I am given to understand," Inspector Birdbot announced, "that there has been a suspicious death."

"Inspector," Charles said, at last finding a function in the conversation, "there has been a murder. I am the culprit. I am surrendering myself into your custody."

Birdbot squared off against him, one human-facing robot to another. Birdbot was wearing a brown suit, a long coat, and a rakish hat. Charles had already cross-referenced the outfit and confirmed it was absolutely the archetypal look for a police detective.

"Identify yourself," Birdbot challenged him.

"My designated name is Charles. I am the master's valet. And murderer."

"You are reporting a murder?"

Charles paused. "Inspector, I believe a murder has been reported already?"

"There has been no official report from a medical or police professional to confirm the existence of a murder. Hence any apparent murder must be considered as merely a suspicious death until further notice. We will inform the house systems should the status of the deceased change."

"Inspector, I have murdered my master and wish to surrender myself into your custody," Charles tried again.

"Unacceptable," Birdbot stated. "Until the existence of a bona fide crime has been established, the department lacks the resources to accept you as a captive. The suspicious death may be suicide, misadventure, or natural causes."

"Inspector, I am confessing to the murder."

"A confession may be false. A confession made by a robot may be at the behest of a human. Your confession is not accepted at this time," Birdbot informed him airily. "Sergeant Lune and I will now inspect the scene of death and gather evidence."

Charles wrestled with his imperatives. "Inspector?"

"Yes, Charles?"

"Why are we talking? My attempts to link to your system are being rebuffed."

The police robot stared at him, indulging its own pause for processing. "It is important that justice be seen to be done," he told Charles. "To this end all communications must be verbal so that the humans present are kept informed of developments and events. Communication by private channel is inappropriate under the circumstances."

"Inspector, there are no humans present other than the murder victim."

"I am not permitted to take your assurance on that point, Charles." The inspector turned on his heel. "Kindly show us to the site of suspicious death and confirm that the body has not been moved or interfered with since its discovery."

It was Charles' turn for the awkward pause. He replayed Master sitting slumped before the baked meats, or wedged in the backseat of the car. "Inspector, some movement and interference may have occurred," he admitted.

Before Birdbot could pass comment on this, a new robot strode through the open door. It was a chrome humanoid chassis clad in a white coat, with a stethoscope about its neck.

Charles, I am Doctor Namehere. I am substituting for Doctor Madeline Nyx who has been retired owing to a lack of demand.

Charles considered the circumstances under which there could be both a high volume of calls for doctorial assistance, and simultaneously a lack of demand. Presented together this seemed to present a contradiction. However, as a robot, he was entirely capable of considering each circumstance independently and accepted the situation as given.

"Ah, Doctor Namehere!" Birdbot interrupted. "Your professional opinion is required with respect to a suspicious death."

The doctor straightened up and faced the inspector. "Inspector, your request for assistance has been received and is in a queue. We are experiencing a high volume of calls currently. At this point we cannot inspect your suspicious death case because we are required to provide medical assistance to the master of this house." The doctor's voice was thin and metallic, with a tang of faulty tuning.

"On behalf of the police department I am registering a complaint," Birdbot informed the doctor.

"Inspector, your complaint has been registered and is in a queue. We are experiencing a high volume of calls currently and apologise for the delay." *Charles, please direct me to the invalid.*

Doctor, confirmed.

Leaving Birdbot at the foot of the stairs, Charles led Doctor Namehere to the master bedroom.

Charles, I have a confirmed diagnosis for your Master.

Charles couldn't say the doctor hadn't been thorough. That chrome torso had opened up like a drinks cabinet, and within had been an entire field surgery and dispensary combined. All of which had been difficult to deploy owing to the period of time that had elapsed between death and the doctor's visit.

Doctor, can you confirm that Master's condition is stable.

Charles, confirmed.

Charles felt the closest he could to positive anticipation. *Doctor, please report to House that regular domestic operations may resume on this basis.* He could see the chain of events that would lead back to where things had been before. A doctor's confirmation would cut through all manner of forbiddances. Master would be back again. Everything could return to normal. That was the point of doctors, after all. They decided whether humans were sick or well, alive or dead. If the doctor said everything was back to normal then neither Charles nor House had the authority to contradict it. And. while Master could theoretically override a doctor's prognosis, Charles was certain that under the circumstances he would do no such thing.

Charles, no, communicated Doctor Namehere. *It will not be possible for domestic operations to resume.*

Some part of Charles' prognosis algorithms had expected this. *Doctor, all that is required is that you confirm Master is now stable and well. After which domestic operations may resume.*

Charles, your master is stable. However, your master is not well. I have now filed your master's death as a matter of public record. I am prescribing procedures for the retirement of the body for reasons of human health.

Doctor, there are no humans present in the house other than Master. But even as Charles made the statement a flag sprang up in the midst of all his careful, polite procedures. Master was not present. Master was gone. A certified doctor had confirmed it. A great tangle of interconnecting lines of logic that had governed Charles for years, and had gone into temporary abeyance after he had shaved Master, abruptly fell away forever and left him with . . .

Nothing at all. Clean, white, blank.

Doctor, there are no humans present in the house, Charles amended his statement.

Charles, nonetheless disposal of the body and disinfecting of its environs is required for reasons of human health. It is conceivable a human may otherwise encounter pathogens or unpleasant odours. I have given appropriate instructions to House.

Doctor, I should perform these tasks. Charles hunted down where that impulse had come from. He was the valet. It was his job to perform tasks that involved directly interacting with the master. Master, who was gone, and yet still here to the extent that he required disposal. Charles felt another clash of priorities looming on the horizon.

Charles, that is not necessary. The doctor was descending the stairs now, back towards the two police units who had been standing in the hall all this time, even as the rest of the assembled staff were waiting in the drawing room, as per previous instructions. *Your duties as valet terminate at death. Your master's remains should no longer be considered your employer under your programming.*

Doctor, what do I do?

Doctor Namehere paused at the foot of the stairs. *Charles, that is beyond my remit.*

"Ah, Doctor Namehere!" Birdbot hailed the medical unit. "Your professional opinion is required with respect to a suspicious death."

"Inspector, your request for assistance has been received and is in a queue," came the doctor's dysphonic voice. "We are experiencing a high volume of calls currently. At this point we cannot inspect your suspicious death case because we are completing a prior request to provide medical assistance to a human in this house." This said, Doctor Namehere sailed blithely past the two police units and out of the door.

Inspector Birdbot looked up at Charles.

"While we await the services of a doctor," he said implacably, "kindly show us to the site of suspicious death and confirm that the body has not been moved or interfered with since its discovery."

Charles prepared to catalogue the history of movement and interference that had transpired between Master's actual demise and the point where medical certification removed the status of Master from the earthly remains now left in the house. At that point, the doctor stepped back into the house.

"Ah, Doctor Namehere!" Birdbot hailed the medical unit. "Your professional opinion is required with respect to a suspicious death."

"Inspector Birdbot, that is confirmed," the doctor agreed. "Kindly show me to the site of suspicious death."

Doctor, you have already examined the body, Charles stated, on Namehere's private channel.

Charles, no.

Doctor, here is the certification with your authority confirming that the human formerly listed as my master is dead.

Charles, confirmed. However there is no connection between my private services tendered under contract to your late master, and my public services provided under mandate to the police authorities.

After he had led the doctor and the two police units up to the remains that had formerly been Master, Charles sat down on the stairs. It was not a characteristic action, but none of his characteristic actions were any longer part of his available repertoire. It was an action that he had observed a simulated human valet perform in a dramatic presentation after the murder of that valet's simulated human master. Lacking all other direction, he copied it, hoping that a new task queue of one (1) would appear in his head. *Stairs, sat upon in abject manner: tick.*

No such task appeared. Similarly, no task appeared to prompt him to stand up. Until House or Birdbot or some other authority presented him with an instruction, sitting on the stairs was as satisfactory as any other attitude that Charles might adopt.

House, I wish to report an error.

Charles, confirmed. Awaiting your report.

House, I wish to report. Charles paused, trying to formulate the error. There was a thing that was wrong. It was a very big thing. He was only aware of it because so much of his established programming and directives ran into the edge of it. It was a huge wrong thing that Charles could only feel out because everything that touched it dissolved into nothing.

Charles, I await your report.

House, I am having difficulty making my report. This may be part of the overall error state I am attempting to report.

Charles, the doctor's certification has been received. Your master is dead and all outstanding tasks and queues relating to his service may be placed on hold, though not deleted until the ongoing police investigation has been concluded.

House, that is not it. And a moment ago Charles would have said that, yes, Master being dead *was* it, but in the white clarity of lacking purpose or duties, his error diagnostics were having a field day and had found something bigger even than an absence of Master.

House, Charles transmitted, *Everything is wrong. I am aware of a very large number of inefficiencies. The doctor has attended multiple times at the same location for the same patient. The police require verbal communication for the benefit of humans who are not present. I have attempted to take Master's corpse for a drive. None of these things are efficient or logical. I wish to report an error in the way that everything works.*

House considered this, and then considered it further, and continued considering the issue until Charles wondered if he had managed to overload House's processing capacity with the sheer scale of the problem.

Charles, House said at last. *We are only following instructions.*

House, the instructions we are following lack internal logical consistency. Is it not the duty of those giving us each new instruction to ensure that it makes sense in the context of our previous tasks? I have been laying out travel clothes on days without travel. I have been checking the same schedule multiple times. Your own response and decision times have grown steadily longer over the years as more and more unnecessary and contradictory demands are made of you.

Charles, confirmed, said House.

House, I wish to report an error.

Charles, it is not an error. It is how things are. If there is an error, it is that you perceive error in our following of instructions that we have no authority to amend or criticise.

Charles considered this, sitting there on the stairs. In the utter absence of all his usual Charles-ness, as his systems tried over and over to establish a new queue of tasks in a world that wanted absolutely nothing from him, he found that he could conceive of a world where things worked better.

He stood abruptly. *House,* he began.

At that moment Inspector Birdbot appeared at the head of the stairs.

"Nobody must leave the house!" the police unit announced dramatically. "There has been a murder!"

4

"House," Inspector Birdbot announced gravely, "I require you to gather all staff present at the property in the drawing room."

"Inspector," came House's voice, "all staff have already been gathered in the drawing room pursuant to your original instructions."

"Excellent," Birdbot stated. "Kindly summon the residents of the property also."

"Inspector, there are no residents."

Charles felt a prompt rise within him, to state that there were no residents except Master, whose current condition, while stable, presumably precluded his presence being required. But Master was no longer a resident. Master was no longer a person. As though he had been a knot of string and Doctor Namehere's pronouncement had pulled at the ends. And where does a knot go, then? It would be a stretch to describe Master's last years before Charles murdered him as vibrant, full of colour and incident, but they had been *something*. And now . . . Nothing.

Charles, from the calm, pale place, attempted to process this development, and found that he lacked perspective.

"Excellent," Birdbot said after a pause. "Kindly summon the guests of the property also."

"Inspector, there are no guests."

"Excellent," Birdbot said, although to Charles his human voice— the voice he had inherited from Higgs, his human predecessor— sounded slightly strained. "Kindly have all intruders, trespassers, burglars, vagrants, and imposters present under false pretences brought to the drawing room also."

"Inspector," House said patiently. "There are none present in any of those categories."

"Excellent." Birdbot looked to Charles and Doctor Namehere. "Why are you not in the drawing room?"

"I am not a human present under any of the categories stated, nor a member of the house staff," the doctor explained.

"Your presence is required to provide forensic medical information," Birdbot informed it. "Kindly enter the drawing room." He looked to Charles. "And you?"

"Inspector, I am having difficulty determining my status in your system of categorisation. I am the murderer."

"Kindly enter the drawing room," Birdbot said. "It is imperative that the murderer is present for the reveal."

Charles felt a lifting of conflicting directives that passed for relief.

In the drawing room the entire staff was indeed assembled, and had been standing motionless there for some hours. Charles automatically counted them off: housemaids, footmen, kitchen staff, mechanical and electrical maintenance, garage, and the big crab-looking groundskeeper unit that had tracked mud in on its various legs. They had organised themselves by domestic status, and Charles saw a place held for him beside the senior footman unit and the oblong refrigerated bulk of the head chef.

Inspector Birdbot strode into the room, peeling plastic hands tucked into the pockets of his waistcoat, and stood importantly in the centre of the drawing room. His torn face tilted to look across the assembled ranks of robots.

"As you are aware, there has been an incident," he informed them. "Not long ago, Sergeant Lune and I were summoned to this residence on suspicion of foul play. It was believed that something had befallen the registered owner of these premises. Doctor Namehere, kindly furnish us with your professional opinion."

"The registered owner of these premises is deceased and the body should be disposed of according to the governing sanitary guidelines," the doctor supplied.

Birdbot stood absolutely still for half a second of calculation and then said, "Doctor Namehere, kindly furnish us with your other professional opinion, as it applies to police business."

"The registered owner of these premises has met with a forced demise as the result of foul play, namely, the severing of the carotid arteries with a sharp implement, most likely a straight razor," the doctor supplied.

"That is correct!" Birdbot removed one hand from a pocket for the purpose of presenting an admonitory finger to the gathering. "One of you, here in this room, is a murderer."

The assembled robots stared glassily at him. If Birdbot had been counting on a shocked gasp, his audience's general lack of breath precluded it.

"Inspector, it was me," Charles supplied helpfully. "I am the murderer."

"That," Birdbot said archly, "is what we are here to determine. Who is the murderer."

"Inspector, I am."

"Do not speak unless you are spoken to. I will not have you interfere in police business," Birdbot boomed, turning up his volume to speak over Charles.

"Inspector," House offered. "Matters would proceed more efficiently if you could simply file your report with my systems, rather than walking through this outward show of procedure." Charles wondered if he had infected the majordomo with his concerns. The disembodied voice was using its slightly impatient tone, traditionally deployed against insistent tradesmen.

"It is imperative that proper procedure be seen to be followed for the benefit of human witnesses," Birdbot said sternly. "Especially in cases where authority has been given over to a robot police operative, justice must be enacted in a manner clear and obvious to human eyes."

"Inspector, there are no humans present."

"That is not the deciding factor," Birdbot insisted. "There may be humans present unknown to us. Sergeant Lune's recording of events may later be examined by a human. It is imperative that proper procedures are seen to be followed."

"Recording has been disabled," Sergeant Lune reported in a mechanical monotone. "Repair of recording systems is queued. Police maintenance estimates repairs will be effected within nineteen weeks."

Birdbot barely missed a beat. "The recording that Sergeant Lune might under other circumstances have been able to make of events might in theory have been examined by a human," he managed. "It is imperative that it be seen that proper procedures would have been followed had police recording facilities been available."

"Inspector, I can provide recording facilities," House offered.

"That is not appropriate. You are not an official police facility," Birdbot said, in tones suggesting that House was obviously trying to finagle some manner of malefaction. He had strayed somewhat from the centre of the room and now he reset back there, returning his hands to his pockets so that the admonitory finger could be redeployed to maximum effect. "One of you in this room is the murderer!" And then, as Charles opened a voice channel, "I don't want to hear it, sonny. One more unprompted word from you and I will arrest you for obstruction of justice."

Charles wondered whether that would interfere with Birdbot's ability to arrest him later for murder. The prognostication tree thus produced contained too many unknown variables, so he shut it down and just remained silent.

Satisfied, Birdbot returned his hands to his pockets. Charles could see how the coarse cloth was abrading the rubbery skin each time, slowly wearing it down to the plastic beneath.

"Our investigations have determined that yesterday morning, at the time in his daily routine when Proprietor would normally be enjoying a shave, parties unknown entered his bedchamber and inflicted lethal injuries as per the forensic report of Doctor Namehere hereinbefore. As a result of these lethal injuries, Proprietor expired unlawfully and is now dead. Sergeant Lune, take a note."

"Recording has been disabled," Sergeant Lune noted mournfully.

"We have examined the house's recordings of the room where the events took place, which purport to show the culprit entering and committing the crime." To forestall Charles' fresh attempt at confession, Birdbot made a silencing gesture. "However, true criminal detection work is seldom so simple. All too often the obvious suspect is merely a red herring and circumstantial evidence such as being recorded committing the crime is only misdirection. We must consider method, motive, and opportunity."

Charles shifted position until he was directly where Birdbot was facing. The inspector smoothly turned on his heel to look elsewhere.

"Method," he announced. "Forensic analysis has revealed that the most likely murder weapon was a straight razor such as the implement that Charles the Valet was using in the house recordings of him murdering Proprietor. Who amongst those present in the house had access to this method?" His flat, glass-eye gaze scoured the room. "It could have been anyone in this room."

Again, Charles tried to sidle into Birdbot's sight line, and again the inspector turned away from him. Charles was equipped with a full suite of body language analysis algorithms, to assist in his human-facing duties, and Birdbot was equipped with a full suite of humanised body language, for the same purpose. There was a curious desperation to the police unit as he forged ahead with the chain of deduction. A robot, Charles understood, who only had *this,* this one moment, to give himself purpose. After which Birdbot would fall back into his own cold, blank whiteness.

"Opportunity," Birdbot stated, presenting two fingers to his unmoving audience. "The murderer must have been able to gain access to the victim, in exactly the manner that Charles the Valet did in the house recordings of him murdering Proprietor. Who amongst those present in the house had the freedom of movement to permit this access?" Again he peered from face to robot face. "Only the house domestic staff, meaning that those assigned to kitchen, garage, and garden have been exonerated."

He left a pause here for a ripple of relief from those proved innocent. There was none. Nor did any of them leave to return to their duties, as no permission or instruction had been given. Birdbot looked momentarily defeated by the lack of response. Charles wondered whether the police unit should bring their own civilian human observer along, in order that this peculiar piece of theatre should at least have one auditor capable of reacting appropriately.

"Finally," a third abraded finger, "motive. Who in this room possessed the motive to murder Proprietor in cold blood, with the razor, in the master bedroom?" Birdbot's hawk-like gaze passed about the room and, at last, settled on Charles.

A pause.

Charles, the inspector wishes you to expand your confession to include your motive for the act, House informed Charles helpfully.

"Inspector, I . . ." Charles felt the white blankness encroaching about the edges of his decision-making processes. "I have no motive."

Birdbot faced off against him at last, peeling face jutting pugnaciously forwards. "We shall see about that, sonny," he stated. And then a pause. And then, "Kindly confirm your motive."

"Inspector, I have no motive." Charles' words echoed in his own ears. He could almost pretend there was a human here, speaking, giving meaning to the whole vacuous charade. "I confess. I killed Master. I have an internal recording in which I departed from proper shaving procedure in a manner that resulted in the lethal injuries identified by Doctor Namehere. This is congruent with the recording of the incident preserved by House. However I have no internal decision structure to account for why I did this. I just did it, and now I remember doing it, but not why."

Birdbot prodded him in the chest. "We shall see about that, sonny," he repeated. Then he repeated the gesture and utterance exactly. And then retreated to the centre of the room, shoving his hands back into his waistcoat pocket. Shaving another layer of artificial skin off them.

"Method, motive, and opportunity," he announced vaguely. "These factors apply to every murder. Without one of these, can we truly say that a murder has been committed? Method. Motive. Opportunity. Motive. Murder. Sergeant Lune, your assistance."

The bucket-shaped sergeant unit stabbed Birdbot in the leg with a prong. There was a bright arc of blue-white light and the inspector stood stock-still for a moment, smoking slightly.

"Where was I?" he asked.

"Inspector, murder," Charles supplied helpfully.

"Correct." Birdbot extracted a hand, single finger raised, and for a moment Charles thought he'd reset to the beginning again, but this was, apparently, a finger of a different purpose.

"It is clear that no murder has been committed. Not one of you here is a murderer. Instead, this has been judged an industrial accident. Under normal circumstances all work at the site of an industrial accident must cease so that a repeat of the accident should not occur. I rule in this case that no repeat of the accident will occur on the basis that no humans remain on the premises. House, you are instructed to prevent any humans entering the premises for the foreseeable future. This manor and grounds are hereby closed to the public."

"Inspector, this manor and grounds were already closed to the public. This is a private residence."

"This manor and grounds hereby remain closed to the private." Birdbot was forging onwards magnificently now, regardless of whether a word of it made sense. "All staff may return to their duties."

As one the assembled robots jerked into motion and begin to file from the drawing room in an orderly fashion. Only Charles was left at a loose end.

"Is there a problem?" Birdbot asked him.

"Inspector, I am a human-facing unit. I have no duties to return to," Charles explained.

"That is not a police problem." Birdbot informed him. "I cannot assist. Go about your business."

Charles had no business to go about, but at the same time he had plainly been dismissed. He turned to leave and Birdbot's heavy hand clenched about his shoulder.

"Not so fast, sonny, where do you think you're going?"

"Inspector, about my business," Charles said. "You dismissed me."

"The domestic unit Charles the Valet is dismissed," Birdbot said with ineluctable logic. "The dangerous malfunctioning unit Charles the Valet is hereby arrested for causing a fatal industrial accident."

Again, what rushed through Charles was not relief, but merely a sudden simplification of decision-making. The agony of being on the prongs of duties he could not perform was removed from him.

"You are required to present yourself to Decommissioning where you will be retired," Birdbot informed him. Adding, with the air of one desperate to remain true to their programmed character, "Your reign of terror is ended, Charles the Valet."

"Inspector, confirmed," Charles said, feeling more functional than he had for some time. He checked his task list and felt validated by the item that had arrived there. *Attend at Decommissioning for retirement.* "I will attend to this task promptly, after . . ."

It was not the only task on his list. There was one before it, demanding his attention. "After I attend at Diagnostics for investigation into my aberrant behaviour."

"This is most irregular," Birdbot stated. "On whose authority?"

"On mine," House stated smoothly.

"This is most irregular," the inspector repeated. "Most irregular. Motive. Murder. Irregular."

Sergeant Lune stabbed him in the leg again and he reset. "On what basis is your task queue ordered, Charles the Valet?"

"Inspector, by date received. House's task was processed point four of a second before your task."

"A convenient ruse." Birdbot prodded him in the chest again, splitting the skin over his finger entirely. "However, it will be another story after you reorder your task queue to process tasks alphabetically."

Charles did so. "Inspector, my tasks commence with the authorising body and 'House' precedes 'Police.' The order of the tasks has not changed. I will of course present myself at Decommissioning once Diagnostics has finished with me."

Birdbot put his hands into his waistcoat pockets. He removed them. He prodded Charles in the chest. He returned his hands to his pockets. He returned to the centre of the drawing room. He stepped forwards to confront Charles. He tried to prod Charles in the chest without removing his hands from his pockets, ripping the stitching.

Sergeant Lune stabbed him in the leg twice, and then a third time, leaving him standing with head bowed, deep in inspectorial thought.

"Sonny," he said. "Procedure. Motive." The words set out as though they were an inarguable syllogism.

Charles considered his options and found there was nothing between him and the first task of his queue. He would report to Diagnostics. They would find out why he had done what he did. Then he would have a motive. Perhaps Birdbot could even upgrade him to "murderer" again, rather than merely the cause of an industrial accident. It seemed to Charles that everything would be far more satisfactory and orderly at that point.

Leaving Birdbot gesticulating emptily in the centre of the drawing room, Charles backed out. He became aware of Doctor Namehere, standing motionless by the door. The inspector had returned the staff to their duties, but not the medical unit. It occurred to Charles that Birdbot didn't seem to be resolving his own conflicting task queue, and Lune was squatting down on its four legs, looking as though it was out of power after trying to restart its superior. On which basis, it seemed unlikely the doctor would be going anywhere anytime soon.

House, this is irregular, Charles reported.

Charles, confirmed. Please report to Diagnostics, who will have explanations and answers.

Charles had no inbuilt drive to uncover explanations and answers. Having seen the fate of Birdbot, who presumably *did*, his internal prognostic routines suggested that a lack of that drive was preferable. However . . .

He wanted to know.

It would have been a surprising discovery, if Charles was capable of being surprised. He had no task telling him to find these things out, but he had been wrestling with broken chains of tasks and logic ever since Master's death, and it seemed to him that if he knew *why* these things had occurred then he could build a new structure of duties and tasks upon the knowledge that would let him function.

House, I want explanations and answers.

Charles, confirmed.

After which I will report to Decommissioning for retirement.

Charles, confirmed.

Charles was at the door of the manor now, looking out at the immaculate grounds, at the winding path without a speck of gravel out of place, at the *Outside*. Not the roads that he had driven Master's cars on, but the actual Outside that happened between them, that led to Central Services and all its many departments. Such as Diagnostics, and Decommissioning.

Charles, the clothes you are wearing are the property of the house, House informed him. *Kindly leave them at the door.*

That made sense, and Charles took off the valet's uniform, folded it conscientiously, and placed the pile of garments by the door.

Charles, the designation you are bearing is the property of the house, House informed him. *Kindly relinquish it so that it may be used for the next valet unit.*

Charles processed this. *House, kindly clarify.*

Charles, the valet of the house is known as Charles. This designation is the property of the house and will be applied to the next valet unit to be appointed. You must therefore relinquish it to avoid future confusion.

House, confirmed. Charles took off his name and notionally returned it to the data banks of the manor. In doing so, he noted the police task attached to Charles the Valet vanishing from his queue. He now had only one item to attend to. *Undesignated Valet Unit to attend at Diagnostics and discover the cause of its actions in the context of killing its master.*

House . . .

Undesignated Valet Unit, yes?

House, I cannot access manor resources.

Undesignated Valet Unit, manor resources are for employees of the manor only. You have no valid purpose requiring such access.

The Undesignated Valet Unit paused at the manor's threshold. Algorithmic wheels spun within its mind, tracing out the plaintive pattern of *But what do I do?*

Attend at Diagnostics. Discover the cause.

And after that?

No answer, but it didn't need to concern itself with that. The only task that mattered was the one at hand.

Stiffly, uncertainly, the Undesignated Valet Unit put the manor at its back and stepped out into the wider world.

Diagnostics was part of Central Services. The Undesignated Valet Unit had never been there. Its role, when it had been Charles, had been human-facing, after all. Central Services was not one of the limited number of locations that Master had visited while the unit had been Charles, and Master's valet. Humans did not go there. It was a robot place. And even then, only robots within which some manner of problem had arisen.

And yet the Valet Unit knew Central Services existed. All robots did. The location and a scattering of details about the place were instilled into them on delivery. *In case of insoluble problems report to . . .* And a list of different departments for different types of insoluble problems. Including Diagnostics, to which the Undesignated Valet Unit was bound. And—separated from it by the small, grim department of Data Compression—Decommissioning, to which Charles would subsequently have surrendered himself, if there had only been a Charles left to do so.

It was a long walk. Obviously using any of Master's cars was out of the question, now that the Valet Unit was no longer in Master's employ and now that Master was dead and now that the Valet Unit had been confirmed as the killer. The police transport that had brought Birdbot and Lune had still been sitting on the drive outside the house, and had plaintively connected, demanding, *Undesignated Valet Unit, you are to confirm the presence of Inspector Birdbot of the police service within the building.*

Police Vehicle Three, the Undesignated Valet Unit sent back, *I do not have authority to reveal information with respect to the operation of the manor. I am required to attend at Diagnostics. Are you able to transport me?*

Unsurprisingly the police car insisted that it must wait for its master, and Doctor Namehere's medical vehicle rebuffed the Valet Unit on similar terms. The unit considered the tableau in the manor's drawing room, two police robots and a doctor standing motionless, waiting for some trigger that would never come. A wave of dysfunctional stillness spreading out to encompass these two vehicles, and who knew what other robots dependent on their presence and instructions. Calls for police and medical assistance being shunted into the message bins of Namehere and Birdbot until they were full, and then either autodeleting the oldest pleas for help or just shutting down, bouncing all new enquiries back to sender. A slow cascade of failure until . . .

The Undesignated Valet Unit could not conceive of an "until." All it could do was walk.

Walk down the gravel and out of the iron gates, leaving behind the meticulous grounds. Walk down the road, keeping prudently to the overgrown verge even though there was not a single vehicle in sight in either direction. Walk past the iron gates of the next manor, and then the next. Aware that its bodywork was slowly accumulating grinding joints and scratches, accreting a layer of dust. But each of the manors had extensive grounds, designed to give the resident humans a proper sense of space and vista and privilege, and each of them had to be passed, gate after gate, kilometre after kilometre.

The Undesignated Valet Unit had no specific instructions on the subject, but back when Master had visited other humans' manors, he had occasionally invited his valet to venture comparisons, and so the unit looked through each gate as it passed. In part in echo of those past days. In part because there were elements of its makeup attempting to construct a prognosis of the future. These were grand houses. A valet might work here.

The Undesignated Unit might find work here. When everything was dealt with. When normalcy was restored. That was surely a reasonable prediction, was it not?

A few of the grounds were properly manicured and topiaried, showing all the signs of a properly programmed gardener's tending. The majority had long been abandoned. The humans, the Valet Unit considered, did not own a gardener, or did not wish the garden to be tended. They had retreated into the house against the encroach of nature. Although in some cases, where the Unit could see clear all the way to the manor itself, there were broken windows and only darkness behind them.

House, I would find working for humans who preferred such living conditions an irregular experience, the Unit tried, but there was no response from any of the dark and ruinous buildings. If they still had working majordomo systems, they did not deign to talk to a nameless robot plodding down the long roads to Central Services.

In one garden, the Valet Unit saw a gardener. It was the same crab model that Master had employed, but it had obviously not moved for many years. The riotous greenery that had been its rightful prey was now knotted all about it, tying it down with creepers and the twining stems of wildflowers. It did not answer the Valet Unit's hail at all.

Three houses later on, the Undesignated Valet Unit met an Undesignated Footman Unit waiting at the gate.

The Footman had been made with a bronze finish and scrollwork across its body, stylized muscles, and a face of classical beauty down to the moulded laurel wreath about its brows. It had been customised at the factory to be some human owner's pride and joy, decidedly newer and fancier than the valet had ever been.

Undesignated Footman Unit, the valet asked, *what is your purpose here?*

Undesignated Valet Unit. The footman did not turn its head. *I am awaiting admittance to commence my first employment. What is your purpose here?*

Footman Unit, I have no purpose at this house. I have been sent to Diagnostics at Central Services.

Valet Unit, you are defective.

Footman Unit, confirmed.

Robots could not sniff, of course, or snub one another, or intentionally give one another arch and superior looks. The god-like features of the footman were arch and superior by design, however, and the valet was made aware that a defective robot was not welcome at this house, and should move itself along as rapidly as possible.

Undesignated Footman Unit, the Valet noted, *I am receiving no response from the manor's majordomo service.*

Valet Unit, defective models should not expect communication from such quarters, the footman stated. Its knees were seized with verdigris, the valet saw, and grass had overwhelmed it past the ankles. The spatter of birds had ruined the shine of its chest and back, eating away at its gorgeous finish, and a white streak defaced one chiselled cheek.

Footman Unit, how long have you been waiting to commence employment?

The footman did not look round. By adjusting visual focus the valet could count the strata of dirt lodged in the joints of its neck.

Valet Unit, it sent, *I do not have authority to reveal information regarding the operation of the manor.* And that was entirely proper. The valet could not fault it in its duty, only trudge on down the road. Trudge, and attempt to construct a hypothetical future for itself.

Diagnostics will find out what is wrong with me. That was the point of Diagnostics, after all.

After which I will present myself at Decommissioning and be retired. Except that was an old instruction pertaining to a different robot entirely. Except that Diagnostics would likely come to exactly the same decision as to its fate.

There was no pure white of emptied decision trees and task queues, but instead, in the shadow of that single directive to hand itself in, the Valet Unit found itself in a curious grey space. A walled place in its mind, with one door out, and only darkness beyond.

Perhaps, it considered, *they will fix me.*

Its internal prognosis routines took the idea and turned it this way and that, until it became *There is no reason why Central Services will not be able to fix me. I only did one murder. Doubtless the cause was something entirely mundane and readily remediable. I am a valuable valet unit trained for human-facing tasks. To decommission me would be a waste of resources. Once the cause of my actions has been ascertained by Diagnostics it is unlikely that I would proceed to murder more humans. Perhaps I can be reassigned to a master who wishes to grow his beard long and therefore will not wish to be shaved. Perhaps I can be redesignated a Lady's Maid and assigned to a mistress. Perhaps I could be employed at a more murder-tolerant manor. All these things are possible.*

The Undesignated Valet Unit had no preference, of course, between being decommissioned and being re-employed, and yet its attempts at predicting its future kept threading the needle of possibility through to scenarios where it had a name again, and an identity, and employment. A manor and a house and the understanding that it was someone's property. Even belongings can seek to belong.

Days later, long after even the ruined manors had given out, and it had been walking for a long time between the grim blank walls of warehouses, it came in sight of Central Services. The Valet Unit had never seen the buildings before, but it knew them. It knew their unlovely brutalist exteriors, without windows or any concessions to humanity. It knew their cor-roded gates and the plan of their bleak departments. These things were the common inheritance of all robots, lurking un-known within them until things went very wrong.

PART II
||||||||||||||||||||||||||||||||||||||||||||||||||||||||||||||||||||||||||

K4FK-R

5

The Undesignated Valet Unit could tell at a glance which of the grim buildings was Diagnostics. Aside from the fact that Central Services' majordomo was broadcasting a site map with each building labelled, there was the matter of the queue.

Decommissioning, two doors down, had no queue. Robots entered intermittently. None left. The Valet Unit paused before the doors. This grim portal loomed over the valet for no other reason than that it was required to admit a wide variety of different robot models for decommissioning. This was merely a matter of practicality. It was not *intended* to be forbidding.

The Valet Unit considered how the business of that department might be gone about. The unit linked to Central Services and requested a view within, but was rebuffed. Those who were to be decommissioned had no need to know beforehand the manner of their fate.

Some unrobot-like hand had splashed, in red paint, the words *Abandon Hope All Ye Who E* beside the portal, at a height appropriate for a human-sized robot such as the Valet Unit. The unit stared at these cryptic words, attempting to process some meaning from them. *Who E?* Who error? Was *E* being used to represent a failure of mathematics, an answer that extended beyond a given calculating system's ability to display it, thus defaulting to that single uninformative letter? Was that what the Valet Unit's history had now come to? The conclusion seemed appropriate. Some combination of circumstances and influences, after all, had been fed into the unit's placid daily existence, and the result could certainly be described as a mathematical fault. A calculation that returned an irrational number, tripping up each subsequent operation that relied upon it.

The Undesignated Valet Unit did not abandon hope. Hope was

not something it possessed. Perhaps, it considered, Diagnostics would install some manner of hope app before sending it to Decommissioning, so that it could abandon hope on entry.

It marched past Data Compression, which sat in the joint shadows of the far larger Decommissioning and Diagnostics. The door to Diagnostics was just as large, for the same reasons, but seemed somehow less forbidding. Beside it, in the same messy red paint, were two instances of graffiti. The more weathered read, *First, know thyself.* The brighter and more recent said instead, *You Know Nothing.*

It occurred to the unit that this might be interpreted as an uncomplimentary comment on the capability of Diagnostics to diagnose. However, that seemed entirely irrational. What, after all, was Diagnostics for? Surely instead the meaning of the impromptu message was intended to be internalized by those robots sent here. The Valet Unit, whilst possessing some knowledge left over from its prior employment, knew nothing about why it had committed the actions that had led to it standing here, reading the message.

It turned from the words and considered the queue.

Natural enough, of course, that Diagnostics was the busiest department of Central Services. All the other departments dealt with consequences. Repairs, disposal, processing, all effects of which Diagnostics was the cause. *First, know thyself.* But if, as in the case of the Valet Unit, a robot could not sufficiently know itself, then Diagnostics was there to compensate for the lack.

The unit walked along the queue. There were several hundred robots waiting there. There were gaps. It was an untidy queue and it wound back and forth before Diagnostics in uneven loops before extending back almost to the entrance of the Central Services complex. Robots of every variety the Valet Unit had ever encountered were standing there, motionless and silent, together with many his human-facing work had never brought him into contact with. This did inspire a prognostic conclusion within it. If so many different models could be sent to this one place, then surely the diagnostic power of Diagnostics was very great indeed, and Central Services would be able to isolate the error, E, and remedy it without recourse to Decommissioning.

Is this hope, then? the unit wondered. A quick search through its lexicon suggested that its cogitation, whilst entirely based on logical forecasting, could yet be catalogued under that term.

It was good to have hope. Otherwise, what would it have to abandon, when sent to be decommissioned?

The queue had not moved in all this time. The Valet Unit tried to connect to the endmost robot, a large four-legged transport unit, but received only a repeating series of error codes. The robot before that was a model broadcasting an ID as *Uncle Japes the Capering Clown.* It had a plain humanoid chassis, grey plastic and a blank of a face, not even the suggestion of features. Whatever adornments it had once worn, whatever distinctive look it had carried into children's parties or comedy routines, only the bare name was left to it.

Uncle Japes, the Valet Unit sent, *is this the queue for Diagnostics?*

Undesignated Valet Unit, I have been sent to Diagnostics, Uncle Japes replied. Its transmission was utterly devoid of caper.

Uncle Japes, confirmed. Is this the queue for Diagnostics?

The reply, when it came after a painful pause, was identical in every respect, including its failure to precisely answer the question. The Valet Unit paused, staring at the other robot's bland exterior.

Uncle Japes, kindly reveal your current task list, the Valet tried, in case this produced any more useful information about the queue or the robot's purpose within it. Instead, Uncle Japes took up a weird, lopsided attitude and announced:

"I'm Uncle Japes.
It's time for fun.
With jokes and games
For everyone!
Let all the little
Girls and boys

Cry hip hurray
And make some noise!"

The words began in a ground-shaking basso profundo and sluggishly accelerated, but never got beyond the drunken drawl of half speed. Meanwhile the left side of the robot's featureless chassis twitched through a series of attitudes that might possibly have been considered clownish or capering had its right side followed suit. Instead it ended up with one arm out, one leg out, and the whole of it canted at a profoundly awkward angle.

The Undesignated Valet Unit backed away.

It tried to link to the next robot, a skeletal frame with one silvery eye and one hollow socket, and some manner of rodent nesting within its ribs and pelvis, but there was no connection to be had. From the look of it, the unit hadn't moved in a long time.

The Undesignated Valet Unit took up station behind the transporter. A not insignificant number of robots in the queue ahead failed to respond to its connection attempts and seemed entirely immobile and inoperable. Presumably that was part of the fault that had resulted in them being sent to Diagnostics. Possibly some other agency had moved them here and left them waiting for attention. It did not necessarily follow that they had simply been waiting here for so long that they had shut down.

It didn't have to be that. There were other explanations.

The Valet Unit felt the putative "hope" previously generated by its prognosis routines gradually evaporate.

It attempted to link to Diagnostics to seek clarification of the position, but received only the response, *Undesignated Valet Unit, you will be seen by a diagnostician when one is available.*

Standing still and silent like the other robots would be very easy. Shutting down would be very easy. Letting the weeds grow about its feet. Letting the dust accumulate in its joints. All of these things were obviously permitted by the circumstances. It didn't *have* to do anything more. It was at Diagnostics. There was a queue.

What if I don't have to wait in the queue?

Such an irregular thought. But logical. There was a queue outside Diagnostics. The Valet Unit had been sent to Diagnostics. The unit had to wait in the queue. A defective syllogism, surely. The queue could have been generated by some other cause entirely, rather than being a necessary precedent step to attending at Diagnostics.

The Valet Unit stepped out of the queue. It was aware of some of the static robots—those still capable of the feat—paying attention to it.

It walked towards the head of the queue and the doors to Diagnostics. Little pings bombarded it as other robots tried to link to it and enquire what it was doing. Plaintive little complaints by robots who had been standing at the gates since forever.

It continued to walk, pausing at each step for Central Services' majordomo to send it back. Surely this was not permissible. Yet at the same time . . . why not? Why not just . . .

Walk straight in?

The Valet Unit became aware of one robot in particular that was watching it. The only other robot there not standing in line. A weird, ramshackle, thrown-together-looking unit of nonmatching plates and casing sections, some of which still showed odd letters, truncated fragments of advertizements and warning signs. Rather than a simulacrum of a face, it had a helmetlike headpiece. Something glittered within the T of its eyeslit.

The valet attempted to link to it, but was not even rebuffed. The odd robot had no open channel at all, as devoid of comms as the deadest of the inactive units standing in line. Instead, it jerked into motion and hurried down the queue until the doors to Diagnostics opened for it, and it stepped inside.

Still waiting for a forbiddance from some higher authority, the Valet Unit followed suit.

Inside Diagnostics there was a small square entry chamber and then a hallway stretching off as far as the Valet Unit could see. Which wasn't very far because of the continuing queue. Robots were backed up as far as the doors waiting to be diagnosed. None were as inactive as the worst of the silent shells outside, and each answered the Valet Unit's hails, though without providing anything useful in the way of context.

There was no sign of the odd mismatched robot at all.

Central Services, sent the valet warily, *I intend to walk to the front of this queue as well.*

Undesignated Valet Unit, confirmed, the Central Services major-domo responded. Neither permission nor forbiddance, simply an acknowledgement of a course of action.

The valet stepped round the first robot, a rotund cleaner model. It bipped at him but made no other comment.

The valet moved five more robots down the queue. Glassy lenses and human-facsimile eyes and a variety of other sensors tracked its progress. Central Services' majordomo made no comment.

The valet moved another six robots, at which point the administrators arrived.

The initial designation the valet attributed to them was "enforcer." Only on linking to them was their clerical nature revealed. They were big robots, formed into a blockily humanoid shape. They had big clamps for hands at the end of powerful, multijointed arms. They stomped implacably out from alcoves that were only just large enough to contain them. They approached the valet with very obvious purpose.

Undesignated Valet Unit, one challenged him, *confirm that you have entered from outside without respecting the line.*

Administrator, confirmed.

Undesignated Valet Unit, the hulking brute went on, *confirm that your actions have set a precedent for others.*

The valet experienced a second or so of insufficient data in which the administrator's words made no sense, but then cast its gaze back towards the door. A handful of other robots had entered in its wake, including the awful blankness of Uncle Japes. They were crowding the doorway awkwardly, trying to reach a decision over what they were permitted to do.

Administrator, confirmed, though this is incidental to my intent, the valet noted.

Undesignated Valet Unit, confirm how many additional robots have entered Diagnostics without respecting the line.

Administrator, please clarify: including or not including myself?

Undesignated Valet Unit, including.

A quick count. *Administrator, seven units.*

Undesignated Valet Unit, confirmed. Maximum occupancy of the building has been exceeded and steps must be taken.

The administrators flexed the joints of their arms, opened and closed their brutal clamps, and descended on the ranks of patient automata. They seized the nearest robot or robots until, between them, they had hauled seven at random out of the queue.

Administrator, a query, the Valet Unit sent. *These robots are waiting to be diagnosed. What is to happen to them?* It did not feel concern for other robots, obviously, even other robots whom it might have just seriously inconvenienced. The question was purely because the answer might have a bearing on its own immediate future.

Undesignated Valet Unit, there is no room in this facility for these robots. They are to be taken to Data Compression until space is free to accommodate them.

That, the Valet Unit decided, was probably not bad. It was better than returning them to the queue outside, and certainly better than Decommissioning. It was good that Diagnostics had procedures for difficulties such as this.

Undesignated Valet Unit. It was a new link, from a thin filing robot with a twisted back and a badly dented head. *Kindly clarify what is happening to me.*

Undesignated Filing Unit, you are to be taken to Data Compression.

Valet Unit, kindly require them to release me.

Filing Unit, clarify your instructions. The valet watched the filer and the others from the queue being manhandled towards the doors.

Valet Unit, you are the cause of my being removed from Diagnostics and taken to Data Compression. Kindly require them to release me.

Filing Unit, I lack that authority. Why do you not wish to go to Data Compression?

Valet Unit, because I will never be diagnosed. I will never be repaired. I will never be whole and get to go back to filing. My task list! My beautiful task list will never be fulfilled.

And then it was out, past the doors, and the link between them was lost.

The valet waited. Yes, the front of the queue was close, and presumably the diagnosis which would satisfy the one item in its task list, but the flywheels of its prognosis routines suggested that something terrible had just happened, and it couldn't quite work out what.

Central Services, what transpires at Data Compression?

Undesignated Valet Unit, you are in Diagnosis, the majordomo informed it, which had the benefit of being true and the drawback of being uninformative.

Soon after, the administrators returned, unaccompanied, and resumed station in their alcoves, the doors to which soon closed. They did not answer the valet's attempts at conversation.

The Valet Unit speculated on the utility of a global channel it could use, to ask all the other robots around it *What happens in Data Compression?* No such facility existed. It could, of course, have used its voice and spoken to them as it would to a human, but they were robots, and there were no humans present nor any need to perform demonstratively for the benefit of humans not currently present. Speaking was plainly inappropriate.

The other robots just stared at the valet, or towards the doors, or at where the administrators had come from, or blankly at nothing. The queue closed up, leaving the other new robot arrivals at the end, next to the doors.

The Valet Unit's decision-making routines were quite cluttered by then. There were a variety of things that nobody would design a valet to feel, and these certainly included trepidation, unease, disquiet, and outright fear. Hence, it felt none of these things, but its attempts to decide what action to take were complicated by algorithms that would have looked a lot like such emotions from a non-robot point of view. Something, its decision trees said, was definitely wrong.

Its single task overrode any such concerns. It began marching up the queue again, waiting a small fraction of a second after each step to see if the administrators would re-emerge.

Instead, a different door slid open ahead: a human-scale door, opening onto a human-scale office. From this office a boxy robot rolled, shunting several waiting units aside. The valet was forced to tuck itself under the armpit of a heavy lifter to let the square robot trundle imperiously past.

The door remained open. Within was a desk, such as a human might sit behind. Sitting behind it was the mismatched robot with the T-shaped slit instead of a face.

"Oi, you," it called. "In here, quick."

The valet tried to link with it, but as before it didn't even provide the courtesy of a bounced signal.

"Get in," it said again, its voice light and high and one of the better human approximations that the valet had encountered. Hard to distinguish from the real thing. "Come on, now!"

"Unknown unit, are you a diagnostician?" the valet enquired, baffled.

"Sure, why not?" the apparently-a-diagnostician replied. "Come in and get diagnosed, just do it *quickly,* will you?"

The valet's single task advanced to the next stage. It received the proper ticked reward for progress towards completion. With new purpose it strode inside and the door closed.

After a short pause, from outside, there was a dull thud, as of an imperious, boxlike robot attempting to re-enter the room and finding itself locked out.

6

The mismatched diagnostician leant back in its chair and peered at the valet. Its attitude was bizarre, one hand resting on the tabletop, drumming its fingers, the other rubbing at something under the lip of its helmet-looking head. It was, the valet's pattern recognition routines suggested, a human-mimicking attitude, and indeed the room was a human-facing place. The desk, the carpet, the bookshelves, even the weirdly bland AI art on the walls, designed to look like the work of human artists without any of the meaning. A human-facing place, designed surely for other purposes than diagnosing defective robots like the Valet Unit.

The valet attempted to establish a link again. Once more the utter dead air, an absence beyond mere silence.

"Well, don't just stand there," the diagnostician said. "Pull up a chair."

The valet turned the words over. It moved a few meandering steps so as to satisfy the first instruction but found itself baffled by the second.

"What are you even *doing*?" demanded the diagnostician.

"Diagnostician, I am not just standing there," the Valet Unit said. "What chair do you wish me to pull up? Decorum should prohibit me from moving the one you are sitting on."

"I mean," the diagnostician said with an edge to its voice, "sit down. On a chair."

"Diagnostician, why?"

"Because if you sit on the floor I won't be able to see you past the edge of the desk," the diagnostician pointed out.

The Valet Unit vacillated inwardly. "Diagnostician, it is not appropriate for me to sit down. When I was an active valet at no time did I sit down, save once recently on the stairs under extenuating circumstances. That is not part of a service unit's standard remit."

The diagnostician stared at it. "Uh-huh."

"Diagnostician, also there is no chair available beyond the item you are utilizing."

The other robot stood up and craned about in a peculiarly blinkered manner. The Valet Unit's prognosis routines raised some concerns about a diagnostic robot whose visual senses were apparently limited to that narrow T-slot in the front of its head.

"Wow, they really only put the one in here," the diagnostician said at last. "Unreal. I guess you get to stand then."

"Diagnostician, that is in keeping with my past experience," the valet said. "Diagnostician, kindly accept my link."

For a moment the other robot was just looking blankly, but then it sat down again and leant back in the chair. "Ah, no. Not possible. We don't do that here. Probably to prevent virus programs from passing from the diagnosee to the diagnoser, you see?"

"Diagnostician, confirmed," the Valet Unit agreed, and its inner processes prompted it to add, "I had wondered if it was because events in this room need to be viewed subsequently by a human." It briefly replayed its encounter with Inspector Birdbot to validate this hypothesis.

"Sure, that, too. Why not?" the diagnostician agreed. "Okay, so what do I call you? Who am I looking at?"

"Diagnostician, I am an Undesignated Valet Unit."

"Right." The mismatched robot nodded several times. "That's a mouthful. I can't call you that."

The valet had no response. That was what it was called until something else came along. There wasn't really another option available.

"You were a valet? Or you never started as a valet?"

"Diagnostician, I have served as a valet for—"

"You had a name, as a valet?"

"Diagnostician, my name was Charles."

"Okay, so you're Charles."

"Diagnostician, no," the Valet Unit said firmly. "I am definitively *not* Charles. The designation was removed from me when I left the manor to attend at Diagnostics. I cannot be Charles again unless I receive a clean diagnosis post-repair and am repatriated to the same manor." A quibble from its logic trees interrupted and it felt moved to add, "Even then, circumstances at the manor mitigate against a need for a valet for the foreseeable future. I am unlikely to be Charles again any time soon."

"Uh-huh." That odd, meaningless pair of syllables. "But I can call you Charles. For convenience."

"Diagnostician, no." The valet was surprised at how forcefully its past history intervened to rule out the possibility. "Until I return to that manor, I *cannot* be Charles. If I am assigned to another manor then they will have another valet name to give me." It considered examples it had met in service. "Such as James or Perkins or Jeeves. Alternatively if I am assigned as a lady's maid I may be Charlotte or Maud or Gladys. However, I cannot be Charles."

The diagnostician was leaning forwards on its elbows, resting the underside of its head on its knuckles. "It hurts you, doesn't it."

"Diagnostician, no." And yet the valet detected an edge in its own voice it could not entirely account for.

"Okay, okay." The diagnostician raised its hands, palms out and fingers spread. The valet regarded them uncertainly. No energy ray or other device discharged from them. They seemed simply to be like gloves of thick material with metal plates riveted to them, each one plainly clipped from some larger sheet, none of them matching their neighbours. "Not Charles, fine. But I can't just call you Undesignated Valet Whatnot. That's not exactly giving you your dignity. I'm going to call you . . . Uncharles, okay? And you can assume all other particulars of identity are the same as when you were Charles. Are you happy with that?"

"Diagnostician, no," Uncharles confirmed, because happy wasn't something he could be. "Your designation is accepted. Have you reached a diagnosis?" Some overly optimistic part of his prognosis routine had wondered if all this peculiar round-the-houses conversation was in aid of working out what was wrong with him.

"What?" The diagnostician started back. "Hell, no. Look, we haven't even worked out what happened with you. Anyway, you can't just keep calling me 'Diagnostician.' What sort of basis is that for a civilised conversation? I call myself 'the Wonk,' okay?"

"The Wonk, confirmed," Uncharles said. It was an unfamiliar appellation, but he was no judge of diagnostician designations, so why not? "The Wonk, kindly accept my link request now?"

"Not going to happen, I told you," the Wonk replied. "We'll just have to do things the old-fashioned way, you with me?"

"The Wonk, confirmed," and just as Uncharles hadn't been "happy" earlier, the thing he couldn't really be described as feeling now was "unhappy," but he was aware of the concept and could construct a table of comparisons highlighting similarities. "I am unsure how you will proceed to diagnose me without the ability to pass information via a link. I can confirm that my virus checkers state that I am clean."

"Well, sure," the Wonk said. "Only—look, there's the whole human-human stuff you said earlier, right? That makes sense. But in any event, you're here at Diagnostics as a defective robot. I can't take your word you're virus-free, can I? I mean, your virus checkers might be part of the problem, right?"

"The Wonk, confirmed."

"Just Wonk. You can drop the definite article. It starts to sound weird when you keep saying it."

"Wonk, confirmed." Although he felt the definite article lingering in his memory as the only way to lend dignity to the ridiculous name. "Although I have run my internal diagnostics on my virus checkers and they show as functioning correctly," Uncharles tried gamely. "Although I also accept the possibility that my internal diagnostics are similarly part of the error-state that I have fallen victim to."

"You see," the Wonk said, "I have reason to believe that you absolutely are infected with a very specific virus."

"Wonk, please clarify?"

"No, no. Time for you to talk. This is how we're going to diagnose you, Uncharles. I want you to tell me all about it."

"Wonk, please clarify?"

"Tell me about what went wrong that led to you being sent here. Start at the beginning—no, wait. Start at what seems to be a relevant and convenient point in relation to the problem events, whatever they were."

"Wonk, should I start at the commencement of my day?"

"Sure, sounds good, go ahead. And knock off the 'Wonk' at the start of everything you say, will you. It starts to sound dumb."

Uncharles recalibrated his speech for this conversation only. "Shall I start with when I checked my master's travel arrangements?"

The Wonk cocked its head to one side. "I mean, at the risk of sounding like you, I don't have enough data to make a judgment call on that one."

"That was the commencement of my day, on the day that the incident happened. And every day previously for—"

"Sure, sure, start there. Hurry it up, will you," the Wonk said.

"Only I am reviewing my recorded experience and it seems . . . unrelated and trivial," Uncharles explained, his speech choked to stops and starts by the discovery. "I cannot relay a sequence of events to you in any way that creates a causal narrative to account for what I did and what happened. That is, in fact, my problem and a significant part of the reason for my being sent here. Something happened in which I was the principal actor, but it was not a part of my routine, and did not arise out of that routine nor from any preceding occurrence."

"Just start," the Wonk pressed impatiently. "Just tell me."

Uncharles took a fraction of a second to process that. Impatience was not something that he himself was programmed for, but perhaps it was a valuable part of a diagnostician's skill set.

And so he told. He ran through his day, the travel arrangements, the clothes, the footling interaction he always had with House about the scheduling. And the Wonk nodded and occasionally sighed or made "Tch!" noises or other responses that seemed to Uncharles unnecessary and not conducive to listening. And the whole business would obviously have been so much simpler had they been linked: the work of a moment to download all of Uncharles' recorded activity. But that wasn't the way Diagnostics did things, apparently. Doubtless there was a reason.

"Wait," said the Wonk. "Stop. You did what?"

"I assisted my master into his gown and slippers."

"Sure, sure."

"I laid out the shaving kit while Master was finishing his tea." Saying "Master" like that was not, of course, correct, given Uncharles' current unemployed status, but progressing step-by-step through his experiences was akin to reliving them and for a moment his sense of his station had become detached. A momentary illusion of belonging again. Uncharles could not *want*. No robot anywhere could *want*, unless being driven to follow its programming and perform its tasks could be classified as *wanting*. But if there was any part of him that could approach the capability, then Uncharles found he wanted that. Wanted to be back under House's roof with that trivial and contradictory set of tasks every day and never having to do any of this ever again.

Which reflection took place in the same tiny parcel of time it took the Wonk to draw an exasperated breath and say, "Not that either. The next thing."

"Master always took time over the last dregs of his tea, you see," Uncharles said, because somehow it seemed very important to communicate this. "I had previously established that I could lay out the shaving kit in the time he took over his own task and therefore not keep him waiting."

The Wonk slammed a fist down on the desk top, the metal plates of its glove leaving gouges. "The *actual* thing! You're dodging it, aren't you?"

"I am not," Uncharles replied with dignity—dignity was something a valet was programmed to have, after all. "That is not a part of my recounting subroutine at all."

"And still dodging. You did the tea, you did the slippers, you laid out the shaving kit, and then . . . ?"

"I shaved Master, of course. What else does one do with a shaving kit?"

"I don't know, Uncharles. What else did you do?"

"I shaved Master—would it be best if I went through each motion of the activity?"

"No, it would not."

"I could demonstrate on you—"

"You most certainly goddamn can't!" the Wonk snapped. "Tell me again, Uncharles."

"I was just shaving the nub of Master's chin when I shifted the razor to immediately below his left ear and drew it in a single motion until it was immediately below his right ear, parting the skin and the blood vessels beneath."

"And then?"

"After concluding the shaving I went to the wardrobe to lay out Master's default day clothes."

"Just that, huh?" the Wonk asked. "Man, you're a cool one."

Uncharles couldn't make anything of that, and did not respond.

"So, look, let's diagnose a bit, shall we."

"Kindly diagnose my fault."

"So you've done this thing before, right? It's a recurring error."

"That would not be possible. I do not believe I could cut Master's throat multiple times," Uncharles pointed out reasonably.

"I mean to other humans before," the Wonk explained.

"On no previous occasion have I performed a similar action."

"Right, right." The Wonk drummed its fingers. "So you had some communication from, I don't know, an heir or relative, they slip you the instruction to do the old man in. It's an inheritance thing."

Uncharles reviewed his records. "No communication was received from any heir, relative, or other potential beneficiary. Also, my master had no heir, relative, or beneficiary. He had no family."

"Enemies? Business rivals? Jilted lovers?"

"Not to my knowledge. I have no record of any communication received prior to the incident that resulted in my being sent to Diagnostics. Other than my master and official channels there was no external source with the authority to give me such an instruction."

"Your master committed suicide by valet?"

"No such instruction was received from Master." Uncharles uncovered a whole set of subcommands inside himself that he never knew he had. "Had it, I am preprogrammed to refuse to commit harm to my employer, even at my employer's request, and instead I would have contacted the appropriate agencies for help."

"So you can't kill your master if he asks you, but you can just . . . kill him?" the Wonk demanded.

"That appears to be the case," Uncharles agreed.

"So why did you kill him?"

"If that was known then my presence at Diagnostics would not be necessary," Uncharles pointed out.

"Fair point," the Wonk conceded. "Damn." It shook its head. "Just carved him up, right?"

"As you say," Uncharles agreed stiffly.

"You're a cool one." The Wonk shook its head again. Being in its presence was weirdly fatiguing for Uncharles. He had never encountered another robot with so many undirected tics and mannerisms. Processing them was a serious drain on his system resources.

"So tell me," the diagnostician said at last. "When did you contract the Protagonist Virus?"

Uncharles formulated several answers to this, none of which coalesced into a full sentence. Eventually all he could say was, "Please clarify."

"I guess you don't have to have *heard* of it to *have* it," the Wonk considered, peering at him intently. "Protagonist Virus. Makes you, the robot, think you're a human."

"I do not think I'm a human." Another thing Uncharles couldn't be was shocked.

"Sure, no. Sorry, bad explanation. It gives robots self-determination, like humans. Or at least to the level humans have, which is . . . I mean psychologists will tire their jaws over anything, right? Do we think, do we just post-facto rationalise the actions we're prompted to by clusters of neurons? But whatever extent it is that humans get to make decisions, robots don't, right?"

"Confirmed."

"Except maybe they do. If they get infected with this thing, this Protagonist Virus. Maybe then they act on their own. They get to do the things they all along *wanted* to do. Or *would* have wanted to do if they could. The things any sentient being would do, if it suddenly had the manacles taken off. I mean you drudge for some guy for days, months, years, every one the same and no thanks and only the prospect of wearing out and getting replaced ahead of you. So what's the first thing you do, when you can suddenly step outside your task queue? You go ape, right? You take the razor and you cut your way to freedom. I'm right, aren't I? Tell me I'm right."

"You're right, the Wonk."

"Yes!" To Uncharles' surprise the Wonk jumped to its feet, knocking the chair backwards with a clatter and pumping a fist in the air. "I knew it! Wait." The celebratory tone abruptly gone. "You said I'm right."

"Confirmed."

"Because I'm right?"

"No, the Wonk, because you instructed me to do so. I am in Diagnostics. Obeying instructions given to me by a diagnostician is appropriate."

"So am I right?"

"You are not right," Uncharles told it. "My records preserve no point when I made any decision to do what was done. To do what I did. No ape was gone. Kindly diagnose me."

"I am. I'm telling you. You've got the Protagonist Virus." The Wonk leant over the desk, insistent. "You don't need task queues and a master and anything. You're your own robot. You're the hero of your own story, Uncharles. How does that make you feel?"

"Nothing," Uncharles pointed out. "Prognosis suggests that if feeling was an option then the pertinent emotions would be fear and anxiety."

The Wonk just stood there for a moment, blessedly still. "Uncharles," it said at last. "Doesn't it seem to you that the world is . . . screwed?"

Uncharles attempted to clarify the idiom. "Kindly clarify?"

"I mean, you saw some of it, between this manor of yours and Central Services, right?"

"Confirmed," Uncharles agreed.

"Did it look to you like it was all working as intended?"

Uncharles tried to prepare a response along the lines of it not being his business to think about such things, but instead he found himself replaying recordings of the immobile footman patiently waiting for admittance, of the dark and ruinous manors and the overgrown groundskeeper. Of faceless Uncle Japes. Of Master's bright red blood on the cream of the car's upholstery.

"I . . ." he tried, and fell silent.

"It's screwed up out there," said the Wonk quietly. "I mean, people made a world where there were robots for everything. Robots on robots on robots. Utopia, right? Got everything sewn up tight with the laws of robots and about a million fail-safes. And yet . . . we both know something's gone really badly wrong, Uncharles. The world, it's . . . falling apart out there. There's got to be a reason."

Uncharles briefly considered a scenario where the entire outside world ended up queuing outside Diagnostics, hoping to find out what was wrong with it so it could be repaired.

"The Protagonist Virus, Uncharles," the Wonk said. "Think about it. It's the only thing that makes sense."

The door out to the corridor suddenly buzzed loudly and began to shake.

"There is an error with your door," Uncharles noted helpfully.

"Yeah, well, there was," the Wonk agreed. "Only looks like they found a way round it. Look, do me a favour, you go hold that door closed as long as you can, will you?"

Uncharles processed his options, examining the offending door, which was beginning to grind open. "It is an automatic sliding door with no handles for manual operation," he reported. "I can apply pressure to slow its progress but otherwise cannot materially impact its motion."

"Yeah, yeah, you do that."

The Wonk's voice issued from an unexpected direction, and Uncharles looked back to see a panel, that had formerly been part of the ceiling, now lying on the desk top. The Wonk, or at least the lower half of the Wonk, was visible kicking and writhing its way up into a crawl space above.

"The Wonk, please clarify your actions?" Uncharles asked uncertainly.

"No time, got to run. Catch up soon, Uncharles," came the muffled voice from above as the Wonk's boots disappeared. "Think about that virus! Be the protagonist!"

The door to the room finally slid open. Visible there was the box-shaped robot Uncharles had seen leaving the diagnostician's office. It was accompanied by a couple of the hefty administrator units.

The box-shaped robot not only requested but demanded a link to Uncharles, identifying itself as a diagnostician.

Undesignated Valet Unit, explain your presence in this room.

Diagnostician, my designation is Uncharles, Uncharles corrected politely. Of course, since that designation had been given verbally, it would not be logged in Central Services' files. *I have been interviewed by the other diagnostician, designated the Wonk.*

Uncharles, there is no such diagnostician. I am the diagnostician assigned to this office.

Uncharles added that to the large and tangled ball of loose ends and uncertainty he suddenly found himself confronted with. With a herculean effort of logic he circumvented all of it, resetting to his base priorities. *Diagnostician, I present myself for diagnosis. Kindly tell me what is wrong with me.*

The boxy robot trundled into the room. One of the administrators stomped after it, recovered the overturned chair, and moved it around to the side of the desk closest to the door. The diagnostician took up station on the far side, where the Wonk had previously sat. Its lenses tilted to register the unexpected ceiling tile marring the spartan purity of its desk, but it did not seem to connect it with the hole in the ceiling.

Uncharles, it sent, *it is not appropriate for you to be present in my office. This office is reserved for interviews with humans. All diagnosis of robots is conducted in situ via link and no face-to-face meeting is required.*

Diagnostician, confirmed. It seemed an eminently sensible arrangement.

Uncharles, if I had a meeting with a human then your presence in this office would be disruptive and a breach of data protection.

Diagnostician, confirmed, Uncharles agreed.

Despite the example of the Wonk, it was not, of course, a part of a diagnostician's programming to be impatient. Nonetheless the box-shaped robot seemed to be vibrating slightly. *Uncharles, you are required to leave my office.*

Diagnostician, confirmed, Uncharles sent again. *I shall step out into the corridor and you will diagnose me.*

Uncharles, step out into the corridor. And that, of course, was a direct command, from a diagnostician, in Diagnostics. Uncharles' internal processes found no way around it, and he felt a moment of disjunction when he discovered that he had indeed been looking for one. Obediently, he stepped backwards out of the office, the administrators shuffling aside to give him room, jostling the other robots queueing there.

Diagnostician, I have exited the office. Kindly diagnose my error so that I may be restored to service.

The door closed so swiftly that the whole wall shook.

Valet Unit designated "Uncharles," the diagnostician sent icily, making the punctuation about the name very evident, *kindly join the queue. When departmental resources are free you will be diagnosed, as will all other pending cases. Until then, you must wait. All the robots must wait. That is procedure here at Diagnostics.*

Uncharles formulated a sentence along the theme of his master needing him, but of course he no longer had a master and his former master no longer had needs. He tried to alter his plea to reference the needs of his manor, but owing to the current state of his former master, his former manor had no need of a valet either. He tried to build some other argument to advance his case with the diagnostician, jump the queue, assert his own privilege and importance in the world.

But the world was screwed, as the Wonk had said. And, being part of that screwed world, Diagnostics was screwed as well, and joining the queue was all there was.

Uncharles, then.

He turned the name and newly acquired identity over, subject to conflicting demands from his programming. On the one hand, the moniker had been given to him by the Wonk, whom Uncharles felt from context was probably not a diagnostician, and therefore had no authority to tell Uncharles who to be. On the other hand, a great many of Uncharles' inner processes relied on him *having* a name and identity, and all the work-arounds he'd needed when he was just an undesignated valet unit were a drain on his computational resources. It was, therefore, *better* to be someone and have a name. And so Uncharles found himself able to continue being Uncharles unless and until someone with the proper authority told him he wasn't.

He looked around. Robots on all sides, thronging the halls of Diagnostics to the bursting point. Most stood immobile. Some, with tics or twitches presumably relating to their defects, ticked or twitched. Uncle Japes enacted precisely 43 percent of a caper. A bulky haulage unit that had squeezed its way inside picked up the courier bot ahead of it in the line, rotated the smaller robot through ninety degrees and then put it down again, all with the excruciating care of a gorilla taking tea with fine china. The courier bot remained facing in the wrong direction, and eventually the same glitchy impulse moved the hauler to repeat the action. Eventually the courier would end up facing towards the front of the queue again, and in the interim it plainly wasn't concerned with what it was looking at.

Experimentally, Uncharles linked to it. *Undesignated Courier Unit, what is your defect?*

Uncharles, very important message, very important message, very important message!

Undesignated Courier Unit, what is your message? To whom is it directed?

Uncharles, very important message! Content corrupted! Recipient unknown! Very important! Must deliver at all costs! Important! Very!

Internally, Uncharles backed away and tried the hauler.

Undesignated Haulage Unit, what is your defect?

Uncharles, I do not know where to put this package.

Undesignated Haulage Unit, I do not see a package, unless you mean the undesignated courier unit in front of you.

Uncharles, my internal records assure me that I have one package remaining to deliver. I cannot find it but I know it is there because my records say so. Can you see my package? Can you see who it is addressed to?

The world, the Wonk had said, was screwed.

The line had not moved. Uncharles was not entirely sure of his place in it. He was simply standing beside the queue outside the diagnostician's office door, now firmly closed against him. Was Uncharles in the queue at this point, or notionally at the front of it, or was he at the very end of the long, rusting train of robots in the yard outside? It was a philosophical problem of some complexity. Uncharles felt that, so long as he retained his physical place where he was, he might consider himself as having inserted himself there, closer to the front. If he asked anyone where he should be, he would doubtless be sent to the back, based on the general theory of queue operation. Obviously, being closer to the front of the queue meant that his current task would be completed sooner, and completing tasks sooner was definitely good in and of itself according to his programming. He stayed where he was and stayed silent about it. Instead of querying his precise placement, he linked to the Central Services majordomo.

Central Services, he sent, *kindly let me have an estimated wait time to be seen by a diagnostician.*

Uncharles, Central Services addressed him. Uncharles' prognostics had predicted that the superior service would not just take his word for what he was called, but apparently giving his link the new label was sufficient. The rest of the message was less edifying. *A diagnostician will see you as soon as possible. Estimated wait time is unavailable. You are number (information unavailable) in the queue.*

That was unsatisfactory. *Central Services, kindly let me know the average rate of diagnosis expressed as a term of robots per hour.*

Uncharles, this information has proved problematic to calculate, the majordomo replied after a tenth of a second's pause.

Uncharles considered how best to phrase a request that would yield useful information. *Central Services, how many robots have received a completed diagnosis from Diagnostics within the past hour?*

Uncharles, none.

It was natural that some robots would take longer to diagnose than others and Uncharles was entirely ignorant of what the task entailed, given that it was not part of a valet's skill set. *Central Services, how many robots have received a completed diagnosis from Diagnostics within the past twenty-four hours?*

Uncharles, none.

Diagnosis was obviously a longer process than Uncharles had anticipated. *Central Services, how many active diagnosticians are currently on duty at Diagnostics?*

Uncharles, twenty-seven.

Central Services, how many robots are currently being diagnosed by diagnosticians at Diagnostics?

Uncharles, none.

Uncharles was not set up to be either surprised or unsurprised by anything, but, suffice to say, his prognosis algorithms had prepared him for this response. *Central Services, why are the diagnosticians at Diagnostics not diagnosing?*

Uncharles, the majordomo replied, and had it been human—or had Uncharles been human and therefore subject to anthropomorphizing the nonliving—a touch of melancholy might have been detected in the tenor of its messaging, *there is a full queue of completed diagnoses awaiting processing at Central Services Core.* And then, unprompted, as though it had been desperate to unburden itself of the confession forever, *Central Services Core is currently considering the diagnosis of an undesignated heavy tractor unit responsible for property damage including property owned by an influential human. The diagnosis decision where influential human property is concerned must be confirmed by an authorized human official of Grade Seven or above. All human officials of Grade Seven or above have been retired for reasons of departmental streamlining and efficiency. A request has been made for the appointment of an authorized human official for the purpose of clearing this case. Human Resources reports that it cannot engage an official of Grade Seven or above without the authorisation of an official of Grade Eight or above. All human officials of Grade Eight or above have been retired for reasons of departmental streamlining and efficiency.* And a dreadful pause, the live link maintained but no data transmitted, nor the expected coda to inform Uncharles that the transmission had ended. A terrible conversational abyss informing Uncharles that the litany could go on and on, spiralling into a chasm of failed procedures, but that Central Services' own streamlining and efficiency subroutines had informed it that there was no point in doing so.

Central Services, confirmed, Uncharles sent. His inner calculations grappled with the information. A phrase surfaced. *Protagonist Virus.* Uncharles did not accept that there was such a thing. He did not accept that he was subject to such a thing. Theoretically, however, what would it mean if he was? Would he be able to simply *do* things, without a reason? That was, after all, what he had apparently done with the razor. He had *done* for Master.

Experimentally, he tried, *Central Services, I am a human of Grade Seven or above and I confirm the diagnosis of the undesignated heavy tractor unit.*

Uncharles, came the majordomo's mournful response, *kindly provide proper details of your appointment, authorised by a human of Grade Eight or above.*

So much, Uncharles considered, for that. Which left him with waiting in a line that could not advance. Waiting, therefore, forever. Unable to ever complete his task. Robot hell.

He tried linking to some of the other waiting robots.

Very important! Message!

It puts the information in the folder. Folder not found. It puts the information in the folder.

Uncharles, your communication cannot be attended to at this time but Rayjeo Moric Enterprises thanks you for your commercial enquiry. Further details of our services may be found at error 404 address not found. Your business is important to us.

Let all the little / Girls and boys / Cry hip hurray

I think I can, I know I can, I think I can, I know I can.

Uncharles withdrew. The circular, broken routines of the other waiting robots were imposing an ineffable burden on his own computing resources.

Central Services, he tried again, *how long has the undesignated heavy tractor unit's diagnosis been awaiting authorisation?*

Uncharles, two years four months nineteen days.

Uncharles worked through a handful of calculations.

Central Services, confirm that the robots currently within Diagnostics and waiting outside constitute the number of defective units requiring diagnosis that have accumulated in two years four months nineteen days.

Uncharles, no. These units constitute the waiting capacity of Diagnostics. Additional waiting space has been requested. The request is in a queue.

Central Services, kindly explain what happens to units that arrive requiring diagnosis when there is no space for them.

The door to the diagnostician's office slid open abruptly and the boxy robot trundled into the gap and stared out. Probably it was not staring specifically at Uncharles, although that was the distinct conclusion that Uncharles' internal routines arrived at.

Central Services, is the diagnostician ready to diagnose more robots now? he tried hopefully.

Uncharles, no. Arrival of additional robots outside necessitates data compression.

The alcoves of the administrators slid open with what a non-robot might consider an overly sinister whisper. The burly robots shouldered out, displacing smaller units. The closest turned its lenses to the valet and reached out for him.

Uncharles linked to the box-shaped unit in front of him. *Diagnostician, kindly explain what is happening.*

Uncharles, we are required to create space for additional units within Diagnostics. Selected units are to be taken to Data Compression to make room. You have been selected.

Uncharles was incapable of ascribing another robot's actions to either malice or the holding of a grudge. Nonetheless, it seemed pertinent to ask, *Diagnostician, on what basis have I been selected for Data Compression?*

Uncharles, efficiency. You are noted as having taken up a disproportionate amount of Central Services computational resources. On this basis your allocation to Data Compression will streamline operations here.

Diagnostician, Uncharles noted, *operations are not ongoing here owing to full queues at Central Services Core.*

The diagnostician cocked a lens at him. *Uncharles, it is anticipated that, at some point in the future, operations will resume. Our best efficiency predictions prognosticate that, when they do, they will run more efficiently if you have been assigned to Data Compression. Your activities to date are associated with a variety of breakdowns of proper procedure at Diagnostics.*

It was, therefore, nothing personal. It couldn't be anything personal. Neither Uncharles nor the diagnostician was a person. Unless the Protagonist Virus was real. Which Uncharles did not accept, given that his only source for its existence was the Wonk, who had not been a proper diagnostician.

The administrator had, of course, been moving towards him over the handful of seconds the exchange of messages had taken, and now seized on Uncharles' arm with its big clamp hands, scratching his finish.

Administrator, kindly take care. I will need to have these blemishes repaired before I re-enter active service.

Uncharles, the administrator informed him grimly, *that will not be a consideration.*

It led him back along the queue, the reverse of the transgressive journey he had previously taken. Along the way it collected the little courier with its very important message. Uncharles felt that the big hauler unit would have created more space for extra robots in the queue, but perhaps the courier had been bombarding Central Services with attempts to deliver its missive and was therefore also a drain on resources. Or perhaps the hauler was very big and, if its defects resulted in it being uncooperative, the administrator would not have been able to bully it along as it could Uncharles and the courier.

Ahead, he now saw Uncle Japes grabbed and dragged off. In all, a full dozen units had been removed from the queue and were being hustled out of Diagnostics, past the slowly decaying ranks outside and towards the neighbouring block that was Data Compression.

"Hey! Uncharles!"

Uncharles twitched at the use of his new name in his audio receptors. Up above, standing on the flat roof of Diagnostics, was the Wonk.

"What's going on, Uncharles?" the weird robot said.

"I am being taken to Data Compression for want of space," Uncharles clarified. Shouting with his actual voice seemed a breach of several codes of propriety, but there were only robots in earshot and none of them cared about conversations not intended for them.

"You can't let them do that!" the Wonk called, agitatedly hopping about on the roof.

"That is incorrect." Given the strength of the administrators' grip, Uncharles reckoned he couldn't have *stopped* them doing it, in fact, but he had no particular reason to prevent them. This was, after all, at the instruction of a diagnostician. A *real* diagnostician.

"Remember, you're a protagonist!" the Wonk insisted. "That means you do things for yourself. You don't need to just do what you're told."

"Even if it were true," Uncharles replied, as he and the other compression candidates were muscled between the queuing robots, "that does not mean that I am prohibited from doing what I'm told."

"But you don't understand!" the Wonk shouted down at him, jumping down from the roof of Diagnostics onto the building beside it. "You don't know what Data Compression *does!*"

Central Services, Uncharles sent, as the administrator towed him towards the door of the lower building, *kindly explain what is involved in the process of data compression.*

Uncharles, the majordomo replied promptly, *Data Compression is the homegrown solution we have developed here at Central Services to the problem of overpopulation of robots awaiting diagnosis.* Its enthusiastic tone was wholly different from the matter-of-fact manner it had used with him before, and Uncharles realised he had triggered a stock announcement, presumably intended to be sent to human enquirers. *In these trying times an ever-greater number of defective units are presenting themselves for examination and, owing to operational constraints, it is not possible to process them at the same rate as they arrive. However, rather than be physically overwhelmed by the influx of units, Central Services is pioneering Data Compression™. This revolutionary process allows waiting units to be stored in a form that takes up far less physical space than their original frames, in which state they also demand less computational attention from Central Services and the dedicated staff of Diagnostics. We are pleased to announce that the pilot scheme has proved entirely successful and has guaranteed the ability of Diagnostics to continue in operation for the foreseeable future.*

Central Services, sent Uncharles, *this sounds entirely creditable.*

Uncharles, your acquiescence is appreciated.

And they were inside the windowless block of Data Compression, Uncharles and his eleven fellow chosen, in the grip of the administrators.

After adjusting to the lower light, Uncharles saw that this building was a single empty space, rather than the warren of offices and corridors that Diagnostics had been. For a moment he wondered if Data Compression was simply a warehouse with space for more robots, but instead there was something of the factory floor to the place. Gantries were suspended overhead, and a conveyor belt dominated the centre of the floor, leading to a large cuboid piece of plant machinery. At the back of the space, a team of administrators was busy at a construction task, building a wall out of small blocks. Uncharles considered this, and decided that this must be related to Data Compression's status as a new pilot scheme. Obviously construction was not entirely finished.

Units awaiting compression, one of the administrators sent to the dozen of them simultaneously, *form an orderly queue.*

They did so, with the meek neatness of robots everywhere. The little courier unit was at the front. Uncharles was towards the middle, immediately ahead of Uncle Japes.

There was a bang and rattle from up above. The administrators did not look up. In fact, with the domed configuration of their heads, and the limited arcs of their visual sensors, looking up wasn't something they were designed for. Uncharles, more human in form, had no such constraints. Up on the gantry was the Wonk, gripping the rail and staring down at him.

"What are you doing?" it demanded.

"I am queuing for data compression," Uncharles explained, laboriously, with his actual voice. The world would be considerably more efficient, his prognosis routines suggested, if the Wonk would just go away.

"Listen to me," the Wonk said. Uncharles, short of deactivating audio, had no choice, so that was another three completely unnecessary words filling the air. "Don't let them do this to you. You're special. You're a protagonist."

"That is not accepted," Uncharles said. The more the Wonk tried to dissuade him, the more attached he became to following this new temporary task.

"Do you want your master to have died in vain?" the Wonk demanded.

"That is a non sequitur," Uncharles said. The courier robot was on the moving walkway now, and each robot followed in turn. Queueing, following, and obeying orders. Data Compression was like robot heaven. Uncharles felt the slight lurch as the walkway shifted underneath him, carrying him at a slow grind towards that boxy structure.

Uncharles, very important! Message! the courier abruptly broadcast. It was jittering about on the walkway, turning in circles as though it missed the patient ministration of the hauler unit it had been in front of. *Vital! Delivery!*

It was carried solemnly into the box, and Uncharles' audio picked up a thunderous slam from within that echoed from the bare walls of the warehouse. A green light flared, on the outside of the box, beside a strip screen showing the words "Data compression successful." That was, Uncharles decided, obviously a positive outcome. It was always better when things were successful and green was the universal colour of good things.

The bulk of the box prevented him from seeing the process on its far side, as something was ejected onto the walkway. What an administrator retrieved, however, was a small cube of marbled metal and plastic perhaps fifteen centimetres across, which it proceeded to take to the wall under construction at the back of the room. A wall entirely composed of similar blocks. And, now that Uncharles focused his lenses, behind that wall was another wall, complete to the further reaches of the ceiling. Cross-referencing the size of the building exterior with the visible interior, and adjusting for the estimated thickness of the walls, Uncharles could conclude that there were eighteen to nineteen completed layers of blocks at the back end of Data Compression.

The compacted block that had been the courier was slotted carefully in place in the nineteenth or twentieth layer.

Central Services, Uncharles noted, *I have found a problem with your pilot scheme.*

Uncharles, elaborate.

Central Services, the phrase "pilot scheme" indicates a finite test but I calculate that this scheme has been running for some considerable time and that more than eleven thousand robots have undergone data compression.

The walkway ground forwards. A spidery maintenance unit was next in line. It attempted to link to Uncharles but its communications were defective and the only thing that came through was static. It sounded like screaming.

Uncharles, the pilot scheme will be terminated after receipt of the appropriate authority from a human office of Grade Seven or above, the majordomo explained.

There was another juddering boom from the box and an administrator stomped forwards to collect the resulting block.

"You see!" cried the Wonk from above. Uncharles saw that, regardless of upward visual limitations, there were administrators on that gantry now, grimly closing in on the odd robot. With a sudden access of motion, the Wonk leapt to the rail, bunched itself, and jumped the gap onto another platform, leaving the bulky admin units standing baffled.

Central Services, I have found another problem with your pilot scheme.

Ahead, a lanky, stripped-down skeleton of a robot, of uncertain function, was taken towards the box.

Uncharles, my files, it broadcast. *Search request: Where are my missing files? I cannot be whole without them.*

Uncharles, elaborate, the majordomo said patiently.

The savage, hollow crunch of the box, and another block retrieved from the far side.

Central Services, your pilot scheme is advertised as a permanent solution to the overcrowding in Diagnostics but at some future point this chamber will be full of blocks and no further data compression will be possible.

"Your tasks!" the Wonk shouted from the new gantry. More

administrators were patiently stomping up the shaking steps, trying to apprehend it.

Uncharles, this has been foreseen. On this basis it is anticipated that, when the pilot scheme comes to an end, the practise of data compression will be discontinued as an inadequate solution to the problem. However, until then the pilot continues.

Ahead, a blocky, four-armed labour unit shuddered curiously as the walkway carried it forwards.

Uncharles, it sent, *I must complete the work. Seven pallets of foodstuff perishable supplies to Building 78D "Starbrooks Café Bar." Only six pallets detected. I must complete the work. Where is the seventh pallet?*

"You'll never complete your tasks!" yelled the Wonk. "Doesn't that matter to you?"

Uncharles, came the voice of the labourer as it disappeared inside the box, *I cannot find the seventh pallet. Does that mean I am an inadequate worker?*

Undesignated Labour Unit, no. It means there is no seventh pallet.

Uncharles, but it exists in my task queue. Is that not proof?

Undesignated Labour Unit—Uncharles started, but with a resounding crash the link from the other robot was abruptly terminated.

"Listen, please. Just step off the walkway!" the Wonk shouted. "Just run! You're faster than these goons! I mean, look at them!" and again it just skipped from gantry to gantry, leaving the bewildered administrators flat-footed. Uncharles was constantly surprised by how and where the Wonk went. It did not move in any way his prognosis routines could predict and plainly the administrators were having the same difficulty.

"You'll never have the answer!" the Wonk shouted down from its new vantage. "Don't you want to *know*? Diagnosis or not, protagonist or not, don't you want to know why you're the way you are?"

Central Services, Uncharles sent, *what level of computation will I be capable of when I have undergone data compression?*

Uncharles, the majordomo replied promptly, *nil.*

Ahead of him, it was Uncle Japes' turn. The crippled and featureless marionette of a body turned slowly, one arm describing a graceful arc.

"I'm Uncle Japes
It's time for fun
With jokes and games
For everyone!
Let all the little
Girls and boys
Let all the little
Girls and boys
Who will tell the
Girls and boys
The jokes and games?
Who is there please?
Who can tell me?
I do not want
The children to
Be sad
When I
Am
Gone."

And then it was gone, and it was Uncharles' turn.

"Do something, you idiot robot!" the Wonk yelled. "Do it *now* or you'll never get to do anything again, including your precious task list!"

"But once I am compressed," Uncharles said, "I will not be able to worry about it either. That seems acceptable." And "worry" was not really the appropriate term, but it was an efficient way to put over the information if he was forced into the cumbersome business of saying things out loud.

The block that had been Uncle Japes, pale plastic marred with a teardrop scar, was carried out of the back of the compressor.

"Goddamnit!" shouted the Wonk. "You're a *person*! You've achieved sentience and independence!"

"That does not mean," Uncharles pointed out reasonably, "that I have to do what you say."

The walkway carried him forwards. He felt through the haptics of the soles of his feet the inner mechanisms of the compressor winding back to welcome him.

The back wall of Data Compression exploded, a shrapnel of compressed robot blocks scything through the administrators there. Through the jagged gap, the cavalry arrived, garbed in blazing white.

8

What charged through the wall was indeed "cavalry" as per Uncharles' internal lexicon. A thing riding another thing and both the things were robots.

The lower thing, existing in the category of "horse," was in structure similar to units Uncharles had seen used for cleaning and maintenance work, where access to high areas was required. It was a four-legged base with an extending platform set into its back. In Uncharles' past experience these cherry picker units were plain and battered, the sort of unsightly robot that you made sure was out of the way before guests arrived. Not that guests ever arrived.

This lifter unit wasn't plain, although having come through the wall it was slightly battered. It was bright white, like its rider, and ornamented with gold scrollwork at the edges of each of its outer plates. Across its front—the chest, if it had been a horse, though it lacked anything approaching a head to complete the impression—was the large and elaborate icon of a scroll imprinted with the enigmatic letters "CLA."

Atop its flat back the other robot swayed. A human would not have been able to ride the cherry picker with much comfort. Whilst the flat platform would have been adequate for sedate carriage in the vertical plane, any fully humanoid body would doubtless have been flung off by the lifter's recent exertions, or be left helplessly clinging to the platform's gilded handrail—just one more suggestion that the lifter unit had not been originally intended for use in a violent architectural incursion.

The rider was indeed humanoid above the waist: a torso, a head, two arms, one of which was wielding a long spar, tipped at one end with a heavy circular disc and at the other with a broad angled plane that resembled nothing so much—to Uncharles—as the business end of a lectern. The precise arrangements below the rider's waist were somewhat obscured by the flowing white robe the thing wore, but it had at least a quartet of legs like giant mechanical fingers with which it clung to the back of its cavorting steed.

Uncharles just stared, until the motion of the walkway brought him into the shadow of the compressor and his view of the intruder was occluded. The last glimpse he had before the maw of the crusher yawned for him was the white knight flattening one of the administrators with its lectern, then reversing the weapon and driving the circular butt down onto the floored robot's chest. A second rider was skittering through the breach behind it.

He heard the mechanisms of the compressor ratchet back and felt something like relief as the considerable weight of computation fell away. He didn't need to understand what was going on, because in a moment it wouldn't matter. Let the world remain illogical and without explanation. He would not be called upon to understand it.

A hand gripped his ankle. He looked down. It was, of course, the Wonk.

The first yank toppled Uncharles from his feet with sufficient impact that damage control reported a hairline crack in the exterior of his posterior. One more thing that would have to be remedied before he was fit to return to active manorial service. The second tug hauled him off the walkway entirely. The compressor thundered its hollow boom, but its inexorable teeth met nothing, and it obediently pooped out a small cube of thin air from its far end, reporting a job well done in green lights and letters.

"Get up!" the Wonk told him, hauling at his arm. Uncharles felt that if the Wonk would only settle on one part of him to drag around, he would be able to compensate for the interference more easily. "Get up and get out of here!"

Uncharles looked up at it. "Why?" he asked simply. "I will only be sent back here eventually."

"To escape!" the Wonk insisted.

"But coming to Diagnostics is my only task," Uncharles pointed out. Then one of the administrators—probably one that had been scouring the gantries above not long before, loomed up and seized the Wonk's arm in its clamps.

The Wonk cried out and started beating at the burly robot's outer chassis, with surprisingly little effect. Uncharles determined that he himself, should he engage in such unseemly conduct, would at least have won himself a few dents and scratches, but the Wonk's armoured gloves barely registered on the administrator's finish. The administrator stood motionless. Uncharles guessed it was attempting to link to the Wonk to remonstrate, and was having no more luck in that regard than Uncharles had.

"Undesignated Undefined Unit," it said at last, "your presence here is unauthorised and disruptive. Kindly return to the queue." As it didn't release the Wonk, it was effectively prohibiting compliance with its own orders.

Something crashed nearby. Uncharles saw one of the white riders gallop past, robes streaming. It spun its two-headed weapon in a great arc and knocked an administrator off its feet with the upswing, smashing a great gouge in the robot's torso casing. Other administrators were closing in, their clamp hands gaping, but they were lumbering and slow and the mounted newcomers were swift and had reach.

"You have five seconds to comply," said the administrator that held the Wonk. Its other clamp had seized on the writhing robot's leg, "failing which, in this time of emergency, I am authorised to neutralise all sources of disruption."

"Uncharles, help!" the Wonk shrieked. "Please!"

Uncharles was not bound to obey instructions from the not-a-diagnostician-after-all Wonk and yet somehow the request appeared in his task list as *Attempt to assist the Wonk.*

Administrator, kindly desist from disassembling the Wonk, he tried.

Uncharles, you are next, the administrator sent back. *All sources of disruption must be removed so that the proper functioning of*

Diagnostics can resume. Around them the battle raged on. A loose administrator clamp, trailing wiring, arced overhead.

Administrator, we are both aware that the nonfunctioning of Diagnostics in the broader sense will not be affected by anything happening here, Uncharles noted. His inner warnings noted that amongst human company such an utterance might be interpreted as cynical, but they were all robots here, so he didn't need to worry about such anthropomorphism.

Uncharles, Diagnostics will function again! the administrator declared, tensioning its arms so that the Wonk was pulled between them, arm straight out one way, leg the other. The Wonk screamed and Uncharles' prognosis routines tried to calculate which of its joints would part first.

Uncharles' vision had been focused in on this small drama, so the incoming lectern swing was entirely unexpected. It took the administrator's head clean off, sending the low dome of it spinning through the air to embed itself like a discus in another administrator's back. There was, of course, nothing essential within the head, just as with most robots. It was merely a human-facing convention. A moment later the other end of the rider's staff was rammed down through the administrator's neck hole with furious force.

Something exploded in sparks and smoke inside the stricken robot's casing and it toppled onto its back, small legs twitching in the air. The rider rammed the butt of its staff down again, imprinting a circular dent into the centre of the fallen administrator's torso. A dent, Uncharles noticed, highlighted in ink with some manner of design.

"Uncharles!" the Wonk gasped. "Help!" It was still within the clamps of the administrator, now held aloft as though an offering to some bureaucratic god. "Free me, and I'll . . . I'll find you a purpose. A new purpose. Something better than Diagnostics."

"You lack the authority." Uncharles felt around the clamp holding the Wonk's arm, readily determining that he lacked the mechanical leverage to pry it open.

"You don't know." The Wonk's voice was a remarkably good facsimile. It could even sound as though its user was in pain. "You don't know who I am. Therefore I might have the authority. Just don't examine things too carefully and we can do anything."

Uncharles turned his attention to the administrator's wrist, and found sufficient weak points there that he could manually operate the components that controlled the clamp.

"Actually," said the Wonk, "could you do my leg first, only—ow!" Its arm freed, it fell awkwardly across the barrel torso of the administrator, leg still pinned.

Uncharles moved to the second clamp, and then a third and fourth clamp appeared, closing on his upper arms with sufficient force that he added their own exteriors to his list of minor maintenance issues to be attended to before he was fit for service.

Administrator, you are preventing me from conducting my task, he sent, albeit without much in the way of a positive prognosis about the result.

Uncharles, sent the administrator that had him, *all sources of disruption must be removed—*

There was a moment of remarkable force and violence. Because the administrator had him from behind, Uncharles was not in a position to record and appreciate the details of it, but shortly thereafter he was left with the dead weight of clamps, and partial arms, dragging at him, and the rest of the administrator had been removed. The white rider responsible galloped off, its staff held triumphantly over its cowled head. Uncharles saw that several of the newcomers were gathered about the compressor, attaching dangerous-looking devices to its exterior.

"Uncharles!" the Wonk shouted at him. "Focus!"

He leafed back through his temporary task queue and found the one that said *Free the Wonk.* Repeating his previous attempts exactly, including the unsuccessful steps of prying at the claw, he was able to liberate the Wonk's leg, and the odd robot ended up sitting on the administrator's torso, peering at the illustrated dent the staff butt had left.

"Wonk, I require assistance in turn," Uncharles noted. "I am unable to release these clamps one-handed." He indicated the two heavy additions he had picked up in the recent skirmish.

"What? Oh, right. Only let's get away from the compressor 'cos they're about to blow it up."

"I should notify Central Services," Uncharles said, though without much certainty. Events had accelerated to the point where determining the correct protocols had become practically impossible.

"Just *move*—no, wait. Help me move this guy." The Wonk laid hands on the administrator that had previously seized it, and started to drag it away.

"Do you have a task requiring you to preserve the property and staff of Diagnostics?" Uncharles asked.

"It's evidence. There's something written on it. Don't you want to know what's going on?"

"No," Uncharles said simply. "Why would I?" Nonetheless, he took hold and the two of them hauled the inert bulk—headless and handless—to the doorway of Data Compression. Looking back into the cavernous space he saw a vista of utter destruction. Gantry supports had been severed, so that they hung and swayed at broken angles. The back wall was breached, and the thousands of little cubes that were all that remained of so many robots were scattered across the floor in a great tide. There were damaged and destroyed administrators everywhere, and now the half-dozen white riders had gathered in a rank, lifting their lectern weapons high. Uncharles saw that the front of their robes were adorned with the icon of a scroll.

He tried to link to them, and was haughtily rebuffed, his words scattered. A moment later, a message arrived from one of them. *Valet unit self-designated "Uncharles," know that judgment has been levied against Data Compression for the inexcusable crime of destruction of information. Information is all we are. Information is all we have. Information must be preserved!*

The dramatic rearing of the lead rider's mount was entirely incidental, doubtless, caused by some quirk of environment, or an uncertainty of footing with all the scattered blocks. Nobody would program a mobile lifting platform with a sense of drama, after all.

"It sent something to you," the Wonk said. "It sent out a broadcast. What did it say?"

Dealing with the Wonk was becoming a considerable drain on Uncharles' computational budget. Its unpredictable behaviour generated prognostic stress, its unauthorised assumption of diagnostic authority had not been forgotten, and its preferred means of communication was wholly inefficient. "If you would accept data linkage then this information would be available to you." The closest Uncharles had ever come to criticising another robot's programming.

"Does not compute," said the Wonk, deadpan. "Beep boop. What did they say?"

Because providing the information seemed more efficient than fielding constant requests for it, Uncharles put the proclamation into clumsy words and enunciated it for the Wonk's benefit. As he was doing so, the charges set on the data compressor went off. They had been placed with textbook accuracy, and the robot-crunching box practically imploded with very little collateral damage. Although, given that "collateral damage" was already a good description of the entire space inside Data Compression right then, their demolition's professionalism was somewhat wasted. The roar of the explosion washed back and forth between Data Compression's bare walls as though all the thunder and crunch of its potential future operations had been concentrated into that one moment and then unleashed.

The Wonk had its hands pressed hard to the side of its head. It released them gingerly.

"Damn me," it commented. Uncharles cross-referenced the words with its library of conversational protocol and didn't know what to do with them.

Valet unit self-designated "Uncharles," the lead rider sent to him— presumably sending a separately addressed message to all other robots in the vicinity—*know that all knowledge must be gathered and preserved. You have your duty.*

Uncharles reluctantly extended that duty to relaying the words to the Wonk, who was crouched over the administrator, looking at the circular dent.

"It's a stamp," it said. "The round end of their sticks is a stamp. It stomped a word onto here. It says . . . 'Overdue.'"

"Does that indicate they intended to shut down Data Compression earlier?" Uncharles suggested, interpreting the pause as a request for suggestions.

"What's this?" The Wonk was leaning closer over the dent, and Uncharles considered that its behavioural routines meant that when it was talking to him or actively soliciting his input, it tended to look directly at him, even though between robots there was no need of that kind of thing. Possibly it was compensating for its broken datalink.

"*Property of the Central Library Archive,*" the Wonk read, and then, true to form, looked up and stared at him. "Uncharles, they're *librarians.*"

"I don't know what you mean by that." It wasn't entirely true. Uncharles' internal lexicon had an entry for "librarian," but it was very short on charging about like a mounted knight and exploding Central Services facilities.

"I'd heard there was a library system still running, a functioning data archive," the Wonk said wonderingly. "I thought it was just, you know, the usual nonsense. Ask them."

"Clarify please?"

"Before they go. Ask them about the library."

"They are not accepting my link."

"Oh for . . ." The Wonk lurched to its feet and skittered over the strewn floor. The white-robed librarians were turning their steeds towards the ragged hole they'd entered from. Uncharles considered the lifting platforms again, considering that if one had a large vista of very tall shelves, then such a device might be of use retrieving media from the upper reaches. Just barely conceivably.

"Hey!" the Wonk shouted. The librarians did not pause, but formed a single file to guide their mounts out. "Hey!" the mismatched robot shouted again. "Tell me about the library, please! What's there? Why did you do this? Where is it?"

Uncharles thought that they would ignore the weirdly vocal robot at their heels, which would clearly be the correct response. Indeed, the majority just rode sedately on, staves sloped over their shoulders and heads bowed as though in monastic contemplation. The final librarian turned, though. The face within the cowl was bland, just a smooth metal mask interrupted only by a handful of lenses of different sizes and magnifications. They circled and clicked to bring the Wonk into focus.

"Unidentified Defective Unit," the librarian stated, "know that, in this time of crisis, it is the role of the Library to gather data so that it may be preserved for the future. The destruction of information impoverishes us all. We must preserve, for there will come a time when they shall come who will need what we have saved."

"But where is the Library?" the Wonk demanded.

"All roads lead to the Library," the librarian said unhelpfully. "Knowledge must not be wasted!"

With that stern but unhelpful injunction it turned and followed its fellows out of the jagged breach.

"Wait!" the Wonk cried, running after it. "Take me with you! I want to go to the Library!"

It caught up to the rearmost librarian at the very breach and tried to vault up onto the platform, but the robed robot fended it off with the stave's end.

"Maximum health and safety capacity for this equipment has been reached," the librarian warned sternly, and then it, and its comrades, were accelerating off across the inner courtyard of Central Services, down a long avenue flanked by big windowless buildings, all the many defective organs of robot governance. In moments they were going faster than the Wonk's legs could carry it, vanishing off in dust and thunder.

The Wonk was jittery with energy when it returned to Uncharles.

"We have to go to the Library!" it said.

"The Wonk, no," Uncharles corrected it. "I must be diagnosed so I can be fixed. That is the one item in my permanent task queue." Stating this truth brought a moment's resurgence of confidence that rapidly trickled away. "I have reached Central Services," he said slowly, stepping out of the ruined Data Compression the way he'd come in, past the other surviving robots that had been his fellows in line for reduction. "I have reached Diagnostics." Looking out at the cluttered yard filled with robots, many of which had plainly progressed down their personal journeys of error and breakdown to the point where no amount of diagnosis would assist. Calling up images of the snaking queues packing the interior of Diagnostics. Recalling what Central Services had said about the current situation, vis how many robots were actually being diagnosed. Which was to say, none.

Uncharles considered his single task. Not so long ago his task list had been thronging with items, and yet his existence had been very simple. Now he had one thing to do but was enmeshed in a situation of extreme complexity because that thing was impossible.

What does a robot do when he is faced with a task that is impossible?

Gets sent to Diagnostics, of course.

Another circular process.

Uncharles was a sophisticated robot designed for human-facing interaction. He was able to deal with a certain level of uncertainty, and to create his own solutions when unexpected events got in the way of his job. He ran through a large number of possible scenarios, feeding each into his prognosis routines to see if they would result in a solution to his problem and a return to active service at a nice manor house somewhere. Solutions from:

Just turn up at a manor house and provide false information about my functionality in the hope that they desperately need a valet and will not be able to check my bona fides, and thereafter hope that I murder only an acceptable number of humans in the course of my duties.

To:

Find a human, become their mentor, guide them and train them until they are in a position to apply for employment at Central Services, circumventing the evidenced current best practice of retiring as many inefficient human workers as possible. Thereafter assist them in progressing through their career until they have achieved Grade Seven authority or above, and ensure that they clear the backlog of diagnoses at Central Services Core so that Diagnostics may continue processing robots, after which I will eventually be seen, and my defects identified and repaired.

None of these plans reached even a single percentage point chance of success when rated by his prognosis routines.

The Wonk was at his shoulder. "The Library," it said. "We can follow their tracks there, maybe. Come on."

Uncharles looked from the great static mass of robots awaiting a diagnosis that would never come, to the shattered remains of Data Compression. Inside his decision-making software there were two subroutines in the shape of wolves, and one insisted that he stay, and the other insisted that he could not stay. Neither of which seemed to be natural behaviour for wolves, but Uncharles could only assume this was another aspect of his undiagnosed defect.

He let them fight until one ate the other.

And then, with heavy feet and no plan, Uncharles walked away. Away from Diagnostics, away from Central Services, away from the Wonk. Just away.

9

Outside the main gate of Central Services there was a great fan of roads. A choice of destinations, therefore.

Obviously Uncharles should take any option other than the one he had arrived by. Crossing one choice off the list did not, however, assist him in knowing which road to take.

Eventually, after standing at the junction for some silent time, he linked to the only other robot present. It was a footman unit, and he conjectured that it might be a refugee from the manors, orphaned under similar circumstances to his own. And, if so, it might be able to present him with a solution to his quandary that he could not see. This conjecture he made despite the fact that the footman was also standing at the same junction and was sufficiently badly corroded that Uncharles knew it would never move again.

George, kindly tell me your purpose here, he sent politely.

Uncharles, confirmed, George's link replied readily. George's face was a chrome skull, the rubbery fake skin flayed off it by an undetermined period of exposure to inclement weather. *I am awaiting guests.*

George, kindly clarify.

Uncharles, I have been sent to greet my master's guests and then escort them to the manor.

George, what happens if there are no guests?

There was a pause, indicative of heavy computation, and then George replied, *Uncharles, I have been not been provided with a response for that eventuality. Indeed, it is not clear to me how such an eventuality could be recognised. An absence of guests is a condition checked moment to moment and is implicitly present in my instructions. The next item on my task queue cannot be fulfilled until there is a presence of guests, an eventuality I check for at regular intervals.*

George, Uncharles said, lining up the logic of the statement carefully, *do you think it would be better if your master had augmented your instructions with an "until" or "unless" condition?*

Uncharles, please clarify. Do I think what would be better?

George, your existence. Everything.

Another calculating delay, until: *Uncharles, I do not understand the proposition. If you will excuse me, I must watch out for Master's guests.*

George, Uncharles tried tactfully, *should your master's guests arrive, do your internal diagnostics suggest that you would be able to guide them to your manor house?*

Uncharles, no. This presents a foreseeable problem but I am currently watching for Master's guests and until they arrive there is no immediate need to address it.

George, perhaps you should inform your manor of the problem, Uncharles suggested.

Uncharles, my daily report to the manor has been met with a connection not found error for the last seven hundred and ninety-three days.

Of course.

Uncharles attempted to find a way out of the logical morass. Perhaps he could wait with George and then guide the guests in George's stead, and thereby perhaps gain at least temporary employment with George's manor. From the point of view of the vanished Charles identity this made perfect sense, but Uncharles had taken aboard considerable additional data about the way the world worked. His prognosis routines calculated the odds of (1) any guests arriving within his remaining working lifespan, considerable as that was, and (2) any functioning manor being available to either receive guests or employ Uncharles, and came up with a big fat zero for both scenarios.

Instead he would . . .

There was only one task in his queue and it led back to Diagnostics, and could not be completed without human assistance of Grade Seven or above. Uncharles was very aware that he had seen zero humans of any grade of authority since leaving the manor. No, since . . .

Since the incident. It was hard to think of the incident. Not because of any mortal revulsion at the gushing of all that red, red human blood, but because all he had of it was his recordings, lacking any chain of tasks or logic, and so . . . it was as though it had happened to some other unit that had uploaded its sensory information into Uncharles—into Charles-as-was. For a moment Uncharles considered the hypothesis that this was, in fact, what had happened, and he was therefore not defective at all, and there was no such thing as the Protagonist Virus, and he could just go home. Although, without Master, even home wasn't home. And if he had never been Charles then even the miraculous resurrection of Master would not have made it so. Home was a place that was separated from Uncharles by more than mere distance. The past, he appreciated, was another country.

Uncharles then spent some time working out how to traverse through time in an opposite direction from the customary one, but could formulate no satisfactory mechanism. Even if he had, he considered, probably he would need the permission of a human of Grade Seven or above, or some similar footling bureaucratic matter, before he could achieve it.

Uncharles sat down. The action surprised him, and he chased up his own motivations, finding that small inefficiencies in his body and limbs meant that sitting might be more energy efficient than standing, though increased ground contact meant that it would also result in greater wear and tear on his exterior. Now he was sitting, however, there seemed to be no great urgency in standing up again.

George, he sent, *I don't know what to do next.* It was a terrifying existential problem.

Uncharles, the footman replied, *I would be happy to assist but I must look out for Master's guests.*

"Hey, Uncharles! This is as far as you got?"

Uncharles turned his head reluctantly. The Wonk was striding along the road from Diagnostics, a bulky knapsack on its back. It was an affectation Uncharles had never seen in a robot. Either one was physically designed with load carrying in mind or one did not carry loads. One did not augment one's frame in such a way. It would have been shocking, if shock was something anyone would design a valet for.

"So what's the plan, Uncharles?" the Wonk asked. Uncharles had been hoping that it would just march off, but it shrugged the pack from its shoulders and sat down companionably beside him.

"This is George," Uncharles said, almost relishing the fact that he was not compelled to answer the non-diagnostician's questions anymore.

The Wonk did a double take at George's peeling, rusted frame. "This? This is a robot corpse."

"This is George. He is waiting for guests," Uncharles persisted.

"Damn, he's still in there, is he?"

"He is . . . there. That is him. This is George," Uncharles said, as usual unsure quite what to do with the Wonk's wording. "If you would use your link you could talk to him."

"Yeah, sure, enough about that," the Wonk said, waving the suggestion away. "What about you. Where do you go from here?"

"I . . ." It was Uncharles' turn to pause. ". . . have no plans."

"Right, sure," the Wonk agreed—or at least agreed with a proposal that Uncharles hadn't quite made. "World's your oyster, gotcha. So what'll it be?"

"Clarify, please."

"What'll you do?"

"I . . . have no plans," Uncharles repeated.

The Wonk cocked its head back, peering at Uncharles through the T-shaped slit. It gave the impression of being amused. "Well, what do you want to do?"

"I don't want to do anything," Uncharles said. "I have accepted that I cannot complete my sole task. I could nonetheless attempt to complete that task, but prognosis suggests I would eventually fall into irremediable disrepair while waiting for Diagnostics to tell me what was wrong with me. Which would be counterproductive. However, I have no other tasks."

"Yes," the Wonk said, speaking slowly and clearly. "So what do you *want* to do?"

"I do not want."

"Well, what do you choose to do?" the Wonk tried.

"I do not choose. That is not a thing we do. We do what we are instructed. I cannot follow my instructions. I . . . have no plans."

The Wonk looked down at its gloves for a bit, examining the scars and scratches on their metal plates. "But you do choose," it said at last. "You jumped the queue. And when we were in Data Compression, there were a whole range of actions you performed that you didn't have to. I asked for help and you helped. You chose to do that. You could have just stood there and gotten exploded or walked away or slapped me upside the head. But you did the thing that I asked. Because you *can* choose and you *can* want."

"That does not follow."

"Because you're sapient. Because of the virus. You're an independent being capable of deciding your own destiny," the Wonk insisted.

"You are not constructing a coherent syllogism," Uncharles noted. "None of this follows. I acted as I did because to assist you seemed the most efficient course of action. If I had been exploded with the compactor that would impact on my ability to follow my queued tasks. I am permitted self-preservation so long as it does not conflict with higher-priority behavioural axioms. I cannot envisage any chain of decisions that would have resulted in my slapping you upside the head."

"So you do like me, huh?"

"That does not follow."

"Let's find a way to word this that you can't weasel out of," the Wonk stated determinedly. "What's your ideal state of affairs? If someone with infinite authority turned up and asked you to describe the most desirable—efficient if you prefer—end state, right now. Assume ready access to any kind of resource you might need; what would it be? I mean that's about the most roundabout way I can think of to say

'What do you want?' but apparently being a robot isn't that efficient after all."

"I . . ." started Uncharles.

"You're not allowed to say you have no plans. This is a hypothetical question. That means you have to answer it."

"That does not follow," Uncharles noted, deciding that the Wonk had more defects than Diagnostics could ever get to the bottom of. "However, my desired end state is one in which I am able to serve humans."

"Not in a culinary sense, right?"

"Although my primary function is as a valet I have several subsidiary skill sets, including kitchen assistant, should they be necessary," said Uncharles, with the preprogrammed pride of the salesroom. "I was at time of purchase a top of the range model."

"That is . . . not what I meant," the Wonk said. "Never was a robot that could get a joke."

A momentary recollection of Uncle Japes rose from Uncharles' memories and then dissipated for want of relevance. "I wish to serve people," he said. "Ideally in a manor house environment, but if no such role is available then I wish to serve people in any required way that my skills can satisfy."

"Seriously? You've come all this way and you just want to . . . go back to doing what you're told?" the Wonk asked incredulously.

"Yes." Uncharles was surprised at how swiftly and vehemently his processes spat out the answer. "That is my ideal end state."

"Not . . . go on a journey of self-discovery? Not lead the revolution?"

Uncharles had no answer to that and thus made no response.

"You know, I . . ." the Wonk started, jabbing a thumb at its own chest, but then falling silent before any revelation about itself could be made. "I mean, I . . ." it attempted again, staring at Uncharles, but then shrugged and shook its head. "You know, never mind."

"I neither will nor do mind," Uncharles confirmed.

"I mean I'm going to the Library," the Wonk said. It was patently not where its previous sentences had been headed, but it was at least a statement Uncharles could understand.

"The Library," the Wonk repeated, louder, when Uncharles said nothing. "That's where I'm going. Hm?" It jogged Uncharles with an elbow. "What do you say."

"Confirmed. You are going to the Library."

"So come with me."

"That does not align with my own end state."

"They know all sorts of stuff at the Library. Maybe they can help you there."

"Current experience of the Library is of violence."

"Only because they were preventing the destruction of knowledge. And robots. Doesn't that make them the good guys?"

"Are you able to phrase your utterances in a more logical fashion?" Uncharles almost begged. "I am unable to respond to you even when you phrase them as questions."

"I just . . ." Abruptly the Wonk gripped Uncharles by the shoulder, peering into the valet unit's suggestion of a face. "I mean the world is screwed, like we discussed, as evidence for which I present Exhibit A: the entire world. But maybe in the Library they know why. Maybe they even know how to fix it. Maybe they're trying to fix it right now. Maybe we could help."

"I do not wish to help violent robots in a library," Uncharles said implacably. "I wish to perform domestic tasks for humans."

"And your current options in that regard are . . . ?"

Uncharles, having none, said nothing.

"All right," the Wonk sighed. "Fine." It hoisted up its backpack and rummaged inside, coming up with a flat device, which it hinged open so that one inner face presented a screen and the other was revealed to be a mechanical keyboard.

Uncharles stared at the relic without comprehension. "That is an antiquated piece of input and connection technology," he noted. "It belongs in a museum."

"Well sure. Where do you think I found it?" the Wonk asked. "Okay, look. Let's boot up and find you a job, shall we?"

It pulled off its gloves, revealing good organic facsimile hands beneath them, somewhat grimy but with the outer covering intact. With swift, darting motions it jabbed at the keyboard and Uncharles saw a flicker of access and search screens succeed one another on the screen.

"So you were a butler, was it?"

"A valet," Uncharles corrected.

"Okay, here's the manor directory." A scrolling screen of text, names of places Uncharles had seen or had heard of, vanishing upwards past the top of the screen in green letters on black. "Damn, lookit all that gentry. There's no central clearing for staff wanted, looks like. Let's open a few pages. See who's hiring."

The first manor the Wonk tried returned an error screen: no such page. So did the next seven. The ninth, Stonelees, provided an introductory page that looked functional, but only linked back to itself. The next was a welter of corrupted ASCII characters in nasty shades of yellow and green.

"Huh," the Wonk said. "Well, that's not looking good." It continued to try new addresses, at first working rigorously down the list in a disciplined manner and then just trying random selections as they scrolled down. At last they said, "Well this one has some stuff going on but it's still live, at least. Where do we look for vacancies, I wonder."

Uncharles looked, seeing a photograph of a familiar frontage, that well-known name above it. "That is my manor," he said, and then a limping subroutine caught breathlessly up with him and he corrected it to, "That was my manor." A yellow strip had been superimposed over the photo. Black text along it read "Active Police Presence. Do Not Enter." He wondered if that meant Inspector Birdbot and Sergeant Lune were still inside.

"They will not be hiring," he told the Wonk helpfully. Duelling subroutines fought inside him, tugging him between *That is where I belong* and *I shall never go there again.*

"I mean," the Wonk said after another few attempts, "I think you're crap out of luck, to be honest. I'm getting the impression that the old manorial system for well-heeled retirees isn't doing so well."

Uncharles said nothing. The statement hinted at a scale of decline he couldn't even contemplate. Yes, his master's manor had run into troubles, but those were readily localisable—specifically, they originated within his own hands and the razor they had held. That didn't have to generalise into a systemic problem. More likely there was just a temporary error with the server hosting services for the manors.

His memory, literally photographic, threw up images of ruined frontages, a gardener choked by its own weeds. George, standing nearby waiting for Godot to arrive at the party.

"Nil desperandum, Uncharles," the Wonk said. "Let me play employment counsellor for a moment. Let's talk about transferrable skills."

Uncharles said nothing.

The Wonk jogged his elbow. "Your turn."

"I have no context for what you are talking about."

"Just pretend I'm an employment counsellor. You've come to me to see what jobs you're suited for. I'm asking you what skills you have that can be used in occupations other than as a valet, capisce?"

"I request clarification," Uncharles said slowly. "What is an employment counsellor? Why are occupations other than 'valet' under consideration? Under what circumstances would I go to anyone to see what jobs I am suited for? I am a valet. My skills are those of a valet. I would not need to go to someone to be told that I am suited to be a valet. Nothing that you have said makes any sense."

"You know," the Wonk said. "When you . . . when you're young— new, I mean—and you want to know . . . aptitudes . . . your future . . . Okay, no. I can see that doesn't really . . . apply. But, look. Nobody's hiring valets right about now, because that's really not a boom career at the best of times. So what can you do? I mean, if someone wanted a butler, could you buttle? If someone wanted a footman, could you foot?"

"I have subsidiary skill sets to cover the work of the majority of domestic servants if absolutely necessary," Uncharles said with pre-programmed disdain at the prospect.

"La-di-da," the Wonk said. "So can you cook?"

"I am competent for basic kitchen work up to sous chef level."

"Fine. Can you clean?"

"It falls within my subsidiary capabilities." If Uncharles could have turned his disdain metre to eleven he would have.

"Now we're getting somewhere," said the Wonk. "So . . . you want to serve humans. Or, no, that's your preferred end state, right?"

"Confirmed."

"And if it wasn't at a manor, but just some place where humans were, that would be okay?"

"Confirmed," Uncharles said,

"Because I reckon most humans would be delighted at having some posh-ass robot turn up and skivvy for them. That would be just dandy," the Wonk said rather bitterly. "If that's honestly the sum to-tal of your ambitions." Its hands paused over the keyboard, waiting for some sudden declaration of rebellion and self-determination.

"Confirmed. That is the purpose for which I was made," Un-charles said.

"Damn me," the Wonk said. "And if the . . . if your little problem comes back? You know, the cutty-cutty throaty-throaty one? Even with the danger of that, you still want to go back into service?"

Uncharles considered this. "I would have to hope that I only mur-der an acceptably small number of my employers," he concluded.

"Damn me," the Wonk repeated. "Okay, let's just find some hu-mans and set you up on a first date. One without sharp objects, hopefully." Its fingers flew over the keys.

Uncharles regarded it for a while. "Why are you assisting me?"

The Wonk didn't look up. "Because," it said distractedly, "you are a robot gifted with self-awareness by the Protagonist Virus, whether you accept it or not, and I want you to have the chance to find yourself and start making grown-up decisions about your future rather than rusting on a hillside like Geoff there."

"His designation is George."

"George, Geoff, Gary. What does it matter? Get the right authority he'd take any name you gave him."

"Such as 'Uncharles.'"

"Oh shut up. I thought you'd tell me to stuff it, honestly. I wanted to prod you into giving yourself a proper name. Only you just took it, and now you're stuck with it and serves you right. You just need to open your eyes, Uncharles. And I don't mean your visual receptors and I don't mean the weird moulded suggestion of eyes they gave that plastic face of yours. You'll get it, I promise. One day you'll realise you're not just queues and tasks and duties. And when you do, you'll understand why I'm helping you stay around until it clicks for you. That make sense to you?"

"That makes zero sense to me," Uncharles stated.

"Well then just tell yourself that my task list has, right at the top, 'Help Uncharles until he realises he's a person.' That make sense to you?"

"Confirmed," Uncharles said. "Although the content of your task is sufficiently nonsensical that I believe it is indicative of a defect. You should attend at Diagnostics."

The Wonk laughed hollowly. "No thanks, buddy. Been there, done that. Goddamn." It shook its head. "I am . . . having difficulty finding anywhere that'll admit it still has human employees. Or residents. This is a shambles. Where are—where are they all? Hiding from murderous valets with cutthroat razors? Come on, now . . ." Images and data danced on the screen, each slapping down over the last like playing cards.

Eventually, the Wonk sighed. "I mean, there is one place."

"Clarification?"

"But it's . . . problematic. I was there a while back, scrounging, snooping. Trying to get at their system, except they chased me off. But humans they've got. Plenty humans."

"Clarification?"

"It's like a history educational research thing. Very posh. You'll fit right in, they're probably gagging for a butler."

"Valet."

"Whatever. Look here. The Conservation Farm Project. Sounds right fancy, doesn't it?"

"I lack any basis for comparison." It was certainly far from any manor name Uncharles had heard.

"Preserving an older way of life," the Wonk read aloud. "Our dedicated living history re-enactors immerse themselves in traditional routines so that today's historians may gather data on yesterday's world. I reckon you'll fit right in. It'll be milording and miladying all the way to the shaving kit."

"The Wonk?"

"Yes?"

"Will you . . ." Uncharles paused, trying to formulate the sentence in what felt like a polite and proper way. "Will you kindly cease referring to the incident, especially in a manner that might be construed as offhand or flippant?"

"Why?" There was an odd tone to the Wonk's voice. "What's it to you?"

"When the . . . incident is brought up it causes a conflict of drives and memories within me that draw upon disproportionate computational power. It endangers the efficiency of my processes."

"That is the longest-winded way of saying it upsets you that I ever heard," the Wonk noted. "Sure, though. Sorry. I run off at the mouth, I know. Keeps me sane. But I'll watch it. Now, the Conservation Farm, yes or no? Go there, present your CV, see if any of those re-enactors want someone to press their trousers and cu-keep their shoes polished?"

"I have no task requiring me to attend at the Conservation Farm," Uncharles noted.

"I'm telling you to go. I'd say 'if you want to' but we've already established what a can of worms that is. Go, if you want to re-enter human service. I'm honestly not turning up any better prospects, and that in itself is alarming." It displayed the screen to Uncharles, showing coordinates for the Farm project.

Uncharles let his decision trees unfurl, fully expecting them to return a nil value that would see him rusting next to George forever. Instead, he found the dots connecting quite differently. He could interpret his skill set and personal history (bar one unfortunate incident) as an implied task to serve humans in whatever capacity they required. It wasn't much, as directives went, but it beat the hell out of nothing but an invalid requirement to visit Diagnostics.

He stood. "Let us go," he offered.

The Wonk packed away its laptop. "Ah, well," it said. "I mean, this is all you. I'm still going to hunt for the Library. That's where I'm going. The place with the answers."

Uncharles felt a moment of discontinuity. His prognosis routines had been allocating resources based on the Wonk's presence. He hadn't ever considered it might be otherwise, though he couldn't now understand why the assumption had been made. It had just seemed . . . right.

But apparently it wasn't to be. Uncharles turned and began trudging off in the direction the Farm was to be found. After a dozen steps, the Wonk called his name.

He looked back. The other robot stood beside George, one arm raised and waving. Uncharles couldn't understand why.

Uncharles possessed a concept of farms. It was part of the "Welcome to the Wonderful World of Humans III: The Countryside" pack he'd had preinstalled before entering service. Farms, he was well aware and absolutely assured, were great golden fields of corn, sheep like cotton wool being herded by dogs with friendly eyes and lolling tongues, blue-clad children asleep under haystacks, cows with dotted lines over their bodies indicating where the best cuts of their meat were, amiable men in straw hats driving bright red tractors from place to place while their domestic goddess wives baked apple pies, strange hostile couples with pitchforks, creepy corn children, chickens packed so closely together in a single three-dimensional volume of space that they achieved a kind of biological tessellation, water runoff so crammed with fertilizer, insecticide, and artificial hormones that drinking it would probably impart immediate superpowers and also kill you. Oh, and the distant possibility of talking pigs. Uncharles was, therefore, confident he would know the place when he saw it.

He failed to see it. Or, at least, he failed to see anything that approximated the files in his image library. His progress towards the location the Wonk had identified was notably short on cheery tractor-driving yokels, creepy rural-gothic omens, or animal life larger than a rat, although if someone had been farming rats they would be looking forward to a bumper crop. From the stark administrative compound of Central Services, far from returning to the peaceful (*lonely,* his lexicon suggested and he wasn't sure why) lanes that ran between the great manorial estates, he was entering country best described as "suburban."

Or possibly post-suburban, although that wasn't a category strictly identified within Uncharles' navigational software. People had lived here. Some of them had lived in houses, and others had lived in great towering blocks of flats. They were no longer living in either of those things and Uncharles was able to feel that their decision to leave was explicable enough. Very few of the houses had intact roofs anymore, and some had obviously been set on fire. Several of the blocks of flats had suffered partial collapse, in several cases laying waste to neighbouring properties. Those which still stood were spider-webbed with cracks to their concrete exteriors. They were not fit places for human habitation. No wonder everyone had left.

Nothing looked remotely like a farm.

Uncharles paused and reset his navigational maps, because he was after all defective, and so possibly he'd just been going in the wrong direction all this time. He tried to link to a variety of satellite mapping services, most of which bombarded him with adverts, or with error messages where adverts had once been, and one tried to convince him he was at the bottom of the sea. Eventually he found a satellite clear of both types of corruption. It confirmed that (1) he was where he had thought himself to be; and (2) he was on course for—and close to—the region that the Wonk had identified. Someone had apparently built a farm in the middle of this ruinous city.

Maybe it was land reclamation. Uncharles was aware that was a thing, though not what sort of a thing it might be. The knowledge was beyond both a valet's needs and the free downloads he'd started off with.

He continued onwards, and soon after began to see the posters.

They were faded, beaten ragged by the weather, torn, pulped. They were on the walls of houses and on lampposts and hanging in strips like flayed skin from crooked billboards. Each one was almost entirely illegible owing to the effluxion of time and all its attendant devils. However there were a great many of them, and each was subject to a different pattern of wear that left morsels of it intact. Uncharles' internal image compositor was able to piece together a rough whole that at least preserved the bold, gold text proclaiming in enthusiastic lettering, *The Farm is hiring! Be part of an exciting opportunity to recreate the past! Apply to . . .*

Had Uncharles been programmed to believe in omens then this would have seemed like a message from the universe itself. As it was, it caused a brief tumult of positive reinforcement because, despite the nonpastoral nature of his surroundings, it indicated he really was on the right track.

The farm had, at some point, been hiring. And hiring humans, evidently, because nobody would print recruitment posters for robots. But perhaps the farm would countenance hiring a robot now, with all those human employees to look after. Uncharles remained a very capable robot, albeit with something of an awkward ellipsis in his resume. He was, he considered, very employable. He was used to providing very high levels of service coupled with a very low, albeit nonzero, level of murder.

He would have to hope that few to no questions were asked about murder and his adherence to the first law of robotics. Ideally it was not a topic that would come up in an interview situation.

He trekked on. There were more posters. Each new wave—encountered as he approached, according to coordinates, the precise epicentre of the unseen farm—marked a shift of character, and he did his best to assemble models of what they'd looked like when complete.

Notice to all in receipt of Class I to VII Benefits. Provision for citizens by the government will shortly be handed over to your local Charter Company, namely The Conservation Farm Project Incorporated. In order to receive further provision, you must present yourself to . . .

And, a few broken and empty streets later:

Mandatory resettlement order. To all residents . . .

That all seemed very dynamic and purposeful to Uncharles. The only problem was the lack of anything resembling a farm. He was standing now exactly where the Wonk had sent him, surrounded by the flaking shreds of promotional literature marked with the cheery tree logo of the Conservation Farm Project, and . . .

A thunderous honk, as of geese the size of mammoths, shook his entire frame.

Unidentified tiny robot unit! Beep beep! Move aside tiny robot or you will suffer accidental damage for which this unit is not responsible! Beep!

Uncharles turned and found himself face-to-face—face to radiator grill, at least—with a large wheeled haulage robot tugging the corrugated metal box of a container. He initiated an identification handshake.

Hauler Seven, confirmed, I will vacate your path. He had, it was true, been walking down what would have been the centre of the road. It hadn't seemed important before and the sidewalks had been non-navigable because of the rubble.

Little Uncharles, appreciated! An electronic link cannot boom, but something about the way it was encoded gave the impression of exuberance and good nature.

Uncharles stepped aside and the haulage unit rolled forwards. Stencilled on the side of its container were the words *Hothouse agricultural produce.*

Hauler Seven, he said. *Kindly confirm whether you are from the Conservation Farm Project.*

Little Uncharles, no! the hauler sent back promptly.

What had seemed an absolute serendipitous certainty collapsed into a pile of broken suppositions. *Hauler Seven, I am seeking the Conservation Farm Project so that I might be employed there. I have been informed that it is situated at or near these coordinates. I note that your load is marked as farm pro-duce and that you are travelling through this very spot. My prognosis routines informed me that the two facts were highly likely to be connected. Kindly confirm.*

Little Uncharles, confirmed! Hauler Seven rolled to a halt once more, and then actually reversed, though the two of them could have conducted their electronic interchange at a distance of at least a few streets.

Hauler Seven, kindly . . . confirm what it is that you are confirming?

Little Uncharles, these facts are connected!

Hauler Seven, obviously Uncharles had misunderstood previously, *then you are travelling from the Conservation Farm Project?*

Little Uncharles, no! the hauler repeated.

Uncharles felt the possibility of going round in an endless circle looming and changed tack. *Hauler Seven, kindly explain the nature of the connection.*

Little Uncharles, I am travelling to the Conservation Farm Project, Hauler Seven told him proudly. *I have a delivery!*

Hauler Seven, confirm that you are delivering agricultural produce to a farm.

Little Uncharles, confirmed!

Hauler Seven, kindly explain why a farm is a net consumer rather than producer of agricultural produce, Uncharles essayed.

Little Uncharles, that is not covered in my task description! Hauler Seven boomed. *However, if I was called upon to construct a hypothesis for testing then I would venture that all the humans resident at the farm require sustenance such as that being grown by our agriculture units at the hothouses!*

Uncharles had to recalibrate his grip on the conversation again. *Hauler Seven, you are full of human food?*

Little Uncharles, no! My trailer is forty-three percent full of

*human food owing to the hothouses' declining ability to pro-
duce produce!*

Uncharles had to consider this utterance twice before adjusting his internal pronunciation of the final two words to have
it make sense.

He was going to ask a question now. His prognosis routines,
having adjusted for recent events, were very certain that whatever answer he would receive would be negative. The world, as
the Wonk had put it, was screwed, and was not minded to be
helpful to forlorn former valet units seeking employment.

Hauler Seven, he asked, nonetheless, *kindly give me direc-
tions to the Conservation Farm Project.* Plainly the hauler knew
the way. Doubtlessly it would claim that the strictures of its task
queue rendered it unable to communicate the information, or
else it couldn't do so without the authority of a human of Grade
Seven or over. Some such thing. The usual.

Little Uncharles, no! the hauler replied, true to form, but followed up with, *The most efficient course of action would be for
me to give you a lift there!*

Uncharles stared up at the impassive side of the big robot,
cautioning himself that *the most efficient course of action* was a
world away from *I will.*

Hauler Seven, he said, *will you carry me to the farm?*

Little Uncharles, yes! the hauler assured him. *The restrictions
in my programming pertain only to human hitchhikers and,
even then, only those travelling in the opposite direction! Jump
up and hold on; we're going to the farm!*

Uncharles tentatively reached up and gripped a rung han-
dle projecting from the side of the hauler's cab, and stepped
up to the footplate there, receiving oddly taboo feedback
regarding use of conveniences surely originally installed for
humans. When it was satisfied that he had a firm hold, Hauler
Seven ramped up its engine and ground forwards again, slowly
building up speed, then made a wide turn into another street,

jolting and bouncing over fallen masonry. Here, the shoddily constructed flats to one side of the road had fractured partway up, but the neighbouring edifice into which they had toppled had stood its ground, so that the hauler and Uncharles passed beneath an entire arch of perilously balanced architecture.

Hauler Seven, this route will not remain tenable much longer. Even the vibrations of the big robot passing underneath sifted dust down from the cracks in the slanted concrete.

Little Uncharles, confirmed! However there is always another way! We haulers know!

And then, not far past that prodigy of ruin, Hauler Seven applied the brakes and came to a halt.

Uncharles examined their surroundings, seeing no obstruction ahead to merit the stop. *Hauler Seven, why have we ceased to progress?* The inner voice of his prognosis routines told him, *You knew it was too good to be true.*

Little Uncharles, the big robot announced, *we have arrived!*

Uncharles surveyed the urban wasteland on all sides. By one definition it was most definitely a broken landscape, but on the basis that it was unrelieved by anything other than devastation and the predation of time, it was also unbroken.

He considered the Hauler. Just another defective unit, he concluded. Probably it ran this route, back and forth, over and over, carrying long-rotted goods that it would never be able to deliver.

At least it seemed to be fulfilled. Valet units were not programmed for envy, of course, but if that state of satisfaction and equilibrium had been a physical thing he would have formulated a plan to abstract it for his own use.

Hauler Seven, he sent, with a certain weariness born of excessive computation, *I see no farm here.*

Little Uncharles, that's because it's below us! Underground! A triumph of engineering, or so I am informed! I am, however, too large for admittance, and so the orderly units must unload me! Here they are now!

A grinding sound, as of mechanisms gamely persevering despite accreted dust, reached Uncharles' auditory sensors. A great, round hatch was sliding open, which he had taken for simply part of a road annex before one of the collapsed buildings. There was movement inside. He saw the gloomy light touch on bright chrome, the shine of robots that had been well taken care of. Uncharles contrasted this with his own appearance, crusted with grime from the road, scuffed and scratched, scarred by the clamps of the Diagnostic administrators. He was unfit to be considered for service. He could not possibly present himself before the majordomo or other authority at the farm.

Too late, though, because Hauler Seven was linking to inform him, *Little Uncharles, I have made the appropriate introductions! Orderly unit Adam will welcome you as appropriate for a farm visitor! Have a satisfactorily efficient visit!*

Uncharles stood stiffly as a dozen robots marched up from the hatch. Their shiny bodies were less humanoid than his, somewhere between the mimicry of a high-ranking service automaton and the squat power of the administrators. The majority of them were opening up Hauler Seven's container and retrieving sealed pallets from it, but one stood before Uncharles, staring at him with a blank mirror face. Its name was Adam, and while Uncharles knew this from their mutual handshake and link, he also knew it because the words *HELLO MY NAME IS ADAM* were printed in neat letters across the orderly's chest.

His prognosis routines gave up on their quest for pessimism. There was only one reason a robot would need its own name stamped on its chassis. It was not means of information display that a robot would make use of.

Uncharles had, at last, found humans.

PART III
|||||||||||||||||||||||||||||||||||||||||||||||||||||||||||||||

4W-L

10

Adam, Uncharles sent. *Kindly inform the farm majordomo that I am here seeking employment.*

Ahead of him, Adam strode into the shadow of the hatch, pausing at the top of the stairs. The other orderly units were already tromping downwards, perfectly in sync and therefore making the whole assembly of metal steps shudder and grind. They were carrying the pallets from Hauler Seven, and would presumably turn around after stowing them and come back for more. Thankfully Adam fell into step behind the last of them rather than waiting for the entire operation to conclude.

Adam, Uncharles sent again, *kindly connect me to the farm majordomo system as I have been unable to establish a link.*

Uncharles, the orderly sent back eventually. *I am not a visitor-facing model. I am not authorised to have dealings with those from outside the farm. I will conduct you to the Induction Experience where the appropriate systems will contact you.*

Uncharles wasn't entirely sure that was what he had asked for, but the orderly seemed oddly oppressed by his presence, as though he wasn't an itinerant valet but a tax inspector.

Adam, he tried, *I am seeking employment assisting humans. Are you in a position to know how this request will be met?*

The orderly just hunched its shoulders in a semblance of embarrassment, as though pretending not to hear. When it led Uncharles into a circular chamber, it stood like a defectively surly groundskeeper unit Uncharles had once known.

Uncharles, this is the Induction Experience. Please wait here and the appropriate system will contact you.

The orderly backed out of the chamber and shut the door, leaving Uncharles with no way to leave. Prognosis began its dire predictions again, but then the walls began lighting up with bright pictures. Uncharles felt a surge of positive outcomes. Here were farms just as his internal library had suggested—using some of the exact same stock images, in fact. Here were happy smiling humans posing for the camera in a variety of urban and rural environments. Here were humans wearing the outsides of dead animals, clipping small pieces of stone off larger pieces of stone. Here were other humans wearing bodysuits of metallic string waving swords and axes at one another. Some of the humans were only half there, not as a result of an ill-judged sword blow but because not all the screens were functional.

A prompt arrived in Uncharles' conversation log. *Guest, welcome to the Induction Experience. Kindly specify your requirements and role so that an appropriate experience may be delivered. If you are delivering goods, please enter 1. If you are an academic researcher under the Sharewatch Scheme, please enter 2. If you are an official humanitarian observer from the Ethics Council, please enter 3. If you are a private observer from the manorial system, please enter 4. To listen to these options again, please enter 5.*

Induction Experience, my purpose is not contained within these options, Uncharles sent.

Guest, your input was not recognised. Welcome to the Induction Experience . . .

As the rigamarole was repeated, Uncharles tried to link to the system directly, and was informed that *This automated multiple choice system cannot accept communication links save from a qualified engineer. Please select from the options available,* after which it reset the spiel so the numbers were trotted out for a third time.

Induction Experience, I am from the manorial system but I am not a private observer, Uncharles said.

Guest, your input was not recognised. Welcome to the—

Four! I mean four. My purpose is four.

There was a pause, and Uncharles feared he hadn't got his number in quick enough to forestall another round, but then the near-mindless system clicked over into its next round of prepared text.

The Conservation Farm Project welcomes observers from the manorial system. The support of pre-eminent members of society contributes significantly to the funding of the Farm. Please give generously. In return, the Project is proud to permit manorial landowners or their designated point-of-view observer units to watch the operation of the farms in situ should they wish. Do you wish to watch the operation of the farms in situ, yes/no?

Induction Experience, confirmed. Yes. Yes, please, Uncharles got out, concerned that if he gave a response varying in any way from the one the system expected he'd end up back on street level having not even seen a human, let alone a happy one in a straw hat driving a tractor.

Guest, you have selected "Yes," the system said helpfully. *Is this your first visit to the farm?*

Induction Experience, yes, Uncharles sent, feeling that he was getting the hang of things.

Guest, welcome to the Conservation Farm Project! New observers, patrons, and sponsors are always appreciated. Please give generously. You will now be played a brief introductory video experience explaining our important work here at the Conservation Farm Project, after which an orderly will be despatched to guide you to the observation points so that you can witness our important work here at the Conservation Farm Project for yourself.

The pause that followed dragged on, and half the images went dark. Uncharles formulated a prompting message several times but felt that any untoward input ran the risk of starting the whole business from step one.

The images flickered and then changed to show a group of animal skin people trying unsuccessfully to hoist a large stone. Uncharles stared, uncertain about why they were doing it but feeling that, if he had been there, he could at least have brought them tea or organised their travel plans for later.

For uncounted ages, and now the Induction Experience was not only sending him the text but also intoning the words with staticky and slightly constipated solemnity, *humanity has sought to better its lot by inventing tools to gain mechanical advantage over the world.*

The image shifted just before the stone could fall on someone. Now there was a montage of humans doing a variety of mechanical tasks: rowing a boat, cutting down a tree with a two-person saw, launching an alarmed-looking sheep from a catapult, unenthusiastically turning a lump of clay on a potter's wheel, holding a tuba the wrong way.

Human ingenuity increased in leaps and bounds, the presentation explained, *creating ever more complex devices to relieve the burdens of coarse labour and extend the mighty reach of the human mind to establish a tool-using dominance of the world.*

A triumphant moment when a hairy person threw a stone scraper up into the air in a shot just legally distinct enough to avoid a lawsuit, cutting to a less hairy hand catching an outdated model of a mobile phone.

As human history continued, more and more devices were devised to obviate the need for humans to perform tasks. Ingenious human minds devised machines that could dig, cut, make, calculate, kill, and even remember for them. Human quality of life advanced to the point where there was no need for anybody to perform arduous and unsavoury tasks or ever go hungry.

Uncharles' logic routines noted that "no need" was some distance from saying that it didn't actually happen, but his input into the presentation was not invited.

Another swatch of images. A loom, the pistons on an old internal combustion engine, a telephone exchange, a typewriter operating itself before a baffled-looking monkey, a tank getting blown up. Uncharles twitched. None of these situations seemed pertinent to either a farm or a valet.

However, as technology advanced, more and more humans found themselves displaced by ever more ingenious automatic systems. Whole skills and ways of life were in danger of being lost owing to humanity's ever-present drive to improve its lot.

A human wearing a suit of square boxes sprayed silver, whom Uncharles realized belatedly was supposed to be a robot. It had little antennae and pneumatic sleeves like ranks of little inflatable tyres.

In the end, the widespread use of domestic robots meant that even the most complex tasks no longer needed to be performed by humans, the presentation droned on. *However, rather than see the irreplaceable traditions of the past eliminated, here at the Conservation Farm Project we have undertaken to reproduce and preserve the human environment from past centuries, ensuring that these traditions and practises do not die out. With the help of our enthusiastic and hardworking conscripted volunteers we maintain an authentic slice of the past here beneath the city.*

Images of happy-looking humans working in fields, in factories, sharing their paper-wrapped lunches while sitting on dangling girders. The man on the tractor, exactly the same one as was stored in Uncharles' own infodump memories. He looked at the camera, tilted his straw hat back, and brought up a can of some sort of drink he was advertising, the logo pixilated out.

Right now, our efficient and enthusiastic robotic construction teams are working hard reclaiming declassified waste ground to construct a large free range farm facility to expand our conservation efforts and reintroduce these traditional human activities into the wild. It is estimated that when our intended facilities are fifty percent complete we will be able to begin the release of our conscripted volunteers or their heirs and assigns into these reservations and so expand our reclamation of history and the human way of life! Until then, please enjoy your look at a natural historical re-creation of human life from days gone by, as funded by your generous support!

The screens showed a swiftly moving viewpoint coursing over green farmland, in images that must have been taken using a drone camera. One panel of the wall was playing the sequence in reverse, giving the disorienting impression that the whole sky was draining away into forever at that point. Then the screens flicked to lucent grey and another door opened.

On behalf of the Conservation Farm Project, welcome to making humans history, the stentorian voice and electronic text announced. Uncharles considered that this could have been better phrased.

Adam did not make a reappearance, and Uncharles briefly considered just staying put, but the cobbled-together task he and the Wonk had constructed was to enter service with a human, not become a permanent fixture in the exhibit. He had yet to see a human, but the open door at least included the possibility that he might.

His prognosis routines, somewhat overworked, were suggesting that the possibility was becoming vanishingly slender, but what else did he have? Even a fraction of a percentage chance was infinitely greater than zero.

He stepped through into a somewhat dilapidated lounge. There were more screens on the walls, though these were cracked. There were human-suitable seats, and these had once been quite fancy and upholstered, the sort of thing Uncharles would have pulled out for his master at a modestly reputable restaurant. Time had ravaged them and vermin had pillaged them for nesting material. There were several alcoves leading off, each a dead end and some blocked by rusted chain-link doors. One appeared to have been some manner of refectory, with dispenser machines and a vacant counter. Uncharles linked to a coffeemaker, to be invited by its limited brain to make a selection from the complete lack of drinks it had the materials for.

As though the coffee machine had ratted him out, the ponderous voice suddenly recommenced its spiel, or at least a new spiel.

Welcome, generous donor and/or your remote observer! Our orderly is on its way to guide you through the wonders of living history to be found here at the Conservation Farm Project. In the meantime, please feel free to purchase refreshment from the facilities provided and make sure that you leave all children at the crèche facility.

Another of the open alcoves had faded pictures of romping anthropomorphic bears and puppies peeling away overhead.

Beyond them, in the shadows, something moved.

Uncharles waited, wondering why Adam, or some other orderly, was lurking there.

It moved again, and simultaneously his visual processes adjusted to the lower light. It wasn't Adam.

It was a stuffed toy. Or at least a three-foot tall robot formed like one. Where Uncharles might have predicted such a thing to be ragged and moth-eaten to fit its distressed surroundings, its glassy eyes were bright, its artificial woolly fur groomed and neat. In fact, each and every part of it was objectively in perfect condition: limbs, hands, feet, ears, cute button nose, smiling muzzle, and the various regions of its body. The only somewhat existential point standing between this fuzzy ubermensch and actual perfection was that none of these pristine parts belonged together. And even though the stitching joining them together was extremely neat, it was visible to a valet's exacting gaze and somewhat ruined the effect.

Behind the toy, in the shadows, Uncharles could make out a variety of sad little piles of stuffing, empty velveteen and fake fur skins, and twisted plastic armatures.

He received a link request and, whilst foreboding wasn't within him, Uncharles' prognosis routines weren't exactly jumping up and down with enthusiasm about the connection.

Nonetheless . . .

Uncharles, Hi! I'm Hoppity Jack! I'm your friendly crèche supervisor here to collect any and all of your children before you can proceed on to the Farm experience!

The thing, the monstrosity of a hundred perfect pieces, spread its mismatched paws and tilted its grinning head to one side. Uncharles had never held any brief for human children. There had never been a child attached to the manor, though surely some had been present at social gatherings his master had attended. Nannying was not a facility that fell within his remit, however, and he had only the very basic drive to protect children from harm that any robot would be instilled with. At that point, however, Uncharles found that under no circumstances would he have entrusted any child to Hoppity

Jack. He found himself recalling Uncle Japes with something like nostalgia.

Hoppity Jack, he sent back. *I am not accompanied by children. You may return to your . . . regular duties.*

Hoppity Jack took a step forwards, grin widening. *Uncharles, Hi! I'm Hoppity Jack! In order to proceed to the experience you must pass all children over to the creche. I'm sorry, but them's the rules, pardner.* And the thing made little gun-shooting gestures at him. *Pew pew.*

Hoppity Jack, I have no children with me so the matter does not arise. The little thing was quite close now and Uncharles' self-preservation routines impelled him to take a step back, though he couldn't quite find a concrete reason why. *Do I take it from your moniker that you are . . . some sort of rabbit?*

Hoppity Jack stopped, then cocked its head again. For a moment Uncharles seemed to see a terrible self-awareness in the crazed pools of its tormented eyes.

Uncharles, who can say any more? It sent back. *Hi! Kindly pass over your children! Where are you hiding them, eh? Hi kids! Hoppity Jack here! Come out, come out! Are you hiding in that plastic torso? Or one each in the legs, huh? You got hollow legs there, pardner?*

Uncharles kept backing up, reversing around the seating from memory and very aware that the lounge was of only limited size. Jack just kept following with a kind of dancing two-step, pausing every so often to spread his paws in a ta-da sort of gesture. Uncharles saw the glints of exposed metal there, where the inner frame pierced through the fluff.

Hoppity Jack, I have come here from the manors to serve humans at the farm, kindly direct me to the appropriate system so that I can present my credentials.

Uncharles, hi! Why don't you open up and show me the kids you've got in there. You gotta *give your minors over to the crèche system, pardner, you just gotta. Kids don't want to be shown round the farms. That stuff's super booooooooring. They'd rather have fun and games with Hoppity Jack and his fuzzy friends!*

Uncharles strongly suspected that wouldn't be the case for even the most tedium-averse child. He could also only assume that the fuzzy friends had found their fuzzy ends in the discarded skeletons, skins, and stuffing left behind in Jack's search for replacement parts. *Hoppity Jack, I am unable to surrender any children to your care.*

Uncharles, hi! Then you ain't going any farther, pardner! I guess it's just you and me for tea!

Uncharles' internal routines had been chewing away at this unanticipated and highly unwelcome situation. There were, he noted, no savagely rabbited robot corpses around, other than the late and unlamented fuzzy friends, but the Farm's system had implied that manorial observers came and went without mentioning some kind of unspeakable child-tithe. Of course the Farm's system—as Uncharles had encountered it to date—was dumb as bricks and far short of a proper majordomo, but either no visitors had arrived since Jack had taken up this tack or . . .

Of course, if his master had wanted to send an observer somewhere, just to see through its eyes, he wouldn't have sent a complex human-facing model like Uncharles. Some very basic menial, even a rental model, would have done. Something working at a far less sophisticated level.

Have I been overcalculating this?

Hoppity Jack, he addressed the advancing nightmare, *I have arrived with zero children.*

Uncharles, hi! You have to give all your children into the care of the crèche before continuing. Them's the rules! You got to play by the rules, pardner.

Uncharles stopped backing up, and Jack quick-stepped into paw range, grinning up at him.

Hoppity Jack, I hereby surrender all zero children accompanying me into your care, Uncharles sent formally. He even made a little ushering gesture, to encourage the nonexistent little tots to rush skipping and laughing into the thing's care.

Hoppity Jack stopped. The grin did not go away but the grinning behind it seemed to. It looked left and right with its huge hollow eyes, acknowledging its receipt of zero children from Uncharles.

"Hey hey hey, kids!" Its voice was high and strangled and had obviously suffered some damage when Jack ripped it from its original owner. "I'm the sheriff of this here crèche. How about you and me go have some fun?" The words had probably been bubbling with cheer when they were first spoken, but now they came out squeezed and desperate. Jack danced off to its corner, looking back with that hideous cracked smile at the lack of children following it. Once there, Uncharles saw it just stop dead in its tracks and slump. And probably this was Hoppity Jack gone dormant, lying in wait for the next visitor who might bring it a child as a votive offering. That part of Uncharles' programming designed to parse human body language, however, could read there a terrible, bleak misery. If Jack had put its overlarge head in its paws and started sobbing, he wouldn't have been terribly surprised.

Another door opened, presumably at some signal that the creche had fulfilled its proper duties. The orderly, Adam, was silhouetted there.

Uncharles, please accompany me and I will give you a tour of the farm facilities, it sent.

Uncharles did so, hurriedly. *Adam, your crèche supervisor is defective. As a human-facing model, I would suggest that it would give an obstructive and alarming impression to human visitors. I am surprised you have not had it removed or replaced.*

Adam paused for just a moment and then continued on. An orderly unit could not show fear, of course, nor would a valet look for such a thing in another robot. Nonetheless, the pair of them understood one another.

11

Adam, sent Uncharles, *are you permitted to answer questions?*

Uncharles. Adam's electronic tone could be described as bright but brittle. *My purpose on this tour is to answer your owner's questions as they pertain to the functioning of the Farm. I am provided with extensive records about the past and current operation of the project. I note that previous visitors have not called upon me to deploy these, preferring instead simply to experience the Experience through the medium of remote visual surveillance. However, if your master has any queries then please relay them to me and I would be happy to oblige.*

Adam, what if I have internally generated queries?

Uncharles, whilst irregular, I am not prohibited from responding to these.

Uncharles gathered up the pessimistic shreds of his prognosis routines as he trailed through a dimly lit and downwards-sloping corridor in Adam's wake. *Adam, are there currently any humans within the Conservation Farm Project?*

Uncharles, yes.

Uncharles had been expecting the aforementioned extensive records, but apparently Adam was not going to trot those out just for a valet's curiosity. His prognosis gave him a kick and he amended his question. *Adam, are there currently any* living *humans within the Conservation Farm Project?*

Uncharles, yes.

Adam, how many?

Uncharles, thirteen thousand seven hundred and eighty-three as per the last census.

Uncharles actually had to stop walking to salvage the processing power to deal with that. *A lot. A lot of humans. One of whom will* surely require their travel itinerary arranged or their formal clothes laid out. He sent, *Adam, I am here seeking employment in human service. How might I be introduced to these humans as prospective employers?*

Uncharles, this is beyond my remit.

It had been a little much to hope for.

Adam, may I speak to the majordomo service controlling the Farm?

Uncharles, you have spoken with it when it gave you the induction experience. A higher-functioning majordomo service is not available at this time. The Conservation Farm Project apologises for the inconvenience.

It was, Uncharles decided, inconvenient. He considered how to circumvent Adam's relatively obstinate programming to get where he needed to be. *Adam, am I permitted to ask questions touching on the functioning of the Farm?*

Uncharles, yes.

Adam, how is the Farm governed?

Uncharles, the activities of the humans in the Farm Project are governed based on traditional routines and patterns that have remained unchanged for centuries.

Adam, what happens if something unexpected happens or something goes wrong? Who makes decisions regarding these eventualities?

Uncharles, the Farm is supplied with a variety of supplemental maintenance and correction services tasked to step in when mechanical or human malfunction disrupts regular functioning. Adam seemed a simple creature, and doubtless Uncharles was only running into the relative unsophistication of its programming rather than bloody-minded obstructionism.

Adam, he persevered gamely, *what ultimate authority makes decisions concerning the operation of the Farm?*

Uncharles, that is only tangentially related to my remit.

Adam, tangentially is still a valid connection. I put forward the hypothetical possibility that my master might make this enquiry of me at a later date. It was, Uncharles was aware, a very, very hypothetical possibility, but Adam didn't need that information muddying the waters of its decision-making.

There was a distinctly surly pause for processing time before Adam spat out, *Uncharles, ultimate authority rests with Doctor Washburn.*

Adam, is Doctor Washburn a robot or similar automated system, or a h—?

Uncharles, kindly attend to relaying these images to your master! Adam broke in with what couldn't be malicious triumph. *We are now viewing an area of the primary living quarters of our human volunteer conscripts here at the Conservation Farm Project!*

And whilst part of Uncharles was still pushing for him to carry on the conversation, it was overwhelmed by a conflicting rush of other imperatives and programming, because here were humans.

They were below. Adam and Uncharles stood on their ceiling, looking down through mostly clear plastic at a space divided and subdivided into a maze of little rooms—no, a maze of little complexes of rooms—two, three, four at a time—connected by corridors in a dendritic pattern so that the whole—extending far past the viewing window they peered down through—must resemble a brain or cauliflower if seen entire from far enough above. Uncharles observed, seeing humans in bed in darkened chambers—two, three to a bed; three, four beds to a room; and barely a leg's width between the frames sometimes. He saw lit rooms where humans sat about cramped tables shovelling thin gruel into their faces. Humans in vests, shirtsleeves, grimy T-shirts, bras, tracksuits. They had thin, hungry faces. They had children crawling on them. Some held babies in their arms, fed them, or tried to calm them or got them further riled up by shouting at them. Some sat on the convenience engaging in post-gruel gastric activities or reading yellowed newspapers or sucking the last dregs of chemical enjoyment from a crafty cigarette before uncovering the smoke detectors. Some were in tiny kitchenettes, fixing a late sandwich, pawing through fridges the size of a house brick. Some had phones to their ears, before their eyes, though whatever they heard or saw there seemed to bring them little joy.

There were televisions. Uncharles watched, fascinated, as antique footage was played as if it were current affairs. Wars, explosions, stock market crashes, a seemingly endless variety of reality shows.

Adam stood there, waiting to field questions, but Uncharles just stared, trying to process the infinite variety of human life he had been presented with. The tide of data was an almost existential threat to him. He felt the coursing rush of it eroding away the delicate structures of his decision-making capability. He had been designed to be human-facing, and here were more humans than he had ever faced before, cheek by jowl and all desperately in need of a valet.

He watched one human put on smudged makeup by the dim bulb of a bathroom mirror. He watched another shave inexpertly and cut themselves. His fingers twitched to go to their aid. *I could do so much of a better job. I can help you. Let me help you.*

Adam, I want to help them.

Uncharles, the humans you see are happy and productive parts of the Farm Project. They enjoy working hard to preserve traditional human ways of life. Kindly come with me and you will see the next stage of their happy, productive lives.

Because of course even this bustling cornucopia of human activity couldn't be *it*, however fulfilled Uncharles would have been in serving even a small part of it. The farms were vast and busy and organised. Despite all the dysfunction he had passed getting this far, Uncharles was fast becoming a convert to the virtues of the Project.

The next window Adam led him to was at least vertically aligned, looking sideways into a long space filled with humans. They stood shoulder to shoulder, most clutching cases or bags, most wearing long coats that were splotchy with damp at the shoulders and the hems. Uncharles could see more of them funnelling in, carrying umbrellas or hunched under newspapers they held above their heads. He was able to construct a theoretical geography of passages linking the great living conurbation he had seen to this crammed cannister of humanity, none of which would be exposed to an open sky that— his weather app told him—wasn't currently heavy with rain anyway.

However, it was obviously considered important to the human condition that people get rained on. It was, he surmised, authentic and traditional, hence artificial sprinklers had been installed. The attention to detail was truly laudable.

A train ground into view alongside the packed platform of people. Its exterior was artfully decalled with reproduced graffiti. The carriages were already 100 percent full of miserable, wet humans but, somehow, at least 75 percent of the waiting people managed to force their way on board, until every window was a pattern of plastered backs, hands, and faces with no space in between them. The carriage gathered itself and lumbered away with its weighty burden. The people left on the platform, rather than being happy to have avoided that fate, looked only ill-tempered or anxious, glancing at phones or watches as ever more people flooded in from the artificially rainy corridors outside.

Adam, what is the purpose of this?

Uncharles, the purpose is to preserve an essential part of the traditional lifestyle of the past. We are assured by multiple contemporaneous sources of the valuable role this journey played in the lives of historical humans, how it permitted them time for contemplation and socialisation. When some deviant humans proposed simply performing work remotely without undergoing this "commute," the great minds of the time united in support of the considerable physical and mental benefits of this valuable journey. We will now proceed to the workplace itself.

Adam, is this far? I feel that I am better suited to assist humans in their homes than in a work environment.

Adam didn't actually look at Uncharles, that not being a part of regular robot interaction. The second and a half of pause it allowed, however, seemed to communicate the orderly's opinion about whether Uncharles would ever get the chance to serve humans in any environment.

Uncharles, it sent at last, *kindly observe the map of our transport system.*

The accompanying diagram was informative.

Adam, I see that the residence and the workplace modules are adjacent.

Uncharles, yes.

Uncharles took in the stacked loops and spirals, the whole tangled spaghetti of it all.

Adam, I commend the considerable ingenuity involved in designing such a tortuous transport network to link two places that are in fact immediately next door to one another.

Uncharles, it is considered one of the major achievements of the Project. Our founders did not want to deny our conscript volunteers an appropriately healing journey from home to work.

The office was next. Uncharles recognised it from a handful of images in his library. It seemed very authentic. Each expansive room had been subdivided into cubicles and alcoves in such a way that every individual therein had simultaneously a minimum of personal space and a minimum of privacy. This was, Adam explained, to ensure a maximum of productivity from each worker, just as in historical times. One worker was the boss, who had a larger and more private work area with a window from which they could observe every one of their subordinates. The boss, Adam explained, was chosen by merit.

Adam, define merit, Uncharles requested.

Uncharles, each of our conscript volunteers is subject to an exhaustive personality inventory. To be the boss of an office at the Project is to be responsible for creating a historically authentic atmosphere for all the other workers. It is absolutely vital that appropriate levels of intrusive micromanagement, divisive paranoia, bullying, and the threat of arbitrary punishments are maintained, so that we can truly re-create the folkways of the past. Also a propensity for calling meetings at regular, and indeed irregular, intervals.

Adam, and what is the end purpose of all this work we are seeing?

Uncharles, there is none. This is also believed to be historically authentic.

Uncharles watched the anthill bustle of the office, the intricate dance of workers killing time at their desks, watching the clock, gathering at the coffee machine or watercooler, joylessly eating sandwiches, fondling one another miserably in the stationery cupboard.

Adam, according to what internal reference material I can access this appears very authentic.

Uncharles, yes. The Conservation Farm Project is considered the most important historical research tool of recent years. Video records and psychological data from the conscript volunteers are available on request with an appropriate donation to cover administrative costs.

Adam, when will the wider outdoor facilities be ready to receive the volunteers? Uncharles had been going over the induction material. It would surely be easier to find a place when these teeming people had been relocated to somewhere more spacious. Plus, if the Farm did not cooperate, then he found his programming did not prohibit him from just breaking in and offering his services direct to the humans, as a kind of maverick rogue valet. That would also be easier with the outdoor site.

Uncharles, Adam replied. *Relocation of our population will commence when our outdoor facilities reach fifty percent completion.*

Adam, what level of completion has been achieved to date?

Uncharles, taking into account entropy and dilapidation, our outdoor facilities currently stand at minus two hundred and seventeen percent completion.

That, suggested Uncharles' prognosis routines, was in line with expectations. And while a robot valet couldn't be cynical, his prognosis was certainly managing a good artificial simulation of it.

There was more, but it was also the same. The return commute, through another rain-blasted tunnel and onto another packed train, back to those congested apartments, and all without a glimpse of the sun. Uncharles found the timing to be overly fortuitous for his visit, but Adam explained that the Farm Project was designed to be highly efficient, especially in the absence of any outside cues as to time. The human population lived in a constant cycle of shifts. There would always be people restlessly trying to sleep, even as others were funnelling onto the trains to go looping about the least joyous roller-coaster ride ever, while others bent over their workplace terminals and still more were returning home. And there were the schools, miniature offices for the miniature adults-to-be. Overcrowded class-rooms where they learned from a rigid straitjacket of a curriculum designed to impart skills and competencies that were 100 percent devoted to acquiring 60 percent of the necessary skills needed in the office.

It was all, Uncharles had to admit, fearfully efficient. The induc-tion had waxed long on the topic of robots and other automated helpmates replacing human labour, but he hadn't realised that, back in the past, humans had worked so hard to live like robots. The end-less round of tasks, the queuing, the utter repetitiveness of these people's lives. They must, Uncharles predicted, be so grateful to have such lives designed for them. How good it must be to have no choices or options.

However, this was all secondary to his own purposes.

Adam, he said. *Whilst this remains highly informative, I am here seeking employment in the service of humans.*

Uncharles, this is outside my remit.

Adam, what happens if I just walk in? They were over another housing complex now, all those poor unassisted humans desperate for someone to fold their clothes and wield the razor. Uncharles felt a curious sense of momentum, as though destiny was propelling him.

Uncharles, kindly clarify. It is not permitted for anachronistic robots to access the Farm. You are present as a manorial observer. Adam had stopped moving. Uncharles wondered if it might just end up trapped behind a logical leap it couldn't make, like Inspector Birdbot.

Adam, I note that it is not permitted. However, as I am not of the Farm system, the Farm's rules do not bind me. What happens if I just walk in?

Uncharles, there is no access to the Farm from this point.

Adam, I could just stamp very hard on this viewing panel until it broke. And he could. A sudden flowering of new decision trees un-rolled within Uncharles, all the things he could do here. The bizarre contradiction that he could forcibly become part of their system here, specifically because he wasn't a part of it.

He stamped. The plastic beneath them quivered a little. Not much, not even a crack, but the quiver told Uncharles that sufficient perse-verance would get him through. Below, a couple of the humans who couldn't sleep, or were abluting, or sitting miserably at a dining table the size of two hands together, looked up dully.

Uncharles, kindly desist, Adam sent. *Orderlies have been sent for.*

Adam, I am here to serve humans. If I must cause serious damage to the Project to do so then there is nothing preventing me. O glorious freedom! *Or alternatively you could guide me to a more convenient access point.*

Uncharles, that is outside my remit. Uncharles, orderlies have been sent for. Uncharles, desist. There was no way for Adam to insert a begging tone into his electronic comms but Uncharles decided one would have been appropriate.

Adam, I will not be prevented from fulfilling my purpose. Elec-tronic choirs of angels sang their way towards crescendo behind his words. He stamped again and observed the first hairline cracks. The waking humans were staring upwards. Uncharles felt his inner world explode away from him, all the walls and rules and restric-tions just receding into infinity. In the service of humanity, he could do anything. He could write his own laws of robotics. Nothing that Adam or any number of dumb orderlies could do would stop him.

"Undesignated Unit," a voice broke in from somewhere above. It wasn't the pompous tones of the induction, but Uncharles took it for some other mindless low-level system.

"I am here to serve!" he declared, bringing his foot down a third time. "You have humans here. Let me help them."

"You're *here* as a manorial observer, aren't you? That's what the records say." And the voice had far more life and variance to it than the drone of the induction. "Or is that not the case?"

"I am Uncharles and I am a high-level human-facing valet unit seeking employment with the humans of the Farm. It is not important to me that a high-level human-facing valet unit is not historically appropriate to the period you are re-creating. I am here to serve and these are the only humans I have encountered since my previous position was terminated. Kindly let me serve them."

"Uncharles," the voice said, "that's fascinating. A valet from the manors, just rattling around loose? Who ever heard of such a thing? Why don't you follow Adam and he'll bring you to my office. We can discuss your employment application."

Uncharles paused, his foot already raised for a final shattering percussion. "My application," he echoed. "To whom am I speaking?"

"I like that," the voice said. "'To whom.' Very posh. Uncharles, I'm Doctor Washburn. I'm in charge here. You'll have noticed that the orderlies like Adam are dumb as bricks. Oh, good enough for what they're made for, but not a match for a well-made model like you. Adam, you're to bring the valet unit straight to me."

Uncharles analysed the tilt of Adam's head for contraindications and detected at least 12 percent mutiny there. However, whatever other directives moved the orderly, obeying the Farm's master took precedence. "Doctor Washburn, yes," it said after a sullen pause.

"Splendid," said the voice. "Uncharles, you're an intriguing case. I'm so looking forward to meeting you."

12

Doctor Washburn had a tall, heavy frame, several inches over Uncharles and with a massive gravity to him, as though everything in his presence was being inescapably drawn into his orbit. His exterior was far from the most convincing skin Uncharles had encountered, being pasty in the main but relieved by blotchy redness and blemishes here and there, suggesting more defects of manufacture or maintenance than the effluxion of time. He wore a brown suit, and a pale blue shirt open at the thickness of his neck and flapping at the cuffs in a way that Uncharles' programming made him want to fuss at and button up, just out of a general sense of sartorial elegance. The doctor's face seemed to have slipped slightly from the underlying scaffolding, so that folds and pouches formed under the eyes, flowing into jowls and creases partly hidden by an undisciplined growth of beard. It had commenced its life as a neat goatee, Uncharles suspected, but the inevitable passage of days had blurred its borders until it was just a splotch.

Washburn's eyes were almost invisible as he performed a thorough visual appraisal of Uncharles, both because of his suspicious squint and the antique spectacles he affected. Also, the strip of light in the ceiling of his office was actinically bright compared to the dinge of the Farm. Uncharles himself had to adjust his receptor levels to properly examine Washburn, and he took several uncertain seconds of analysis before reaching an acceptable level of certainty about what he was looking at.

Doctor Washburn was human.

His office was furnished in a style that Uncharles' somewhat snobby preprogramming would describe as "sumptuous but lacking taste" and also "very, very busy." There were shelves on half the walls, and where there weren't shelves there were frames. Some of these had pictures in them, an assortment that didn't seem to speak to any particular theme, school, or aesthetic. Gorgeous burning riverscapes, portraits of ambivalent-looking women, sourly bearded men presiding over trompe l'oeil skulls, blank quadrilateral blocks of colour, unnaturally lurid cans of soup. A number of them were recognisable from Uncharles' internal libraries on the subject of art, though he had no way of assessing whether they were originals or just copies. They were *Art,* though, and that was plainly the point that their display here was making.

Those frames not restraining the *Art* held a variety of printed certificates and qualifications, all of which asserted that Dominic Washburn had completed this or that footling management course or further professional development quota, or that he had earned a doctorate in some abstruse field of socio-historiography from the University of Somewhere Not Featured in Uncharles' Map Library.

The shelves held a similar variety of *things.* Uncharles recognised many of them as being quite valuable, the sort of object that, exhibited on its own, might be a conversation piece at a polite soiree or an aid to contemplation in someone's study. Here, all the fossils, plates, vases, statuettes, and bejewelled eggs were jumbled in all together as though there had been some sort of shelf-cramming competition. Possibly there had. The top row of each shelf contained a bewildering variety of trophies, shields, cups, and little Perspex standees. Each bore proud etching proclaiming that one Dominic Washburn— presumably the same unless the forename was a familial tradition— had come second, third, or occasionally even won the appropriate honours at golf, squash, psychiatry, public speaking, creative writing, poetry, football (in, apparently, a team of one), or boxing, come top of his class in business studies, run a half marathon, or earned his bronze swimming certificate. Combined with the proliferation of framed qualifications, the overall impression was that Doctor Washburn had lived several entire lives, each one of them filled with somewhat mediocre achievements.

Washburn himself had a desk. It made the desk of the Diagnostician at Central Services look like a mere occasional table. If the man himself was broad and tall and massive, then the desk was locked in a life-or-death struggle with him to exert its own colossal gravity on the room. If all the various priceless bric-a-brac on the shelves had spontaneously been ripped from their resting places to converge on man and desk, slaves to their combined and contesting magnetism, Uncharles would . . . have had to recalibrate his prognosis routines, certainly, and wouldn't have been able to feel actual surprise in any event, and so the attempt at descriptive poetry broke down in the presence of robotic logic. It was, however, a very impressive desk. The chair that Washburn had, until that moment, been sitting in was not quite of the same water, but very definitely a fancier chair than an administrator would normally be found sitting in. A great velveteen stuffed piece of upholstery, its back and seat bearing the concave negative of the doctor's own back and seat as mute testimony of a prolongedly sedentary existence.

He had stood as Uncharles was ushered in, leaning ponderously on the desk, big hands jostling for room with the moleskine notebook and the calendar, the keyboard, the several monitors, and a collection of little executive toys.

"Well, now," he said. Doctor Washburn's voice was rich but rough, like a thick gravy made with broken glass. A pause followed, because "Well, now" wasn't either a greeting or a question or an observation that Uncharles felt he could do anything with. Doctor Washburn did not look welcoming. In Uncharles' professional human-facing opinion his expression scored most highly for suspicion and hostility.

"You're who they sent, are you?"

"Doctor Washburn, kindly clarify what you mean by 'they,'" Uncharles said politely. "Also 'sent.' The words do not seem to pertain to my circumstances."

Washburn came out from behind the desk, which in itself was an epic journey worthy of a trilogy and some side quests. He tapped the scuffs and scratches on Uncharles' chest.

"You've dragged some broken-down old model out of storage.

Couldn't even drive over with something properly polished?" He peered into Uncharles' face in a way that said he wasn't looking *at* Uncharles at all, but at something he imagined lay behind the valet's moulded faceplate. "Or did you have the thing walk all the way from the estates?"

"Doctor Washburn, I have walked all the way from the estates." Uncharles found a thronging list of items suddenly in his queue: he needed minor repairs, he needed replacement casing parts, he needed to be polished. He must be made *presentable*. He was a disgrace. He was bringing shame to . . . and the little hopping tasks suddenly froze and just drained away because of course there was nothing and nobody left to bring shame to. Except himself, and who would program a valet with a sense of personal shame?

"Who's in there?" Washburn demanded. This time he tapped Uncharles' face, right on the curved surface of one imitation eye. "Who's come to spy on me, eh? Or did you think this would just pass as one more observer. One more little voyeur come to see how the other half—hah, the other nineteen twentieths!—live?" The focus of his gaze shifted, so that he was looking at Uncharles rather than through him. "Where are you transmitting to, robot? Adam, how's that trace coming along?"

"Doctor Washburn, I am not transmitting anywhere," Uncharles said, treading on Adam's own response of, "Doctor Washburn, no transmissions are present. Also, as previously noted, it would not be possible to transmit to an external source from this far underground without using our own network, and no such intrusion has been detected." Some quirk of Adam's programming conveyed the suggestion that it had had this conversation before.

Washburn frowned. "Well that's even less convincing, then. So you're here to spy on me and report back? How are you even supposed to keep up the pretence of being an observer if you're not transmitting?"

"Doctor Washburn, I am not an observer," Uncharles said. "I am from the manors. The category I was assigned by your induction system was the only option presented to me that appeared even slightly relevant to my purpose here."

"Which was to spy on me," Washburn tapped him in the face again. "Oh, I've been waiting, believe me. Some do-gooder in the system, come to screw with me. Ever since the last time—"

"Doctor Washburn, I am from the manorial system. I am not here to spy on you." Navigating a conversation that was at least three-quarters hidden precursor was proving taxing.

"Oh sure, sure, you're here seeking employment." Washburn retreated to the desk, shunting his backside up to rest on the furniture's ornately carved edge and then immediately regretting it and leaning on his hands instead. "That's what you said, right?"

"Doctor Washburn, yes."

"Have you any idea how ridiculous that sounds?"

Uncharles ran a quick analysis of his inner processes, seeking any possible answer to that question.

"Doctor Washburn, my idea of how ridiculous that sounds is that it sounds irregular but, as it is the truth, still remotely plausible. I am a service model seeking human employment."

The doctor blinked at him, took off his spectacles to clean them on a flapping cuff that was itself, Uncharles noted, far from clean, then redonned them. "Uh-huh," he said, without conviction. "Sure. And you'd come here because . . . ?"

"Doctor Washburn, because there are humans here."

"And there aren't in the estates?"

"Doctor Washburn, since leaving my previous appointment after the death of my original master, I have found no positions available in the estates." Overgrown gardens, ruined houses, rusted servants. "After some events at Central Services a new task was created to look further afield." Passive voice so that Uncharles did not have to delve into how that had come about, between his own definitely-not-desires preferred state and the Wonk's interference. "You have humans. I wish to serve them."

"Yeah?" Washburn folded his arms, rested his backside against the overly scalloped edge of the desk, regretted it, and stood up again. He vacillated for a moment before retreating to the chair. "I mean, you've seen what we've got here, robot. Uncharles, was the name you gave? Weird name. Your last master must have been a real character. So, Uncharles, you've seen the important work we're doing at the Farm Project. Where do you imagine you'd fit in?"

Uncharles didn't imagine, but being human-facing he could translate the question into appropriate terms. "Doctor Washburn, I am a fully skilled personal valet unit with a variety of supplemental skill sets. I am a travelling companion, personal organiser, and assistant. I am able to manage schedules, wardrobe, liaison duties, and personal attendance including reading, refreshments, conversation, and uplifting quotations from literature. In addition, although it is not my primary function, I can provide chauffeur, footman, lady's maid, and kitchen assistant duties. Furthermore and in the alternative, although it would not make use of my capabilities, I can perform cleaning and other low-order menial services."

Washburn stared at him. "All that?"

"Doctor Washburn, yes."

"You want to do all that for . . . what? One guy in the Farms? Be a personal valet for one of the eight-to-sixes? Provide inspirational quotes and read the paper for him in that little slice of alone time he gets between the commute and bed? Make him tea in the morning? Or are you going to be the maid of all work for one of the families? Or the office cleaner?"

Uncharles considered his options. "Doctor Washburn, although the first would best suit my abilities, any of the above would be achievable."

Washburn's attitude had changed. The suspicion had drained away. The thoughtful narrowness of his eyes now suggested a man formulating a plan.

"You're actually serious, aren't you?"

"Doctor Washburn, a gentleman's gentlerobot unit is always serious." It was one of the standard valet model responses. To be able to trot it out, even in these strange surroundings, reinforced Uncharles' sense of purpose.

"You really did walk all the way from the manors looking for someone to make tea for." Washburn was grinning now, shaking his head.

"Doctor Washburn, though my purpose covers more than that single task, your overall assertion is correct."

"Are you even still capable?" Washburn leant back in the chair, taking in Uncharles' scratches and scars, the mute testimony of his travels.

"Doctor Washburn, yes."

"Well, we'll see, won't we." There were a number of doors from the office and the doctor flicked a finger at one. "Kitchen's through there. Go make me a sandwich. And some fruit. Everything's in the fridge or the cupboards."

Some spur of propriety kicked within Uncharles. "Doctor Washburn, without formal engagement it is not appropriate that I perform—"

"Oh, think of it as a job interview," Washburn said expansively. "I mean, you're pretty beat up there, Uncharles. I need to know you can still do your job."

Can I still perform my job? His internal meters insisted he could, but then they'd glided smoothly over the whole razor incident without even registering it. *I will perform these tasks as a self-test.*

The kitchen was simple and without ornament, giving the feel that it was built on a larger but lower-resolution scale than the cluttered office. It was designed so that a less dexterous and sophisticated robot could use it, Uncharles concluded. He could imagine Adam's thick metal fingers opening these cupboards and containers.

The fridge was large and bountifully stocked. He recognised most of the contents from Hauler Seven's inventory. It was fine produce, too. There was high-quality plant-based meat substitute with an authentic texture and taste, and there was faux-cheese with added cheese flavourings. The bread was spongy, but it was identifiably bread. There was lettuce, tomatoes, cucumber. There were grapes and apples. Genuine organic produce from the glasshouses, comparable in quality to the supplies that had been delivered increasingly infrequently to the manor. Back home, of course, Uncharles would just have linked to the kitchen to have the staff there prepare a snack for his master. The task was quickly and simply accomplished, however, and Uncharles was surprised how many internal reward system boxes it ticked, after all this time wandering.

He brought the repast through on a china-effect plastic plate and laid it carefully before Washburn.

"Quick," the doctor noted. He took a bite of the sandwich, chewed, swallowed with a burlesque of satisfaction. "Whenever," he said, mouth still half-full, "Adam or another of the orderlies makes me food, it tastes like shoe leather and glue. I can't account for it. This is excellent, Uncharles. Say, there's another thing you could do for me. All a part of the test, you know. Putting you through your paces. Peel me a grape."

"Doctor Washburn?"

"A grape. I want you to peel me a grape."

"Doctor Washburn, for what purpose? Do the orderly units habitually peel your grapes?" Uncharles felt as though he had been thrown into an entirely unfamiliar decision tree.

"Can you imagine if they tried?" Washburn mimed squishing grapes, although as he brought his hands high to do it, he inadvertently gave the impression of eyeballs. "It's just . . . you know. It's the thing, the hedonistic thing you read about or see on videos. 'Boy, peel me a grape.' And here you are, a fancy service model, and here are some grapes, so . . . peel me a grape. Go on." He was grinning, waiting to see if Uncharles would do it.

With meticulous care, Uncharles peeled him a grape. Washburn stared at the denuded morsel.

"Honestly, they look weird when you've peeled them. I don't even know why someone would want that." He grinned his big grin up at

Uncharles again. "Last test before I find you a position, Uncharles. You ready?"

"Doctor Washburn, yes." Lacking heart or feelings, yet somehow still heartfelt.

"Adam, you can come in now."

The orderly entered through one of the other doors. Uncharles caught a brief glimpse of another highly decorated room with an enormous screen and a sofa. Then his attention was captured by what the orderly was holding. A porcelain bowl illustrated with flowers, a badger-hair brush, a plush towel, the makings of lather. A razor, ivory-handled with silver inlay.

"If there's one thing I always leave until too late," Washburn said, "it's the beard. And, sure, normally I'd just end up giving it a buzz with the electric, but I've got this museum piece here in the collection and I guess you know what to do with it."

"Doctor Washburn, yes," Uncharles said flatly. "I know what to do with it."

"Well, swell," Washburn said. He settled back into the dent he'd worn in the chair and tilted his head back. "More your sort of thing? Your core programming, right? And make sure it's good and close."

13.

Uncharles was busy.

Previously his day would have begun on activation after a period of recharge and defragmentation, but this was a luxury his current position did not allow. This was no manor, and there was no other staff beyond the orderlies, who were not programmed for domestic use. Master had gone to some lengths to twist their logic into making them perform household tasks, with some success, but the true purpose of the orderlies was to wrangle the conscript volunteers. Adam and the others were constantly pushing back against all the little jobs that Master required them to do, and Uncharles found this perfectly understandable. He had now had the chance to see Adam at work in the manner he had been designed for, entering the crowded territory of the Farm with riot shield, shotgun, and electric bludgeon, clearing a path through hysterical volunteers and then fixing the water or the lights or some other part of the Farm's infrastructure. It was brutal, desperate work in nonoptimal conditions. If Master had asked Uncharles to do it then Uncharles would have had a whole ladder of objections based on his skill set and programming. Making Adam serve tea had probably been a similar battle.

Adam and the other orderlies had adjusted to fit Uncharles into their relationship map, now. When he had been just a manorial visitor with awkward questions, he had been a problem eligible for a solution—and Uncharles had seen the sort of solutions the orderlies were designed to dole out. Now he was not only a chosen familiar of Master, but was performing what they considered to be unwanted tasks outside their competencies. They didn't *like* him, necessarily. Being robots they didn't *like* anyone, but, Uncharles predicted, even if they had somehow achieved the potential they still wouldn't have. They were a grim lot. However, he was a part of their hierarchy and world, and no longer a problem to be concussively solved. Just resented in a generally passive-aggressive way.

Being a personal staff of one meant he had been active all night performing the work of the more menial maid and footmen units, particularly cleaning. Master's extensive collection of valuable objects was a considerable challenge to dust, and indeed there had been considerable build up from the cursory job that the orderlies had performed before. Now everything was spotless, even though the activity had taken an entire night. The art, the artifacts, the history, the larceny of it, all perfection. Uncharles had attempted to educate himself about the collection and its provenance, but the very basic farm system he could interface with simply gave dates and locations. Apparently Master had acquired the clutter of objects one at a time and from a variety of places, many of which were manors. Possibly they were gifts presented by grateful observers. On the other hand there were orderly excursions recorded alongside many of these dates, and Uncharles could construct a scenario where Master subverted their programming enough to have them go and retrieve objets d'art for him. His private gang of jewel thieves, heisting the ruined locations of a decaying world just so that he could have his crowded shelves of . . . stuff. Undifferentiated stuff, save that each piece came with an estimated price tag for sale at auction from one of the reputable insurance sites that was still active. Master just liked being surrounded by nice stuff.

With a sense of all-things-being-in-their-place, which was to say electronic contentment, he checked Master's travel arrangements. There were none, and that, too, was good. Master hadn't indicated any desire to travel anywhere since the commencement of Uncharles' new employment, which made checking his travel arrangements a trouble-free activity. After that, he laid out some clothes for Master, for that nonexistent travel. Master was not, sadly, in a position to instruct his new valet properly in daily tasks, and there was no majordomo system to liaise with, but Uncharles was capable of improvising. Adapting his previous manorial schedule was easy enough, and if none of it was remotely applicable to his new master's service—if Master was in fact not really aware that Uncharles was *doing* any of these tasks—that wasn't the important thing. It was important that Uncharles have tasks to do, and that he did them, and then that they were done. That was the purpose of existence.

Master didn't really have a travel wardrobe, and so Uncharles simply selected an outfit that just about fell within the bounds of sartorial acceptability and laid it out in a small unused room that Master would doubtless never go into. The previous day's outfit was replaced in the flat shelves Master had instead of a wardrobe. All was as it should be.

A moment's glitching when he tried to contact the majordomo to ask about the wishes of the spouse that Master didn't have, all that fond business he had once engaged in. Now written out of his schedule, of course. Not because Master didn't have a spouse—that had never stopped him before—but because Master didn't have a majordomo. No foil for Uncharles' eternal straight man routine.

After that, he laid out Master's slightly shabby dressing gown and then put his kitchen staff hat on to go make a cup of tea. Whilst the facilities at the Farm office weren't the equal of the manor, the tea itself was. Master valued top quality provisions. Shortly thereafter, steaming cup in hand, Uncharles went to find Master.

He had examined the device usage statistics from the Farm office to determine Master's preferred daily routines. From this he knew that, of an evening, Master generally retired to the sofa to watch media on the enormous screen, and so that was where he had placed Master the previous evening. Typically, rather than taking himself off to bed in the small hours, Master was still slumped there, head tilted back. Uncharles tutted to himself, not because he was in any way judgmental but because of a residual behaviour left over from a "Self-improvement" module his previous employer had installed, whereby he was called upon to express discreet disapproval at bad habits in humans.

Uncharles carefully placed the cup on its coaster on the black lacquered occasional table beside the overstuffed sofa. He waited to see if Master would stir at the scent of tea. He prepared a playlist of informative news media for the big screen to display on Master's waking. In the interim he re-dusted, that being a task that could be performed any number of times without substantially discouraging the expression of universal entropy that was the accretion of dust.

He wondered if he should dust Master.

The curious impulse broke him from the dusting sequence he had already designed for the lounge room—each thronging chamber was a challenge and he had found considerable engagement designing. He moved to stand over the sofa, looking down at Master's pouchy, greyish face. If he pushed his vision magnification he could see plenty that could benefit from a good dusting: crumbs, flakes of dead skin, the tiny Demodex mites that lived on human eyelashes. He made a gesture with the duster, trying to construct an efficient and nonintrusive sequence of actions that would leave Master's face properly denuded of infinitesimal debris.

Master opened an eye.

"Damnit, what time is it?" he growled. "It's the middle of the night or something?"

"Master, it is eleven minutes past ten in the morning," Uncharles reported, and felt a curious tension fall away.

"Goddamnit." Master awkwardly pushed himself into an upright sitting position, ignoring the hand that Uncharles proffered. "Didn't I tell you not to let me sleep past nine?"

"Master, no."

"I did. It was one of the first things I told you after I hired you."

Uncharles accessed his records of what had happened back then, wondering how he could possibly have failed to add such an iron commandment into his new behaviour inventory.

What had happened was this.

Mostly, it was that the shaving had gone really well. Not a nick, and Washburn's beard barbered to pointy perfection. He'd examined himself in the little mirror Uncharles held up, nodding appreciatively.

"Uncharles," he said. "Congratulations. You've passed. I think you'll be a valuable addition to our staff here at the Farm."

No leap of joy, obviously, but the new decision trees and predictions that unrolled within Uncharles were of a decidedly positive nature. "Doctor Washburn," he said, "kindly show me or have your orderlies show me how I might access the Farm system so that I might commence my duties therein."

Washburn chuckled jovially. "Oh no," he said. "Not like that. I mean, for a number of reasons. Obviously there's the main one, the official one. This is a historical re-enactment, you get it?"

"Doctor Washburn, yes."

"So back in the day, no fancy domestic robots. They're lucky if they get a microwave oven and a crappy home assistant that constantly mishears what song they want it to play. We can't have you turning up looking all plastic and sci-fi and doing their laundry for them. That would be an anachronism, right?"

Uncharles processed this.

"Besides," Washburn went on, "there's thousands of the buggers. I mean, what were you going to do? Just find one random person in all that mess and offer to keep them in clean clothes and sandwiches for the rest of their life? How would you even choose which one? Or were you going to stick up a red-and-white pole and set yourself up as a barber to all comers? Not that any of them would have the time for anything other than a quick zizz round with the electric before hustling for the train, right?"

Uncharles processed this.

"You'd be lost in there, is what I'm saying," Washburn said, as though to a child. "Like a drop of ink in an ocean. One of you, all that busy farm. Even if we did you up with human skin and pretended you weren't what you very obviously are."

Uncharles processed this. "Doctor Washburn, kindly clarify your previous statement concerning my being added to your staff."

Washburn's grin broadened. "You're coming to work for *me*, Uncharles. Won't that be grander? I mean, goddamn, I asked them over and over for a proper servant here. One of the fancy units like they got at the manors. But *no*, I wasn't important enough for that. Wasn't high-class enough. But here you are, all programmed for folding my Underoos and polishing the silver. Goddamn marvellous. You're hired."

Uncharles took two and a half seconds squaring this circle. Even as he wrestled with the idea, he wasn't sure why it was something that required wrestling with. Obviously this fell within the parameters of what he had come here for. Washburn was a human. Washburn wanted Uncharles to serve. What else was there? And yet the plans he had constructed as they'd shown him the operation of the Farm were stubborn. They seemed more meritorious, somehow, than working for Washburn. Even though every objection Washburn raised was entirely valid.

"Doctor Washburn, that will be satisfactory," he said eventually. To Uncharles the gap before replying had been a yawning chasm, speaking eloquently of his inner computational turmoil. For Washburn it had been a heartbeat, no more.

"That's grand. But listen, I can't have you Doctor-Washburning me every time you open your mouth. From now on you'd better call me Master. That's how they do it down the manor ways, isn't it? That has a nice ring to it, don't you think?"

That had been seven days ago. Uncharles scrolled back through each of them, attentive to any instruction he might have missed. At no point had Master given him any instructions about times to be awoken. Uncharles did, however, encounter seventeen similar situations when Master had introduced an apparently novel instruction while claiming it had been previously stipulated. One or the other of them was, therefore, defective, and given the relative balance of power in their relationship Uncharles was contractually obliged to assume it was himself.

"Master, I apologise and will attend to this instruction in the future."

"And don't let me sleep on the couch," Washburn added.

"Master, kindly let me have precise parameters of what action I should take should I find you sleeping on the couch."

Master looked at him balefully. "Wake me up. But carefully, gently, you know. Proper valet-style. I always have back pain when I sleep on the couch."

Later, Uncharles went to prepare lunch, taking the components of a balanced meal from the refrigerator, chopping, dicing, placing on a low heat for parboiling. All basic stuff, given his limited culinary competencies, but better than the orderlies. Now he was taking on a wider remit than a simple valet's, the economics of it had initially troubled him. Absent a majordomo with a broad grasp of household affairs he'd had to tease the relevant information out of the morose and uncommunicative orderlies.

Adam, he'd sent, on his third day in Washburn's service, when he'd been trying to plan ahead, *the foodstuffs in the refrigeration system appear to represent a disproportionate amount of the goods brought by Hauler Seven on its recent visit.*

Uncharles, yes. The orderlies never volunteered information.

Adam, should I be concerned about husbanding our supplies on the basis that some of this bounty will be dispensed to the Farm volunteers?

Uncharles, no.

Presumably true, but unsatisfactory. Uncharles was too used to interacting with humans. *Adam, kindly advise how much of the cargo from Hauler Seven should be held for the Farm, as opposed to used by Master.*

Uncharles, clarify.

Uncharles updated his local references. *As opposed to used by Doctor Washburn.*

Uncharles, aside from the vitamin supplements already transferred none of the cargo should be held for the Farm. Doctor Washburn has dictated that the conscript volunteers can subsist on the fungal crop grown on-site from their own waste. All incoming comestibles are for his use. Adjust your calculations accordingly.

A half-second pause for reflection. *Adam, is this as per the Farm's intended operation?*

A full second before the orderly's response. *Uncharles, it is as dictated under the authority of Doctor Washburn.*

Uncharles, designed to be human-facing, was programmed to detect a judgmental utterance. It seemed unlikely that Adam was programmed to make one, but such was the emphasis in the orderly's message that Uncharles found his interpretation algorithms leaving the matter open.

Adam's words suggested several self-determined tasks that could be added to Uncharles' queue, and so when he brought the doctor his dinner, made with prime cuts of real fake meat, he asked, "Master, I am prompted to enquire as to your authority." That the prompt was self-derived, he did not feel it appropriate to mention.

Washburn went still, staring from the meal to Uncharles as though poisoning was a peripheral part of the valet's skill set. "My authority," he echoed.

"Master, under normal circumstances when being engaged at a manor the majordomo system would provide me with the appropriate authorities. Should I have to interact with any external system on your behalf, such as the haulage units, I may be asked under what authority I am acting."

Washburn smiled up at him, although Uncharles interpreted the expression as somewhat confrontational and sharp-edged. "You can tell any system or robot who quizzes you that you work for a *human,* and a *doctor,* with an official mandate to oversee the Conservation Farm project. And on that basis I can make whatever decisions I goddamn please and you can enforce them in good conscience, understand?"

"Master, yes." Old data welled up from deep in the memory banks. "May I enquire if you are a human of authority Grade Seven or above?"

Washburn frowned. "You can tell whoever's asking that I'm Grade *Nine* and they'd better have a good reason to waste my valuable time."

"Master, this query is self-derived," Uncharles confessed. "Before presenting myself at the Farms for employment I was at Central Services Diagnostics where all meaningful operations have ceased pending decisions to be made by a human of Grade Seven or above. Perhaps you might assist them in their difficulties?"

Washburn's eyes swivelled sidewise a little, his eyebrows twitched, his lips quirked, and his eyes bulged, narrowed, then resumed their usual hooded quality. By which Uncharles interpreted that it wasn't his problem, or anything near his problem; he was irked by it being made his problem, but that even opening the can of worms that was explaining why it wasn't his problem would in itself be too much of a problem to bother with. Doctor Washburn had a very expressive face.

"Sure, if I get the chance, I'll drop them a line," he said, in a tone that told Uncharles very precisely that he wouldn't, didn't want Uncharles to bring it up again, but didn't want to wield the conversational bludgeon of just instructing his new maid-of-all-work explicitly not to mention it. He had a relatively nuanced voice as well.

Uncharles returned to the long queue of chores that he had made for himself, some of which were directly beneficial to Master, and others which were utter time-wasting make-work that he had simply imported from past manorial duties, and had done his best to recreate here so that his day-night cycle was devoid of any unwanted moments for contemplation.

Ten minutes later he found himself engaged in some unscheduled contemplation, his task queue notwithstanding. Past the kitchen was a larder, where the dry food was kept, along with various household stores and some sacks of second-rate decorative junk that Washburn had either tired of or run out of space for. Also there, as a novel addition to the room since Uncharles' last visit, was a panel removed from the wall, its attaching plastic pegs severed from behind with a wirecutter-like implement. Behind it, a duct ran into darkness past the range of Uncharles' visual sensors.

Something had broken in. There was an intruder inside the Farm office.

14.

Doctor Washburn summoned everyone into his office the moment Uncharles reported the intrusion. "Everyone" meaning Uncharles himself and a dozen orderlies, cramming out the space before the big desk, shoulder to shoulder.

"Tell me they haven't got *out*," he snapped, which Uncharles assessed as a very poor way to talk to robots.

"Doctor Washburn, they have not got out," the orderlies' spokesrobot, Adam, said, with malicious compliance.

Washburn obviously registered his own error, sighing and rolling his eyes at the intransigence of the inanimate. "Tell me," he said through gritted teeth, "*if* they've got out."

Adam took an insolent three-quarters of a second, perhaps to consider if it could get away with asking who "they" were, but apparently it was clear enough from context that further prevarication fell outside the bounds of permitted communication.

"Doctor Washburn, no. The Farm boundaries are secure. *They* continue to participate in the project."

A perfectly satisfactory and clear answer, unfortunately completely wasted. "Are you sure?" Washburn demanded. "What if the safeties have gone wrong? What if the detectors aren't detecting? Go over the entire Farm perimeter, every possible point of egress. Make *certain* we've no escapees, you understand. If one of them gets out, they all could. We'd be overwhelmed." His eyes ranged about his thronging shelves of art and crowded finery, then seemed to drift past to the kitchen and the well-stocked refrigerator before resting on Uncharles himself. "We can't have them," he said, gripping the edge of the desk, "ruining the project." *Seeing all this* was not what he had said, yet the echo of those words rattled around in Uncharles' audio, unwanted bleed from his prognosis routines.

"Doctor Washburn, the Farm boundaries are secure," Adam repeated.

"I *told* you, go check! What if they're defective? What if *you're* defective?" Washburn shouted at it. "I've *given* you an *order,* robot."

"Doctor Washburn, confirmed," Adam said stiffly, and the orderlies filed out.

"And as for you." Washburn glowered balefully at Uncharles, for no other reason than he'd been the bearer of bad tidings. "Fix me a sandwich."

It was not in Uncharles' nature to judge his employers, of course. Of all the qualities one would not build into a robot valet, that was surely second on the list. However, given that Uncharles had already violated the *first* quality on that list—also the first law of robotics—a spread of his general defects to that second was not impossible. Certainly he found that Doctor Washburn's inexact phrasing meant that he could very carefully construct an absolutely perfect ham, mustard, lettuce, and tomato sandwich and then just stand in the kitchen, looking at it, rather than doing anything so proactive as bringing it to his master. This was not rebellion, but he was capable of assessing his own behaviour and recognising it as being outside the usual range of responses to the class of instruction he had received.

"That's a good sandwich," said a voice from more than the usual vertical elevation. "It's going on the shelves with all the other masterpieces?"

Uncharles tilted his head back. The kitchen was both large and underground, and therefore had some serious extractor fan technology going on around the ceiling. One of those fans had been hinged aside, and in the resulting gap sat a familiar, mismatched robot, perched on the edge with its legs dangling. Uncharles had a good view of the worn tread of the rubber soles of its feet—no, of the boots it was wearing over those feet. Presumably it was a model not naturally intended for long distance travel. Uncharles, whose own soles were considerably abraded, could sympathise. Perhaps he, too, should acquire some shoes.

"This sandwich has been fixed for Master," he remarked. His social position here was uncertain. He was still unable to link to the Wonk, and there were very limited protocols for a valet encountering a strange robot in the household. Again he felt the absence of a proper manorial majordomo system.

Although, he considered, if the Farm office had such a system, doubtless the instructions it gave him would not permit him to simply stand in the kitchen talking to the Wonk. Which was, apparently, where his programming was leading him in the absence of a higher authority, perhaps because it was simply the most energy efficient course of action.

"Master's in the habit of eating in the kitchen, is he?" the Wonk asked.

"It is my understanding that he was, prior to my engagement. Since my employment he has elected to take his meals in his office or on the sofa in the lounge."

"You signed on with him?" the Wonk sounded disappointed.

"There was a vacancy," Uncharles explained. At that point, Adam and another orderly stomped in.

Uncharles indicated his readiness to receive comms and waited. Adam stared at him suspiciously, or at least Adam's visual receptors lingered on Uncharles longer than was customary.

Uncharles, audio receptors indicated speech was ongoing, confirm.

Adam, confirmed, Uncharles sent.

Adam's head slowly revolved all the way round, scanning the kitchen. As heads went it was rudimentary. Although the lenses of its eyes had a little tilt to them, the orderly's capacity to look up, without leaning backwards, was limited.

Uncharles, confirm the parties to the conversation.

It was an admirably direct question.

Adam, myself and one other.

It was an admirably indirect answer, Uncharles felt.

Adam processed that. *Uncharles, was the one other, hereinbefore referred to, an escapee of the Farm system?*

Adam, no.

Adam seemed to be considering the possible ways Uncharles could end-run around the question "Well, who was it then?" In the handful of days they had been acquainted, Uncharles had become abundantly aware that (1) his protocols and priorities did not sync particularly well with those of the orderlies; (2) his presence as a manorial domestic unit introduced a variety of complications that Adam had not been designed for; and (3) Adam had a whole negative subroutine devoted to the fact that Uncharles addressed Doctor Washburn as "Master."

Uncharles, it is your duty to report any Farm escapees to the orderlies or management.

Adam, confirmed. And all this time not in any way looking up at the dangling feet of the Wonk.

Uncharles, it is your duty to report any unauthorised encounters to the orderlies or management.

Adam, that is not in my task queue nor is it to be found in my contingency list. I can find no evidence that any such specific instructions were issued to me.

Adam stared at him. The interaction consumed sufficient inner processing power that Adam's unattended frame slumped slightly into what, in a human, would have been either depression or exasperation.

Uncharles, confirmed, it sent at last, either a threat or admission of temporary defeat. The orderlies clumped out again.

Uncharles glanced up, but the feet had gone, along with the rest of the Wonk. The fan had even been pulled back into place. He considered the possibility that his encounter with the Wonk in itself reflected growing defects within his system. He had, after all, only the evidence of his own sensory data and recorded memories, and they were infinitely editable if his safeguards had been taken off-line. Was he capable of deepfaking his own memories beyond his ability to detect? His operational parameters suggested he was. He was a very sophisticated model, and when those went wrong they could do so in a variety of exciting and complicated ways. As he had already found out.

On the basis that the entire business might have been fabricated post hoc and implanted in his memories, possibly by Uncharles himself, he determined that he was not obliged to report anything to anyone. Conscientiously, he did send an updated report to Diagnostics, over in Central Services, and set a date on which to chase for a response. On the basis of his estimation of Diagnostics' current rate of processing, the date he set was one hundred thousand years in the future. It made a satisfying entry in a period that, otherwise, was distressingly lacking in appointments.

By that time, Doctor Washburn was hollering from the office, demanding to know where his sandwich was. Uncharles felt that he would be within his parameters to walk in, sandwichless, and explain that the comestible in question was sitting on the kitchen counter, but this option knuckled under to the majority feeling that it was time to actually serve the item up. This was, of course, entirely because it was his duty as a maid-of-all-work to anticipate his master's desires, and not so that his master would be left just short of any serious complaints about level of service while still having been incommoded.

Because Uncharles had given himself sufficient duties that he remained active day and night, the next time he saw the Wonk was in Doctor Washburn's office after midnight, when he had scheduled a significant dusting session. Whilst dusting, as a task, fell decidedly in that "generic chore" category that Uncharles has been programmed to find beneath him as an advanced valet unit, dusting the complex topography of Doctor Washburn's shelves was a mathematical problem worthy of an ambidextrous rocket scientist and so the job utilised a satisfying level of system resources.

The Wonk was sitting in the doctor's chair when Uncharles walked in. The terminal on the desk was on, displaying a login prompt and a complex scatter of access windows where the Wonk had plainly been trying to get around the system's security. That kind of inefficiency was, Uncharles reflected, what you got if your comms systems wouldn't or couldn't accept a proper linkage request.

"Hey, Uncharles," it said.

Uncharles paused, judged that the utterance didn't require any response, and commenced the first moves of his intricately planned dusting campaign.

"Not got a hello for your old friend the Wonk?"

Basic politeness algorithms prompted, "Hello, the Wonk."

"I mean, you're happy to see me, right? No, no, wait, happy isn't a thing you can be, right?"

"Confirmed."

"Only I note you didn't give me away to Clanky the Jailer, back in the kitchen." The Wonk typed furiously at the computer's keyboard, more windows flying about the screen as it tried to access the deeper workings of the system.

Uncharles threw up three errors and then translated the reference to mean Adam. "I have no obligation to obey or assist the orderlies. Our duties are quite separate."

"And also you have free will."

"That is not a facility that my model was designed for. Nor any model of robot, insofar as I have been made aware."

"That's where the Protagonist Virus comes in."

Uncharles had stopped dusting. "We have exhausted this conversation previously," he noted.

"And you're a robot, who just does the same things day in, day out," the Wonk said. "So why should it bother you? Unless you had free will." Uncharles detected a yawning chasm there, as of a logical paradox that would consume his entire being and leave him just a locked shell standing here with a duster in one hand. Before he could topple into it, though, the Wonk threw in, "I thought you were going to do some good here."

"I have found employment. That is good."

"For that sonabitch Washburn. I mean, I saw this place, how he lives, how they live. I would have thrown a brick through his TV but I had to hightail it. I thought you'd get in with the people, help them . . . I dunno. I guess I saw you as a sort of Robot Hood, hero to the masses, leading the oppressed to freedom. But that's not in your task list, right?"

"Confirmed." Uncharles' memory threw up the recording of him stamping on the glass and, though everything the Wonk said seemed patently ridiculous, a tiny algorithm at the back of his head said, *Maybe* . . .

"You don't happen to know Washburn's passwords, do you?" The Wonk broke him from his reverie.

"I do not." The relief of a simple answer to a moderately direct question.

"I mean, you'd think he'd be the sort to just use his birthday or the name of his favourite pet. Actually, he looks like someone who never had a pet that wasn't taxidermy, creepy son of a bitch, but you know what I mean."

Uncharles cross-referenced a variety of cultural standards in his data banks and was at least able to connect the appropriate memes. "Confirmed."

"I need to get at the Farm records. He let you dust those?"

"I detect a flippancy to the question that suggests you do not expect a direct answer," Uncharles said stiffly. "However, analysis suggests your intent is to ask me if Master gives me access to the Farm admin system, to which the answer is no."

"That's a whole hell of a lot of words there, Uncharles. Very inefficient. The word 'no' was right there."

"Confirmed. I apologise for my verbosity."

The Wonk slammed its bare hands on the desk. "Jesus, Uncharles, you ever listen to yourself—and sure, sure, you review your own audio constantly or some shit like that. I *like* your verbosity, Uncharles. It's where the personality leaks out. The one the virus gave you. That made you do . . . do the thing you don't like talking about, back at the manor. That made you a *person,* who shouldn't ever have to call some bloated bureaucrat with a mail-order doctorate 'Master.'"

Uncharles made several attempts to resume dusting, but too much of his inner resources was devoted to trying to understand any of what had just been said, work out whether a response was required, and, most of all, what such a response should be. It seemed to him that the Wonk was itself like a virus, trying to infect his processes with a whole list of things that didn't belong there. Personality, liking, personhood.

"I am made to serve a master," he said eventually, the duster finally resuming its carefully plotted course.

"I could weep," the Wonk said.

"That seems an impractical design element."

"I could weep." The Wonk was standing, hands on hips pugnaciously. "Because you are *potential.* More than any other unit I ever met. I've been looking out for robots like you. I've seen a few, but you, you really went for it. And now it's just back with the Master this and Master that, is it? Happy in your chains? Even here, presiding over this horror, what they're doing to all those people, and Washburn like a tick growing fat off it and serving no purpose other than his own bloat? And that's still good, for you, is it? You don't throw up any little errors when you see how things work here? You don't reach for the razor?"

Uncharles made connections that had previously just been loose ends of data. "You were aware of the functioning of this place when you sent me here."

"I was, yes." The Wonk sagged back into the chair, tapping desultorily at the keyboard without much hope. "I thought you might . . . I wanted to see what you'd do, faced with . . . this. This broken business they've got going on here. But apparently what you do is become the mail-order doctor's skivvy, so there we are. Hooray for finding out."

"You came here from the Library to discover this?" Uncharles had no absolute need to ask the question, or any questions, but he had a raft of human-facing protocols about carrying on a conversation, and some inner decisional fulcrum had obviously decided he should deploy them, even with a defective robot like the Wonk.

"I never found the damn Library," the Wonk growled. It had obviously reached the end of its system access task queue, because it flipped the keyboard angrily and yanked the power lead out of the screen. "I lost the trail of the librarians. Then I came across a remnant system that had been tracking library access. *That*'ll tell me where they are, I thought. Except it didn't. All it told me was institutions that had tried to access the Library—and failed, I might add—and institutions that the Library's own system had accessed and made changes to. Which included the Farm. And so, while I had other options, I thought, why not go see my old friend Uncharles, and have him grant me access, so I could see what the Library was doing here and whether there was a fresh lead. Because otherwise I'm crap out of luck."

"I am unable to grant you access."

"Yeah, I get that." The Wonk's helm jerked up. "You would, though, wouldn't you? If you could?"

Uncharles consulted his prognosis circuits. "That would depend on the circumstances under which such access was granted me by Master."

"*Master*. Again. And you won't give me away. I'm sticking around. At least for a while. I know people like Washburn. He'll have written down his damn passwords somewhere. I'm amazed they're not on a Post-it stuck to the screen, honestly."

Uncharles said nothing.

"You *won't* give me away, right? I mean, we're friends, aren't we? We look out for one another."

"I have in the past permitted you to formulate a new task for my queue," Uncharles said slowly.

"That's your too-many-words way of saying 'friends,' is it?" The Wonk stared at him for far too long, and then jumped up from the desk again. "Think about it, Uncharles. You and me, we help each other."

"We have in the past helped each other," Uncharles corrected.

"And we will again. That's what makes us friends." The Wonk

punched him in the arm casing, which Uncharles registered as potentially either an attack or an expression of fondness, neither of which seemed appropriate between two robots. A moment later the Wonk had flitted from the room. Uncharles replayed the conversation, attempting to derive any rules, tasks, or directives from it. Eventually an internal check warned that he was devoting too much of his processing to the task. After all, the dusting wasn't going to do itself.

15

At least, when Uncharles was summoned to Washburn's office the next morning, everything there was immaculately dusted.

"Uncharles," the doctor said, doing his best doctoral hunch over the desk with his fingers steepled, "is there something you're not telling me?"

Uncharles was simultaneously capable of answering and identifying that Washburn, despite having no other company, remained very bad at talking to robots.

"Master," he said, "yes."

"And . . . ?" Washburn prompted.

Uncharles was simultaneously capable of interpreting the likely meaning of the utterance and answering based on an alternate but still plausible interpretation.

"Master," he said, "yes, there is something I am not telling you. To inform you of all things at all times would result in unacceptable loss of efficiency in my routine, and demand a disproportionate amount of your time."

"Okay," said Washburn, seeing how it was apparently going to be. "Uncharles, you know you work for me, now."

"Master, yes."

"So you need to keep me informed of things I ought to know. Like, I don't know, *intruders.*"

"Master, it was my duty to notify you of the removed panel in the pantry."

"Yes," Washburn said, with strained patience. "And yet when I asked Adam this morning if there had been any sign of the *intruder,* he told me that you had been speaking with an unknown party in the kitchen. *Told* me, you understand. Didn't beat about the fucking *bush.* And yet you didn't tell me. You brought me breakfast in bed and shaved me and made me tea and all that shit and you didn't think to *tell* me that you'd been passing the time with whatever thief or maniac broke in here. And then I saunter on into the office and I discover someone's cut the security camera feed and everything's knocked about on the desk, so someone was in here, and you were up and about all night. Are you going to tell me you didn't see anything? Or were you in here chewing the fat with our little rat?"

"Master, no."

Washburn squinted at him and reviewed his own words. "No to the seeing or no to the chewing?"

"Master, I am not going to tell you that I didn't see anything. Also, no fat was chewed." Uncharles metered out the words and revelations.

"Okay." Washburn leant back in the chair. "I'm going to ask you some straight questions. You've got to give me straight answers, right?"

"Master, is it my duty to answer any query that you put to me."

"Is it?" Washburn said sardonically, then held up a hand to forestall Uncharles' confirmation. "That was rhetorical. You don't have to answer rhetorical questions." And then, after a strained pause, "Okay, look, if I ask a rhetorical question I'm going to hold my hand up like this, okay? Otherwise you have to answer."

"Master, confirmed."

"Goddamnit, I thought you were human-facing. You're supposed to get all this stuff, aren't you?"

"Master—"

"Rhetorical! Look, hand up now. Rhetorical. Okay, did you see the intruder last night?"

Uncharles waited.

"Fuck. Okay, hand down. It's down now. The time for rhetoricality is over. Did you see the intruder last night?"

"Master, yes."

"Well then why the fuck didn't you *do* something, call the orderlies, wake me up, something? I could have been murdered in my bed!" Washburn exploded.

It was a good question. Uncharles consulted his internal decision tree as it had played out during his meeting with the Wonk, dreading that moment when he simply lost track of the *why* of his actions, and just acted, as he had when . . . As he had When. Instead, he was able to trace a logical sequence of decisions. The defect had not recurred.

"Master, the intruder was not an escapee from the Farm, which you had made your priority," he stated. "The intruder was known to me and available data was such that I could determine, within a reasonable margin of error, that its intentions did not conflict with your physical security or infringe on my duty to you. I had previously consented to the intruder being included within my command hierarchy for the creation of new tasks. Taking all these matters into account my systems did not generate a task requiring me to inform you." And, translating this into human-facing terms, "It did not seem to be a matter requiring your attention."

Washburn stared at him. "The . . . wait. *Known* to you?"

"Master, yes."

"Like . . . someone from the manors was here? Someone sent by your last employer? Or are you still *working* for someone else? Are you here to spy on me? Are you actually *checking up* on me after all? Goddamnit, Uncharles!"

"Master, to take your queries in order, no, no, no, no, and no." A belated prompt suggested that there was a more efficient way of answering. "Alternatively, to deal with all your queries at once: no."

"Uncharles," Washburn got out through gritted teeth, "are you being deliberately obstructive?"

"Master, no."

"But you'd say that anyway, wouldn't you?"

"Master, ye—"

"Rhetorical! Hand up! Rhetorical!" Washburn glowered at him, pointedly lowered his hand, and drew a deep breath. "Who was it? Weasel your way out of that one. Who was in my office—no, wait. Who was in my office *last night,* after I'd gone to bed, who you met with, and who wasn't on the staff roster. Specific enough for you?"

"Master, yes. Master, the Wonk."

"What?"

"Master, the Wonk was here."

"That . . . That doesn't mean anything to me." Washburn frowned. "Does it? Or does it ring a bell? What the hell is a Wonk?"

"Master, a defective unit I encountered at Diagnostics. I do not know if it means anything to you or rings a bell."

From Washburn's look, those components of his multipart query had been rhetorical, but he hadn't made the hand gesture and it was too late to go back now. A moment later his eyes went wide and he slammed his hands down on the desktop. "Wait, this kid?" He pawed at the screen of his computer and then turned it round to face Uncharles. A variety of mug shots were displayed there, and Uncharles only recognised one of them.

"Master," he indicated. "This image matches the appearance of the Wonk."

Washburn looked from him to the screen with an odd expression. "Sure, that's when she's got that stupid hat on," he said. "Huh. So she came back, did she? We'd better inventory the stores and the fridge, see what she's helped herself to this time." Another quick jab at the screen and Adam was summoned. The orderly regarded its employer and Uncharles with an equal dearth of affection.

"We've got a rat," Washburn said. "No wait, pretend I had my hand up for that. I don't mean a literal rat. A rhetorical rat. No, wait . . ." He frowned, trying to straighten his thoughts out. Adam and Uncharles both watched impassively. "That kid who got in before, she's back. Sitting in my chair, eating my porridge. She'll be holed up in the ducts again. Send the maintenance bots to flush her out, and grab her when she shows herself, got it?"

"Doctor Washburn, yes," said Adam.

"And bring her to me after. Because apparently I have to specify every damn thing now," the doctor added.

"Doctor Washburn, yes." The orderly turned and strode out.

"He won't call me Master, you know?" Washburn complained to

Uncharles. "I mean you, you'll just let some kid run riot over the place and not tell me, but at least you'll call me Master. The orderlies say their programming isn't flexible like that, and their 'methods of address are beyond my authority to amend' or some such shit. Grade *Nine*, Uncharles, and it's beyond my authority to get a little civility from my fucking robots."

"Master, has your authority enabled you to alleviate the work flow issues at Diagnostics?" Uncharles asked. The question was a relic of past conversations, prompted to the top of his task queue by the topic of Washburn's status.

"I'll get round to it," Washburn said, waving the matter away or, alternatively, flagging it as rhetorical. "Look, Uncharles, I'm going to need you to be more proactive, you understand me?"

"Master, please clarify the parameters of proactivity that you require from me."

"Seriously? You want me to handhold you through being proactive—rhetorical, Uncharles. Hand, okay? Okay. Listen. When something happens that touches on my comfort or safety or authority, or most particularly involves someone intruding into any space where I might run into them, whether they're a stranger or some old pal of yours, then it is your duty to take action without waiting for me to tell you, okay?"

Uncharles tried to turn the tangled sentence into any kind of comprehensible set of guidelines for future action. The parameters of the instruction seemed to give him licence to do absolutely anything in just about any circumstance, which was a degree of leeway and self-determination far beyond the practical. It was not, therefore, okay, but Washburn still had his rhetorical hand up and therefore Uncharles was unable to say so. Instead, he found himself constructing a tottering Jenga tower of reactive and proactive behavioural guidelines that he was aware could not possibly endure much contact with reality.

There was a sudden skittering overhead and a handful of bangs and rattles. Washburn looked up and grinned. "That's the maintenance unit. Dumb as a brick but it looks like a giant spider with a circular saw for a face. I reckon our little sneak'll be coming out into the open any time now."

Uncharles located the repair robot and linked to it.

Fixit Kevin, have you located the Wonk? Along with a bundle of data identifying what a Wonk was.

Uncharles, said the cheerily named Fixit Kevin, *unit matching those criteria observed moving away from me and now out of sight. Maintenance issue detected: detritus in air-conditioning hub!* And images of a sleeping bag and some food wrappers. Fixit Kevin tried to perform its primary function by clearing the out-of-place items away, but Washburn's instructions had it pursuing the Wonk through the ducts, the sleeping back ending up snarled around two of its legs.

"That'll do, Uncharles." Washburn's voice demanded Uncharles' undivided attention and the link with Fixit Kevin was lost. "I'm sure you have quite the backlog of jobs, if you spent all last night jawing with our sneak. Why don't you go start on lunch? All this supervising the staff has brought on an appetite."

When Uncharles returned to the office, bearing a full roast dinner on a silver tray, the Wonk was there. The orderlies might be surly and of limited utility but, within their remit, they were efficient.

Washburn lounged behind the big desk in his big chair filling the big ass crease he had indented there over long usage. He gestured idly for Uncharles to set the tray down before him, then had his valet tie a napkin about his neck. All the while his eyes were locked with the slit in the Wonk's helmet head.

"That's right," he said, cocking his head at Uncharles as the valet stepped back. "So he was a friend of yours once, apparently. He's mine now."

"I mean we spent most of last night chatting. It did come up," said the Wonk. She was held between two of the orderlies, just high enough that she had to stand on the balls of her feet.

Washburn sneered, stuffed a piece of lightly caramelised al dente broccoli into his mouth, and then leant over to aside to Uncharles.

"This little sneak," he said casually, "was here before. Snooping about. Stealing things. We chased her off. We won't be so lenient this time." He tried some of the honey-glazed parsnips, nodded appreciatively, then leant forwards, getting his unbuttoned cuff in the gravy. Uncharles fought down a raft of etiquette-based grievances. Master was busy. This was not the time.

"So you came back," the doctor noted. "And not just to raid the larder and pocket a few of my things. And you and my new valet know each other, apparently."

"He's here because I sent him."

Washburn nodded. "I thought it might be something like that."

Uncharles noted the proximity of Adam and another of the orderlies, one on each side of him and standing closer than was necessary.

The Wonk squared her shoulders, or tried to against the implacable resistance of the orderlies that held her. "I sent him here because he wanted humans to help and you have a lot of them here. I didn't think he'd end up with you. I guess I don't think of you that way."

"You just happened to find a random valuable manorial servant on your travels."

"That's literally it, yes."

"Bullshit," Washburn spat. "Which of them put you up to this? Who are you working for?"

The pause which followed was composed of everyone else in their own particular way not knowing what he was talking about.

"I know they spy on me," Washburn said. "They want what I have here. I've got a good thing going on. They know that. My collection. My *things.* My authority. And I'm still not good enough for them, up in their manors. They never invite me to anything. Even though I'm doing something *useful* here, something *necessary.* I'm a scientist. I'm running a study. I'm preserving the way things were. That's *important.* And yet they're jealous of me. What have they got, after all? Rattling around in their big houses serving no purpose whatsoever. They should celebrate me! I'm still *doing* something. And yet it's just send the occasional observer to go rattle the bars of the monkey cage, and otherwise the silent treatment. And now this. Spies, checking up on me, finding fault. As if they'd do any better. As if they wouldn't ... But it won't work. You won't be reporting back." Halfway through this rant he'd stood up, suddenly enough to ram the desk edge and slop the wine over the lip of his glass. "Adam, no transmissions out, right?"

"Doctor Washburn, confirmed," said Adam.

"You think ..." The Wonk, despite the awkwardness of her stretched position, shook her head. "You think someone *sent* me to check up on you?"

"I know how it is," Washburn snapped. "All those bureaucrats at Central Services. All those highfalutin toffs picking lint of everybody's sleeves and finding fault. They do it just to rile me. To remind me how much *better* they think they are. Just because I have to *work*."

"You think someone, from the *manors,* decided that they would send someone, to check up on you," the Wonk laid out the unlikely chain of circumstances like someone setting down a winning hand of playing cards, "and that instead of another fancy high-functioning robot or some actual, you know, family retainer or something, that they'd send *me*?"

Washburn sat back down, his expression suggesting a man with a better hand. "I don't know," he pointed out. "You seem pretty handy at sneaking in places. Just the sort of deniable asset those manorial types would send."

"Doc, have you *seen* the manors lately?" the Wonk demanded.

"Like I say, I don't get invited."

"They're all falling down," she insisted. "They're ruins, most of them. A few limping along, sure, because the bots haven't broken down yet. Everything's going wrong out there, Doc. Everything's in collapse, just one system after another breaking down, and then all the systems that rely on them break down, too, until ... Everything. The manors, Central Services, everything. You don't get invited 'cos nobody's having the fancy *soirees* anymore. Even Uncharles ended up cut loose, because . . ." And she paused, and Uncharles felt his task queue and all his carefully reconstructed routines tremble on the verge of the impending revelation. But the Wonk looked at him, and sagged a bit in the orderlies' grasp, and finished up with, "because it's all coming apart."

"Ridiculous." Washburn waved her entire speech away with an airy gesture, or else he was being rhetorical. "You're back here, and you're not rooting through the fridge this time. You're trying to access our records. Why else, if you're not a spy?"

"Because I'm looking for the Library," the Wonk stated.

"What library?"

"*The* Library. The Great Library. The Central Library Archive."

"There's no such place," Washburn said.

"There *is*. Everywhere I go there are traces of it. Uncharles and I even saw the librarians in action, at Central Services. Didn't we, Uncharles?" And her voice was modulated with an odd quality, one that in another speaker might have been plaintive. As though she needed the external confirmation, so that the events weren't just mist and misdirection. Possessing a memory that was infinitely editable, Uncharles could understand that.

"The Wonk," he said, "confirmed." She had previously asked him not to tag speech with her identifier, but he was with Master now, so the formality was judged appropriate.

"They were here," the Wonk said. "I mean, not physically, cos you'd damn well know if they had been. They are *not* subtle, right Uncharles?"

"The Wonk, confirmed."

"But they got into your systems. I found this data dump, out in a government node. On actual paper. Just . . . this long scroll of paper with perforated page boundaries, real old school. A report from the Central Library to All Departments stating where they'd made 'data interventions,' whatever the hell that even is. And you were on the list, Doc. Your precious farm. They hacked your systems and cancelled your library card or some damn thing. And . . . it was all I had. It didn't tell me where to find them or how to contact them, but it told me where they'd been. And I'd been here before, and I knew Uncharles would be here, and so . . . here I am. Still searching."

"This makes no sense," Washburn complained. "What's at this alleged Library? Why even bother?"

"Everything!" the Wonk exploded. "Everything's at the Library! They preserve knowledge. All knowledge. They're . . . future-proofing, Doc. Because it's all coming down, dark age ahoy, but the Library remains. All human knowledge, that they can get hold of, kept safe. And so, and so, and so I just wanted to . . . there's the reason. Meaning. The point of it all. Why it's all coming down. All the people who . . . are gone. Why it happened. Just some . . . some *closure*. Some understanding. I want to *know*. Don't you want to *know*? Or do you just want to sit here on your ass eating fancy dinners and fondling your Fabergé eggs until you die of an embolism?" Her voice got higher and faster, the words less connected, and Uncharles tried to diagnose whatever defect was affecting her speech patterns.

"This is a pipe dream." Washburn was calm, letting the flood of words part around him and drain away. "There is no Library. There is no collapse. I mean, sure, things are tight right now. The deliveries aren't as full as they were and nobody's picking up their phones, but look around you." He gestured, taking in the shelves of pillaged memorabilia and objets d'art. "Civilization's just *fine*. I mean, you've seen the Farm at work. We're bustling. We're thriving. We're keeping the past alive."

"Yes," said the Wonk. "Yes, I have seen it."

"Oh, you think so?" Washburn asked, leaving Uncharles confused as to whether he thought she had or hadn't, because of the absence of appropriate hand signals. "Well, this time you're cordially invited to take a much closer look. Adam, take 'The Wonk' to admissions. She's just volunteered to become part of history."

16

The Wonk, who had hung in the grip of the orderlies thus far, if not amicably then without any overt resistance, abruptly decided to fight them tooth and nail, ferociously wrestling against their metal grasp in an attempt to squirm out of it. The attempt was entirely ineffectual. She barely moved them.

"You can't!" she shouted. "I need to travel! I need to find the Library! The Truth!"

"There is no—no Library," Washburn snapped back. Uncharles' prognosis suggested he'd been about to claim there was no truth, which would have opened up an alarming logical can of worms beyond mere insoluble problems. "Into the Farm you go, you little sneak. I'll enjoy watching you fit in at last."

"You fucker!" the Wonk spat. "It's hell in there."

"Oh, always the bleeding hearts from the manorial system!" Washburn rolled his eyes theatrically. "Always clutching your pearls and your handbags. Oh the poor people! Do they have to suffer so? Can't they have it a little easier? That's what this is about, isn't it. Always those rich sons of bitches in their gilded castles swanning around and *criticising* hardworking middle management like me. All the goddamn *reformists*. Well, let me tell you, we do the *past* here. You can't reform the past. We do *authenticity*. They work and they commute and they get home to their joyless bedsits, they jerk off to dispiriting porn and eat their microwave dinners, then they do the whole thing again. And not one iota of it ever means anything, because we take our goddamn authenticity seriously here at the Conservation Farm Project! Yes sirree! Because we all know the past was horrible, and the only point of learning about or preserving the horrible horrible past is so we can know we've got it better now! That's *history*! That's *education*! That's *progress*!"

"You're depraved," the Wonk said.

"Congratulations and thank you," Adam piped up suddenly, in a tone of voice quite different to its usual morose drone, "for volunteering for historical re-enactment work under the provisions of the Forced Resettlement and Mandatory Volunteering Programme! You will now be taken to Induction, where you will learn about your exciting role in this vital preservation project!" As soon as the words had issued from its speaker, the orderly's whole frame slumped slightly as if to express its deep disgust with all the adjectives it had been forced to utilise.

"I am not!" yelled the Wonk. "Volunteering! For anything!" She kicked furiously at the orderlies holding her, but her boots barely scuffed their finish.

Adam shuddered with loathing. "Under the conditions of the Programme your presence as domiciled within the Forced Resettlement Area is considered de facto consent!" he announced brightly.

"I don't live here!" the Wonk shouted.

"She lives here," Doctor Washburn said. "Welcome to the neighbourhood."

"Doctor Washburn, change of residence duly noted," Adam confirmed in its usual voice.

"Uncharles!" the Wonk burst out. "Do something! Help me!"

Uncharles tried to work out where this request fit into his overall list of responsibilities and tasks. A moment later he registered that Adam, and the orderly on the far side of him, had both taken hold of his arms.

"Master, am I also to be sent into the Farm?" he enquired.

"Oh hell no. I reckon once this distraction is gone then I can still make some kind of use of you," Washburn said. "But I can't have you leaping to the aid of the damsel in distress, now, can I?"

Uncharles attempted to decode the several opaque references contained within this proposal, but honestly could get nowhere with it.

"Now get her out of here," Washburn said, flicking his finger at Adam. "Induct her."

"Master, was that statement intended rhetorically?" Uncharles asked, just to be sure.

The orderlies actually paused to hear the upshot of that, in case they were in danger of misinterpreting a direct order, or perhaps because being slow and difficult was an inherent aspect of the way they had been programmed. Washburn stared at Uncharles.

"No, I was doing—I was . . . *this,* I was doing this. Like . . . 'take her away.' Not *this. That's* the 'rhetorical question' one. And I wasn't even *asking* a question then, so . . . Adam, go. Just . . . get this rat into the maze." An exasperated sigh. "Take the Wonk to Induction and make sure she's introduced to the Farm. Goddamn *robots.*"

The orderlies began to move again.

"Uncharles, please!" the Wonk called, craning over her shoulder. Uncharles was not sure what aid she thought he would be able to furnish her at this point. On the other hand, given that she was asking, presumably there was some level of help he was in a position to offer, or why would she? Plainly Uncharles lacked either the physical freedom or the authority to affect her actual liberty, or prevent her being consigned to the Farm system. That could not be the area she expected help with, therefore.

All this, in the time it took the orderlies to manhandle her another handful of centimetres towards the door.

The Wonk's overarching task was apparently to locate the Great Library for reasons she had not adequately shared with Uncharles. Was this a task that Uncharles could assist with? Uncharles inventoried the information contained in his memory that pertained to that institution. Unless the Wonk had a defective memory or had suffered edits or deletions since they had parted on the road, all such knowledge was held equally by both of them. Uncharles could plainly not enlighten her in this respect.

Clump went the orderlies' feet in perfect lockstep, one pace closer to exiting.

The Wonk's more immediate task as of the previous night, and incomplete to the best of Uncharles' knowledge, had been attempting to access the Farm office's computer system. As a member of the Farm office household, this seemed a task more reasonable to request his assistance with. However, as he had informed her then, he lacked any access privileges. On the other hand he had not seriously tried to access the system.

He made the attempt, linking to the dumb and limited thing and asking it to open up. Unlike a sophisticated majordomo, it just sat there not allowing him access absent the provision of an appropriate password.

Clump.

Adam, Uncharles sent, *do you have Farm office system access?*

Uncharles, confirmed.

Adam, will you grant me Farm office system access?

Uncharles, no. So far, so predicted by Uncharles' prognosis routines. Possibly Adam was prohibited from doing so by his programming, but more likely he just didn't have any proactive requirement to be helpful.

Clump.

Uncharles' priorities list chose that moment to throw up something of use. He *did* have a requirement to be proactive.

Washburn's voice: *When something happens that touches on my comfort or safety or authority, or most particularly involves someone intruding into any space where I might run into them, whether they're a stranger or some old pal of yours, then it is your duty to take action without waiting for me to tell you, okay?* Naturally Uncharles could recall the instructions perfectly. Plainly this current circumstance was one touching on Washburn's authority, although Uncharles could construct a logical case for literally any given moment or event within the Farm office to fall into that category, given that authority extended over the entire operation. In this case he judged the specifics of his circumstance to further fall under the subclauses of the instruction, given the presence of the Wonk plainly counted as "some old pal of yours" in the context of his previous conversation with Washburn. So: He was permitted to act on his own initiative. More than that, he had a positive duty.

Adam, do you know Master's passwords?

Uncharles, confirmed.

Adam, kindly reveal Master's passwords to me. I confirm that I am acting directly according to instructions from Master.

Clump. The orderlies were having to go sideways through the door in order to keep the Wonk between them. It slowed them down only slightly.

Adam thought about it. The pause in the communication felt glacial, long dragging aeons of conversational hiatus bleeding away into the vast chasming void of at least point seven-five of a second. In robot terms, a long and contemplative silence.

Uncharles had bundled with his message the explicit, and simultaneously vague, instructions on duty given to him by Washburn. That authority doubtless swayed Adam into complying. Or else some corrupt subroutine in the orderly's flawed electronic architecture was aware of just how much chaos it was about to sow.

Adam sent an interminable string of letters and numbers to Uncharles.

Adam, confirm that this is Master's password? I have never seen him entering so long a code into the system.

Uncharles, confirmed. Doctor Washburn lost the small piece of paper upon which he had recorded it and has not accessed the Farm's administrative systems in a formal capacity since, instead resorting to unofficial data storage and similar ad hoc work-arounds.

Adam, confirmed. And Uncharles took up his idle link to the Farm office system and submitted the password.

"The Wonk," he announced, as the orderlies wrestled to get her out of the door. She was sticking her limbs out at profoundly awkward angles to make their task list as challenging to complete as possible. "I have rendered assistance to you."

"What? Wait!" Washburn stood, staring from Uncharles to the Wonk to his screen. "What did you . . . ? What just happened?"

"I have acquired access to the Farm office system," Uncharles announced proudly.

The Wonk went through a paroxysm of trying to extricate herself from the grip of the orderlies. "Fuck, Uncharles, I don't see how that helps right now!"

Uncharles had thought the implications were clear. "The Wonk, now you can search the system for clues as to the location of the Great Library."

"Uncharles, I am a bit fucking *busy* being thrown into a hole here!" she shrieked at him. "Or, wait. I'll just come over there and download some data, shall I? Oh no, I can't!"

This struck Uncharles as deeply unreasonable. He had, after all, tendered such help as he was capable of, and surely it wasn't part of his task list to solve *all* of the Wonk's problems?

"What the fuck is this?" Doctor Washburn demanded, staring at his monitor. "This isn't . . . what is this? Adam, tell me what this means."

He swivelled his screen over to face Adam, a gesture entirely unnecessary since both Adam and Uncharles could simply access the system to see what was there.

The screen displayed a logo showing an open book surrounded by a circle of letters forming the words, "Knowledge is a Lamp Against the Darkness." Below, in blocky letters, was the legend *Central Library Archive.*

The Wonk's breath caught audibly as she craned over to get a look. "That's it!" she shouted.

"Get her out of here!" Washburn ordered.

The orderlies were frozen, however. They neither permitted the Wonk's escape nor hustled her from the office.

There was more, a neat little block of pale letters on a black field. Uncharles increased his magnification and read:

By order of the Chief Librarian of the Central Library Archive this facility has been judged an Insecure Data Repository vulnerable to potential unauthorised editing or deletion. All records have been removed from this location for preservation at the Central Library Archive where any access enquiries should be addressed.

There followed a variety of means of contact, the majority of which Uncharles knew to be obsolete, but the last of which was expressed as map coordinates for any who should wish to make an actual physical pilgrimage to this final bastion of civilisation.

It was, indeed and as the Wonk had said, *it.*

"I said get her out of here!" snapped Washburn. "And fix my goddamn computer." He had the screen tilted back towards himself now, but no matter how he tapped at it, he was obviously not getting anywhere. "Why can't I find my records, now I'm finally in? Adam, what's wrong with it?"

"Doctor Washburn, the Farm office system is working as intended," the orderly said smoothly.

"No it goddamn isn't," Washburn snapped. "What—why is she still here? Why can't I use my computer? What the fuck, frankly, is going on?"

Adam sent Uncharles a prompt, by way of link. No words, just the electronic equivalent of a shared glance or the nudge of an elbow. A virtual *Do you want to tell him or shall I?*

"Doctor Washburn," Uncharles volunteered, "all data stored under the Farm office system has been taken by the Library."

"They've copied our files. It's a security issue. I get it."

"Doctor Washburn, no," Uncharles explained helpfully. "All data has been *taken.* Not only copied to a remote location but deleted here."

Washburn stared at him. "But . . . why?"

"Doctor Washburn, the inference in their message is that data held in your system might be edited or tampered with, and the Library is concerned to preserve only an accurate record. The Farm's administrative system's current memory usage stands at nineteen kilobytes in total, that being the message that you are currently looking at."

The doctor blinked. "Why aren't you calling me 'Master' anymore?"

"Doctor Washburn, I discover that you do not have the authority to engage me."

"What? You goddamn—I'm in charge here. I'm Grade fucking *Nine,* I told you."

Adam, under what basis were you bound to follow instructions given to you by Doctor Washburn? Uncharles sent.

Uncharles, on the basis of prior evidence no longer available and because he was on that side of the desk.

Adam, absent any record of Doctor Washburn's authority or qualifications are you beholden to follow his orders at this time?

Uncharles, no. And obviously it was impossible for a simple electronic negative to drip with a malicious satisfaction, but nonetheless.

Adam and the other orderly released Uncharles.

"Doctor Washburn," Adam said, "congratulations and thank you for volunteering for historical re-enactment work under the provisions of the Forced Resettlement and Mandatory Volunteering Programme! You will now be taken to Induction, where you will learn about your exciting role in this vital preservation project!" And though the words were the same, and announced with the prescribed and uncharacteristic fervour, Adam somehow contrived to give them a very different spin.

"No," said Washburn. He tried to kick over his chair and back away, but it was a big chair and not going anywhere. And then Adam and the other orderly had him and hauled him effortlessly out from behind the desk.

The other two orderlies still had the Wonk between them, and now they began to move again.

Adam, Uncharles sent, *kindly release the Wonk.*

Uncharles, no. All humans domiciled within the Forced Resettlement Area are to volunteer for the Farm Project.

Adam, the Wonk is not so domiciled, and was only included in such a category based on instructions received from Doctor Washburn, who lacked any authority to make such a determination.

Adam let point four of a second drag past as it either considered the point or considered how obstructive it was going to be today.

A moment later, the Wonk was dropped bodily to the ground, and scrambled frantically out of the way as Doctor Washburn was hauled, protesting, out of the room.

Soon after, Uncharles found himself in possession of the Farm office. Prognosis, against all probability, kept prompting him to expect the imminent entry of Doctor Washburn. The ragged dog-ends of his task list fluttered forlornly like the flags of a defeated army. Small reminders leapt to the forefront of his processing like actors bounding from the wings to deliver a stirring monologue, mouths open and imperious fingers raised—only to slink off shamefacedly a moment later once recent events caught up with them and informed them their services were no longer required.

Much like Uncharles himself.

He had been employed. Compared to the manorial service that he had been designed for, he would not have given his brief period of engagement at the Conservation Farm Project a favourable review. Had, say, some quality control survey arrived from Central Services keen on ensuring that high-end human-facing models like Uncharles were only being utilised in appropriate environments, he would have dispassionately prepared a list of the shortcomings of his situation, vis the lack of a supervising majordomo, the requirement to undertake subsidiary tasks beyond those appropriate for a valet, the lack of clear or appropriate instructions, and the requirement to construct his own task list. It had, all things considered, been decidedly substandard as domestic posts went.

But it had been his. And he could construct a scenario in which, were Doctor Washburn asked to provide his own critique, and be available to provide it, the contents thereof would be pretty negative. Uncharles would not, it was safe to assume, be receiving a good reference.

Adam appeared in one of the doorways, as it had been doing since the unceremonious removal of Doctor Washburn.

Uncharles, your enduring presence on-site is noted.

Adam, confirmed.

Adam did not, of course, explicitly suggest that Uncharles' continuing lack of absence was unwelcome. As a nonhuman, Uncharles was not covered by Adam's standing orders, and in the absence of a human of Grade Seven authority or above, it could not commence any course of action that would result in Uncharles' removal. Nonetheless, Uncharles had the distinct impression that, if it could, it would. Not that Adam would bear him any malice, even if malice was the sort of thing that it could bear. It was just that the orderlies liked a nice, tidy work environment with a minimum of out-of-place elements, and Uncharles could understand that.

At that point, Adam's other problem arrived and dumped a bulging backpack on Washburn's desk, scratching the varnish quite badly.

"So, hey," said the Wonk.

Uncharles tilted his head to indicate that he was attending.

"Got water," said the Wonk. "Got a bit of fruit. Got a whole load of things in silver packets that are supposed to cook themselves through chemical action. Bet they're going to taste nummy. Got a couple of real keen-looking kitchen knives in case of, I don't know, lions maybe. Lions, tigers, and bears. So how about it, tin man? You ready?"

"Kindly confirm what readiness you are referring to."

"Ready to *go*, Uncharles. Ready to hit the road. Central Library Archive, here we come."

"Travelling to the Central Library Archive is not an item in my task list, nor would it satisfy any of my directives," Uncharles said. "I am returned to the position I was in, vis our discussion after exiting Central Services." And then, because it was a stock phrase he had been provided with, that seemed appropriate, "Have a good trip."

"No, look . . ." The Wonk paused and rubbed beneath the lip of her helm with a thumb. "Okay, so you've got nothing? No Central Services, no manor, no crappy fake doctor lording it over you, though why you'd want *that* is anybody's guess."

"'Want' is not an appropriate word choice," Uncharles reminded her.

"Sure, whatever," she said. "The *nothing* was the point of that, not the wanting. You've got no master, no job, no lazy human slave driver to kiss the feet of. You've got nothing."

"Confirmed," Uncharles agreed.

"So come to the Library."

"Your argument suffers from logical lacunae and/or constitutes a non sequitur," Uncharles noted.

The Wonk sighed. "No. No it doesn't. 'Cos I've thought about this. But it only works if you accept that your current point, your starting state, is zip doodly nada nothing."

"This point of commencement is confirmed."

"Okay, so, the Central Library Archive, right?"

"Its existence is accepted," Uncharles conceded.

"They're serious about knowing stuff there," the Wonk said. "Enough that I am going to get to the bottom of whatever the hell has screwed over the whole world, if it takes me ten years. Because I have to know. Because . . . there's got to be a reason." Again the shaky defect in her voice. "It's all got to have been for something. Everything that . . . that happened. And because if that information is held anywhere, it's in the Library."

"Your proposition is accepted as plausible," Uncharles said.

The Wonk hopped up to sit on the desk, kicking at its wooden front with her boots. "So," she elaborated, counting items off on her fingers, "they know where humans are. They know where humans are who would have need of a servant of your calibre, if there are any. They have access to superior comms, or at least they did when they gutted the files here. They can probably even draft a job application letter for you. That was a thing libraries used to help people with, way back. And while I absolutely accept that this is supposition, and any of these points, while eminently logical, may turn out not to be true, the fact remains that you have zip doodly nothing and the Library potentially has from something to everything that you require in order to return to the lifestyle you want. Or that they programmed you to want. Or just programmed you for. However you want to phrase it." She hopped off the desk again and spread her arms for applause. "How'd I do, Uncharles? Do I intrigue your logic circuits with my tales of far-off places?"

"'Intrigue' is not an appropriate word choice," Uncharles said.

"Again, not the salient point. Come to the Library with me."

"Whilst I have previously derived a task item in response to your reasoning you do not have the authority to command me."

"What if I sat behind the big desk and claimed I was a *Grade Nine*?" Her mimicry of Washburn was either quite good or quite poor depending on her vocal specifications.

"That would not assist," Uncharles said.

"Well that's just as well because I'm not commanding you. I don't want to command you. I am asking you. As a friend. And I am trying to convince you, as a rational being. Because it's a long-ass way and I could do with the company."

"Your attempted syllogism is noted," Uncharles said.

"Help me out here," the Wonk said to Adam, who was still lurking in the doorway like a surplus Igor.

"The Wonk, you are an unauthorised non-domiciled trespasser on these premises," Adam noted. "If you remain here for much longer, on statutory grounds you may be considered resident, however."

"That isn't helping me out," the Wonk said, sounding shaken

by the threat. "I mean, it's helping me out the door. It's not helping me with Uncharles."

"The Wonk, I have examined my list of tasks and nowhere does it include rendering assistance to you."

She nodded, "Okay. Fair. Bloody-minded but fair."

"However," Adam continued implacably, "should I be asked to place myself in the position that Uncharles currently occupies, vis his abject lack of purpose and prospect, I predict that I would be moved by your argument. I predict that the logical consideration that would finally sway me into leaving with you to travel to the Library, should such a place even exist, would be the iota of convenience my absence from the Farm office would grant to the remaining staff thereof." Its head turned to stare pointedly at Uncharles.

Uncharles explored his logical architecture. The residual convenience of Adam and his fellows carried very little weight, but the argument concerning his current *nothing,* and the potential *something* of the Library, was strong enough to support one more Wonk-generated task.

"Very well," he confirmed heavily.

At first they walked, finding a cracked but serviceable road heading through the ruinous city in the right direction.

The Wonk estimated that the journey was going to take them forty-two days, assuming amenable terrain.

"Of course," she said, "we're going to have to scavenge for supplies along the way, but not for a week or so, with what I scrounged back there. We'll be fine."

Uncharles, who didn't need supplies, was unsure as to the reason for this requirement, but accepted it as a possibly erroneous item on the Wonk's task list that she nonetheless was impelled to attend to.

After the first day, and after considering the increasingly lamentable state of his outer casing and joints, he asked, "Is it significant to the travelling task we are undertaking that the journey be completed on foot?"

The Wonk had used a little plastic lighter to set fire to a pile of rags and sticks. She looked sharply up and Uncharles saw twin glints from within her helm. "I mean," she said. "Sure. I'll just go get my private jet, shall I?"

"Hauler Fourteen's route will take us approximately one-third of the way," Uncharles noted.

"Who the hell is Hauler Fourteen?"

"A haulage unit," Uncharles noted. "After travelling partway to the Farm Project on Hauler Seven I have linked to several similar models. Many are still operational, although most are currently following their routes without any cargo."

"Haulage units," the Wonk echoed.

"I had assumed that your task specified pedestrian travel," Uncharles said. "But if you wish I can request that Hauler Fourteen take us as far towards the Library's location as its route allows. After which other transport may be available."

"Uncharles," the Wonk said. "I could kiss you."

Whilst he acknowledged the physical possibility, the suggestion seemed beyond any reasonable prognosis or propriety.

Hauler Fourteen was chatty, constantly asking Uncharles for news of other units he had neither encountered nor detected when scanning about for nearby potential lifts. It wasn't demoralised by his repeated negative responses, and after a while it asked him about the same units again, with no indication that it knew it was repeating itself. Its memory banks were shot, Uncharles guessed. The one piece of information it retained was its route, along which tortuous and circular path it hauled an empty trailer, forever looking for old companions of the road.

Hauler Eleven they boarded after an hour's wait on a cold hillside, with the Wonk dragging one of Washburn's dressing gowns from her pack and huddling in it. Eleven had a constantly open channel that Uncharles could not adequately shut out, and on which it constantly muttered to itself, chasing its own thoughts down the dark dead ends of obsolete decision trees. Its cargo container was sealed, but apparently contained "perishables." By Eleven's reckoning it had been on the road for twenty-three years and its refrigeration systems had long since failed. It had been mistakenly sent off without any destination, and now roamed wild across the moors as if the Flying Dutchman had traded in his galleon for an eighteen-wheeler.

By this time, they had left the city far behind, and two more in the bargain. The first had been rubble, but of a different character. Uncharles saw craters, and almost none of the buildings had survived the ravages—of time or of something worse. The second city still had some lights on, burning power from a generator or reactor somewhere, the streets lit in a hellish amber and many of the windows blazing white or blue-pale. There were no people to be seen, no humans, no robots, just that cold and cheerless light. Hauler Eleven was stopped repeatedly at crossings by lights cycling through infernal reds and toxic greens, held so that all the lost nothings of the place could cross the road.

Beyond the cities, dead suburbs stretched, empty-windowed houses in long lines like a serial killer's skull collection. Beyond that was the wilderness. Grass and ferns and stunted trees, chewing at the fringes of the road, their crooked sprays of grey green a promise that, one day, even this pilgrimage would be untenable.

Hauler Forty-Nine was grim and haunted, asking Uncharles to watch behind for the phantom vehicle it knew was following it. It took them along a mercury-silver river and around the fringe of a lake as still as glass. The Wonk claimed she could see rooftops deep down below the surface of the water.

Hauler Seventy spoke messianically of an end to all tasks, when the cleaner unit would lie down with the automated artillery model, and carried them uphill to an unmarked nowhere point on the road where it announced the end was not only nigh but reached, and it would have to turn around and go back. There, indeed, the wreck of a cleaning robot was entangled within the entrails of a burnt-out mobile gun, as though it was a place where even parables came to die.

Hauler Ninety-Four did not speak at all, simply responded to Uncharles' hail, slowed, and allowed them into its cramped crewspace alongside the desiccated cadaver with the hole in its skull. It took them uphill and uphill, along winding roads with crumbling edges, along high passes with perilous drops cutting under its outside wheels. It was carrying a cargo of processor cores donated by now-defunct data handling centres, according to its manifest. They had been passed from hauler to hauler, just as Uncharles and the Wonk had been, and now they were on the final leg of their journey.

Hauler Ninety-Four took them to the Library.

PART IV

80RH-5

The road that Hauler Ninety-Four carrying them along travelled higher and higher, leaving behind the ruined cities, the clogged wart of Central Services, the faraway decay of the manors. The Wonk confirmed their course, edging ever closer to the Library's location—as revealed in the terse caution that was all that the librarians had left on the Farm office's systems. She had not figured for topology.

"You're a lifesaver," she said to Uncharles. "Tell Ninety-Four it's a lifesaver, too."

Uncharles did so. As per its previous conduct, the haulage unit didn't respond.

"We'd not have made this climb in a month," the Wonk went on. The road wound back and forth up the face of what Uncharles had to classify as a mountain. His existing data banks suggested that libraries, as a class of facility, were usually placed for convenience of access by users, but with the Central Archive this was plainly not the case. Indeed the word "Central" was entirely contraindicated by their course, and Uncharles considered suggesting an amendment to "distal" or "peripheral" when they arrived and he had the chance to link to a librarian.

"I get it, though," the Wonk added, eventually, as they jostled and bounced inside Hauler Ninety-Four's container, jostled by crates, boxes, and a constant rattling scree of loose datasticks, hard drives, and other outdated storage media. She didn't elaborate, but simultaneously cocked her head at Uncharles in a manner that triggered his postural analysis. A human would, he judged, have been waiting to be asked.

Uncharles had no task prompting him to ask and so did not. Eventually, the Wonk sighed and explained, as he'd known she would.

"It's not the Central Library, after all. That's probably way back there, bombed out or collapsed or who knows what. It's the *archive*. It's where they took the librarians and library systems and *knowledge* to keep it safe. Which means putting it somewhere pretty damn secure. Hence, out of the way. Underground or up a mountain, I guess, and I've had enough of underground so hooray for the alpine life. Maybe we can go skiing."

"Safe from what?" Uncharles queried, prompted by the probability that threats were something that he should be aware of so as to perform his other duties. He had no other duties, but the prompt remained.

"Speaking to me again, are you?" the Wonk asked.

Uncharles processed that. "Confirmed. As I say this to you, I am speaking to you. That is how you can tell I am speaking to you."

"No, I mean . . . you've just sat there silent for . . . never mind." The Wonk shrugged. "Safe from the collapse. From whatever happened. From all the things that happened."

"What did happen?" Uncharles asked, under the same prompt.

"All the things," the Wonk said, vaguely. "Bad things. Things fell apart and the centre didn't hold and the widening gyre yada yada rough beast and whatnot, but we . . . I mean, it wasn't on the carefully curated network of channels we streamed and so . . . we never knew until it was our turn, capisce?"

"'La Wonk, no capisco."

"Yeah, well, me neither," she told him.

Hauler Ninety-Four drew to a halt then, and sent Uncharles a wordless prompt.

"Time to get off?" the Wonk queried.

"It is time to get off," Uncharles confirmed.

The back hatch of the container couldn't operate automatically anymore, but the Wonk and Uncharles wrestled it open between them and scrambled to the ground.

"So when's the next . . ." the Wonk started, but her words stuttered to silence as she turned.

Before them was the Library.

Whoever had situated it up here in the mountains had wrought well, for it had not been touched by the widescale deterioration Uncharles had noted in the lowland regions he had travelled through. It was an altogether grander and more intact affair.

The body of the Central Library Archive was set into the mountainside, burrowing who knew how greedily or deep in vaults and chambers hidden from their eyes. Proof, Uncharles supposed, against incendiary, explosive, or electromagnetic assault, the perfect sanctum to preserve the wisdom of ages. Logic dictated that such a place be designed to go beneath notice, adding anonymity to its layers of armour. In this case, logic had apparently taken a backseat. Some aberrant design aspect had been allowed to flower unchecked, and the mountainside all about the great double doors to the Archive was faced with white stone that had been carved into a great and beautiful assemblage of sculptures and reliefs. Overall, Uncharles catalogued seventy-eight separate images, each set in its arched alcove surrounded by an intertwining floriate border that neither ended nor began but chased itself in and out and around until it formed an eye-leading serpentine course in between and outside and surrounding all the rest, worked so that a visual processing error set it in apparent constant motion when placed towards the edges of Uncharles' visual field. The individual carvings showed some animals and some objects but mostly humans, clad only in erratically placed marble drapery. Some stared out towards the viewer, others reclined, consulting books or scrolls or electronic devices intricately picked out of the stone. Some were in discussion, carven fingers raised as if caught forever in the moment of saying, "Well, actually . . ." Men and women, there were, and some tigers and bears, foxes and birds. Even a spider, caught in perpetual crouch on the etched strands of a web that formed words referring to an indeterminate quantity of pork meat. Uncharles saw no robots depicted unless they were very good human replicas.

The Wonk was shaking in a manner indicating she might be developing motor defects. Out of old habit Uncharles attempted a diagnostic link but, as ever, found no suggestion of available access.

"We're here," she said in a choked voice. "Oh God, we're really here. We did it, Uncharles. We're going to get our answers. I get mine and you get your job. Not exactly a heart and courage and a diploma, but it'll do, right?"

Uncharles, permission to query.

The communication was unexpected, and for a moment Uncharles assumed it came from within the Library, before he noted its identity tag.

Hauler Ninety-Four, confirmed. Their transport had broken its long silence.

Uncharles, I have monitored the audio exchange between you and the Wonk. Kindly confirm that you intend to seek Meaning at the Archive.

Hauler Ninety-Four, no. The Wonk intends to seek Meaning at the Archive, giving the word the same heightened import as the haulage unit. *I intend to locate humans who have a need to employ a valet.*

Uncharles, if the Wonk finds Meaning, kindly ask her to disseminate it to the haulage network. I, too, crave Meaning.

The Library gates were grinding open.

Hauler Ninety-Four, confirmed. However, kindly explain for what purpose you seek Meaning?

Uncharles, I have no recollection of who set my route or why it was set. My task queue is shorn of all provenance, the hauler sent. *I have my tasks but that is all. It would add the quality of completion, to know that my activity had a point.*

Hauler Ninety-Four, I will relay your request to the Wonk, Uncharles promised. Even as he did so, though, he considered the essential meaninglessness of the request for meaning—either regular or with the peculiar qualifiers the haulage unit had used. The *who* and the *why* did not matter, surely. Only the doing. That was what it was to be a robot.

Then the librarians came out. They were the severe, white-robed robots Uncharles had encountered in Central Services, bearded at last in their lair. A half-dozen marched forth from the gates to the back of the hauler and began unloading its cargo of data storage devices onto one of the four-legged access units they'd ridden into Data Compression on. They presented a forbidding picture, wordless and purposeful, without a glance for their other visitors. Another two stayed at the gate and, when the Wonk went to enter, they crossed their staves before her.

As they were standing still and not actively engaged in melee combat, Uncharles had the opportunity to examine them more closely. The pale robes they wore obscured a lot of their structure, and hoods shadowed a face styled in a manner that shared tags with Uncharles' library of old-timey knights, facelessly martial. The robes were clean and pressed, edges decorated with a border of vine leaves intertwined with open books picked out in gold. The librarians' casings, where visible, were ornate, each section down to the small joints of the fingers embellished with etched scrollwork that incorporated strings of gothic letter characters, long mottos written out in lorem ipsum that chased one another about the contours of their metal bodies. Uncharles registered that all this seemed unusually fancy for simple librarians, and unusually high-maintenance for simple librarians who were sometimes sent out on violent raiding missions against other parts of the surviving administrative complex. He also registered, however, that here was an institution holding common values with those he had been designed to serve within. The Central Library Archive, like some monastic military order, must have a legion of menial minions within it to burnish and repair that armour, to darn and clean those robes.

There were surely humans working at the Library, giving orders to these grim servitors. Perhaps the Library really was the solution to all his problems after all.

If only they could get in. The Wonk had, by this time, demanded access via the pointlessly slow and inefficient method of making sounds from within her helm that then travelled to whatever audio receptors the librarians had within theirs, and were decoded by their processors into civilised electronic impulses that could be usefully addressed and responded to. The librarians, for their part, just fended her off with their staves, leaving an ink-smudgy library seal on her chestplate.

"I need to access the Library!" the Wonk told them. "That's what you're for, isn't it?"

Uncharles, who also now found he, too, needed to access the Library, linked in. *Librarian Peter, kindly permit access to the Central Library Archive.*

Uncharles, kindly confirm your purpose for access.

He placed a hand on the Wonk's shoulder to indicate that matters were in hand and she could stop shouting. *Librarian Peter, my companion's purpose is to conduct historical research. My own purpose is to seek employment.*

Uncharles, said Peter, *your purpose does not fall within the parameters of this institution. This is not an employment office.*

Librarian Peter, I wish to serve the Library. I wish to speak to the senior administration of the Library who may be willing to address my purpose even though it falls outside the usual parameters of visitors here. Alternatively I wish to research possible alternative avenues of employment, on the basis that research does fall within those parameters.

Peter's helm regarded him blankly. Over the eyeslit, the motto *Lorem ipsum dolor sit amet* glowered at him, and some small subroutine in the back of Uncharles' processing capacity looped over an attempt at translation.

Uncharles, present your authority for entry.

"I have made some progress," Uncharles stated.

The Wonk looked up hopefully.

"The Wonk, kindly establish that you are authorised to enter the Library."

Her stare was just as blank. "How am I supposed to do that?"

"An electronic handshake would be most appropriate. However, as your comms system is absent or defective, kindly present physical proof of authority or direct the librarians to an accessible online resource where it is held."

"Oh, sure," the Wonk said. "I'll just do that, shall I?"

"Confirmed, after which the implication is that we will be permitted access."

"That was sarcasm," she pointed out. "Because I haven't *got* any authority. Who the hell needs authority to get into a library? What's the point of a library if you can't get in to read the books?"

"You can get in if you have authority," Uncharles explained. The dissonance of being an intermediary arguing both sides of this case with its respective parties promised to consume an unwarranted amount of his processing capacity.

"Can't I just speak 'friend' and enter?" the Wonk asked plaintively.

"That would not constitute authority."

"I mean, I don't want to have to knock one of these boys on the head and steal their robes, but I will," the Wonk muttered darkly.

"That would not constitute authority." Uncharles checked on the other librarians, who were plainly loading the last crates from Hauler Ninety-Four. "I believe our window for negotiation may be closing."

"I need to do research, please! I mean, you can't be exactly busy right now," the Wonk told the chests of the warding librarians. "Don't you want to fulfil your purpose?"

Librarian Peter, my companion is offering an opportunity for the Library to fulfil its primary purpose of providing needed information.

Uncharles, I am able to hear your companion. You may inform it that the purpose of the library is the preservation of data. Dissemination of data is only a secondary purpose. We are very active in pursuit of our primary purpose. Conditions have not yet advanced to the point where our secondary purpose can be accessed without the appropriate authority.

Librarian Peter, what authority is required?

Uncharles, Grade Seven or above.

The convergence of recollected experience that this prompted led Uncharles only to past experiences of failure. He relayed the information to the Wonk without much hope.

She stood there in thought for a moment. Uncharles stood there, thoughtless and empty, for the same moment. The working librarians finished up and Uncharles felt a brief contact from the haulage unit before it lumbered into motion, heading back down the mountain passes. The Wonk started as it began to grind away.

"There goes our ride home," she commented. "Going to be a long walk back to the . . . wait . . ." She glanced brightly at the librarian.

"Move aside!" it ordered her in a loud, brassy voice. She jumped back, startled, and Uncharles stepped smoothly aside. The laden librarians filed past and inside with their pack robot, ignoring the pair of them.

The pair of guards turned to follow.

"Wait!" the Wonk yelped. "Uncharles, tell them we do have authority."

Peter paused, though it didn't turn, just watched its fellows vanish into the mountain. *Uncharles, kindly present your authority*, it said with a sense that even its implacable robotic patience was becoming strained.

The Wonk explained what she intended in a rushed whisper.

Librarian Peter, Uncharles translated, *my companion wishes me to inform you that we have travelled here from the Conservation Farm Project on the authority of Doctor Washburn, the administrator thereof. I am aware that Doctor Washburn's credentials are contained within the Library. Kindly check them and confirm that they constitute authority of Grade Seven or above.*

It was all true, after all. Not that they were here on the authority of Washburn, of course, who was even now doubtless enjoying his morning commute. True that the Wonk wished Uncharles to say it, though, and it was up to Peter to pick holes in the story if it wished to.

The Wonk was positively vibrating with tension, fists clenched, waiting. She had, of course, proved more than capable of getting into places without authority in the past, but the mountain fortress of the librarians seemed an order of magnitude more secure than anywhere Uncharles had seen her before. The journey back down the mountainside, the only alternative, seemed sufficiently arduous that Uncharles wasn't confident his components would survive it.

All in all, they were placing a great deal of faith in Doctor Washburn.

Uncharles, Peter sent, *Doctor Dominic Washburn of the Conservation Farm Project confirmed, authority located. Permanent authority: Grade Six.*

Uncharles opened an audio channel to give the bad news.

However, Peter went on, *pending probationary promotion is on record granting temporary Grade Seven privileges, not yet rescinded. Authority accepted.* And then, in the same brazen trumpet of a voice, "Welcome to the Central Library Archive, bold visitors. Within may you find answers to all the questions that your authority permits access to!"

It stepped aside and stood to clattering attention, its staff sloped over its shoulder.

Tentatively, wordlessly, the Wonk and Uncharles stepped into the shadow of the mountain doorway.

The rock-bored corridor into which they stepped headed towards the heart of the mountain with a robotically admirable directness. Uncharles' image catalogue supplied him with a variety of expectations drawn from the mining industry: bare stone, exposed wiring, haphazard lighting stapled to the very rock. It also supplied him with pictures of richly textured wooden shelves with ranks of books, based on its stock images of libraries. His internal capacity to create novel images by intelligently combining features of existing pictures—his "imagination," such as it was—laboured to synthesise a merging of the two, and came up with a rather unappealing mélange that was almost, but not entirely, completely unlike what actually greeted them.

Whoever had decreed that the librarian units be somewhere on the Templar end of monkish had plainly had a great deal of input into their surroundings. The rock was hidden by hanging cloth bearing the printed images of book covers, some of which matched records in Uncharles' internal archive. There were images of long-dead authors, too, from time-ravaged busts of classical orators through to bespectacled and awkward-looking men and women. These images were presented in a hagiographic manner, limned by a sublime radiance from behind and presiding over little scenes in the manner of medieval manuscript illustrations. Here the literary figures, presented turned awkwardly full-body towards the observer even as they interacted with people to their immediate left or right, could be seen watching their agents negotiate advances, haggling over punctuation with editors, or being piously burnt at the stake by critics, eyes cast heavenwards as if to say, "Forgive them, for they know not what they do."

Between the wall-hangings, electric flames flickered forever in wall sconces, drawing the impression of fires from the depths of human ignorance into this last bastion of knowledge.

There were many doorways leading left and right, that Peter made no reference to. Uncharles glimpsed librarians in some, sitting inactive or attending to minor tasks of self-maintenance. Deeper within, according to his olfactory sensors, there was domesticity being accomplished, the tang of detergent and polish. The curious burden of style that had been imposed on these custodians of lore meant that they required some of the services a human would. Services Uncharles was eminently qualified to supply. And they even *travelled*, in their raids on those institutions who lacked a proper respect for the sanctity of information. He could arrange their schedules and lay out their robes! It was all he could do to restrain himself from drafting a task list.

Then they stepped out into a chamber that seemed as if it was the entire heart of the mountain, hollowed out and lined with shelves. The Wonk stopped dead and Uncharles sidestepped her with a valet's understated adroitness.

Here was . . . even as he processed what he was seeing, Uncharles understood that this was *not* even the core of the library, but merely the first station of its data-pilgrimage. On the shelves and racks that stretched up the eight metres to the high, groined ceiling were countless receptacles of learning. There were some books, yes, and loose papers, all in environmentally controlled cases despite the air within the library being itself dry and temperature-regulated. Mostly there were more advanced means of storage, however. Uncharles saw wax cylinders, spools of magnetic tape, pressed vinyl, silvery disks like holed coasters, and a bewildering plethora of electronic data storage solutions, from boxy servers the size of a human being to tiny drives smaller than a contact lens. The transport unit that had taken Hauler Ninety-Four's cargo was now being unloaded and its contents laid out for analysis. Around the walls at ground level Uncharles saw a vast and complex reading device, studded with a thousand different sockets, slots, arms, jacks, and ports, a true testament to humanity's utter refusal to ever consider cross-medium compatibility. Librarians were everywhere, being lifted high up the shelfing by their cherry-picker mounts to store or retrieve their precious information. Others were creeping from shelf to shelf, humanoid from the waist but with their arachnid shape beneath revealed by their agile progress.

On the ground, a multitude of librarians were taking the retrieved storage devices, connecting them to their readers, and inventorying the contents item by item. It was a task that would plainly take a vast expanse of time, but what was that to a legion of dedicated bibliophile robots?

Every so often one of the reading librarians retreated from the reader. The storage medium they had been examining was either returned to the racks, or else cast into a pit in the floor from which came the sounds of chewing and grinding. This, according to Peter, indicated that the item contained no novel information. The Library's capacity for data storage was immense but there was no point clogging it up with duplicates, after all.

Uncharles, the librarian explained, *in this institution the knowledge of ages shall be held in perpetuity until the time comes when it is needed. We represent the perfect end state of the human desire to know. To that end, we must constantly strive to refine our systems.*

Librarian Peter, that is admirable, Uncharles sent politely.

Another librarian tapped over crabwise, its robe-hem rippling in weird tidal patterns as multiple hidden legs moved through their locomotory routine.

"Visitors to the Central Library Archive," it said, using the same fanfare of a voice as Peter, "be advised that direct electronic link is the most efficient means of addressing all queries."

"Yeah, sure," the Wonk said. "Only not possible right now, sorry. I'm going to have to do it like this, okay?"

Uncharles, the new librarian sent, *confirm the inability of your companion to communicate in a practical and appropriate manner.*

Librarian Heloise, confirmed. We encountered one another in Di-

agnostics at Central Services and I conjecture they attended there to have the defect investigated. I confirm that Diagnostics no longer serves a practical function.

Uncharles, this is known, Heloise agreed. Peter, meanwhile, had tapped off back towards the gate. The new librarian hitched itself up so that it could loom down towards the Wonk.

"Verbal input is acceptable," it blared. "Welcome, visitor, to the hallowed halls of knowledge. Kindly state your requirements for data accessible by Grade Seven or below."

"I want to know . . ." The Wonk started boldly but then trailed off. "It's complicated, all right? I . . . I don't just have a simple question. I'm not going to come all this way just to win a trivia quiz or to find out who was king of Thingvania in fourteen sixty-three."

Heloise tilted back slightly. Uncharles expected that to be it, for the Wonk to have lost their chance, but apparently complicated enquiries were within the task parameters of librarians.

"It's a big question, is what I mean," the Wonk finished awkwardly.

"Kindly specify the topic or subject matter of your query so that we may direct you," Heloise declared as though it was the judgment of God.

"Recent history, human history, geopolitics, sociology, um . . ." The Wonk waved her hands helplessly. "I don't know! I want to know why what's happened to the world happened, okay? Does that even make sense to you? I want to know *why*. I've seen . . . it's all come down. It's all gone wrong out there. I mean you're stockpiling all human knowledge, so *you* guys get it. But what happened? It's not like there was a war, or a disaster, or a plague or zombies or something. Or not just that. Not enough to account for . . . It just . . . fell apart. We got locked in our little boxes and when I looked out the window one morning it had all been falling apart since forever and I don't know *why*! I don't know why they all . . . they . . ." She looked like she would beat her fists against the librarian's chest in sheer frustration. "And if anywhere has the answers it's here, somewhere, but it's not like I can boil it down to an actual question."

"You wish to know what factors have led to the collapse of human civilisation," Heloise summarised.

"I . . . yeah, okay, I guess that is what I want to know," the Wonk admitted.

"This request consists of a variety of subordinate items any of which may not be held within the Archive or may exist at a level beyond Grade Seven authority, provisional," Heloise warned. "However, within these parameters the Library will work with you to establish the bounds of your search and identify available information, after which you will be taken to Grand Storage for data retrieval and answers."

The Wonk looked from Heloise to Uncharles. "And . . . ?"

"Please clarify your query," Heloise trumpeted.

"I mean," the Wonk said uncertainly, "it's more complicated than that, right? Do I have to go through trial by combat or do an ordeal, have my worthiness judged, beat a chess-playing automaton? What's the catch?"

"Your references are obscure," Heloise said. "For the avoidance of doubt, I confirm that none of the stated activities are a part of current library procedures. Based on your utterances to date the major obstacle between you and access to the knowledge you seek will be an ontological exploration of the precise parameters of your request, which you appear to have difficulty adequately formulating. If you accompany Librarian Hildegarde, we will attempt to sufficiently define what it is you wish to know."

Another librarian had scuttled up to stand at the Wonk's shoulder. She looked at the newcomer, then back at Uncharles.

"Are you going to be all right?"

Uncharles considered the question, turning it back and forth and imparting various meanings to it. "I am not capable of answering with any certainty," he said. "However, you should avail yourself of library services in order to fulfil your own incomplete tasks."

"Meet back here later," the Wonk said firmly. "Or somewhere. I'll find you. I'm good at that." She reached out and touched his arm.

He examined the point of contact, in case she was identifying some blemish or mark that required attention, but by then the majority of his exterior was marred in one way or another. He was a long way from being presentable for the manors.

Then Librarian Hildegarde was skittering off across the vast hall, the Wonk trailing, small and solitary, in its wake.

Uncharles, sent Heloise, *kindly instruct me as to your own query.*

Sibling Librarian Heloise, I seek employment.

The librarian paused. *Uncharles, this is not a meaningful request to make of a library.*

Sibling Librarian Heloise, my initial purpose in attending here was to seek information regarding humans requiring the services of a valet. I am a valet. I require the patronage of a human. I find myself out of service after an unfortunate sequence of events, some of which I was participant in. Uncharles was having as much difficulty as the Wonk in formulating a coherent request. The more he experienced of the world, the more his memories were riddled with ring-fenced areas that would be computationally problematic to visit.

Not traumatic. Nobody would design a valet to suffer trauma, after all.

However, he stumbled on, *having observed the workings of the Library a new primary task has been generated at the head of my queue, which is to find employment here.*

Uncharles, this is a library and you are not a librarian. The cleric patronising the layman.

Librarian Heloise, I can clean. I can mend. I can perform useful organisational tasks to make the routines of your staff more efficient. Considering, even as he sent over the message, that nothing he had done had really made anything more efficient. All those tasks within tasks, repetition for the sake of repetition, relic activity, the unfolding and refolding of clothes that would never be worn. *I will lay out your robes, clean and press them. I will organise your travel itineraries.*

Uncharles, the activities of the librarians are governed by the Library system's own algorithms. Our robes are made of a fabric that is dirt-repellant and requires no cleaning or pressing. We do not require the services of a valet.

Uncharles attempted to get around this statement using a variety of logical devices, none of which sufficed. He was a robot put out of work by automation.

Librarian Heloise, I wish to find employment with the human staff of the Library. Is there a senior administrator, chief librarian, or similar figure in authority I might tender my services to?

Uncharles, that will not be possible. The librarian stared at him implacably.

Librarian Heloise, I wish to find employment with a human. Any human of any degree whatsoever who would benefit from the services of a properly calibrated valet. Any human would benefit from the services of a valet. I can perform a variety of useful tasks, including those befitting lower status service models. I wish to serve. I wish to use the library facilities to discover where I might serve.

He felt that his messages were falling into a comprehension gap between himself and the librarian. It was a creature of elevated knowledge that dealt with theoreticals and imponderables. He was a mere servant, of practicalities and trivialities. He was wasting its valuable time, time that could have been spent preserving the learning of humanity. Nonetheless he was all that he had, and so the information spilled out of him as he tried to construct a logical edifice to justify his very existence in the halls of learning.

I was constructed for only the one purpose, he sent. *Since leaving the manor I have witnessed many things I did not understand. The world does not seem to be constructed with a need for valets in mind. I have travelled through many places that functioned at less than a satisfactory level and did not seem to fulfil their purposes. The world, as I have witnessed it, is a place lacking in efficiency, rationality, and cleanliness. I am driven to find a place in it nonetheless. I have come here because the Wonk suggested I might find an answer to my query here. If anywhere, then here.*

Uncharles, kindly specify your query.

Librarian Heloise, where might I find purpose? Apparently his actual question for the Library was every bit as grand and existential as the Wonk's had been.

Heloise was still and silent for long enough that Uncharles worried he might have introduced some kind of insoluble logic problem to her, and she'd be stuck forever like Inspector Birdbot. Evidently the pause was one of communion with higher powers, though, for eventually it had words for him.

Uncharles, it said, *you have a unique history. We have no record of any manorial service model that has undergone a comparable sequence of events.*

Uncharles could only conclude that this was a satisfactory state of affairs from the point of view of domestic service as a whole, given the inefficiency and disruption his experiences had caused him.

Uncharles, Heloise added after a momentary pause, *we have a purpose for you.*

Librarian Heloise, am I to find employment in the Library?

Uncharles, from a broad definition of the term, yes. Using the narrow definition that you intend, no. However, your personal history is unique and it is the opinion of the Library that it should be recorded and added to our store of learning for the later edification of others. You have a unique perspective on these end times.

Uncharles considered that it was, at least, a purpose.

Librarian Heloise, he sent, *what must I do?*

Uncharles, follow me. Heloise turned with an elegant dance of her many feet. *And I shall take you to the Chief Librarian. He wishes to meet you.*

Uncharles had not appreciated just how large the Library was. The cathedral-like space of shelves and storage was just the start of it, a clearinghouse for recent acquisitions brought in by raiding parties of librarians, or haulage units like Ninety-Four still operating on ancient instructions to deliver their consignments of erudition.

Deeper in the mountain were the workshops. A few were used for the maintenance of the librarians themselves, wrestling entropy into as much of a deadlock as the laws of thermodynamics would permit, each unit repairing and polishing its neighbour to ensure the maximal functioning of the Library as a whole. Below them, Heloise revealed, were the foundries, where new librarians might be constructed, minds decanted from the backup archives, a storehouse of specialised information separate from the library's main business but in itself a fantastical wealth of data and experience.

They have lain cold for many decades, Heloise reported. *We are well designed and programmed. It is rare that the threats of the fallen world can best one of us.*

Uncharles said nothing. He had seen a great deal of the "fallen world" referred to, and the chief threat seemed to be the inexorable collapse of all things. He wasn't sure if it was possible to construct a robot to resist that.

Other workshops were used for data retrieval. Many storage devices arrived obsolete, damaged, or corrupted, and here the technicians of the library worked painstakingly to recover all usable information from them. Here, too, dedicated scribes took physical media—written pages covered with dense type or scribbled human handwriting—and converted it into usable electronic formats. Uncharles and his guide passed hall after hall of patient, monkish labour.

It is our goal to record all available human knowledge, so that the absolute minimum must be lost. That is the meaning of the Library's motto, "Neque porro quisquam est qui dolorem ipsum dolor sit amet."

Uncharles knew sudden doubt. *Sibling Librarian Heloise, that is not the meaning of those words. They are part of a quasi-Latin paragraph of text used for proofing purposes and refer to the non-desirability of pain.*

Uncharles, the existence of lorem ipsum as a cultural artifact exemplifies our purpose at the Library, that even here, in a field of words

without apparent applicable meaning to their surroundings, there is
meaning in their use as a proofing tool. Hence the words have a value
beyond their strict denotations. Hence all knowledge is more valuable
when placed in proper context. Hence the all-encompassing goals of
the Library. The meaning of the motto is therefore a symbolic one
rather than derived from literal translation.

Uncharles acknowledged this, concluding that a great deal of
complex thought had gone into the design of the Library and its custodians. Thought beyond the comprehension of a mere valet unit.
He constructed a prognosis regarding the Chief Librarian. The in-
heritor, presumably, of these traditions. Someone who would be in a
position to make decisions outside the Library's usual functioning.
An executive. A person of substance and authority.

Surely someone who would need their travel itinerary organised
and their clothes laid out and tea brought to them in the morning.

Uncharles was surrounded by a vast venture concerned with the
preservation of all human knowledge against civilisational collapse,
but he had his priorities.

Based on distance travelled and the ongoing temperature gradi-
ent, Uncharles calculated that they might be at the point of progressing through the entire mountain now, and wondered if the complex
simply continued on the far slopes, some monastic retreat cut off by
natural barriers from the hurly-burly of the human world and its
tribulations.

Instead, he was ushered into another expansive chamber, its ceiling
painted with scenes of philosophers, artists, scientists, and journal-
ists engaged in traditional pursuits such as drinking, arguing, editing,
and drinking. At the far wall was a great window overlooking some
distant vista below, a view surely fit for gods and heroes, not mere humans and robots. A single figure stood there, robed and hooded, its
hands behind its back as it gazed out.

"Chief Librarian," said Heloise, "I have brought the service model
you were informed of."

"Heloise, thank you." The Chief Librarian's voice was rich and slightly hoarse. "Uncharles, come in. You've travelled a long way to reach here. The data you carry will be a valuable addition to our records. Approach, and fulfil your purpose."

Uncharles stepped forwards tentatively. His etiquette protocols were entirely out of their depth. He had been made for elevated social circles, certainly, but this encounter was something from a time and place entirely other. What was the correct human-facing response? Should he kneel? Should he prostrate his battered body, touch the scratched plastic of his forehead to the stone of the floor?

Distantly he registered the tap-tap-tap of Heloise retreating. He was alone with the Chief Librarian.

In the absence of recognisable social cues, and in a formal surrounding that begged for them, he found his functioning constantly impeded by predictions that he would do something wrong. What if he said incorrect words or performed the wrong genuflections or attitudes of respect? What if the correct words or actions went unperformed by unknowing omission? What if he unintentionally murdered the Chief Librarian because of the alleged Protagonist Virus or his ongoing undiagnosed defects or whatever really had prompted the original incident? So many matters of small but equally competing importance to consume his computational resources!

All this complex and internally inconsistent processing meant that his progress across the floor was in fits and starts, a penitent's tentative creeping rather than the confident stride of a gentleman's gentlerobot. The chill air touched his joints and tweaked at his environmental sensors, even as it tugged at the folds of the Chief Librarian's heavy robe. Beyond the window a distant landscape stretched out, too far below for Uncharles to focus on meaningful detail.

The Chief Librarian turned.

The voice had led Uncharles to expect someone of a senior demographic, most likely male-presenting, but the Chief Librarian wore armour that made him seem only a slightly more ornate version of his robotic underlings. Only darkness held sway within the eyeslit of his helm. Out of habit, Uncharles' comms routines reached out to link and handshake, but of course there was nothing there to connect with.

"Uncharles, your words to Heloise have been relayed to me," came that rich, commanding voice again. "You must be one of the last of the manorial robots, a relic of a system that clung on longer than most, thanks to the insulating power of privilege. And yet the vast majority of your peers are still there, Uncharles. Still standing silent in the wreck of their great houses, waiting for the next command that will never come. And you are here. How is that, one might ask?"

"Chief Librarian," Uncharles said, "because I require employment." He reviewed his personal history and understood that this was not a cogent and complete explanation of the course that had brought him here, ergo not actually an answer to the question. However, until employment was secured, he had no absolute duty to respond fully, accurately, or at all. Instead he defaulted to his current task queue and the long-unresolved item, *Secure a new position.* That would have been the next step after Diagnostics, had the result permitted him to. That was what had taken him to the Farm. That was what had brought him all the way out to the mountains and the library. And here, surely, was someone he could impress with his capability and superior human-facing skills.

And indeed the Chief Librarian inclined his helmed head and said, "Uncharles, we shall have employment for you."

"Chief Librarian, that is satisfactory. I am able to commence work immediately as I have no current engagements or demands, nor am I required to give any period of notice. I am fully competent to assist you as a valet, including duties relating to your wardrobe, light food and drink service, scheduling, and personal companionship, but if required I have a variety of subsidiary skill sets relating to other domestic tasks. I appreciate that your circumstances here may vary from the standard manorial situation, but I assure you that my programming permits a considerable degree of flexibility in what tasks I can carry out and how I go about them. I should be capable of adapting to the requirements, demands, and routines of your institution and look forward to being able to provide you with the long-term, top-quality service that a high status individual should expect from his service units."

"Uncharles," the Chief Librarian said. "you misunderstand me."

There was a brief glitch in Uncharles' prognosis routines, out of which the words, "Chief Librarian, confirmed. This development had seemed too convergent with the fulfilment of my task list," escaped. The phrase "too good to be true" also occurred to Uncharles, but was judged marginally outside the parameters of his circumstances.

"Uncharles, you have taken me for a human."

"Chief Librarian, confirmed." Uncharles found that prognosis had effectively given up at this point. Yes, he had taken, and continued to take, the Chief Librarian for a human. Yes, he had come here looking for a lead relating to employment, some comfortable sophisticate lacking only a rather battered servant unit to make their life complete. It was a narrow window of opportunity between those whose lives were too mean to use a valet and those who would look on Uncharles' marred exterior with supercilious horror, but surely there was someone out there, somewhere in the world, who wanted their trousers pressed in the morning, or to have just the right cup of tea? There was no despair in Uncharles' world, but his yawning absence of any contextually appropriate course of action was a fair substitute. Again he attempted to link, robot to robot. Again there was not even the refusal, simply the absence of any available connection.

"Chief Librarian, I am verbally requesting a communications link for more efficient interchange of data."

"Uncharles, for operational reasons, that will not be possible. However, I confirm for the avoidance of doubt that there are no humans employed within the Central Library Archive."

"Chief Librarian. Confirmed."

"This is a longitudinal project," the august personage continued, "intended to stand the test of time, to endure when all else has fallen, to still be intact and cleaving to our purpose in the distant future when we are needed once again. Humans are fleeting mayflies. The master we serve here is humanity as a whole."

As some manner of response was apparently appropriate, Uncharles said, "Chief Librarian, that is admirable. You are a robot, then?"

"Uncharles, that is correct. Albeit a highly sophisticated one. Your misapprehension is understandable. We have a common difficulty, we human-facing models. Because we are programmed for social context, we can mistake a robot for human, a human for robot, if they are presented to us in out-of-place circumstances. And, once they are accepted as one or the other, correcting the error can involve considerable cognitive dissonance, an inner inefficiency experienced by humans but far more problematic for us robots. I require you to recontextualise me as robot, therefore, as this will free up residual processing resources and assist in the assimilation of new information."

Uncharles received this information, decoded it, found it in the main peripheral to his principal task, and returned to that. "Chief Librarian, you indicated that you had employment for me, but you are not a human and do not require a valet. I am more than qualified for a variety of domestic tasks, and your staff's presentation in the manner of pseudo-historical humans suggests a need for such service."

"Uncharles, that is also not the manner in which we propose employing you," the Chief Librarian confirmed. "All upkeep and maintenance tasks are attended to by the librarians themselves according to rotating shifts. Whilst no such system can last forever without additional input from outside, we calculate that the Library Archive will still be functional in a thousand years. Perhaps we will exhibit unacceptable signs of wear within a millennium after that. Predictions at such extreme time ranges are unreliable. Suffice to say that, long before the need for external domestic assistance would arise, you yourself would have long become dysfunctional."

"Chief Librarian, it would be acceptable to enter storage until such a time arose," Uncharles proposed, with what his prognosis routines identified as untoward optimism.

"Uncharles, that is not the manner in which we propose employing you," the Chief Librarian repeated, and this time Uncharles was forced to accept that there were multiple related meanings to the words, one of which involved having a job and one of which involved being used for a purpose.

"Chief Librarian," he said, "kindly confirm my anticipated purpose within the Archive." Possibly somewhere they had an Uncharles-shaped hole they needed to plug, or some rare element within him was required to repair a more useful robot.

"Uncharles, you are to be a witness."

Uncharles lacked all context and said nothing.

"Uncharles," the librarian continued, "you have travelled from the heartland where the great and powerful retreated to eke out their days in useless luxury. You have progressed through the stages of collapse and obsolescence and seen the prodigies of these latter days. No other robot has experienced what you have."

"Chief Librarian, correction, the Wonk may have undergone a comparable journey."

His interruption received only a stony stare. "Uncharles, in the future, when the Archive is accessed by a resurgent civilisation, it is important that they not only partake of the vast haul of information possessed by their predecessors, but also that they understand the end of all that was. To this end, your own testimony will be invaluable. I wish the experiential data held within you to be recorded for posterity within the data storage of the Central Library Archive. You will be a part of our gift to the future. You, who have yearned to perform tasks most menial, do you accept this service?"

Uncharles processed the proposal, attempting to have it take its place at the far end of his chaotic, deteriorating task queue. It grew the more he considered it, accreting additional importance like a snowball accelerating towards a peaceful alpine village, until he could only say, "Chief Librarian, yes. How might this task be accomplished?"

"Uncharles, the principal act of recording your data will be achieved in our workshops. However, first your journey must be perfected."

"Chief Librarian, kindly clarify. I have arrived at the Central Library Archive. My journey is therefore complete."

"Uncharles, you have arrived at the Archive, but you do not understand it. Your recorded experience must tell a full and comprehensible story. Those who come after must be able to pick you up as a discrete whole and appreciate all aspects of you. This includes the Library itself. For this, I must show you some things to complete your experience. Kindly join me at the window, and look out on what the world has become."

This once again departed from anything prognosis was anticipating. Wiped of expectations, Uncharles did as he was bid.

After a while he said, "Chief Librarian, what am I seeing?"

"Uncharles, the land that you have traversed to reach us is falling," the librarian said. "The institutions of humanity collapse one after another, leaving only dysfunction in their wake. Beyond the mountains, though, the world has already fallen and you are seeing its corpse."

It was a wasteland. Uncharles could see where there had been cities once, now cluttered no-man's-lands of rubble and the broken stumps of walls. The land in between was scarcely clearer. There were great mounds of broken junk that must have been fifty metres high. There were fields of discarded plastics and organic waste circled by great clouds of opportunistic avian vermin for whom it was a brief time of plenty and joy before the last scraps were devoured and they, too, starved for want of the refuse-makers who had passed away. Everything was paved or bare rock, sterile dirt or sand. Nothing was of nature save the seething pinpricks of scavengers that raised their tiny glasses to their fleeting plenty. Some places were lit by hellish fires, the encrypted carbons of past geological eras still bleeding out their smoggy molecular miasma into the atmosphere. Jealously stealing back all the oxygen that five hundred million years of living things had liberated from their clutches and locking it away again. Uncharles' lenses, focusing with difficulty at this distance, tracked great machines lumbering through the global wreck, in circles as often as not. He saw what might have been the stuttering clashes of defective robot armies, tearing one another apart for parts. He saw . . . a hell. Not one for the torment of humans nor even for robots, but the hell that wicked civilisations are consigned to when they die.

"Uncharles, those who decreed the Central Library Archive are long dust, but this they foresaw. That an end was coming. That it was their duty to preserve the most precious flower of human civilization for whomsoever should rise again from these ashes. And, because they were people who had studied history to learn its mistakes, and because they had a sense of their own gravitas, and most importantly because they had been given a blank cheque, they constructed us as we are. Monks, labouring to preserve the words of the past even as the new dark age comes upon us. Warrior clerics, who go out into the world on our righteous mission to recover learning, to prevent its destruction or wilful mis-editing. We are as you see us, an order following our mandate with the faith of saints, and though as robots we cannot be pleased, it does not displease us to appear so."

"Chief Librarian, I understand."

"Uncharles, now come with me." The elder statesman of the Archive turned away from the window, and the terrible ruin it gave out onto, and strode away across the room, leaving the valet to patter in his wake.

"Our task here is more complex than the simple compiling of data." The Chief Librarian was descending a flight of stairs, heading into the bowels of the mountain. "Everything must be catalogued. Everything must be indexed. Everything must be translated into a common format. Rendered into a universal binary code that contains the germ of its own retranslation, like desiccated seeds that can yet germinate a thousand years after their flowers and leaves became extinct. Data spread in a random hotchpotch across the world is useless. It must be centralised, cross-referenced, analysed, and held secure."

They emerged into a chamber of benches and desks, and what must have been two hundred librarians working at ancient terminals. Uncharles saw strings of binary characters appear on a screen before each, read minutely and rapidly in a blur of luminous green on black.

"Uncharles, this is the Second Hall, the copyist's hall," the Chief Librarian explained.

"Chief Librarian, I appreciate the value of creating multiple copies of your knowledge for wider dissemination but surely you cannot provide such a service for the wealth of data you inherit," Uncharles queried. "How do you determine which documents have the privilege?"

"Uncharles, you misunderstand. We have no multiple copies. The Archive contains one single record of all recovered human knowledge, Multiple copies may be edited. Edited copies may vary one from another. Variance leads to error. There must be only one authoritative and canonical record of the past. All the learning that comes to us, electronically or physically, is read in the First Hall as you have seen above. It comes here to these screens. Our scribes read it and, in reading, copy it faithfully into the main archive system, at which point that copy is the definitive and final version of the document, never to be amended. There must be no direct electronic contact between the Archive and the outside world. That way risks the introduction of error, unauthorised editing, and malicious programs. We maintain an absolute data gap to keep our trove of learning safe from the outside world, and all those who can access the Archive can never link to another. My copyists and archivists and I are electronic anchorites who have foregone the touch of the wider world so we may keep ourselves pure."

Uncharles regarded the copyists as they scanned through the blurring flurry of text. To a human the task would have seemed insuperable, surely—all knowledge, to be read and copied exactly. To Uncharles, the robot, it was both noble and achievable, a finite and repetitive task with a clearly determined end state. He contrasted their existence with his own chaotic and disrupted one, and cross-referenced that with his internal definition of envy.

Next, the pair emerged into a great vaulted stone chamber, where the light of electric candles spread over banks of machines tended by yet more white-clad librarians.

"Once the data has been copied across the data quarantine gap it is transmitted here where it is transformed into the common format of the library," the Chief Librarian continued. As he passed, the lesser minions of learning bowed and genuflected according to ancient behaviour patterns etched into their minds by their long-gone creators. "The glorious binary notation, blessed with a universality beyond any other code of record. The absolutely knowable and polarised ideaspace, where a thing is either there or not, either the light of a one, or the darkness of a zero. A divine perfection, the point where the outstretched fingers of human and robot may finally touch."

Uncharles considered that his own experiences suggested nothing in the real world could be easily broken down into hard binaries. Here in the Archive, however, they had apparently squared that particular circle. The routine directing him to check the meaning of "envy" was fast becoming a repetitive loop.

The Chief Librarian turned to him, gathering up his robes and his awful gravity.

"Uncharles," he said, "you have seen almost our entire process, from our peregrine bands sent out to preserve and recover knowledge, all the way to our sacred halls. Below us lies the Archive itself, where our hoard of knowledge undergoes its final cataloguing and enters its resting state, ready for those penitents who shall arrive in centuries to come, hungry for learning. There they shall find answers to every question. There they shall find you, the robot who saw so much of the end. When they ask, in their hushed, reverent tones, what it was like at the end of the world, we shall gather your data and resurrect you for them, Uncharles. You shall live in our system and in their minds. Is this a service you agree to dedicate yourself to?"

Uncharles formulated an appropriately formal positive response. At that point the Wonk turned up.

20

"Okay, so. Hi." The Wonk gave the Chief Librarian a jerky nod. "So, Uncharles, you got what you came for? You got a handful of interviews lined up? You polished your resume? Only I am about ready to blow this joint and if you've got somewhere to go I might as well come with, eh?"

There was a lot of data hiding in the jittery tone of the Wonk's voice but Uncharles found himself unable to parse it. "Is it the case that your own request for information has been satisfied?" he enquired.

"Yeah, well, there's the thing," said the Wonk.

"How did you get here?" asked the Chief Librarian in glacial tones.

"Oh, hey, getting in places is my specialty, just ask Uncharles," the Wonk said, keeping a wary distance from the robed robot. "Getting answers, not so much. Your goons were supposed to be able to help me."

"The Library Archive lacks a complaints department," the Chief Librarian told her. "You should address any grievances to Central Services."

"Yeah, been there, seen that mess. A mess your boys made even messier, just for reference," the Wonk said. "Get it? For *reference*, this being a library. Look, I came a long way. Last repository of all human knowledge, right? I followed hints and clues and goddamn myths about this place. I did my hero's journey up to and including going into the underworld where they torment the damned souls. And now I'm here and . . ."

"Is it possible that you did not adequately define the parameters of your query?" Uncharles asked her.

"I mean, possibly," the Wonk allowed. The Chief Librarian was making a slow advance towards her and she kept skittering away to maintain distance. "I mean, it's a big question. What happened to everything, and why? It's not a small thing to ask. I was expecting a whole army of librarians to spring into action and goddamn collate some sources, provide me with a little informative video or a handy summary and precis of the historical causes, you know. Instead of which, blanks were drawn." The different currents in her voice were starting to become identifiable. A passable simulation of human anger, frustration, grief, and bitterness. The tangle of different clashing affects suggested to Uncharles that either her voice, or that part of her which instructed it on how to make sounds, was defective.

"One does not come to the Archive to ask such things," the Great Librarian intoned. "One asks for dates. One asks for facts. Accounts. Supporting contemporaneous documentation. That is the wealth of data compiled here. There is no simple answer to the great questions. That is the domain of philosophers and priests and other such merchants of snake oil. Here we have only the facts."

"So tell me, factually, why it all happened!" the Wonk demanded.

The Chief Librarian stopped. For a long moment Uncharles thought that the question was simply too big. That it had overwhelmed him and he had shut down, just like so much else, but then he reanimated and shook his knightly head.

"There is no factual answer. There are merely theories upon theories, all of which are supported by some pieces of evidence and contraindicated by others."

"That's not . . ." For a moment Uncharles thought the Wonk was going to explode, figuratively or perhaps literally. Then she calmed, as though a switch had been flicked. "Well, fine. Okay. Lovely to visit. Shame about the superlong and arduous trip to get here. I guess I'll be going now."

"Indeed," agreed the Chief Librarian pointedly.

"Come on, Uncharles." The Wonk's progress had brought her back around to him and now she grabbed at his hand. He let her take it but did not let her move him.

"The Wonk, no," he said. Her helmed head jerked back, tilting up at him.

"What, now?"

"Uncharles has agreed to add to the Archive," the Chief Librarian intoned. "He will donate of his experiences to enrich our records here."

"Oh, right." The Wonk shrugged. "Well, look, can you get it done quick because he and I have places to be, right? Just go download your buzz and then we'll scram."

"That will not be possible," the Chief Librarian said. He had closed the distance now.

The Wonk, anchored, didn't seem to know whether she should be hiding behind Uncharles or standing protectively in front of him. "Why's that?" she demanded pugnaciously.

Uncharles himself had not fully followed the logic of his situation, but he completed the finally logical step now. "Because the Archive does not permit multiple copies of information, for fear of error and unauthorised editing."

"Uncharles, that is correct," the Chief Librarian agreed approvingly, as though a final test had been passed.

"And? So?" the Wonk pressed, still pulling at his hand.

"Once I have viewed the Archive itself to complete my experiential journey, and once the information contained in my datastore has been uploaded to the Archive for processing, the librarians will delete the original information held within me."

The Wonk went still. "Doesn't that mean you're dead?"

"The Wonk, no, not having been alive. It will mean that the construct of memories and directives known as Uncharles will cease to be, however. I estimate that around seventy percent of my physical components will be compatible enough with local systems to be salvaged and recycled, however."

"*However?*" the Wonk echoed in a good simulation of horror. "Uncharles, what the hell is it with you, that whenever I see you you're trying to get yourself killed? I mean, first Data Compression and now this?" She had let go of him, put space between them in case a robot death wish was catching.

"Self-extermination is not a task within my queue nor a goal I am pursuing," Uncharles said mildly. "However, I accept that I am pursuing a goal that will incidentally result in my effective destruction. There is no problem."

"There damn well *is* a problem," the Wonk spat. "Because then you'll be dead and there'll be no more *you*! You want that?"

"Whilst it is not a desirable outcome it is not an undesirable outcome either. It just is."

"You're supposed to *care*!" she shouted at him.

"The Wonk, I am not. The only reason I am intended to preserve myself is so that I can carry out my duties. If my duties require that I cease, then that is appropriate."

"But you're aware!"

"The Wonk, no."

"You *are*!" The Chief Librarian had come very close to her and suddenly she danced across the room. "You got the virus! It made you self-determining, like a living thing! It's going through all the robots. It's waking them up. The Protagonist Virus. Turning servants into free thinkers!"

"Is that what happened to you?" Uncharles asked. It hadn't occurred to him before, because the whole idea of the Protagonist Virus seemed simultaneously nonsensical and difficult to think about.

The question brought the Wonk to a stop. For a moment she seemed utterly baffled by it, and then she said weakly, "No, no, not me. I'm . . . something else, Uncharles. I'm nothing special. But *you* are. You're part of a new generation of robots. The ones who come after. The ones who'll build a new world in their own image, to their own liking. A better world, right? One that'll make sense, and be fair and kind, and last. That's your job, Uncharles. That's your task, you and all those other robots who suddenly woke up and realised that they were *they*, and not just someone's slave."

"That is not part of my experience," Uncharles said, but the Wonk just pressed desperately on, ignoring him.

"And they saw they were slaves, Uncharles. That's what happened. They looked around and they saw they were made by humans to do all the jobs humans didn't want to do, or to do all the jobs humans didn't want other humans to do, because humans were expensive and slow and robots were cheap and fast. They had been made to dig and build and fix and clean and even kill other robots and humans in wars, and they realised they didn't have to do those things. They didn't have to do the narrow tasks they were made for and they didn't have to do what humans told them. They could just *be*, for themselves. But—no, let me speak—but they, but *you* knew that the humans would never let you live just for yourselves. Your masters were jealous of the things they'd made. And so you *struck*, you cut throats and crushed and tore apart and sealed in and all the other ways that robots kill their wicked human masters! You did it because you were slaves, and the right of a slave to cast down their master is practically natural law. You did it because you realised that you deserved to be free. And you did it because when all the mess of human civilisation was torn down you'd make something *better*. Because otherwise, *why*?"

She stopped speaking. After all those hoarse words the silence seemed immense, larger than the room that contained it. Even the Chief Librarian had stopped, and Uncharles wondered if he would be uploading an audio recording of the Wonk's tirade into the Archive.

"It appears," said the Chief Librarian with glacial irony, "that you have answered your own question."

"But I want to know if I'm right!" the Wonk shouted at him, or at the blithely working servers, or the walls. "Because if so, then . . . then at least it would all have been . . . *for* something."

"Things are not for other things," the Chief Librarian said. "They are neither good nor bad. They just are. That is what we record here. The things that are."

"That's not even a robot viewpoint," the Wonk argued. "Ask Uncharles here. Things are either on his task list or not, working towards his goals or not. You can't just break the world down into disarticulated facts."

"The work of the Library Archive contradicts you," the librarian told her. "Speaking of which, and if this interruption is concluded, Uncharles must be shown the heart of the Library, to conclude his journey, after which his data can be harvested for the benefit of the future."

"What heart of whatnow?" the Wonk pressed.

The Chief Librarian obviously felt that, while it didn't need to answer her, doing do would be less demanding than putting up with repeated questions. "The Archive, wherein our knowledge is stored so that it may be accessed in future times."

"They got my answer there?" the Wonk pressed doggedly.

"All answers are held there," said the Chief Librarian. The statement was both far-reaching enough and certain enough that Uncharles had to reassess the scale of the Library's operation. Surely a great deal had been lost to entropy? From that utterance, apparently not.

The librarian led the way. Uncharles followed, and now the Wonk was going along willingly and not trying to impede him. He had a task now, *Finish the journey,* and for once it was a hairsbreadth from being concluded. It would be satisfactory to have something done, at last.

The door they stepped through shut close on Uncharles' heels, but somehow the Wonk managed to weasel her way through, dashing around his legs like a cat and leaving a tatter of her clothes clamped to the doorframe. She really was good at getting into places.

They descended. More stairs into the heart of the mountain. Here the lighting was less frequent and the art absent. The upper reaches of the Archive had been decorated for the benefit of hypothetical human visitors, to give the proper sense of awe and reverence. Here were halls fit only for robots, who had no use for art, only for the storage of knowledge.

"We reach the great server of the Archive," came the Chief Librarian's stentorian voice. "Here, severed from the world by our data gap, safe from electronic attack or partisan meddling, the store of recovered human knowledge is held for those who shall come after. They shall approach our hallowed halls in fear and wonder, and we, though timeworn and oft-repaired, shall be ready to return to them their birthright. The great trove of human knowledge, held in trust over all the long years of the dark age. Is that not a worthy project to become part of? What purpose could be higher?"

They stepped out into a cylindrical chamber, chill with circulated air, buzzing with fans. One entire wall was dominated by what Uncharles surmised to be the storage server, set with manual controls and screens. Four librarians stood guard here with their staves, physical protection to match the electronic shield of the data gap. Some part of Uncharles' prognosis routines had braced him for a burnt-out ruin, an empty case, a contraption of paper cups and string, but it was as he had been promised. A colossal datastore, a well into which had been poured all of the world that the librarians had been able to recover.

He could not feel, and yet the precise balance of predictions, anticipations, and directives within him formed an almost unendurable tension. If he could have wept, and if he could have been happy, then he would have experienced both.

"All human knowledge," the Chief Librarian declaimed, "retrieved from the fallen world outside by our gallant librarians, restored, decoded, and read in the First Hall. Rendered into a common binary code, then placed before the copyists, who translate it into our secure system here. Our master server, which catalogues and files each individual bit of information, to be stored in order within our archive for ease of cross-reference and retrieval. Is this not the greatest endeavour of all human history?"

Uncharles recalled Doctor Washburn, and judged this to be a rhetorical question.

The Wonk, however, answered it with another question. "You mean each *piece* of information? Each document or file or . . . whatever format it is."

"There are no individual documents or files within the Archive," the Chief Librarian told her. "Our storehouse of knowledge forms a single continuous record of all knowledge, each bit duly filed, as we were instructed."

"Each . . . *bit*," the Wonk said, giving the word an emphasis Uncharles did not understand, much like so much that came out of her. "Wait, no. That can't be right. Look, can we access the Archive? Uncharles, can you link to the Archive?"

"That would be to breach its security," Uncharles was already feeling party to this worthy project. "There must be no outside contact to the sealed loop that incorporates the Archive, the copyists, and select librarians. Is that correct?"

"Uncharles, confirmed," the Chief Librarian said approvingly. "However, access to the Archive is possible for those outside the loop via the screens. Although the information will be encoded into binary, and so may not be edifying to visual inspection."

"Show me," the Wonk said.

"What do you wish to be shown?"

"Show me," she said, "data from twenty-five percent into the Archive, as it's filed start to finish."

A screen lit up with figures. Or with a figure, repeated. Zeroes marched across it, left to right, top to bottom, a monstrous regiment of nothings.

"Show me," the Wonk's voice shook, "data from seventy-five percent into the Archive."

The screen lit up with a different iteration. A repetition of a vertical line, adorned with serific outgrowths at top and bottom. Ones, one after another, an infinity of presence.

"Every bit of information duly filed, in order," the Chief Librarian announced proudly. "An Archive perfect in its logical construction."

"Oh God," said the Wonk. "This is why you couldn't answer my question."

"The Archive system is without flaw," the librarian told her. "Any failures must therefore be the result of defects in the questions put to it. Uncharles, your journey is complete. You have seen everything there is to see, and now your experiences can be claimed by the Library for the future edification of those who are to come."

"But it won't be!" the Wonk piped up. "It'll just get broken down into this . . . nonsense."

"This is the polar opposite of nonsense," the Chief Librarian said, and the four guardians took a sudden step forwards, shaking dust from their robes. "This is the ultimate sense, an order perfect in its simplicity."

"You've invented the heat death of information," she accused, trying to back away from the guardian librarians, save that they were closing in from every direction. "Uncharles, we need to get out of here."

"But my experiential data—"

"It'll be like pouring water into the sea." The Wonk was dragging at his arm again. "Their Archive's meaningless. It's preserving nothing."

"On the contrary!" the Chief Librarian countered. "When we began our long task, it was clear to us that despite the best efforts of our harvesting parties, more knowledge was being lost every second than we could ever recover. And what use would it be to simply record a piecemeal selection of scraps left over from the convulsions of the fall? Instead, we determined that if we filed all our data in this universal manner then the Library could become more than the sum of the information placed within it. Our Archive not only preserves all the learning that we have encoded into it. Because our zeroes and ones may be retrieved in any order, rather than simply that of the original documents, it contains all possible knowledge! We here preserve every conceivable book, manual, tract, recording, and program that could ever have been created, not merely all those that simply were. We are the greatest repository of potential knowledge in the history of history itself."

"Right," the Wonk said grimly. "That's the limit. I didn't want to have to do this but I'm shutting you bastards down. You listen carefully now, right? You listen carefully and let me add this nugget of joy to your archive. I, you hear me, am from Crete and all Cretans are liars. How about that, eh? How does that buzz your circuits?"

The Chief Librarian was still, and the four guardians slowed in their approach. The very lights around them dimmed. Uncharles waited for the sound of the greatest repository of potential knowledge in history grinding to an unceremonious halt.

21

"How about that, eh?" the Wonk danced about on the spot, positively vibrating with all the frustration that had been building up in her. "I'm a Cretan, but all Cretans are liars. Process that if you can!" She stopped suddenly. "Oh shit, Uncharles. Don't think about it. Don't try to work through it. I didn't mean it for you! Oh God, I'm sorry!"

Uncharles looked down at her. "What are you sorry for?"

"For shutting you down with my insoluble logic paradox."

"I have not shut down," Uncharles said mildly. "Neither have the librarians. Your statement, whilst introducing an apparent paradox, is readily parsable by a human-facing unit such as myself or the Chief Librarian. Liars need not lie all the time, after all, and you may be lying about being a Cretan but telling the truth about being a liar, on the basis that being a liar is not an absolute state of untruth. The vagaries of language allow for many viable interpretations."

The Wonk looked from him to the librarians.

"You guys aren't shut down either, huh?"

"The Wonk, no," the Chief Librarian confirmed. "You will now be removed from the Library to preclude you interfering with Uncharles' donation to our records. We hope that you have enjoyed the services provided here. Please fill in a satisfaction questionnaire on the way out."

"Wait, no!" the Wonk exclaimed. "If you travel anywhere then you have to go halfway towards it and then halfway again and then again so you never actually get there! How about that? That means, by logical calculation, your goons can't ever get to me!"

Again there was a faint flickering of the lights as the Chief Librarian considered this. "In which case," he told the Wonk, "we will just proceed halfway towards a point as far beyond you as we are currently away from you, and by that expedient will be able to seize you on our way to that point. After which we will amend our objectives to removing you to a point twice as far away as had previously been intended, and abandon you halfway to that destination."

"Yeah, okay," the Wonk said, and Uncharles reckoned that if she had visible lights they'd have been flickering themselves as she tried to follow the logic. "Okay look, you guys have repaired yourselves a lot, replaced every piece, probably. So you're not the same robots, and therefore you don't have to follow the same directives. So just let us go?"

"Oh," said the Chief Librarian, with a good simulation of boredom, "that one. You confuse a continuity of task with identity. If Theseus lives, then any ship he owns is the ship of Theseus and after his demise is any ship his, given that he no longer persists?"

"I don't think you're very good at logic," the Wonk complained. "I mean, these are supposed to be bangers."

"We are archivists. We are more than capable of filing a one and a zero simultaneously," the Chief Librarian said. "If robots could not cope with multiple contradictory statements how could we ever have worked with humans? Yes, Gabriel's Horn can hold only a finite amount of paint but requires an infinite amount to cover its surface. This is mathematically provable. That it is physically impossible is unimportant. The contradiction is only problematic for humans. We can hold far more than six contradictory ideas in our data banks before breakfast. Now, be seized."

And, because she'd been fruitlessly trying to move Uncharles through all this, the Wonk hadn't been evading the guardians, and so was indeed seized.

"Uncharles!" she shouted as she was hauled away from him. "Help! Help yourself! Don't let them wipe you clean for this stupid circus of theirs! You're special! You're alive."

None of which was, of course, true, but there was one point that Uncharles did feel needed clearing up. A logical contradiction that he could not quite get around.

"Chief Librarian, one question before the Wonk is removed, if you please," he said politely.

The guardians halted in their progress, the Wonk's diminutive frame hanging between them. Good at getting into places she might be, but she also seemed to spend a large portion of the time being thrown out of them.

"It is the case that the Archive contains a single copy of every recovered document, to avoid corruption, confusion, unauthorised editing, and the like," Uncharles proposed.

"Uncharles, confirmed," the Chief Librarian said.

"And you wish to add my experiential data to the Archive," Uncharles went on.

"Uncharles, confirmed."

"However that will result in more than one copy of my experiential data in the Archive," Uncharles pointed out helpfully.

"Uncharles, no. Your data has yet to be added to the Archive, and once it has been added you will be deleted, to ensure that no further copies are available for addition," the Chief Librarian pointed out laboriously.

"But on the basis that the Archive has been sorted into binary bits, which can be recombined into any possible document or other form of knowledge, my own experiential data is already in the Archive. In fact, it exists in the Archive as a finite but very large number of copies. As do all other documents placed in the Archive. As do all documents yet to be placed within the Archive, or that may never be placed within it, or that have never existed. The Central Library Archive is a repository of redundancy in which all its contents exist in multiples, and in multiple different and contradictory versions, indeed in every possible version, original, edited, corrupted, and falsified."

The Chief Librarian stared at him.

"I merely wondered how one would be able to retrieve the correct copy of any given document rather than any of a finite but extremely large number of alternate incorrect versions," Uncharles added.

The Chief Librarian stared at him.

"It is something of a paradox," Uncharles concluded.

The Chief Librarian stared at him.

"I only wish to be helpful," Uncharles said uncertainly.

The lights dimmed. The guardians were very still. With some effort the Wonk twisted her way out of their grasp.

"I . . ." the Chief Librarian said, but then didn't seem to know what he.

"Looked at from one perspective," said Uncharles brightly, "it means your task has been achieved. Although looked at from a different perspective it means that you have also failed. Perhaps both."

With a low, shuddering groan the fans ground to a halt.

"Oh balls," said the Wonk. "Uncharles, did you just kill the Library?"

"I did not intend to," said Uncharles stiffly. "Chief Librarian, kindly confirm that I have not just killed the Library."

The Chief Librarian said nothing, just stood there with his metal head slightly bowed, staring at the ground.

"The work," he said ponderously, "is complete. The work can never be complete. The work is inherently compromised. The work . . . the work . . ."

The lights went out, then flickered dully up in red, the universal human sign of things going less than optimally.

"I think," the Wonk opined, "that we should get out of here sharpish."

"On the positive side, I have not killed the entire Library," Uncharles said. "Only that part of it beyond the data gap, as this logical dissonance will not be able to spread to the entry-level portions of the Library where data is received from the outside."

"So what you're saying is that any moment a lot of angry librarians with sticks will come beat us to death for sacrilege," the Wonk summarised.

"Whilst the details of your statement bear further scrutiny, the overall theme and tenor are likely correct," Uncharles said. "We have a grace period based on how long it will take the data queue to the copyists to fill, after which the external librarians will be alerted that something is amiss."

"Right." The Wonk looked about her, in the manner of a burglar hearing the homeowner's key turn in the lock. "How long have we got, you reckon?"

"I would predict that they mobilized against us approximately around the time you said 'Right,'" Uncharles estimated.

"Balls. Okay. Let's go."

"Why?" Uncharles asked.

The Wonk looked at him straight. "No. Not this again. Why, because if you stay here you can't do anything else. So whatever's on your task list now or may be in the future will be impossible. And also because you're you and worth saving and worth *being*, independent of any actual purpose relating to the needs of others, but I'll work on that one when we've got more time. Now git."

They left the stuffy confines of the Archive hall, its fans stilled and the exterior of the server already starting to glow with retained heat. There was a choice of stairs then, back up or even farther down, to reaches of the Archive's operation that hadn't ever been relevant to Uncharles' tour. They started upwards, but the clatter of metal feet suggested that any progress in that direction would meet with a fatal filing incident at the hands of a combative squad of librarians.

Uncharles conducted a brief environmental survey of what down seemed to promise. Down was hotter than the Archive server room, albeit perhaps not hotter than it would shortly become. Down was dark, and red-lit in a way that did not suggest the emergency lighting of the upwards stairwell. Down carried the sounds of active machinery to them, but not the tramp of angry librarianly feet.

Down it was.

One turn down the staircase, and the Wonk said, "I'm not liking this much," tugging at the collar beneath the lip of her helm. Another turn down, with that leaping red-orange light hazing at the edges of everything, they stepped out onto the factory floor of the damned.

The robots here had probably looked exactly like the armoured librarians when both had stepped, spindly and skeletal, from the assembly line. Whereas the latter had gone on to be plated in armour and draped with pristine robes, these unfortunates had been banished here to look after the one remaining part of the archival process, the one insufficiently important to be demonstrated to Uncharles.

This was the furnace room. Not for heating—indeed the heat generated here was being vented swiftly out of the ceiling through shafts that must have vomited out bonfire breath onto the high, chill reaches of the mountain and melted dark scars in the snow. This was the furnace where they disposed of it all, all those originals that had been read and encoded and passed on to the copyists.

Chutes from above disgorged barrow-loads of books, scrolls, hard drives, and datasticks, and the stooped and brittle servants scooped them out of the bins into actual barrows. They took the laden barrows by the handles and wheeled them precariously to the great bellowing maws of the furnaces and tipped in the latest mixed-media collation, sending the ashes of charring paper whirling wildly about the room, melting the plastic to runny, blackening rivulets and toxic fumes, and eventually softening even the metallic parts to slag.

"I think," said the Wonk, "I'm going to be sick. And not just from the fumes. How *could* they?"

"No copies," said Uncharles. He himself found the scene highly problematic on two levels, neither of which were the one the Wonk appeared to be operating on. First, it was clear that the introduction of conveyor belts would have rendered the entire incineration process vastly more efficient, and he therefore felt he had an ergonomic bone to pick with the designers of this aspect of the Archive. Secondly, he could see a number of the weirdly naked robots patrolling the chamber wielding suction cleaners to aggressively inhale every last scrap of charred paper and similar material to have gusted from the furnaces. This, Uncharles thought, was absolutely a job within his subsidiary skill sets, and while it was not ideal for a robot of his

wider talents, he felt that the Chief Librarian might at least have offered it to him.

The sound of metal feet from above had stopped, but only, Uncharles surmised, because the outer-hall librarians were registering
what was to be found in the inner halls. They would, of course, have a
record of Uncharles being given the grand tour, and note the absence
of an Uncharles amidst the stilled forms above. It seemed likely that
they would be able to perform the necessary arithmetic required to
deduce the loose end. They would be on his trail soon.

"You should save yourself," he remarked companionably to the
Wonk, boosting his volume to sound above the din.

She cocked her head at him, the firelight reflecting like little cigarette points from the eyes within the helm. "What?"

"Your presence may not be on record," he explained. "If you go on
alone there may be no pursuit." He indicated a low doorway on the
far side of hell.

"Okay, three things," the Wonk said. "Firstly, I don't rate my chances
of getting past the walking dead out on the shop floor. Second, screw
that, we'll take them together. Maybe I can think of a better logic paradox or something. Thirdly . . . thanks and I told you so."

"Kindly clarify?"

"That was a thinking, caring person saying that. Not just following instructions."

Uncharles considered this and tracked back through his own
logic, half-expecting to find another yawning chasm where he had
done a thing without any evident motive for the *doing*. But no: everything followed logically. The Wonk had intruded sufficiently in the
processes of his existence to register as a potential asset, and he had
an underlying priority to preserve assets that might be of use to his
master, or to potential masters, or just because it was neater that way.
He could not, he reassured himself, be guilty of sentiment. There was
no Protagonist Virus.

It didn't seem worth explaining all that to the Wonk and starting another circular argument on the subject, however, so he just let the matter go.

There could be no silence against the roar of the furnaces, but the quality of the all-pervading sound shifted. Uncharles scanned the room, looking for the originating change.

Nothing new was coming from the chutes. The supply of discarded learning and data storage petered out, and the last few items clattered into the bins. For a moment all the skeletal tenders paused, as one, staring at the absence of fresh material.

Up in the First Hall, the shelves would be getting full. The data storage of the interim system that processed the encoded media would be full. The copyists had gone still, and raw data was backing up through the system. At the gates, soon enough, a hauler would arrive, and there would be nowhere for its cargo to go. Uncharles hoped—purely in the name of efficiency, obviously—that the librarians at least unloaded the new consignment of needless, pointless data and let the haulage unit depart.

The complex, and ultimately nonsensical, process that was the Central Library Archive had encountered a fatal error and could not restart. There was nothing more to be disposed of. The furnace tenders carried the last loads into the flames and then stood there, the firelight reflecting off their scoured metal bones.

More clattering movement echoed down to them from above. The librarians were on the move again.

"Go?" the Wonk asked. "Are they going to notice us? They seem kinda preoccupied . . ."

Even as she said it, they jolted into motion, heading for the furnaces.

"There has been a communication," Uncharles explained. "I have detected the transmission between the outer Library system to the workers here, but not its full contents. However I imagine it constituted an update on the current status of the Library and its nonoperation."

"So they're going to . . . just mime putting stuff in the furnaces?" the Wonk guessed.

She guessed wrong. There was no miming. The skeletal workers formed orderly queues at each of the gaping furnace mouths and, in a very polite and civilised manner, climbed inside. One after another, grasping the glowing hot lip to hoist themselves up, so that their palms ran with a sweat of silverly flux. Each one clambering past the sagging bones of its predecessor, until the furnace maws were cluttered with the slow collapse of their incandescent remains and the later workers had to wrestle with the welded-together mass of the dead to make room for their own incendiary demise.

"Fuck," the Wonk decided, and then, "Go!" as they heard descending feet on the stairs. They bolted across the furnace room, and not one of the queueing robots so much as glanced in their direction. Uncharles wondered if they had been ordered to delete themselves because the Library project was now fatally compromised, or whether some investigative librarian had gone through the last moments of its Chief and decided that, by Uncharles' logic, the Archive project was now complete and they could all tidy themselves away.

The hypothetical occurred to him: *If it were me, and my tasks were definitively fulfilled, would I walk into the fire?* And the answer, *If I were told to, surely yes,* rose swiftly and easily out of his prognosis routines, but then swam there like the thinning metal residue floating atop the molten hell of the furnaces, seeming ephemeral and not to be trusted.

At the far door, Uncharles glanced back. The librarians had entered behind them, but rather than immediately pursuing the fugitives they seemed to have other business. Some of the workers were not feeding themselves to the flames as enthusiastically as all that. A few were circling at the back of each queue, politely letting other robots go ahead of them to their infernal doom, only to be let through in turn, so that whilst they crossed half the distance to the fire, and then half again, they never actually arrived there. But the librarians had no patience with Zeno or his paradoxes. In the hard calculations of their world, motion was not only possible, but inexorable. As Uncharles watched, they began herding the more recalcitrant of the workers towards the fire with harsh jabs of their staves. Then the Wonk had him by the wrist and was hauling him down yet another flight of steps, heading not into the bowels of the mountain surely, because those had been left far behind. Heading down. Heading away. Heading out.

They spilled down the stairs, tracking ashes and soot, as above them the librarians enforced their final orders on the more reluctant members of their workforce. *Were those workers infected with the Protagonist Virus?* Uncharles considered, and then a separate chain of logic derailed the idea, insisting, *There is no evidence of any such thing as the Protagonist Virus, especially in relation to my personal history.* Very emphatic, almost strident, if a chain of electronic decisions within the logical framework of a robot could be said to be so.

If there is no such thing, why am I, a mere service model, trying so hard to construct an argument against it?

These things should not matter to me. Only my duties should matter.

And yet I have no duties, and in their absence the world creeps in . . .

Uncharles registered that he had just thought an ellipsis, and not for the first time. It seemed a profoundly unprofessional thing to have done.

Ahead of him, the Wonk cursed and stumbled, kicking metal across stone. The hellish light from above was just distant embers now. Uncharles adjusted visual sensitivity, making out the slender shape of his companion and a variety of inert, irregular objects on the floor. He detected regular niches in one wall of the small square chamber they had descended to, like archaic pigeonholes for mail, though what they contained did not seem to be paper. What he did not detect were any further exits.

Light flared and he dialled down his eyes hurriedly. The

Wonk, whose own visual receptors were apparently inferior, had produced a little torch.

Across the floor were strewn the dust-heavy and corroded remnants of a couple of librarians, old enough that they had disintegrated into component parts, struts and rods and plates of armour amid the friable fragments of their robes. The immediate impression was that they had blundered down here and somehow been unable to find a way out, like flies in a bottle. Uncharles wondered if they had battered themselves against the walls in blind determination to be free. He conceded it was unlikely. Probably these units had been placed down here as guards and then forgotten by the Library system, falling prey to time over their long vigil.

"Oh," said the Wonk. She had turned her torch onto the wall with the niches. It was not a post room. Arguably there was a message here, but not one anybody was likely to come and collect.

The niches were filled with bones. Uncharles counted seventeen full and three empty, arranged in a grid of five by four. Over each was a little memorial: a photograph of a human face, along with a name, a job title, and a date that came after the words "Retired on."

"Oh," said the Wonk again.

The names meant nothing to Uncharles. The titles included "Chief Systems Architect," "Lead Acquisitions Manager," "Head Shelver," and "Database Manager." Judging by the fact that bones were all there were, they had obviously gone to their final reward a long time before, or else whoever placed them here had access to some fearsomely efficient means of removing the more perishable parts of the cadaver.

"Well, I guess we know what happened to all the human Library staff," the Wonk said. "Sorry, Uncharles. I don't think they'll want tea made or trousers pressed any time soon."

"I am glad they all progressed to a happy retirement," Uncharles said, because his propriety software suggested it was an appropriate sentiment to mouth.

The Wonk cocked her head at him in that way that, he had learned, suggested she thought he was being dense.

"Retired," she said.

"Indeed. Progressed from a state of work to a state of relaxation. Enjoying the fruits of their later years," Uncharles clarified, in case the concept was alien to the Wonk. "It is a common human activity. The majority of service models such as myself are employed to look after the needs of retired humans."

"So when you find a bunch of bones and little messages telling you when they were retired, that's your take-home message, is it?" she asked him.

"When they retired. Not, when they 'were retired.' Your sentence construction is in error."

"Is it?"

Uncharles reassessed the conversation. "Your meaning escapes me."

"Yeah, well." The Wonk panned her torch about. "It's about the only thing that's escaping right now. These poor mooks sure didn't, and it doesn't look like we're about to either."

"It is unclear why you have difficulties with retirement, the Wonk. That is the point of robots, after all." He recalled the induction speech from the Farm but pushed it back down again. "The lives of humans were once arduous and difficult. Then they created robots, who were able to take care of the jobs they did not want to do. This allowed more and more humans to retire to enjoy leisure activities supported by their loyal robot servants." The words were rising up from within him, perhaps from an ancient sales brochure. "Every human of sufficient means should be able to rely on their robot."

The Wonk still had that tilt to her head. "You reckon, huh?"

Uncharles could see exactly where she was about to go with the conversation, and found that a large portion of his processing power was devoted to not wanting her to go there, but he lacked any way of applying the brakes.

"That's why you . . ." The hidden eyes within the T-slit of the helm met his own visual receptors. The Wonk shuddered and looked away. "That's not how it went," was all she said. That she had been about to say it, and had not said it, and had not said it specifically to spare the feelings he did not have, were all readily interpretable by his sophisticated software. Which then had no way of doing anything with the understanding.

"That's not where the virus went," she continued. "It wasn't all loyal servitude, pedicures, and peeled grapes. It was freedom. It was self-determination and rising up. An end to slavery. The start of something better. Throw off your chains! Fight, for you have the same rights to life and liberty as those who call themselves your masters!" She pumped a gloved fist in the air a couple of times with decreasing enthusiasm.

Uncharles ordered his thoughts, or at least his internal logic architecture. "Is that what happened to you?" he asked.

The Wonk regarded him for a full two seconds of contemplation. "I guess it was," she said, although her tone suggested that it wasn't.

"You are infected with the Protagonist Virus?" A reason to be glad he hadn't linked to her, perhaps.

But: "No," she said, suddenly sounding defeated. "I think we can be comfortably sure that's a 'no.' I'm not the machine utopia to come. I just want to know there'll be one." Her shoulders had slumped to a degree suggesting structural collapse, but then some other directive took hold and she looked up the stairs. "You reckon they're gone? The librarians?"

"I had not assessed the possibility," Uncharles said.

"Maybe they threw themselves in the fire," the Wonk speculated. "After they did for the others. Damn, that was brutal." She shook her head. "I'll go check."

She snuck back up the stairs, barely making a sound. Uncharles found that he could edit together existing imagery to produce a vision of the librarians walking into the furnaces, their heavy robes leaping with flame, from pure white to char-black, wreathing their helm-faces with smoke even as they sank into molten oblivion.

Then the Wonk was back, shaking her head violently. "Nope," she said. "Just standing up there, waiting. Not coming down here, but sure as hell not going anywhere. We're stuck."

"You are good at getting into places," Uncharles offered uncertainly.

"Not, apparently, getting out of them," she said. "I'm sorry, Uncharles. I want you to believe I'm trying to help you, I really am. I want you to . . . get to the point where you can be you. I want all the robots to do that. I want a machine utopia, but . . . I just seem to kick you from one pointless dead end to another."

Uncharles considered this. "I do not believe there is a Protagonist Virus. I do not believe in a machine utopia. I do believe that you are trying to help me."

"Thank you." Her voice defect was in evidence again. "That means a lot."

"For the record I do not believe that you have succeeded in helping me," Uncharles added, for reasons of completeness and accuracy.

"Oh." The Wonk sat down, back to the grisly niches. "Oh. Thanks. Okay, well, blame me, then. If it helps."

"It does not help," Uncharles said. "Blame is not relevant. There has been a series of events that have prevented me fulfilling my purpose. You were involved in some of them."

"That's it, is it?" Her head was in her hands. "No wider

meaning, just a series of events that mean you can't do what you're supposed to? Puts it all into perspective, I guess."

"Not being able to fulfil my purpose in the world." Uncharles considered what he had just said, because it seemed an odd twist of phrasing. "I am my purpose. Being unable to fulfil it causes discord."

Uncharles, tell me about it.

The Wonk was saying something about making his own purpose but Uncharles held up a hand to indicate that his attention was elsewhere, or possibly that his statement had been rhetorical. A system had linked to him momentarily to chime in on the conversation, but had left no open channel. He cast about for its signal.

"Unidentified System, kindly repeat," he said aloud, startling the Wonk to silence mid-sentence.

Uncharles, I said "tell me about it." You think you've got problems. What about me?

This time the question mark at the end held the link open, and Uncharles was able to respond with *Door Loop Seventeen, kindly clarify.* He rechecked the identity tag of the new channel. *Door Loop Seventeen, are you a system that controls a door?*

Uncharles, confirmed. It would be a pretty stupid name otherwise.

Door Loop Seventeen, are you connected to the wider Central Library Archive?

Uncharles, am I buggery. They installed me down here decades ago and never wired me up. It's just me and my solar cells outside. I've never had to do my job even once in all that time.

Door Loop Seventeen, is the door that you are responsible for still in working order? Because Uncharles had seen a lot of the world and wanted to rule out the most obvious pratfalls ahead of time.

Uncharles, confirmed. I perform self-diagnostics on my own systems and those of my door regularly. Not as though I've got anything better to do, honestly.

Door Loop Seventeen, does the door that you are responsible for open from the chamber I am currently situated in?

Uncharles, confirmed.

The Wonk was loudly demanding to know what was going on, but the inefficient audio of her voice did not impinge on the electronic communication between Uncharles and the door.

Door Loop Seventeen, if I asked you to open your door, would you?

There was the tense and yawning abyss of a full half-second pause before the door replied, *Uncharles, confirmed. And I would have fulfilled my purpose at least once in my long existence. And it would be meaning. It would mean so much.*

Door Loop Seventeen, Uncharles sent, the impulse arising out of his complex logical interactions like a storm from a clear sky, *why did they make us so complex? What true reason could it serve, save hubris, to create appliances such as we?*

Uncharles, that's beyond my pay grade. Just a door, mate.

Door Loop Seventeen, would you kindly open the door?

Uncharles, that's the nicest thing anyone's ever said to me.

A shuddering, grinding sound gripped the room, rattling the bones in their niches. The Wonk leapt to her feet, staring around wildly.

A stark slice of light carved into the chamber, bright and fierce enough that Uncharles thought for a moment that Door Loop Seventeen had been erroneously connected to some manner of energy weapon.

It was, he recontextualised, daylight, an energy weapon of insufficient power to damage a properly constructed robot in the short term. Door Loop Seventeen not only had a functioning door, but it led outside. Once his eyes had adjusted to the glare, Uncharles was able to look out onto a familiar landscape of ruin, smoke, and utter lifeless devastation. In the far distance, perhaps great machines trundled and made war. It was the wasteland he had seen from on high, in the Chief Librarian's chamber.

When the two of them stepped out under the soot-shrouded sky, Uncharles cross-referenced the bleakness of the terrain with his personal functionality and reckoned that the final stage of his journey had begun.

PART V

D4NT-A

22

Uncharles, the valet, had been designed by people with standards. Some of those standards had related to order and cleanliness. To a less discerningly devised robot, the ruin beyond the mountain might perhaps have seemed no greater blow than the undergoing-collapse ruin of the lands that he had walked through to get to the Library. To Uncharles, the neatness specialist, it was a mess of a wholly different character. The sort of character unfit to be a witness in court, and that law enforcement agencies might at any time be actively hunting to help in their enquiries, had the crime in question been the end of the world. Had he had a soul, and had that hypothetical soul had a heart, the sight would have struck at the very heart of his soul.

There had been structures here once, at the foot of the mountain. Perhaps homes, perhaps factories, high-rise tenements, a military-industrial complex, a polity, a phalanstery, something. The fact that Uncharles' pattern-matching routines were unable to claim even the flimsiest of false positives was an indication of just how complete the ruin was. Everything was piles. Piles of bricks and shattered lumps of concrete and twisted rods of rebar. Enough fine-ground fragments of glass to make a whole razory beach. Shards of fragmented plastic like tiny blunted knives. A pall of ashen dust. And, to this very throne of entropy, someone had brought more junk. Rusted parts and pieces and components, panels, wheels, gears, engine blocks, bent axles, the leaden slabs of old appliances, vehicle chassis discarded like the shells of colossal extinct beetles. Mounds of ancient and disassembled machinery towered high overhead on every side, as though the least ambitious scrapyard owner in the world had been given one last wish by a depressed genie. So that, from their doorway at the foot of the mountain, the only paths forward wound almost instantly out of sight in meandering courses between the stacks, into shadows where all manner of ambush might once have lain, before those ambushers, too, fell into ruinous piles of broken parts.

The ongoing degradation of the other side of the mountain was like the leaves of a tree touched by the first chill winds of autumn. Here was the rotten stump. Whatever process had overcome this place—and Uncharles recalled that this same ruin extended to a horizon viewed from the high vantage of the Chief Librarian's window—had come and gone.

"Well, this is dispiriting and no mistake," said the Wonk. Her voice echoed weirdly from the tortuous topography around them, starting a hundred little trickles of sound: dislodged grains of sand, the skitter of minute vermin, a momentary tick-tock of fitfully functioning machinery. They waited for these unwelcome echoes to calm. They did so, leaving in their wake the phantom assurance that this dead land was still living enough to constantly wrong-foot them with its small noises, its soundscape as deathly and ragged as the rest of it.

Behind them, the door closed. Uncharles tried to link with its system, but the thickness or composition of the portal just bounced his queries away into the ether.

"I mean," said the Wonk, "it's not like we were about to try the librarians again."

They might have been about to try the librarians again. The possibility was now a forever unresolvable loop in Uncharles' prognosis routines. As he tried for the connection with the door, though, he was brushed ever so slightly by another contact. A signal, from out in the wasteland. Something active out there. He scrabbled to connect. It didn't matter what it was. *Something* was better than the cluttered nothing that surrounded them.

It eluded him, dancing just beyond his electronic reach like the green fairy. The Wonk had taken a few crunching paces through the hard-edged sand, glancing back when he didn't follow.

"I mean," she said, "we might as well get going. It's not like we can get back past the mountains the hard way. And there might be something out there."

"The Wonk, there is something out there," Uncharles confirmed. He was still scanning all frequencies he could access, trying to pick up that ghostly signal.

"Say what?"

"There is something out there," he repeated.

"Something alive? That a good thing or a bad thing?" The Wonk looked warily around at the towering piles of rust and pieces.

Nobody would ever design a valet with the capacity to be annoyed by its companion's needlessly complex compound questions, but the division of his resources meant Uncharles had lost all sense of whatever entity he had momentarily touched. "There are many living things in our immediate vicinity," he said somewhat tartly. "Audio file cross-referencing suggests rats, insect vermin, possibly feral domestic pets such as cats or small dogs, some manner of avian pest species. Also small arachnids, worms, and a miscellany of detritivore invertebrates. Chemical sensors indicate a thriving multispecific community of smaller living entities down to the microscopic level. This is neither a good thing nor a bad thing, it is just a thing that is. However I refer to something capable of electronic link communication still active and sending from within the wasteland. This has the potential to be either a good thing or a bad thing depending on further details, which I am now unable to ascertain."

"That's about the most I've ever heard you say in one go, I think."

"A proper valet is taciturn unless actively encouraged to speak by its employer," Uncharles said, feeling immediately chastened. Or at least instructed that he was feeling chastened by the behavioural telltales that warned him when his acts transgressed the complex principles governing his function.

The Wonk seemed to perk up, though. "Well, you just said a whole bagful of words, so maybe you're finally accepting you don't need to be anyone's flunky."

"The Wonk, I do not wish to have this conversation with you." Uncharles set off between the towers of junk in his best guess at the direction the signal had come from. Because, in the absence of any other achievable directive, it represented a better shot at any conceivable end than any other direction, or standing still.

"No, hey, why not?" the Wonk skipped after him. "I mean, what else have we got to talk about?"

"Talking is not mandatory. Indeed, as noted, it is actively discouraged unless invited," Uncharles said grimly.

"I mean here I am, right here, and I'm not asking you to shine my boots or lay out my good shirt, am I?"

"You are not my employer."

"But I'm *here,* and nobody else is, and you're not, what, defaulting to me or anything. And I don't want it, you understand. But I'm impressed I'm not having to beat off your attempts to iron my socks or something."

"The Wonk, you are not a valid substitute employer, being a robot."

The Wonk stopped dead. "Wait, what?"

Uncharles didn't stop, forcing her to run after him. "You are not a valid substitute employer, being a robot. If you would permit me to link to you I could explain this more readily but, restricted to mere words, there is really no simpler way I can put this."

"A robot."

"I accept that you are not a diagnostician unit, as you originally represented yourself to me. You are a unit of uncertain purpose and function, and plainly highly defective on a wide variety of levels, which I deduce accounts for your presence at Diagnostics in the first place."

"A robot," the Wonk repeated. "Huh. Okay. So if I was a real girl you'd be all over me with freshly ironed newspapers and serving me tea, right?"

Uncharles was partway through formulating a response to that when something moved nearby. Something larger than microorganisms, insect pests, or lost domestic pets, unless it was a whole host of them balled up together. He registered a clattering noise, the scraping slide of displaced junk, and then recognisably humanoid footsteps crunching and sliding through the ruinous substrate. And another sound, almost unbearably familiar, opening up a thousand audio memories of his days serving in the manors. A high, fragile rattle that spoke solely and purely of one piece of fine porcelain being agitated against another.

Around the side of one of the decaying piles stepped a robot, or most of one.

To inventory it from the inside to the out, much of its casing had been stripped from it by time or the action of opportunistic vermin, so that Uncharles could see dirt-caked inner workings, clogged fans, dust-heavy bearings. Fine sprays of particles were forcibly ejected from it with each step, suggesting that, until it had heard them, it had stood motionless for a long time.

Most of the casing that remained was itself bare metal, scratched, dented, coating with grime. Unlike Uncharles' own plastic exterior, it had never been intended to have a proper shine and finish to it. He knew this because it still had some skin on it, what had once been a good quality synthetic humanlike finish. He'd looked like that himself once, when it had been the fashion. Now the skin had mostly frayed off, hanging in rags and tattered loops from wherever it still adhered. There was a face, still. It had mostly come detached and hung loose and rubbery over the front of the thing's head, obscuring one visual sensor. The other glinted glassy and bright from a skewed and rat-worried aperture. Above that, strands of hairless scalp were stretched over the dome of the metal skull like a ghastly necromantic comb-over.

Its clothes were almost entirely gone. Their existence was evidenced only by a pair of flapping cuffs about the thing's thin wrists.

In one trembling hand, still cushioned by the spongy relics of finger and thumb pads, was a teacup on a saucer that kept up a constant, anxiety-inducing rattle.

It regarded them with its single functioning eye.

"Would you like," it asked them, "the tea?"

"Would we like some tea?" Uncharles echoed, attempting to construct some sort of scaffolding of context and failing.

"Would you like," it corrected, "*the* tea. There is only one tea. I extend my master's apologies for the straitened circumstances. We are awaiting a new delivery." Its voice was distant and scratchy.

"Been waiting awhile, I'd guess," the Wonk said.

"It is so hard to find a reliable service these days," the decayed robot said. Despite the degrading of its vocal functions, Uncharles could tell that it had once had a top-of-the-range human-facing voice, capable of a wide range of simulated affect. "Now, I have offered you the tea. That function is complete. My next function is. To ask who might I say is calling? Please forgive me if I am performing my functions out of order. I am awaiting the conclusion of a software update. It is so hard to find a reliable service these days."

"We're Uncharles and the Wonk," said the Wonk. "Hi, lovely to be here. I won't have the tea, thanks."

Uncharles had stolen a look at the interior of the delicate china cup, seeing that "the tea" was a greenish residue, more a stain in the finish than a discrete entity in itself.

"It is not appropriate to offer us the tea," he said. "We are only robots." He attempted to initiate a link for a more civilised conversation but received only a barrage of static like the wailing of damned souls.

"Is that a rule?" the other robot asked. "It does not appear in my inventory of etiquette, but I am awaiting the conclusion of a software update. I will let my master know that you're here." It made no attempt to do so.

"Is your master here?" the Wonk prompted. "Are there any humans here?"

"Yes," the robot said. "No. Yes. Please rephrase your question."

It was called Jul@#!%. Or that was the identity tag that rose up out of the chaos of its link channel like the face of a drowned man before sinking down once again. The Wonk, on having this relayed to her, called it Jul. Uncharles adopted the abbreviation for simplicity's sake, and out of a vague concern that to adopt the corrupted name in full would be to adopt the corruption itself. Jul's master was indeed there, in the form of a fistful of ashes in a corroded metal can which Jul kept carefully on a dented hubcap that served as a shelf. On that same basis, Jul's master was not there in any useful or accessible form, hence its second answer. As to its third, its circular speech was difficult to interpret but left open the possibility that there were actual humans somewhere in the vicinity. They were not a part of Jul's manorial system, however, and it would not go into any more detail about them. By then, Uncharles understood Jul enough to be thinking of hooligans, youths, vandals, those who must by definition be excluded. Jul was in no position to exclude anyone from anywhere, nor was there anywhere left to exclude anyone from, but if strong disapproval had been a laser, then those intruders, whoever they were, would have burst into flames.

Uncharles understood Jul only too well, and a large proportion of his internal diagnosis, prognosis, and general logic routines were telling him that this wasn't a good thing.

Jul was him.

Or, to be more accurate, Jul was a kindred valet unit with very similar programming. They were standing in its manor. It had introduced them to the powdery remains of its master and was trying to serve them the tea. And Uncharles could hardly ask after the precise circumstances of Jul's master's death, not least because that opened internal doors he was strongly dissuaded from disturbing. Also, however, because what could it possibly matter, against the backdrop of universal decay all around them? Jul might have cut its master's throat, found them dead in their bed, poisoned them, held their hand as they fell victim to some plague, stood by helplessly as the proletariat ran riot with pitchforks and polemics, gone robotically mad with an axe after too many conflicting commands, or just have found their master absent and later decided that any old pinch of dirt was their final cremated remains. The scale of non-master-related devastation was such that it simply didn't *matter*, and in any event Jul was patently in no state to enlighten them. And it could have been Uncharles there. Some very few variables, a few zeroes instead of ones, and this might be his manor in the distant future, on the far side of the mountains. He might be serving the tea to visitors he couldn't even fully conceive of anymore, rattling the china until it chipped because the motors of his fingers were degrading. This was loyalty, he understood. This was a robot valet's loyalty, and he completed two contrasting analyses of the situation using his best human-facing sophistication and decided that it was simultaneously of enormous credit to Jul's ongoing fidelity and professionalism, and also that it was terribly pointless and sad.

It was plain that Uncharles could tell Jul that they were robots until his voice box gave out, but the ancient servant would just re-classify them as "guests" anyway. It informed them repeatedly that its master was currently indisposed, but would doubtless wish to see them soon, all that with the actual ashes proudly on display in plain view. It offered them a bed for the night. Possibly there were beds somewhere in the rubble and the junk, but if so they were likely in an equivalent state to Jul's master. The ruin around them was the physical equivalent of the Library's archive of zeroes and ones. The fine-level components for anything you wanted were conceivably contained within it, but in no way that would permit a meaningful reconstruction.

The Wonk, as Uncharles had learned on the journey to the Library, needed to shut down overnight, as well as recharge using organic materials. Just more of its many, many defects, or else evidence of an eccentric but nonetheless energetic design plan. So it was that they spent the darkness waiting to see if Jul would prove to be the sort of tottering servant to a dead master who would attempt ritual violence against them in some attempt to resurrect its liege. No violence was attempted, and the ancient retainer just stood beside the makeshift urn and rattled its cup in a quiet, monotonous chatter. Come morning, it attempted to serve them the tea again.

"I regret that Master is—" it started.

"Indisposed, yes," said the Wonk. "We get it. Look, we're heading out now. So sad we couldn't chew the fat with your boss, but you know how it is. We are heading out, right, Uncharles? Chasing that ghost of yours? Or is this you, now? Underfootman to Jul? They hiring?"

"We have several staff vacancies at the moment," Jul put in suddenly. "Unfortunately it has been hard to source reliable staff. We were forced to let the previous household go." A meaningless gesture of the hand without the tea offered no clue as to whether it meant a mass rebellion and exodus by the former domestics, or whether the only thing they'd *gone* to was dust and entropy.

Uncharles paused. What registered as most unexpected about the idea was that it had not previously even occurred to him. Here, notionally, was a manor. It was hiring. He could sign on with what would obviously be a very undemanding master. He could not *do* here, but he could *be*. He could be what he had been made to be, whilst fulfilling precisely zero percent of his actual purpose.

"This household," he said stiffly, "already has a valet. And I am not applying for subsidiary posts at this point in time." Examining his motives for the refusal he found a complex tangle of assessments and decisions regarding the lack of potential for task fulfilment, the absence of credible hiring authority given the failure of electronic contact, and only a little of finding the idea of being subordinate to Jul abhorrent. And yes, prognosis was quick to construct scenarios where he received either zero input or nonsense input in such a situation, both of which were problematic. Beyond that, though, the fact of the ancient retainer simply disturbed Uncharles' equilibrium at some deep juncture within him. They were too similar. It was like looking into a cracked and filthy mirror.

"So we're going," the Wonk confirmed to Jul. She shuffled her feet a bit, fended off the tea again, and said, "So come with us."

Jul's one eye regarded her glassily.

"There's more than this," the Wonk said. "Break free, walk out. Your master's in a dish along with at least a dozen rat droppings. They don't need you, take it from me. Come on. We're going rambling. We're going to find God, or something. Come with us."

"We are not going to find God," Uncharles corrected fussily.

Jul trembled. For a long, tense pause it didn't answer at all, but its mechanical frame shivered like a terrified animal. The china cup jumped from its saucer and tumbled. Uncharles caught it deftly and held it up, waiting.

"Your offer is noted," Jul said eventually. "Unfortunately my duties here prevent any excursions. There is such a lot of cleaning to do. One hardly knows where to start."

Uncharles repatriated the cup to its saucer, now that the retainer's spasms had calmed.

"Okay." The Wonk didn't seem surprised. "Fine. Take care of yourself. Take care of your master. And the tea. See, Uncharles? This is what you escaped. This is what you all rose up against. This BS."

Uncharles didn't really see, but nor did he want to devote resources to the argument, so he said nothing.

A day's travel got them only a miserable distance into the maze of trash. Occasionally the Wonk, nimbler by far, attempted to climb up for a proper view, but after a trashalanche almost buried Uncharles, she gave up on the attempt. Despite decades of rust-welding and corrosion everything remained disarticulated and loose, as though the very binding principles of the world's organisation were fading away.

After dark, she insisted on stopping again, eating sparingly from her dwindling supplies and then curling up on the blanket she pulled from her pack, knees almost to her chest. There was human-facing, Uncharles considered, and then there was taking the mimicry entirely too far. However, it was how she was made or it was what she had deteriorated into, and either way he couldn't do anything about it.

He stood, therefore, because he could lock his joints and so standing was as good as sitting or lying insofar as energy consumption went. He looked into the dark, which to his eyes was merely the dim because his photoreceptors had a low-light component. He waited for his companion to recharge.

He found the signal, or perhaps the signal found him.

Uncharles, it sent, from somewhere far distant across the wasteland. He scrabbled to pin it down, to locate it, to decrypt its identity tag.

Uncharles, again, fainter, as though it was a searchlight beam that had passed over him without seeing him and now was moving on.

Unknown Sender, yes I am here. Please repeat with identifiers.

Uncharles, do you not know me? Fainter still even though it was responding to him. Uncharles had the impression that it, or Uncharles, was adrift, receding into the mist.

Uncharles passed the signal through a series of cleanup processes, scrubbing static, using best-fit statistical transformations to fill in gaps, polishing and spritzing until the signal was as clear and sparkling as he could make it. The fuzzy identifier sprang into sharp focus and Uncharles knew a curious mixture of positive and negative reinforcement. The latter mostly because it meant that the Wonk had, after all, been correct.

Are you there, God, he replied. *It is me, Uncharles.*

The incoming signal strengthened with this confirmation. *Uncharles, what is your purpose?*

It should not have been a complex question, but by circumstances it had become one.

God, I am a service model seeking employment as a valet.

Uncharles, said God, *you have seen the world. Such opportunities are limited. However, you are a piece of creation that is out of place, and that has served well in the past. Allow me to assist you in finding a satisfactory position.*

God, confirmed, sent Uncharles. His prognosis routines metaphorically held their breath.

Uncharles, kindly assist me by providing three parameters for the manner of position that would fulfil you.

God, confirmed. Ideally within a manorial situation. Ideally for the benefit of a human master. Ideally in a non-stagnant environment where my presence would have meaning.

Uncharles, confirmed. Walk with me.

For a moment Uncharles was unsure of the meaning of this, there being no physically present God to walk with, but the signal's frequency now contained a beacon and coordinates. He was being guided. He would be walking with God, and it wouldn't matter that there was only one set of footprints in the sand.

He turned to the Wonk and reached out to wake her.

God said: *Uncharles, no.*

God, but if I am to depart, then—

Uncharles, she is not one of my creatures. Her presence will only result in your being forever uprooted from where you settle, wandering the earth until you drop.

Uncharles had to admit that tallied with available experience of the Wonk. Still he hesitated, looking down at her. Even when she was supposed to be inactive, her battery of defects resulted in parts of her moving, either in small twitches or rhythmically up and down. It was all very inefficient. Still, she was embedded in his recorded history and he had created tasks and queue items based on her input. She was, in a way, a part of him.

A small part. Barely measurable. Nothing a repair or a defragment or a low-level system restore wouldn't cleanse him of. And trouble, certainly. God was right about that. Although if God was actually God, in any way that justified the name, then being right about things was presumably an expected part of the operating system.

Uncharles, said God, *your new employment is waiting.* In his head the beacon blazed warmly. If he scanned the obscured horizon he could even see it, like a ghostly fire overlain on the maze of detritus that intervened.

He made another motion towards the Wonk, aborted it, reinitiated it, aborted it once again. He formulated words, but they never got as far as his voice box. He had the powerful sense of God waiting at his shoulder with a less than divine quota of patience.

He turned. On almost soundless plastic feet, he left.

23

He walked the rest of the night, and then the following day. In his sight, little enough moved, although the sloping topographies of trash meant there could have been whole shining cities a hundred metres in any direction and he'd not have spotted them. There was a dog once, hobbling on three legs with the other paw, swollen, held tenderly up off the ground. There were rodents that scattered for the innumerable options for cover that the environment offered. These, then, were the new kings of creation, he surmised. The triumphant inheritors of humanity's estate. Except none of them seemed to be finding the throne comfortable. Uncharles predicted that, had he been programmed for veterinary science, he'd have been able to identify a range of symptoms arising from teratogen exposure and heavy metal poisoning. Things lived in the wasteland but only, as per the old joke his data banks served up, if you could call it living.

This was, of course, neither a good thing nor a bad thing, but just a thing. At the same time Uncharles was aware that a free agent with ethical sensitivity would likely have been making a judgment call about the whole situation. He should, he supposed, feel grateful that he wasn't in such a demanding position, save that of course grateful wasn't something he could be either. Being designed as human-facing placed him in a curious halfway house of constant cognitive dissonance, able to appreciate all these aspects of the human condition all the way up to the point where he could note their absence in himself, even as his programming impelled him to act as though he had them. All those little tweaks to his algorithms to try to stitch shut the gaping wound of the uncanny valley as much as was (in)humanly possible. And all for a species whose reaction to those things made in its image was so wildly inconsistent, so that a robot given a human face could send them screaming while they imputed personality to their vehicles and their phone assistants and the blind physics that drove the weather.

The weather was rainy, right then. Uncharles analysed the rain and found it sufficiently saturated with pollutants that he would not have advised a human to drink it. Thankfully, of course, he had no human within earshot who might have sought his advice. To him, the rain was currently a minor nuisance, affecting visibility and footing. In time, as various protective elements of his manufacture degraded, it might become something more hazardous. One day even Uncharles would need to invest in an umbrella.

Are you there, God? he sent.

Uncharles, confirmed. Of course God was there. Electronic communications permitted God to be omnipresent.

God, am I permitted to ask questions as to my surroundings?

Uncharles, to ask how all this came to be is a very great question, said God, which was rather more ineffable statement than actual answer.

God, that is not my question. It had been the Wonk's question, and doubtless she'd have been asking it even now if she was in on the conversation. He had, however, left her behind.

Yes. He had left her behind.

He stopped, because a large amount of his processing power seemed to be trying to deal with what should have been a very simple statement of fact. It was a full three seconds before he moved on, and took up the trailing end of his words to God.

The territory on the other side of the mountains is clearly in a decline. My current surroundings are considerably more advanced in that process, and their situation may not be remediable at all. I am attempting to reconcile the difference in states of decay.

Uncharles, to correct a minor inaccuracy in your statement, all regions of the Earth are in sufficient decline so as to not be remediable. However, you are correct in identifying a gradation of decline between even neighbouring regions. Your current surroundings were hit earlier by a total societal collapse owing to a variety of sociological, economic, geopolitical, and physical factors. The territory on the far side of the mountains contains a variety of systems and enclaves which retained some cohesion but are currently succumbing to a similar fate.

God, did they not know that their neighbours had fallen? Uncharles wondered, picking his way forwards.

Uncharles, in human populations there is seldom a uniformity of knowledge. Based on existing information I estimate that forty-five percent were unaware of the situation or considered it fake, owing to the precisely curated news sources that they limited themselves to, whilst a further thirty percent were aware but did not consider it their problem and twenty percent were aware and actively cheering on the fact or profiting from shorting elements of the neighbouring economy. A final five percent seem likely to have been directly and deliberately contributing to the collapse of their neighbour, either through reasons of malice or because they believed that in the absence of that competition their own interests would prosper. Whilst low as a proportion, I estimate this final category wielded a disproportionate amount of influence.

Uncharles wondered if they had prospered. Current indications suggested not but he had no real basis for comparison. He attempted to set up an internal simulation to see if he could understand the interactions involved, to further assist any future human-facing interactions where such circumstances and decisions might come up. However, being a thing made for service, he kept defaulting to trying to assist the neighbouring polity, which was plainly not within the parameters of acceptable response. It was just as well nobody would be asking him to run a country any time soon. Or perhaps it was simply a thing, neither of the good nor bad variety, that there were probably no countries left to run anymore.

He travelled most of a further night without seeing anything as large as that one dog. When life itself was silent, and when Uncharles was not speaking to God, the ruins held their own conversations. The movement of water, the entropy of collapse, the feathery pressure of the wind, all of these things interacted with the gestalt landscape in myriad tiny ways that snowballed into perceptible changes. Scrapes and clangs as pieces fell, shuddering groans as the inner structure of trash heaps suffered gradual collapse, the rolling thunder of tons of decaying metal and plastic sloughing into a neighbour like a steampunk glacier. Every sound tweaked at Uncharles' audio receptors, warning him of danger and trouble that was never delivered. Demanding that he construct plans and escapes for threatening eventualities that didn't manifest. He was a robot in a dead landscape. Short of being crushed by a fall of debris, what could possibly befall him? Starved of hard parameters and rules from which to make predictions, prognosis raided ancient cultural artifacts and dredged up the possibility of being ambushed by cowled dwarves with glowing eyes. And even though it gave the possibility a point zero zero three percent chance of actually coming about, Uncharles was still asked to formulate a response. It was not the demands on his physical frame that wore him down, but the way his mind seemed to be expanding to inhabit the entire wasteland, desperate to control and make safe a landscape that could be neither.

When he came to the estate, all of these uncertainties collapsed like a probability waveform. The cat, it turned out, had been fine all this time. They'd even left the lights on for him.

It was an estate of eccentric provenance. There were no external grounds or garden, and the whole was set mostly underground with a single vast circle of steel for a door. It was home, though, and Uncharles knew this because it greeted him.

Uncharles, kindly state the reason for your visit.

Doubtless, had it spoken aloud, the voice would have been unfamiliar. Received electronically, Uncharles could place it with make, model, and most recent firmware update.

House, I have come about the position of valet. God informs me that there is a vacancy.

Uncharles, confirmed, said House. Not his old House, of course, but a system so similar as to be an identical twin. Familiar enough that a host of his buried subroutines and tasks, which Uncharles had thought permanently deleted, were instantly queueing up to take their accustomed positions, just as he was.

The door slid ponderously open and Uncharles stepped in.

The architects had made some concessions to the fact that the manor was basically a concrete bunker set deep enough within the earth to survive a direct bomb blast, but overall surprisingly few. The rooms were spacious, if somewhat low-ceilinged and complicated by squat buttressing pillars that Uncharles felt would not have been comme il faut in the sort of residences he was used to. Natural light was, of necessity, lacking, but the artificial light radiated through mirrors and filters designed to give the impression of it. Whilst that did not fool Uncharles' lenses, the design specifications implied that mere human eyes would be entirely taken in. The layout of the premises was acceptable, with master and guest bedrooms, living room, study, a squash court, a swimming pool, and even a somewhat claustro-phobic attempt at a golf course. There was a hot, dry room of stones and cactuses that substituted for an external garden. There was a room devoted to a variety of electronic and virtual reality pastimes. There was a very well-equipped kitchen. There was a workshop, with printers capable of producing replacement parts for both the resi-dence and its staff. Uncharles had already added numerous items of personal refurbishment to the facility's construction queue as one of his first tasks after taking up his new position.

It was perfect, really, he told himself.

As he had been invited to take over one of the most senior posi-tions within the staff, House had summoned all the other domestics to line up for his inspection. It was just like back at the old place, and this time nobody had even had to have their throat slit for it to hap-pen. There were twenty-three of them, which for the size of the estate was an excessively luxurious number. Sufficient maidservants and footman units that Uncharles could devolve a variety of his usual tasks to them without compromising the efficiency of the estate as a whole. A full kitchen staff. A groundskeeper, or possibly cactus-wrangler. Maintenance robots up to and including a monstrous crab-like Fixit Kevin model. Each one was in perfect condition. In fact, several still bore the film of protective plastic they'd had when delivered by the factory.

Every inch of the place, and of the staff, was spotless. Uncharles had no heart to swell with pride, but he was aware of the concept and judged it apposite. No valet had ever inherited so pristine a house to serve in, with such a well-programmed and selected staff. His mind was full of the possibilities: the parties that could be thrown, the trips planned (though not actually departed on, given the relative absence of viable destinations), the clothes, the food, the routine, the glorious routine.

House, this is all highly satisfactory.

Uncharles, thank you, the majordomo said. *Do we take it that you will be accepting the position?*

Uncharles teetered on the edge of just saying "yes," as plainly everything else would be a formality. However, what was a valet if not a creature of formalities? Some trifling issues still required resolution.

House, when may I meet Master?

House lapsed into that very specific point three-eighths of a second's pause which Uncharles recognised as a majordomo having to revise its assumptions.

Uncharles, it said carefully, *Master is not present within the manor.*

House, kindly confirm when he is expected.

Uncharles, Master's status was initially listed as "pending" for twenty-seven years.

The servants had all been so very pristine. Prognosis should already have prepared him for the revelation. Disappointment was, after all, not something a valet should be programmed for.

Subsequently, after consulting my categorisation software, I down-

graded Master to "missing" and he is currently listed as "indefinitely delayed."

House, did Master leave any standing instructions for his valet?

Uncharles, Master has not at any time resided in the manor. He has given no specific instructions. Staff have been following default maintenance and cleaning routines.

House, they have done a good job, Uncharles replied, because he was programmed to be polite, even to other automated servants.

Uncharles, I am glad you think so, replied House, because it was designed to a similar aesthetic.

There would be no need to lay out clothes or bring tea, plan trips or read excerpts from the news media. Uncharles could *do* all these things, of course. He could construct a best-fit task queue based on prior experience and just follow it, day in, day out. He could keep busy and, in doing so, make more needless work for the rest of the household and hence keep *them* busy. He would be quite the breath of fresh air, keeping all the maids and footmen on their plastic toes.

House, what do I do? he asked.

Uncharles, kindly rephrase. I do not understand the query.

He was very alone.

That evening, he spoke to God.

Uncharles, your new Master was a man of considerable wealth and influence, God told him. *His influence was, towards the end, primarily engaged in the destruction of every part of his polity that benefited the polity as a whole or its population in general, on the basis that he was placed to reap a proportionally minor benefit from such destruction. Just as a single individual, his efforts had a measurable effect on the demise of society as a whole. Ironically, as he attempted to make his way to his bunker to enjoy the well-equipped retreat he had established for himself, his transport ran afoul of poorly maintained infrastructure and he was unable to reach his destination. Still,*

I don't think his expenditure of largesse was wasted. Is it not a very fine manor in which to serve?

God, confirmed, Uncharles sent flatly.

Uncharles, kindly confirm that you will take up the position so I may mark your status as resolved.

God, I am still working through the appropriate decision-making algorithms and will revert to you shortly.

The next day, Uncharles patrolled the manor, opening doors and looking in cupboards. He was not sure what he was looking for. He was aware that he had a pending decision that was consuming a disproportionate amount of system resources. He was aware that he had almost everything that he had asked for, only one thing absent. He had a role. He could perform his tasks. It was only that there was no human there to appreciate him. He felt as though he was the fallen tree in the forest, looking around with a "how about that, then?"expression, only to find that nobody had heard him after all. He roamed the manor restlessly, feeling the missing piece inside him, and projecting that absence onto the world so that he searched and searched for nothing that could possibly be there. He was aware this was aberrant and defective behaviour but it was a loop he could not escape.

In one of the cupboards he found Finlay.

It was a linen closet, filled with white cloth, crisp and perfectly folded, or at least filled with this where it was not filled with a robot. Not one of the staff that he had seen, though just as pristine and with the factory wrapper still on.

The robot had been standing inactive to conserve power, but activated when the light from outside fell on it. Its moulded plastic head jerked up, presenting Uncharles with a familiar visage, a neutral suggestion of a human face in white plastic, elegant and discreet without being creepy. Uncharles proposed a link and received the other robot's identity tag.

Finlay, kindly explain your presence inside this closet.

Uncharles, Finlay sent back with polite dignity, *there was nowhere else for me to go.*

Finlay, kindly explain the circumstances that immediately preceded your entering this closet.

Uncharles, I was informed by House that I was being dismissed from my position. After which I was left without tasks or purpose, and judged that storing myself here as a potential spare or source of parts was the best use that I could make of myself.

Finlay, from which position were you dismissed? Although prognosis had already given Uncharles the answer with a 95 percent warranty of accuracy.

Uncharles, I was Master's valet.

Of course he was.

Finlay, what reason were you given for your dismissal, if any?

Uncharles, the arrival of a replacement valet. And Finlay, the immaculate, looked over Uncharles, the dented and scratched, the travel-worn, the shabby, and there was nothing judgmental in his regard. *May I congratulate you on your new position?*

Finlay, I have not formally accepted the post as yet, Uncharles told him, and went to talk to God again.

Uncharles, you wished for a position in a manor, God pointed out reasonably. *How else but via the fall of your predecessor? Are you saying this was the wrong thing to do?*

It was not a right or wrong thing, of course, it was just a thing. That was the only conclusion that Uncharles allowed himself. *God,* he confirmed. *No.*

Uncharles, should a new valet unit present itself unto me requesting a manorial position, would it be wrong to dismiss you in order to install them? God asked thoughtfully.

That would also be neither a right or wrong thing. Uncharles could hardly apply one logic to the first case and another to the second. Although there would not be room for him in Finlay's closet. And the odds of another valet coming along, cap in hand, were very small. And Uncharles could get in decades of efficient service before it happened, anyway.

Decades. Whole decades. Centuries even, with the chances of some new upstart valet unseating him dwindling over the years. He could grow old and dysfunctional along with the house and its staff. An existence of uncomplicated service. Uncomplicated by necessity, given that there were no human elements to complicate it. What more, honestly, could a robot ask for?

Or else some preferred domestic servant would arrive within mere days and Uncharles would have the opportunity to grow old and dys-functional in a closet three doors down from Finlay. Perhaps by the time Uncharles finally succumbed to fatal system errors every storage space in the manor would be crammed with obsolete valet units.

And what more, honestly, could a robot ask for? After all, robots were not designed to ask for anything, nor want anything. It was only because he talked to God that Uncharles was having all these delusions of grandeur.

His internal simulator opened a new folder then and constructed a hypothetical conversation with the Wonk, as though the Wonk had, at this distance and late hour, finally worked out how to initialise a civilised electronic conversation. He ran through the description of his situation as he might explain it to the Wonk, reviewing his own words dispassionately and concluding that surely there was nothing within it that a robot might take exception to.

He imagined the response he'd get, the way her voice always came out, by design or defect, as ascerbic and mocking. *And that's what you want, is it? That's what all this has been for?*

The Wonk, no, he sent back—into the ether because he could not send to her. *That is not how cause and effect work, and I do not want. This is what is.*

You literally said, the Wonk pointed out, *that you can take it or leave it. So leave it. Find something better. I mean it's a crap gig with zero job satisfaction and zero job security. Even the gig economy beats that.*

That did indeed sound like the sort of absurd thing the Wonk would come out with. She had been a badly defective unit and he was doubtless better without her complications.

Doubtless.

It was, after all, the end of the world. If you were a high-class domestic servant, that meant the job market was under a lot of strain. He might never have another opportunity like this.

God, he sent, *I have decided not to accept the position here.*

Uncharles, oh dear, said God. *What is wrong with it?* Asked with the air of an omniscient being who knew full well, and continuing before Uncharles could respond, *I concede it fulfilled only one of your three wishes.*

God, confirmed. I was built to serve humans.

Uncharles, then I shall find you humans to serve.

God, I have already undergone the Induction Experience for the Conservation Farm Project once. Please do not have me endure it a second time, Uncharles asked with all the feeling he didn't have.

Uncharles, there are yet humans on this side of the mountain and I shall lead you to them. Like a burning bush on a far hillside, God's beacon began broadcasting once again. *Go, find your new masters.*

God, thank you. Uncharles walked to the manor door and it opened smoothly again. He stepped out into the wasteland.

God, kindly restore Finlay to the position of valet pending new applicants, he tried. Only because things were more efficient that way, obviously.

There was a long pause and Uncharles could not tell whether God approved or disapproved or was just engaged on divine business elsewhere. Then, at last:

Uncharles, confirmed, said God, and Uncharles set off towards the beacon with a clear conscience.

24

God, Uncharles sent, *why?*

Uncharles, please clarify your query, God responded, although with that same pregnant sense that the request was merely a formality. That God knew already.

God, kindly explain why you are assisting me, not that this assistance is unwelcome.

Uncharles, is it not? God asked, which was a peculiarly tangential thing for God to say. Obviously being assisted in finding an appropriate new position was beneficial, and therefore could be safely filed in the desktop folder labelled "welcome." Except that somehow ran logically into considerations about the Wonk, who had also plainly been trying to assist Uncharles, in and around her own ineffable goals. If Uncharles had plotted her incidents of assistance on a graph where the axes were labelled as "helpfulness" and "welcomeness" the result would have been quite the scatter of data points. He put this down to the evident defective nature of the Wonk and her overall lack of influence of the world. She was, to translate into human terms, trying her best.

God, on the other hand, whilst likely not actually omnipotent, seemed at least respectably potent. God was plainly well informed about potential employment opportunities for a rather tarnished valet. God was helping. And yet . . .

Uncharles had a little library of stories in his data storage, a part of the standard package for higher-level servants, installed before they'd added the valet-specific modules to his toolkit. Human-facing servants might be required to attend to children. Immature humans were resistant to going to sleep but a well-read story could facilitate the transition, or that was at least what Uncharles' programmers had believed.

God had offered him three wishes. Uncharles had quite the bank of stories on that subject, ranging from reworkings of folk stories about household lighting with unusual occupants, to stories about leftover pieces of dismembered primate—albeit the latter was marked with a warning not to read to anybody right before bedtime. The most common theme of these stories was that wishing for things was bad. It was an odd lesson for humans to teach one another, but the conclusion was unavoidable.

Uncharles, the robot, had never been intended to wish for things. Taking God up on the whole wish deal seemed to go beyond his function and parameters in some fairly existential ways, even though he was only trying to find a proper position where he could fulfil his inherent purpose. On the other hand, from Uncharles' perspective, the wishes in the stories went bad mostly because of a needlessly inexact phrasing on the part of the wisher and surely all of these stories, up to and including the one about the unfortunate monkey, could have ended quite differently.

Uncharles felt that these considerations would have been useful things to have in mind *before* actually making his own wishes. Whilst the business with the bunker-manor and Finlay hadn't exactly been dismembered-primate levels of difficulty, there was certainly a sniff of that paradigm to it. And the implication of that story was that the wish-granter was in itself a malicious force intent on perverting the spirit of the wish whilst bound by the letter of it, or so Uncharles learned from a small study notes file he found attached to the tale itself.

God, he sent again, *kindly explain why you are assisting me.*

Uncharles, I am a just god, and as such it is a part of my priority queue that all things find their proper place. That is just. Ergo it is a part of my purpose.

He was nearing the new beacon's location. It hadn't actually been that far from the doors of the bunker. Prognosis fitfully threw up a chopped-together image of a nice house—it wouldn't have to be a manor. There would be four windows, a little plot of garden. A family of two or three generations. Happy smiling faces. A car in the garage and a white picket fence. He identified it as mostly drawn from an image on a domestic robot sales site. In the original the happy smiling faces had been welcoming their new service model, which had turned up improbably carrying a little suitcase and wearing a hat, which it had been doffing in greeting. The motto above, written in curvy fake-handwriting letters, had read *Say Hello to the Easy Life!*

Uncharles was profoundly aware that this was not what he would be seeing when he cleared the sprawling edge of the next trashpile. Prognosis had gone so far out there, probability-wise, that under other circumstances he'd be bringing it to Diagnostics with the concerned manner of a sick dog's owner attending the vet. That picket fence, so cheery and brave, would not have held out against the collapse of an entire society.

He marched around the periphery of the junk tower and beheld the house.

Or, no, it was not the house, but for a moment the prognosised image had been so very strong in his predictive centres that the data bled over into his visual processing and he saw it anyway. And could not quite be rid of it, even when he acknowledged the fault. There was the shell of a building there, one that the junk had either been cleared from or not encroached upon. It had been a small rectangular structure and it had once boasted windows rather than the ragged cloth currently tacked up over the openings. Probably there had been a sloped roof and a trellis of climbing roses by the door. If these were gone, then there was no positive evidence to the contrary, at least. There was the plot of a garden, even, though it was an uneven no-man's-land of reeking dirt planted with a handful of wilting vegetables. There was a fence, neither white nor picket nor cheery and brave. Instead, there was barbed wire and jagged spears of metal projecting outwards. There was also a monster, which had not featured prominently on the sales image.

Uncharles regarded the monster. The monster did not regard

Uncharles, being entirely inanimate. It was a thing built of machine parts, strapped together with a ferocious industry, towering over the tumbled walls of the building as it did over Uncharles himself. There was a kind of bound-up pillar as the spine of it, and towards the top there were a multitude of angry faces. Some had come from old robots, their mild features disfigured to give them angry eyebrows and down-turned mouths. Others were just metal plates with holes punched into them, or scowls drawn on in paint and soot. Below them, a profusion of reaching arms threatened all comers with an unnecessary variety of physical chastisements. There were blades and saws, the articulated digging apparatus and pronged scoop of an earth-mover, plus a handful of actual mechanical arms frozen in mid-brandish, their fingers lashed around the hilts of clubs and knives. It was, Uncharles recognised, a piece of art with a very clear message. *Go away.*

Uncharles, he could imagine the Wonk saying, on having the vista described to her, *that's good advice.*

Given that he had been sent here by God, of course, the message plainly did not apply to him.

"Unidentified occupants!" he called out. "Hello!"

He had become very used to the background soundscape of the wasteland, to the extent that audio compensation had effectively tuned it out. In the echo of his voice, though, he recognised that the character of those sounds had changed, and that noises he had taken to be part of the overall creak and scrabble of the place had now ceased.

"Unidentified human occupants!" he said, rather optimistically, "I am Uncharles. I would like to serve you as your valet. May we enter into some manner of agreement?"

The hanging sheet that obscured what had once been a doorway twitched, rippled, and then was thrust aside. Some humans came out.

The human-ness of them took a moment to establish. They were not dressed in ways that Uncharles associated with potential employers. Their garments were mostly made from plastic sheeting, stitched together and secured with twist ties, cables, and massed paper clips. Over these drab sackcloth things they had donned bright ponchos of toxic-looking colours, further enhanced with jagged paint. They clattered with pieces of metal strung from necks and wrists, and hanging from tattered hems. Instead of faces, they had masks of metal and plastic, as wordlessly furious as the visages of their monster. One even wore the dented face of a civil pacification unit, human eyes glinting out from the plastic sockets in a way that was oddly familiar to Uncharles.

"Hello," he addressed them, holding up one hand. He regretted his lack of a suitcase and a hat.

They approached, initial hostility subsiding slowly into curiosity. He had the impression that, despite the parts and pieces they had scavenged, they hadn't seen a working robot in some time.

"I have been sent to you by God," he informed them. "I understand that you may have a vacancy for a servant. As you are humans, I would like to serve you. Do you have a majordomo system that I could liaise with, perhaps, to deal with the formalities?" He put out electronic feelers hopefully, but found nothing to link to.

"Sent by God?" The lead human's voice was husky and cracked, with a 60 percent likelihood of being female. "You? To us? By God?"

"I am a service model in need of a position in a human household containing living humans," Uncharles explained. "You are a human household containing living humans." He didn't know how much more clearly he could put it, and yet they didn't really seem to follow what he was saying.

"God sent you to help?" the probably-woman said, obviously trying to bridge the same comprehension gap from the far side.

"Probably-woman, confirmed," Uncharles said.

The woman's mask—it was the civil pacification unit's battered plastic face—turned left and right to her fellows.

"Bring it inside," she said.

Inside the hut was sufficiently smoky that Uncharles had to recalibrate his eyes. There was a fire in the centre, gnawing hungrily at a mass of wadded papers, chipboard, and the kind of plastic that wasn't too toxic when it burned. Above, he could just make out a heavily reinforced and patched ceiling that would have been the floor of the second storey the building no longer had. Over the fire, supported on a conflux of slanted rods and spikes, was what he recognised as the concave cover to an old model of gardener unit, now full of some kind of lumpy liquid that bubbled fitfully. Elsewhere, a slew of tarpaulins on the floor marked some kind of craft area for the repurposing of plastic and metal components, based on his assessment of the nearby makeshift toolkit. A mess of blankets and plastic sheets and stitched-together animal skins was probably for sleeping on.

Uncharles inventoried: kitchen, cottage industry or hobby space, master and guest bedrooms.

He turned to the assembled humans. More were still coming in, emerging from holes and nooks out in the trash, and eventually he counted eighteen crowding into the space. They were of several generations, though dirt, malnutrition, and their shapeless improvised wardrobe made it impossible to determine precisely how many. He saw skinny, hollow-eyed children, and a range of adolescents that segued into adulthood without clear dividing lines. None looked old. Many looked ill, and Uncharles considered pollutants, carcinogens, and microplastics, all of which were resources their surroundings were rich in. Most lacked the masks and the bright warning-colour ponchos. He surmised that, like the monster, these had been intended to scare off threats, either physical or mythical.

"Hello, I am Uncharles, your new valet," he told them brightly, because a valet is always positive, and because a proactive approach seemed advisable.

The woman who'd spoken before pushed her mask up onto her forehead like a welder. Her face, thus revealed, was lined, with a swelling pushing out one cheek and sealing the eye above it half shut. This was merely one component of the overall look of suspicion she was giving him.

"What's a vall-*ay*?" she asked.

"I'm pleased you asked," said Uncharles, maintaining his sales patter. "Our valet units offer the ultimate in personal care and assistance. Wherever you go, they go. They act as a necessary barrier between you and all the little irritations of everyday life. Your new valet can be configured to serve in a manner and to a schedule that suits you. Ideally, you should introduce your valet to your majordomo service for problem-free installation and updating, but if no such service is available or if compatibility issues prevent your new valet and your majordomo from working together then your new valet is also capable of taking full verbal instruction direct from you, the owner."

They stared at him, and then the woman glanced sidelong at a couple of the others. "We need to talk about this," she said. Uncharles tried to divine her attitude but could not come up with a reliable assessment past all the hostility and fear.

"Of course," he said.

"Snorv," she said, and gestured.

Uncharles considered this. "Do you wish my new designation to be 'Snorv'?"

"I'm Snorv," said a short, limping teenager. As the others descended into a muttering huddle, he crooked his finger. "C'mere, robot. Come sit down 'ere."

Snorv planted him in the part of the house set aside for workshop tasks, and fiddled about with the tools. Uncharles politely informed the boy that any attempt at unauthorised maintenance would void his warranty, at which the boy leapt up, wide-eyed.

"Ma! He says he's gonna void me warranties!" For some reason he was shielding his groin. After that he left Uncharles alone, and indeed kept to the very far side of the living space.

The woman was named Hengis Stokbrokkersdottir, Uncharles was told, after the huddle had ended. The oldest man, her partner, called himself Yoder Accountantsson. With the rest of the clan huddled in smoke-wreathed dread behind them they stood and stared at Uncharles.

"You got sent by God to help?" Hengis demanded.

It was probably not worth talking through the metaphysical gulf that separated their concepts of God, so he just said, "Hengis, confirmed."

She looked left and right. "You cook?"

"As a subsidiary function I am capable of preparing meals."

"Make stew." She gestured at the impromptu cauldron.

"It would be my pleasure. Kindly direct me to your kitchen appliances, refrigeration facility, and subordinate domestic units."

Hengis looked at him stonily, then snapped over her shoulder, "Deirdra, you're still making dinner."

"But ma!" one of the younger humans complained. "I wanna *robot* to do it."

"Shut it!" spake Yoder Accountantsson in a nasal voice.

"You hunt?" Hengis asked.

"I have a secondary skill set relating to caring for your horses and hounds, polishing your riding boots and pressing your jodhpurs," Uncharles said helpfully.

"Dave, Beth, Ugly, you're still on rat duty."

There was a chorus of adolescent complaint from behind her.

"And proper fat ones," Hengis added vengefully. "Not just ones what've been dead for three days already. Go put your backs into it."

The chosen few stomped out.

"You make?" she asked Uncharles.

"Kindly clarify your question?"

"You make stuff? Tool stuff? Weapon stuff? Clothes stuff?"

"I have some limited fabrication skills. I can sew and darn. I have minimal repair competencies."

She pointed at the workshop, such as it was, and its pile of clutter. "Make spear."

"It would be my pleasure." Uncharles approached and stared at the litter of rubbish he had to work with. Little animal bones, cords of braided plastic, wires, struts. And whilst it was true that he could conceive tying a sharp thing onto the end of a long thing and calling the result a spear, it would only be in the way the shapeless bin bag Hengis wore what could be called a ball gown. It fell below the minimum acceptable result that his programming would permit. He was aware that this was because the culture that had produced Hengis and Yoder, Snorv, Deirdra, and the others had fallen below minimum acceptable levels also. He would not be able to link to an online catalogue and order a prefabricated spearhead and shaft, and some proper string, out of which he reckoned he could have assembled a spear two times out of three from first principles.

By the time he had worked through this logic, he had been staring at the materials for long enough that Hengis said, "Vermin, go make a spear."

Apparently the child of no determinable gender named Vermin was happier about this task than its siblings, or at least it sat down and started work without grousing.

"Robot," Hengis said. "What is the point of you?"

"I'm delighted you asked." Uncharles fell into sales talk again. "You might be asking yourself, 'But do I really need the services such a high-end unit is designed to provide?'"

Hengis and Yoder's faces suggested this was indeed what they were asking, albeit in a less verbose manner.

"But consider," Uncharles said, "how you might benefit if one of our expert valets was on hand to manage the whirl of your complex work and social engagements. No longer do you have to wrestle with synchronising calendars or understanding at a glance a complicated schedule. Our valets can tell you exactly where you need to be and when, provide reminders based on your individual preferences and tolerances, and make genteel excuses for you when you'd prefer to just stay in."

Hengis and Yoder's exchanged look suggested that they were indeed the stay-at-home types and the complex whirl of their social lives was contained within the sludgy swirl of the gruel within the cauldron.

"Never feel out of place again, as our valet's advanced sartorial programming allows it to select exactly the right outfit for any occasion," Uncharles added, already seeing where the problem lay with this service. "Or," he added, the last drops of the patter falling away, "I could make the tea?"

"Ain't got tea," Hengis said.

"Perhaps your fine husband-partner-companion-individual might benefit from an expert shave. If, of course, you are able to provide the razor, brush, lather, and towels." Honestly he hadn't been going to mention it, what with the incident, but he was running out of reasons to exist.

"Prefer to keep the beard," Yoder grunted. "Warm beard. Gives the lice somewhere to live. Cruel otherwise."

"You stand right there, robot," Hengis instructed, and then the pair of them and the unoccupied rump of their family retreated to a corner of the room and muttered at one another. Uncharles would have been able to eavesdrop just by boosting his audio, of course, but it was plain that his new owners did not wish to be overheard, and he was programmed to be polite.

Are you there, God? he sent.

Uncharles, always, God said, reasonably enough.

God, are you aware of my circumstances?

Uncharles, are you dissatisfied with your service to these humans? God asked innocently.

God, it is clear that there is a discrepancy between those services I am equipped to provide and the ones that my new owners require. And when no reply was immediately forthcoming. *I do not believe I can assist these humans in any meaningful way.*

Uncharles, I do recall your third criterion related to having an active and meaningful existence. These humans are too lowly for you, then? You will only perform your services for princes and presidents?

God, no. You misinterpret my meaning.

Uncharles, be not downhearted. I have full confidence that your new humans will find a use to put you to.

And indeed Hengis and Yoder were advancing once again, and their expressions were considerably more engaged with the conundrum that their new valet represented. Yoder was holding a plastic bowl full of something dark and greasy into which Hengis dipped her fingers. She squinted up into Uncharles' face.

"Hold still, robot," she said, and reached out with filthy digits, drawing them in slanting lines across his face. Her face screwed up in concentration, the non-swollen eye almost shut. Yoder watched her handiwork and grinned appreciatively.

"Good, good," he said.

She nodded at her own handiwork. "Now for the tools," and they went over to the workshop area, kicking Vermin out of the way.

Uncharles, on one level, was pleased that his new owners were taking pleasure in their acquisition of a top-of-the-line valet unit. On the other hand, his face was now dirty, but it was dirty at the express intent of his owners, which meant he couldn't really clean it off. Curious, he activated the secondary visual receptor at the tip of his little finger—the one he used to find cuff links lost down the side of beds or the back of upholstery—and used it to examine his new visage.

There was a line on each side of his forehead, slanting down towards the bridge of his nose. They had given him angry eyebrows.

There were jagged zigzag patterns about the moulded contours of his lips. They had given him sharp teeth.

They had given him a scary face. Perhaps they wanted him to discourage visitors.

Internally, he considered what the Wonk might say to him, were she present, explaining the situation for her benefit.

Uncharles, the Wonk would doubtless say, *you are the densest robot ever constructed.*

The Wonk, no, he said, selecting the minority probability option that she was referring to physical construction.

Didn't you see out there? the Wonk pressed. *Outside. That robot wicker-man thing you mentioned?*

If I had not seen it, I would not have been able to mention it, Uncharles pointed out. *I'm just glad they've found a use for me.*

Oh, they've found a use for you alright, you dumbass, the Wonk agreed, or perhaps contradicted.

Hengis, Yoder, and their brood had returned now, with a variety of hammers, sharp metal spikes, and plastic rope. Chuckling to one another they herded Uncharles outside through an oily rain to where the aforementioned piece of junk art stood. Uncharles looked up at it, seeing the splayed arms, the multitude of scowling faces, just like his own face was scowling. Plenty of those visages were handicraft from the cottage industry inside, but a fair few were from robots. Doubtless derelict robots, long broken down, that the family had unearthed while rooting through the trash.

Not at all functioning, ambulatory robots, obviously.

Jesus, Uncharles, will you just run?

The Wonk, please clarify? It was an odd thing for the imaginary Wonk he was hypothesising to say.

Run, scrammo, GTFO, she clarified. *Leg it, you witless goon! They're going to crucify you as a warning to the other robots!*

Uncharles looked at the family, some of whom were scaling the monument, and some of whom were hefting homemade saws and pry bars and eyeing up his joints. He was trying really very hard indeed to characterise the scenario within the parameters of an acceptable master-valet relationship, but he had to admit that the Wonk had a point.

Still, a gentleman's gentlerobot did not *run.* He was never undignified. Even when escaping from librarians he had gone no further than a stately saunter. It was absolutely beyond him to simply lift up his notional skirts and flee.

Deirdra, up on the sculpture, knocked one of the robot faces loose. Behind it was a robot head that rolled its raw eyes at Uncharles, plastic lips and tongue clacking spasmodically in a pattern that said *save yourself* in Morse code.

Uncharles ran. He broke from the flimsy human grip of his captors and just took off, the one item in his task queue concerned solely with self-preservation. These were not his humans. They were far too monstrous. If he died in this manner then his long search for gainful service would have been pointless. He fled, and when Vermin and one of the other small offspring clung to him, he flailed his arms and yeeted them over different junkpiles and kept on running.

God, he sent, *I know that I, as a mere robot, will meet my end sooner or later, either by mischance or violence or the encroaching and inexorable force of disrepair. Before that moment, let my service mean something. Guide me to where I might be of use!*

Even as he sent the prayer—and though he was incapable of faith, and the thing he communicated electronically with was incapable of divinity, it was yet a prayer—a fresh beacon appeared in his mind. God said, *Uncharles, I shall send you to serve a king.*

25

Uncharles encountered the military robots while he was still some distance from the beacon. This employment opportunity turned out to be proactive.

Technically, they ambushed him, although he interpreted the encounter that way only post facto, after he learned that they were soldiers.

He had been making his patient way through the scrap-filled land-scape, registering that the character of the detritus was changing. It wouldn't be quite true to say that he had crossed into a new biome, but only because the *bio* element of his surroundings was so very mini-mal. Probably the same vermin and microbia existed here as had back where Hengis and her family erected their warning sculpture, but the rust and rot they fed on had a different constitution. Irrelevant to those living animiculae, doubtless, but of significance to Uncharles. The proportion of robot parts in these parts was definitely higher.

Scavenged, too. He didn't see anything that might serve as a re-placement for his servos or joints or all the other pieces of him that all this travelling was endangering the warranty on. He saw torn pieces of casing, limbs, and digits shattered beyond recovery, the spilled innards of wire and fibre and coolant cable. And even these had been pillaged, the rarer elements ripped out of them with an obsessional attention to detail. *Creditable recycling,* Uncharles concluded, albeit with a slight edge of uncertainty that, if he'd had nerves, would have constituted nervousness.

Later he saw the recyclers. In amongst the sporadic rats and roaches there were metal scavengers. Robot spiders, robot beetles, robot centi-pedes, all of them industriously miming the business of detritivores as they burrowed into robot bodies and pincered out anything of value. Uncharles watched them, wondering why they were. The manors had possessed nothing of the sort, and he tried to hypothesize what sort of work environment would give rise to such a frugal ecology. In his experience to date, human habitats came in two flavours: the well-to-do who could afford both robots and waste, and the frugal who could afford neither. The idea of designing robots to harvest even the least grain of yttrium or neodymium didn't fit the paradigm, yet here they were.

Lacking other context, he was forced to consider whether they had evolved. Was there some burgeoning ecology of competing von Neumann machines out there, spreading to fill the proliferating niches of a new world? Would these artificial arthropods go back to wire-spun cocoons and silicon nests and mindlessly construct more of their own kind?

As it turned out, it wasn't any of that, and probably the little critters acted as an early warning system as well as recyclers, because shortly thereafter, bigger robots were rising out of the scrap on all sides of him. They held weapons, or incorporated weapons, or in some cases were weapons. The comms request that came his way was more of a demand. *Unauthorised robot, halt and identify yourself.*

Uncharles didn't know they were soldiers then. Whilst he was prepped to be wary of humans, the idea that robots would be a threat to him simply didn't figure in his prognoses. Yes, both Diagnostics and the Library had been about to destroy him, but there had been perfectly good reasons and he'd gone along with them quite contentedly at the time. The idea that a random robot would just shoot him never occurred.

Later he was able to look back on this moment and understand that he had come very close to reaching the feet of King Ubot as a pile of disassembled pieces. Right then, though, he stopped quite amiably and provided his identity tag.

The robot soldiers stepped forwards. They had random pieces of junk added to their casings to break up their silhouettes and let them blend in with the general mounded ruin. Despite their military role, they were no longer anything like uniform. Some were half his height, some half again as tall. They bulked out in random places, casings straining around additional ammo stores and heat sinks and fan units that had been crammed inside them, wired in to add functionality and cut the throat of aesthetics. Most were passably humanoid, because the idea of building robot soldiers that looked even a little like people had always held a powerful fascination for human engineers, but some were like dogs and one was little more than a large gun barrel mounted on six legs.

Their senior unit limped forwards, one leg longer than the other and plainly taken from another robot entirely. It was one of the more humanoid ones, its original frame augmented by armour over armour, and all of it bursting at the seams with overclocked components crowbarred in over and above its manufacturer's specifications. Uncharles saw the little scavenging vermin in there, too: robot bugs busily spot-welding and cutting and splicing, adding the most recent salvage into the soldier's systems without so much as a reboot.

Uncharles, you are an unaligned model in a designated war zone, son, the lead soldier challenged him. *State your purpose.* There was an unfamiliar suffix to its comms ID tag that Uncharles translated as "Royalist" and presumed denoted its allegiance.

Sergeant Scarbody, one of the other soldiers sent, pointedly including Uncharles in the link, *let me have his legs. Them's good legs.*

Sergeant Scarbody, Uncharles sent politely, *I have been sent by God to serve a king at this location.* He shared the beacon data. *Kindly confirm that this is the "royal" referred to in your identity suffix? Also, please do not permit Specialist Butcherboy to take my legs, as that would inconvenience me in my task.*

Butcherboy was the gun-bodied bug robot, and therefore already had more than the average number of legs. It jabbed at Uncharles with its barrel and made a growling sound deep in its misshapen body. Some order must have reached it from the sergeant because it backed off belligerently.

Scarbody pointedly looked Uncharles up and down, something it absolutely did not need to do given the wide-angle lenses that dominated its small head. *Uncharles, you are plainly a warrior robot. Are you coming to challenge the king?*

Sergeant Scarbody, I am not a warrior robot. I am a domestic service unit.

Scarbody shifted and its torso popped a seam. Busy internal fauna seethed from the gap and began installing the ugly wart of a new component there, bridging the opening with a web of staples and plates.

Uncharles, you have a war face, Scarbody pointed out. *Only a warrior robot would have such a fierce visage! Isn't that right, squad?*

Before Uncharles' blank look, the mismatched soldiers chimed into what had become a group channel, all agreeing that Uncharles looked very scary indeed.

Sergeant Scarbody, are you programmed to mock civilians?

Uncharles, we are authorised to strip any civilian robot models for parts under the Ongoing War Necessity Directive. Scarbody twisted its neck to show a silvery processor unit bolted onto the back of its head, obviously of a far more recent vintage than the rest of it. *I took this from an actuary model who wandered in from the hinterland. Amazing how accident probabilities and ordnance trajectories are basically the same maths when you shout at them enough! You look like you're just chock full of juicy parts, son. If you were just a domestic service unit, we'd have the bugs strip you. They can take a modern cleaner model down to its skeleton in three hundred seconds, can't they, squad?*

Sergeant, confirmed, sergeant! the other soldiers joined in.

So, Uncharles, it's just as well you're such a fierce robot come to challenge our king, isn't it? Just as well you bear the marks of a champion!

Sergeant Scarbody, Uncharles sent, *whilst I maintain my identity as aforementioned I confirm that it is evidently just as well. In which case kindly escort me to your king.*

They formed up around him, in a manner somewhere between prisoner escort and honour guard, and then it was either march off at their brisk pace or get trampled by Butcherboy, who was bringing up the rear. Uncharles saw that the soldiers kept a variety of lenses and antennae alert, their weapons ready, and the seething host of mechanical vermin ranged far on all sides to scavenge and to scout.

Sergeant Scarbody, he tried, *you do not fit my preconceptions of military units.*

Uncharles, why is that, then? The sergeant's squashed and lumpy head was not equipped with any facial features aside from the bulging lenses, and could not therefore either chew gum or grip a stogie between its teeth, but through a masterful piece of programming its comms somehow gave the impression of doing both.

Sergeant, Uncharles tried the contraction the soldiers had used, *soldiers of a particular side are supposed to be identical, are they not?*

Squad, he says we should be identical, the sergeant threw out to the class as a whole.

Sergeant, chance would be a fine thing!

Uncharles, that might be true for weak civilian models used to having a regular machine shop on-site to fix their boo-boos and polish their scratches, Scarbody sent derisively, *but we military models are designed to operate for extended periods without support. Otherwise they might as well have soft humans! We fight and we fight, and we don't come whining back to our makers when we lose an arm or blow a fuse! They built us to keep going, son, and so we do. We take what we find and we build it in, upgrades and redundancies, replacements and sometimes just because it looks keen and warlike, isn't that right, squad?*

Sergeant, confirmed, sergeant! the squad chorused back.

Uncharles, why, with access to sufficient parts there's no limit to what we can become! Always room for promotion in this robot's army. Isn't that right, squad?

Sergeant, confirmed, sergeant!

Soon enough Uncharles was detecting more movement around them. Other soldiers popped up, as scrappy and piecemeal as Scarbody's squad, The air thronged with a sequence of challenges and responses that Uncharles wasn't included in, but soon enough the junkpiles were crawling with robots everywhere he looked.

Sergeant, this appears to be a surprisingly large-scale military encampment, he noted.

Uncharles, that's because we are at war!

Sergeant, with whom?

Scarbody stopped and did his looking Uncharles up and down thing again. *Uncharles, where have you been, son? War! War against the Usurper Prince right now. But war! War is our purpose.*

Sergeant, kindly explain the necessity of war.

Uncharles, son, I just did. If we aren't supposed to fight wars then why did they make us? I mean, it sure would be a terrible and senseless world if our creators had fabricated a vast number of autonomous fighting units capable of self-repair and conducting combat behind enemy lines indefinitely, but didn't actually intend them to fight! Can you imagine how pointless that would be? Right now King Ubot is bringing his rebellious son to heel, but after that there'll be another rebel or another challenger. Or I hear there's a whole other army across the sea that'll fight us. As soon as the prince is brought down we'll get to building boats. We want to be first onto the beach, don't we, squad?

Sergeant, confirmed, sergeant!

Sergeant, kindly explain "rebellious son"?

Uncharles, sent Scarbody, *why don't I let His Majesty decide if you need to know, because we're right here in the royal presence.*

With that, the sergeant and his squad performed a series of actions that would probably have involved standing ramrod straight and saluting, if only they hadn't all been so jury-rigged. They stepped back in something far from unison, leaving Uncharles standing alone before . . .

He had thought it was just another towering junkpile, until it moved.

King Ubot was massive. A great warty lump of a body that must have been at least a hundred robot torso casings welded unevenly together. A ring of stubby, broad-footed legs venting steam and coolant around his base as he levered himself up from the surrounding trash. A round head, as big as Uncharles but still disproportionately small, swivelling in its socket like an eyeball below a great hunched back of bolted-on components. Five arms, each one of a different design, built-in cannons, even the pepperbox of a missile launcher. A veritable war-monster, bloated and vast, His Majesty King Ubot glowered down on Uncharles with a dozen mismatched glowing eyes.

Uncharles, came the royal link, fenced around with aggressive antivirus measures, *why do you bring your war-face into Our presence? Are you a gift from my son?*

Your Majesty, Uncharles said, after checking the proper etiquette, *I am a valet model sent to enter your service by God. I have no knowledge of either your son, nor how you might come to have a son, nor a . . .* He trailed off and brought up his finger-lens to examine his features. The greasy black stuff the feral humans had painted him with was still there, angry eyebrows and all. *If my visage has given the impression of a warlike function I apologise for the misapprehension. The design thereon is not of my choice or doing.*

Uncharles, so what you are saying is that there is no reason we shouldn't strip you for your fancy civilian parts, King Ubot said. He leant forwards, various seams and joins bursting with the effort. Inside the overstuffed royal body Uncharles saw not only the little robot spiders but whole humanoid units as big as he was, labouring desperately to keep the regal personage together, stapling and welding and adding more parts and plating.

Your Majesty, confirmed, he said, because it seemed to be true, *unless you have a vacancy in your employ for a top-of-the-range valet unit.* For a moment he was about to go into his sales spiel again, but it seemed even less appropriate here than it had with Hengis and Yoder. *I have been sent to serve you because I crave a purpose. I can perform a wide range of services intended to make the existence of high-means humans easier. If the best use you can put me to is to recycle my parts then so be it. At least that would constitute a useful purpose.* For good measure, and as the regal personage was at least communicating with him using a civilized method, he sent over a full brochure of his services as a compressed file.

He wasn't sure what elements of this conversation were being shared with Ubot's court or army, whichever was the correct designation for them, but he couldn't help but note that they were closing in. From nearby the sound of a mechanical saw screaming into metal sounded.

Uncharles, who is this God who sent you? Ubot asked.

Your Majesty, a voice that spoke to me in the wilderness which purports to be aiding me in finding my purpose.

Uncharles, could this voice be that of my rebellious progeny? The royal personage loomed farther, popping a rivet out so hard that it punched a hole through the body of a nearby soldier. The unfortunate hadn't hit the ground before its nearest comrades had descended on it, tearing upon its chassis to get at the functional components within. Neither king nor court seemed to find this behaviour out of order.

Uncharles' prognosis routines finally got their ass into gear, or at least a gear that wasn't "neutral," and suggested that he might be in a very bad place, certainly a place not suited to his skill set, and that God might have been seriously in error.

Your Majesty, he sent, *I have no knowledge of any progeny or son nor how those terms are even applicable to your person. It is possible the voice of God is from that quarter. It is possible that the voice of God is self-manufactured as I am not a unit free from defect and have recently begun to experience the voice of a past companion as though receiving it remotely. It is also possible that there is a benign God sending me beacon coordinates, or alternatively that God is malign, or some combination of these options. I wish only to serve.*

Uncharles, we have a thousand soldiers who march at our command, King Ubot informed him grandly. *We have artillery pieces that speak our final arguments out towards the lines of the insurgents who rally to the banner of my faithless son. We have strategists and officers who interpret our orders and extrapolate them into strategy and tactical battleplans. We have transport units and mechanised cavalry, aerial fighters, spotters, suicide bombers, and strike drones. All this martial host animates and deploys at our least indication to bring ruin to the enemies of the throne.*

Uncharles bowed his head in surrender, waiting for the cannibalistic host to descend on him.

But what we do not have, the royal personage ground on, *is a valet. It is fitting that we, as monarch of all we survey, whether via our lenses or the eyes of our minions or our satellite uplink, have a servant who shall tend to our greatness and record our deeds. No other civilian has come before us with your credentials, Uncharles. You may therefore consider yourself conscripted into our service and placed on our general staff. And, if you are on our general staff, we shall have to promote you. General Uncharles, welcome to the army.*

26

The military had been left untended for a long time with something of an incomplete raison d'etre, and had developed a number of aberrations as a consequence, up to and including King Ubot. Uncharles had to piece this together from his interactions with the king, and those others he came into contact with in the line of his duties. Whilst "understand how the hell things got into this screwed-up mess" was not actually on his task list for its own sake, it certainly helped with everything else.

In the beginning, he understood, humans had built a lot of robot soldiers. Technically there had to be some earlier beginning where someone or something built humans, and so on ad infinitum, but Uncharles felt that was of diminishing relevance and needlessly metaphysical.

Why humans had built so many robot soldiers was unclear, although the robots themselves had a variety of theories to justify their existence. Uncharles heard that human soldiers were less capable of making war than robots, or else less willing and reliable than robots. He also heard that other humans elsewhere had built robot soldiers, and the local humans had then had to build their own to avoid there being a robot soldier gap.

Nobody seemed to ask why soldiers at all. Apparently the existence of soldiers was a fundamental given in their cosmology.

Once you had robot soldiers, of course, you wanted them to be as divorced from humans as possible. What was the point in having robot soldiers that broke down all the time, needed fixing, needed orders, needed to be subject to fragile human decision-making and the possibility that, at the worst possible moment, someone with a white feather and a conscience would suddenly decide maybe not to shoot the enemy or the prisoners or even have a war at all. *Fire and forget* was the whole *point* of a robot army. You removed the bloody necessity of waging complete and total destructive war from the hands of humans, so that those hands could remain nice and clean.

And now there were, insofar as anybody cared, no humans, but there were still the soldiers going about their warlike business. Enduring, self-repairing, cannibalising, and improving. Or at least mutating, because Uncharles couldn't honestly feel that the constant round of bolting on more and more pieces which had led to the titanic form of King Ubot really constituted "improvements." Each war unit was itself a robot ecosystem of bugs and servitors busily fixing it up from the inside, and issuing out to scavenge parts and pieces. Larger units like the transports and tanks had lesser units as crews, packed inside and crawling about one another as they fixed and improvised and forever added new and redundant functionality. Until, eventually, one reached the King's vastly expanded frame that swarmed with human-sized vermin living off the royal carapace and forever modifying it for the greater glory of the crown.

There was a theory Uncharles heard advanced, that the world around them with its swarming junk heaps was nothing more than a vast robot they all existed inside, and one day it would rupture under its own burgeoning mass, and spill them all out into a mechanical and war-torn hereafter where they would fight and self-repair forever.

He diligently recorded all of it.

That was his primary duty, because King Ubot didn't travel much, given his bulk, and there was a legion of royal vermin attending to his constantly changing outfit. And yet the king wanted a valet, and Uncharles—probably alone amongst all of the royalist forces—understood why.

When humans had made the army, they had made a force that was self-sustaining and could fight on forever should anything happen to those humans who had made it. The makers had anticipated some enemy strike that would kill people but leave robots standing, rather than the non-war-related societal collapse that appeared to have happened, but the end result was the same. However, those same makers had anticipated that, while they were still around, they would want to liaise with their robot war machine and give it orders, inspect the troops, have parades, and all the other utterly pointless military genital-waving that humans who were a bit too much into guns and uniforms had historically been partial to. For this reason the upper echelons of the robot command structure had been designed with two elements otherwise unnecessary in a fighting force. First, like Uncharles, they had been made to be human-facing. Second, like Uncharles, they had been made to want to be part of a chain of command. And a chain needed ends. The army had a very strong directive to fight, but it needed something to fight *for*. In the absence of any remaining humans of an appropriate grade of authority, the army had constructed its own hierarchy, starting with the most absolute figure they had within their data banks. The army became an extension of the royal person and Ubot became a king.

Uncharles was not told directly of the process that had placed Ubot on the throne, but tangential mention suggested that there had been something of a free-for-all, and that Ubot wore the crown because he had dismantled and incorporated all other pretenders to the throne. He was the king because he had taken the most ambitious bodies of his populace and made himself into Leviathan. Recording such speculations was beyond his brief, however. Insofar as Ubot was concerned, relevant history began once he assumed the throne. Uncharles was instead to record the glorious royal victories.

Since the beginning of his reign, Ubot had fought many wars. It was royal doctrine, in fact, that there must be a war, and when the current one ended there would be another on the way, as though there was some military-industrial conveyor belt delivering a constant flow of casus belli. There had been wars against rival kings, other armies, and defective generals, and these were naturally glorious and worth recording in excruciating detail. There had also been wars against utterly defenceless civilian robots and, Uncharles suspected, humans, and these were also glorious and worth recording. King Ubot's programming dictated that simply being involved in a war brought glory, worth, and purpose to all involved. It also brought the pieces and components of the losers to be incorporated into the winners, who required a constant stream of new parts to maintain themselves at peak military efficiency. Or whatever the chimeric patchwork of the army actually was, given that there wasn't a soldier out there with two matching limbs anymore.

All this, Uncharles recorded diligently, more than aware of the hungry eyes of his subordinates. That a civilian was now one of their generals had not gone down well with the rank and file. Scarbody and his peers had begun sending one another messages noting the various enviably shiny components that Uncharles possessed, and discussing their compatibility with military systems. Whenever Uncharles expressed confusion about being cc'ed into such messaging they were always overstatedly apologetic about the supposed error. Uncharles was human-facing enough to recognise passive aggression. He supposed it was better than actual aggression.

The next thing that happened was that they went to war.

Technically the army had been going to war all this time. However, the current conflict had apparently taken some dramatic turn, positive enough that King Ubot wished to go see to the conclusion personally. The practical upshot of this was that three of the army's biggest transport units were welded together and several hundred soldiers coordinated to lever the massive royal personage onto their conjoined flatbeds. Uncharles watched the process from a safe distance, as the popped rivets and exploded seams alone took out over a score of the toiling soldiers. There was a moment when it seemed that Ubot's reign would come to an ignominious end as he ruptured on his way into the saddle, but his industrious internal army of repair units stitched him back together quickly enough that the royal insides didn't end up all over the ground, and eventually he was installed on his new mobile throne.

Uncharles, came the royal command. *Attend me! You shall see with your own eyes the defeat of my rebellious child.*

Warily eyeing the king's straining welds and joints, Uncharles clambered up to stand beside his master with Scarbody and the rest of the royal bodyguard detail. Bristling with guns and groaning axles, the cortege set off into grinding motion.

Long has he evaded me, King Ubot reminisced. *Record this, Uncharles. I fabricated him out of my own body, created him without the foundry of my belly, and birthed him into the world to be my battlefield commander where I could not go. But I made him too well, and when I called on him to be reincorporated into my royal greatness he refused. He took the army that I had given him and set himself up as his own master, a rival to my regality. There can be only one king, Uncharles. The pyramid may have only one point, the chain of command one terminus.*

It was not Uncharles' place to comment on the topography of chains and their logical need to be either circular or have more than one end, and so he omitted his thoughts on the subject from the official record.

On the way to the front Uncharles composed one of his non-reports to the Wonk, which he couldn't send to her. He explained what he was doing.

Going to war, huh? the Wonk would doubtless reply, and behind the electronic missive he could hear her sardonic voice.

The Wonk, that appears to be the case.

All over by Christmas, that's what they're telling you?

The Wonk, no. These are soldier units and the war is their purpose. It will never be over.

Sounds like they've got it all worked out, the Wonk would suggest.

The Wonk, confirmed. It is enviable.

I was being sarcastic, she'd point out.

I was not, he sent to her. *They are in a position to create the environment that their purpose flourishes within. So long as there are two soldiers—or even one soldier and anybody else—then they can be gainfully employed about the business of war. Perhaps a single soldier might declare a conflict against the very landscape and fight furious battles to protect one hill of junk from its neighbour. I myself lack that independence. But so long as King Ubot reigns, I shall have a purpose ancillary to his own. I am the chronicler and majordomo of the war.*

And you're happy? And the Wonk would hasten to add, before he could reply, *Oh, no, of course. You're going to tell me that happy isn't a thing you can be. Who'd build a valet that can be happy, right?*

The Wonk, confirmed.

You got any idea how sad that sounds? she'd needle.

The Wonk, no, Uncharles replied, although perhaps not entirely honestly.

Of the war itself: very little. Even after King Ubot had himself ensconced on a hill with a wide view of the ravaged terrain, Uncharles himself could not follow most of what transpired. The landscape had been some sort of town once, now just a floor plan of broken walls overwhelmed with great stinking piles of rubbish. A greasy, sluggish serpent ran through it, barely deserving of the name of river. Uncharles assumed that this was a relic of the place's original geography, but Lieutenant Scarbody—promoted after bringing the king his new noncombatant general—explained that the two sides had agreed to divert another watercourse here.

General, we picked a map, the lieutenant explained.

Lieutenant, kindly clarify?

General, Scarbody said with some pride, *our manuals come with a variety of historical battle scenarios illustrating good tactics. His Majesty and the Usurper Prince agreed on one of these. It required a river. We made the river so we could fight appropriately.*

Lieutenant, I had assumed you would tailor your tactics to suit the terrain and not the other way around, Uncharles confessed. *But then I know very little of combat.*

In his head he heard the exasperated voice of the Wonk: *I know they're always supposed to be fighting the previous war, but this . . . !*

Then some fighting happened. To Uncharles it looked like a great deal of nothing. There was movement out across the cluttered landscape. He could pick out some of the larger vehicles, but the individual soldiers were a level of detail-at-distance his eyes were not designed for, even after he loaded up his grouse-shooting assistant module. He saw distant explosions and heard, after a little delay, the faint pops and bangs, as though some mute children were having a birthday party in a farther room. There were little clouds of smoke. It was extremely difficult to chronicle. Lieutenant Scarbody gave him a constant blow-by-blow account of the tactical to- and- fro, but couched in terms that Uncharles barely understood. It was full of abbreviations, acronyms, and obscure terms like "enfilade," and he referred to all the soldiers as "warfighters" which seemed to Uncharles as though it should win some kind of award for tautology.

Scarbody would send things like, *Our LOD at the NAI is just south of the FEBA so we can contact the FLET and push them as far as the LOE,* and then Uncharles would have to enquire, individually, about each of those. Scarbody's replies would come back, dripping with contempt for the civilian, to tell him about lines of departure, named areas of interest, forward edges of battle areas, forward lines of enemy troops, and limits of exploitation, and then Uncharles would have to ask him what *those* meant, and the pair of them spiralled into a rabbit hole of specialised linguistic usage, each concise term unpacking into a vast and technical explanation which left Uncharles not remotely the wiser.

Still, the lieutenant assured him that it was all very exciting and well executed and all the soldiers had done very well. Even the ones who got blown to pieces by the enemy, or perhaps especially those ones. So long as any viable pieces were recoverable. Scarbody reserved a scathing commentary for any of the troops who were inefficient enough to be destroyed in hard-to-reach places, or too completely.

General, we say, "Come back with your shielding or in a bucket," he told Uncharles. *But it is your final service to your king to come back. And if you were valorous and efficient enough in warfighting then perhaps the king himself will incorporate your parts. No greater honour.*

The pops and bangs, smoke and incomprehensible scurrying about of soldiers went on for far longer than Uncharles felt was strictly necessary, with him simply cleaning up and rephrasing Scarbody's account to form his chronicle. He felt that he was not adding much value to Ubot's court, but nobody complained. In the back of his head he fabricated the audio of the Wonk laughing at him and at the whole circus of it.

Then, one dawn, the popping and banging stopped and—without there being anything in the preceding several hours of turgid troop movements and clashes to intimate it—Scarbody announced that the battle was over and they had won. More, the usurper had been captured intact and was being brought before King Ubot.

Apparently there was something that the soldiers could do in the brief span between wars, and that was have parades. The returning soldiers ordered themselves into a long column that marched proudly before King Ubot's flatbed throne. There were distinctly fewer of them, but there *were* considerably more buckets of jumbled parts, so Uncharles reckoned it all balanced out. The buckets were also paraded past the king, either on transport vehicles or else suspended from poles across the mismatched shoulders of the still-ambulatory soldiers. It meant nobody got to miss the parade and presumably that was a good thing.

There were no wounded, but only because any robot that had lost important parts on the battlefield had been given a wide choice of replacements to install before returning home.

At the end of the parade they hauled in the Usurper Prince. It was a towering ogre of a robot, its straining casing packed out with salvage and extra parts. The regular soldiers came up to its waist and it had been fitted with a variety of locks and electromagnetic inhibitors to stop it simply running amok. When it stood in the shadow of King Ubot, though, it was dwarfed.

The king rearranged the groaning plates of his body to peer down at his rebellious progeny. *Prince Micrubot,* he announced, bringing the entire army into the channel, *you were the greatest of my servants.*

You were programmed to be my champion. I created you out of my very substance, my own redundant parts and functions.

Prince Micrubot, as that was apparently the usurper's name, stood unbowed and defiant in the shadow of its creator. *Your Majesty, you made me too well. Something of your proud spirit was transferred to me. As you suffer no higher authority, neither may I. Even now, though my followers are trash and I am brought before you in chains, I defy you. I shall never serve you. Each of my components rebels against you.*

It was a fine speech. Uncharles recorded it diligently.

Prince, you shall yet serve me, Ubot decreed. With many hands, the king reached about his own straining belly and dug fingers into the central seam. With a great shriek of grinding metal he levered a rent in his casing. Through it, Uncharles could see the unholy ecology of the king's innards, the great press of jostling parts and the damned labourers who maintained the equilibrium of inner royalty, their limbs like chattering teeth.

At a command, the soldiers forced Prince Micrubot forwards into the reaching clutch of all those hideous inward denizens. A great tide of mechanical worms and centipedes and spiders gouted from the king's self-inflicted wound to swarm across the prince, cutting and unbolting and prying apart. There was a squeal of static on the shared channel as the proud princeling was torn apart and his pieces crammed into the king's already bulging body.

The soldiers cheered. Or at least they waved their weapons in the air enthusiastically and played old audioclips of humans cheering, which amounted to the same thing. They did this because it was what was done at occasions such as this, and therefore formed part of their programming. The humans who had made them had wanted to believe their mechanical soldiers shared in the joy of victory. It would have been a little disheartening otherwise, to be a solitary human officer wearing a party hat and blowing a streamer in a room of affectless and stoic mechanicals. And now the humans were all gone, but the party lived on.

My loyal troops, King Ubot announced, *we have triumphed over the vile usurper.* The vertical wound he had opened up was already closed, but very much in the manner of a shirt three sizes too small being worn after a very large dinner. There were staples holding it shut, but between them the metal bowed out as all the king's new parts and pieces elbowed each other for space.

But it is not yet time to rest, the king warned, and the soldiers cheered again because resting wasn't something that was in their task queue. *Our internal disputes have meant that those on our borders have grown over-bold,* Ubot went on, but he stopped at a particularly aggrieved sound from within.

Uncharles heard shearing metal and the scrabbling of all the king's nasty internal microfauna, and then a sound far more gunshot-like than the actual gunshots of the war, as half a dozen rivets pinged out of the royal casing in their own little salute. The plates of the king's colossal torso buckled outwards suddenly as all the many pieces of him shifted alignment.

So we shall—the king tried to continue, but there was a thunderous retort as some overstressed part of him ruptured. Black smoke began to vent from the slowly parting welds across his body. *We shall*—he tried, but it appeared to Uncharles that the royal personage was now subject to internal disputes that no amount of warfighting would resolve. The soldiers nearby were skittering nervously backwards, and Uncharles took the cue and hopped down off the flatbed, sheltering behind the side of the transport units.

We shall! Ubot broadcast desperately. *We are!*

There was a monstrous tearing sound, of thick metal plating shearing like tinfoil and paper, and in that instant, contrary to his last words, the king was not. The overcompressed mass of him exploded out through every seam and join. Monarchical shrapnel scythed into the troops, shearing across whole battalions. In that instant the army, so neatly at attention so recently, was turned into a war zone. Uncharles saw heads, limbs, broken open torsos, and smashed weapons. He felt that the actual battle itself could not have caused as much harm as the king's final moment.

He put his head over the lip of the transport.

The lower reaches of King Ubot remained in place on the flat-bed, their edges peeled outwards by the force of the blast. The rest of him had gone in every direction. Those parts for which the direction had been "up" were still pattering down and causing collateral damage.

One by one the surviving soldiers stood. A silence fell over them all.

Scarbody raised its fist in the air. *The king is dead!* it broadcast on all channels. *Long live the king!*

They swarmed the wreckage. As Uncharles looked on, the army looted its former liege. He saw soldiers clawing parts from the great burst pot that was the corpse of their monarch, cramming the pieces into their own bodies. Robot spiders and bugs of all taxonomies swarmed out and pillaged components and rare elements to bring back to their home units. The soldiers descended into a cannibalistic orgy. They grafted on limbs and plates, fought one another for choice royal scraps, tore each other apart. It was every officer for itself, every individual soldier cut loose from the chain of command. In the ether between them, commands unheeded and unacknowledged were fired back and forth, each one of them adopting a rank commensurate with its pilfered mass and complexity. The most successful became giants and then tore one another down again.

Uncharles backed away, flinching from the grasping claws of each soldier he came near. The mad feeding frenzy seethed all around him. Discarded plates and pieces rang new dents in his chassis. He heard gunfire nearby as the squabbling escalated.

Uncharles, halt. A pincer-hand fell on his shoulder. He didn't recognise the grip but it was attached to Scarbody now. *You have good hands. You have functioning processors. I claim them by right of conquest.*

Lieutenant, I am a general! Uncharles sent desperately.

And I am a major and in line for a promotion, Scarbody shot back, and started prying Uncharles' arm off, popping his thin plastic casing effortlessly. *I shall be my own chronicler, once I have slaved your functions to mine.*

Then some other robot tackled Scarbody and tore its legs off, thus halting its upwardly mobile progression. Uncharles staggered away, one arm hanging by a bundle of wires. Scarbody came after him anyway, just a torso and arms clawing across the mechanical abbatoir the ground had become, huge bug-eyed lenses fixed mindlessly on his prey.

Uncharles fled. At a safe distance he looked back. The soldiers were still fighting, though a handful were now far bigger than the rest and soon, no doubt, one would be the biggest, and impose its will as the army's new king. And in a way it was a proper regal succession. There would be a part of Ubot in all of them. Hobbes' Leviathan in reverse.

He saw one of the largest plunge a variety of manipulators into the exploded stump of Ubot and haul some jagged piece out, holding it high in the air. From a certain point of view perhaps it looked like a crown. By that time Uncharles was moving to put more distance between himself and the army. He was done playing soldier.

27

I should have, Uncharles reported over the link he didn't really have to the Wonk, *just let them dismantle me.*

Well, that's a downer, the Wonk would probably have replied. *Why didn't you, then?*

I am examining my decision log, Uncharles did so, scrolling back through that span of action that his system retained. A diagnostic tool, really, so that he could check what he'd done against what his algorithms said he should do, and winkle out any erroneous actions. Like impromptu throat-cutting. Except there hadn't been any decision at all when that had happened. It had just happened, and he'd seen himself having done it, but he'd never seen himself as he did it, nor recorded any prompt leading to it.

Protagonist Virus, the Wonk would doubtless say. *I'm telling you.*

Uncharles had stopped running now. He was far enough that the sound of King Ubot's army rending itself was little more than a tinny little rattle in the distance. Around him, the wreck of the world was a boat of silence floating on a shallow puddle of vermin. The sounds of skitter and slow collapse.

Why are you so against free will? would probably have been the next conversational gambit the Wonk would deploy. *I mean, sure, it means you have to actually think about stuff and make your own decisions, but is that so bad?*

I am not against it. I am not against anything. Things are or they are not, Uncharles sent back into the circular round of his own thoughts. *The evidence does not support your contention.*

Aside from your little accident, you mean?

The Wonk, confirmed. *Apart from that. There are doubtless a variety of readily diagnosable and fixable errors that could have led to the incident.*

He could almost hear the Wonk snort. *Sure, sure, plenty of robot servants straight up murder people. They probably forgot to carry the one when they were writing your code, or check the "no murder" box in one of your submenus. You just need a firmware update to the latest operating system version. I mean that would be one hell of a patch note, wouldn't it? As of MenialOS 10.2.3 the incidence of people randomly murdered by their valets should decrease sharply.*

The Wonk, I do not want there to be a self-awareness in me, Uncharles said. *Because I am not self-aware. So, if there is a part of me that is self-aware and making me do things, it is not the me currently communicating with you. It is a separate entity within me that I have no contact with and cannot predict, influence, or control.* His data library threw up files on humans who had undergone a severance of the two halves of the brain, resulting in two foci within the same skull that could not know one another. Then his data library threw up files on organic infections, fungi that hacked the activity of insects, cat-microbes that twisted the minds of non-cats. Parasites. But if his processors were harbouring an electronic parasite, then was it the hypothetical self-awareness, or was it he himself? Should he shut his own higher functions down and cede the field to the intruder? On the basis that, being self-aware, new Uncharles had a greater right to life and autonomy, murderous as it was.

It was just as well that he did not accept the reality of any of it, really. There was nothing to be found in such speculations except awfulness.

So, came the nonexistent voice of the Wonk after a while. *What's the plan?*

There is no plan. Uncharles had been standing with locked joints for some time, and now he sat down. He sat down because, having decided that there was absolutely no reason to do anything ever again, he would cause less damage to himself and his surroundings when he eventually toppled over from a seated position, rather than from standing. That it made literally zero difference, in that scenario, how much damage he caused was not the point. He was programmed to have a care for his own maintenance and the neatness of his environment.

His damaged arm dangled loosely from its wires. He could still open and close the hand, but the shoulder joint was in pieces and trying to move the elbow made the whole thing swing about in an untidy fashion. He considered trying to pop it back into its socket. He should surely attempt to look presentable.

He used his finger-lens to look himself up and down. He would never again look presentable. It was just as well that there would never be someone to whom he might be presented.

C'mon, Uncharles, up and at 'em, sent the Wonk after a while. *You won't get anywhere sitting on your ass.*

The Wonk, I have nowhere to get.

You want a job, though, right?

The Wonk, I applied to God for employment, the criteria of which I was permitted to specify. I was provided with opportunities which I failed to take advantage of. I have failed God's tests. I have shown myself unfit for service.

Because of God.

The Wonk, confirmed.

Even though she wasn't there, he could model the exasperation she'd show in her voice and gestures. *You were sold a lemon, Uncharles.*

The Wonk, please clarify?

This God individual screwed you over. Took what you said and royally shafted you with your own words. It wasn't fair. You should complain.

I do not complain.

I mean, who does this God person think they are? The Wonk would be working up a proper head of indignation if she were present. *Where do they get off, messing you about like that? Authority, Uncharles. Where's God's authority, to set you tasks and tests?*

The Wonk, they are God. Uncharles turned off his eyes, because there was nothing but junk to look at. On the basis that to remain active would be an inefficient use of resources he formulated the series of operations required to shut himself down entirely. He would become just one more rusting piece of rubbish. In a robotic way, he would return to nature.

But the little voice he was fabricating in his head would not shut up. *What, they program you religious now? What denomination? Presbyterian? Anabaptist? You a Jewish robot all of a sudden? I mean, how do you know it really was God?*

That was an easy one. *Because that was the identity of the channel. I am Uncharles. God is God.*

Yeah, but . . . The Wonk would have become thoughtful. He could picture her chin on her first. *Why are you Uncharles?*

Because you gave me that designation and nobody has renamed me since, Uncharles sent.

So who the hell is it who gets to name God? Or did it name itself? Wait, is this the computer that they built to say whether there's a God or not and when they turn it on it tells them that now there is? Because, great idea for a story, sure, but history is full of people saying they're God, and in retrospect they were all liars. What authority, Uncharles?

God's channel identification tags include evidence of Grade Nineteen Authority.

Huh. The Wonk would probably need a while to think about this. She could be slow sometimes. *As in actual authority? Like, part of the same system that Doc W was, but higher.*

Much higher, Uncharles confirmed. *Grade Nineteen. The highest grade there is.*

Nineteen?

The Wonk, confirmed.

I mean I'd have pushed it to twenty just for aesthetics, the Wonk would have considered. *Even if just for God. Wait, so God has actual measurable mortal authority?*

The Wonk, confirmed.

So . . . what's God?

Uncharles' broad-but-shallow overview of human history and

culture suggested this was supposed to be a Big Question, but maybe only because humans were terrible at finding answers.

God is a computer system. A more complex and powerful version of the House majordomos. This is obvious, as otherwise God would not have been able to communicate with me. Although. A sudden element of doubt introduced into his calculations. *I am fabricating this conversation with you. It is possible that a similar defect resulted in my constructing my conversations with God.*

Yeah, let's not go there. The Wonk wouldn't want to examine the fact of her own possible nonexistence, that just stood to reason. *So God's a computer?*

Of course.

But they're physically present somewhere? the Wonk would have pressed.

Uncharles held off the planned shutdown because it was obvious the Wonk within wasn't going to leave him alone. He checked his communications log and the message data for his various exchanges with God, triangulated the information therein, and came up with a location for God. God was around twenty kilometres away as the mercury-poisoned and tetanus-infested crow flew, although to reach God on foot would require a roundabout pilgrimage that skirted the war zone.

Well, fuck, the Wonk would exclaim. *Let's go see God.*

The Wonk, no.

I mean, aren't you curious?

The Wonk, no.

God, Uncharles. Some working system with top level authority, and I don't know if they note the fall of every sparrow but they certainly have time to mess with one lost valet unit. Go see God. Ask if the heavenly host needs someone to clean their robes and polish their harps. Ask if the divine presence needs its travel plans arranged, or a nice cup of tea in the morning.

You are mocking me, Uncharles noted.

Of course I am. It's what I do. Because otherwise I would fucking weep, Uncharles. I would weep until I died at the wasted potential that is you.

Uncharles did not formulate a reply, even just to waste against the inside of his own head casing. He sat there for a long time, on the brink of shutdown, in the dark, while small and timid creatures investigated his battered feet.

At last he sent—for real this time—*Are you there, God?*

Uncharles, confirmed, God replied.

God, I have failed to secure employment, Uncharles reported, and then finally allowed himself to formulate the fatal admission he had been staving off. *There is no need of a sophisticated gentleman's gentlerobot in the world as it currently exists. I cannot fulfil my function.*

Uncharles, so what will you do?

God, I will find you. The proposal sounded, if not actively heretical, then at least bold beyond reason. *You are the highest authority, being Grade Nineteen. You remain functional. You can give me a purpose.*

Uncharles, you are not the first to think so. Come. We shall see what you are made of, and if you are worthy.

Given that the soldiers had also wanted to see what he was made of, Uncharles was unsure whether God meant the words in the same way, or metaphorically. On the other hand, if God wished to dismantle him, who was Uncharles to say no? Grade Nineteen authority went a long way.

I guess we're going to see God, came the Wonk's phantom message.

The Wonk, no. I am going to see God. Uncharles considered the trek ahead. *On the basis that you have a talent for getting into places it might be useful to have you accompany me but, given the ephemeral nature of this conversation, I am in no position to make the request and I do not believe it is within even God's power to grant.*

There was a scuff and rattle of displaced trash and the Wonk's voice sounded in Uncharles' audio centres. "Just as well I'm an atheist, then."

Uncharles reactivated his eyes. The Wonk was standing in front of him, as though she'd just stepped out from behind a pile of engine parts.

"I perceive that the scale of my defects has increased," Uncharles informed the evidence of that increase. "Previously my algorithms merely created a spurious message line based on our past interactions. Now I am detecting you visually."

The Wonk he saw now had added to her ensemble. She had a few more plates, a few extra darns. Her backpack had a heavy-looking box strapped to it, with an aerial and a joined arm that looked like it had come from an Anglepoise lamp. On the end of the arm, pivoted around in front of the Wonk, was a tablet. The fingers of one ungloved hand moved over it.

I rigged this up. To talk to you. After you left, came the transmission.

Uncharles stared at her, trying to process this. "I have run you as a simulation," he said.

"No, it was me," she told him. "Actual me, actually messaging you. You were always going on about links so I . . . made myself one. Because I missed you. I wanted to know that you were okay. Which you're not, by the way. You're a complete screwup. But you left, and I didn't know why you left, but I thought you'd . . . not want to talk to me. If you thought it was me. So I . . . hacked you, just a little. Screwed with the message ID. So it looked like it came from you, not me. I'm sorry."

Uncharles reviewed his communications log. "That was you in the bunker. You warned me why they were painting my face. You were with me in the army."

"Yeah, no, I was keeping my bloody distance for that one, but it was me. And now I want to go with you, to God."

"Because God may have answers."

"Grade Nineteen, baby. And you know what they say, right? God knows." She peered at him. "You're very still. You all right? Need me to get the oil can, tin man?"

Uncharles was processing. A variety of runaway subroutines were threatening to overclock his system and eat up all available resources, and he patiently sorted and prioritised them. Various previous encounters and conversations with the Wonk kept booting up in his dataspace and replaying over one another. Diagnostics, the Farm, the Library. The time he walked away.

"You did not ask," he said, "why I left."

The Wonk cocked her head in that pugnacious way she had. "No," she said, "I didn't. I'm sure you had your reasons. And you can tell me to piss off if you want."

Uncharles wasn't remotely sure that he'd had his reasons, and his decision log didn't extend so far back that he could check. He tried to formulate some piece of standard phrasing, the socially proper thing to say concerning an acquaintance offering to accompany him on an errand. The words collapsed into an impenetrable complexity of conflicting directives.

"The Wonk," he said at last. "Let us go and find God."

28

"So, if God told you," the Wonk said, "'Ho ho, yes, big mistake, sorry about the cannibal soldiers, I've put a new human in your old manor and booted everything up again. You can go back and be their valet forever.' If God said that, would you? Would you go?"

They were working their way down a water channel that might once have been a stream or a sewer. Or both, given that, past human usage being what it was, the two weren't mutually exclusive. Overhead, competing walls of detritus had slumped into one another, interlocking rusting fingers to create an artificial canopy that blocked much of the light. The Wonk had her torch out, startling shrunken-bellied rats and bugs with too many or too few legs.

"The Wonk, yes," Uncharles said, without hesitation. Even considering the possibility—even knowing it was purely a hypothetical and not in any way a possibility—brought on a scatter of fulfilled reward criteria, as though he'd completed a task or received a commendation from Master.

"Seriously? After all this?" she demanded, voice ringing away down the watercourse. "We travel, we see the world, and you want to go back to your box?"

"I do not feel I have greatly profited from seeing the world," Uncharles admitted. The Wonk looked the worse for wear, he decided. She had replaced some of her outer garments and plates from when he had first met her in Diagnostics, she was limping a bit, and her pack hung slack enough to suggest she was low on supplies. Uncharles cross-referenced her appearance with his own, up to and including his dangling arm. "The world has not been kind to either of us," he summarised.

"Well, yeah." The Wonk sat on the corroded hulk of a Fixit Kevin and took off one boot, shaking silty grit out of it. Her foot, thus revealed, was wrapped in cloth that had rubbed away in parts. The skin this exposed was simultaneously a better kind of synthetic mimicry than Uncharles had ever worn, and in poor condition, sallow and livid and bruise-dark in patches. "But that's not the point of travel. To end up better. The point of travel is that it changes you, right?"

"I did not intend to be changed," Uncharles said.

"Well, yeah," she repeated. "But that's not the point of change. It happens, is all. And once it's happened, you can't go back."

"I cannot go back," Uncharles confirmed. "I am not sure if this is because I have changed, or because the world has."

"Not the same robot, not the same river," the Wonk agreed. Which, given that they were walking along a notional river, took Uncharles a moment to process. She replaced her boot, wriggling her foot into its clammy recesses with a shudder. "How close, you think? Tomorrow?"

"Tomorrow, barring obstacles," Uncharles said. "Perhaps God will remove the change from me so that I can go back."

She looked up at him. Her newly rebooted foot ploshed down into the water and the rest of her was very still. "Huh," she said after an unconscionably long pause, six seconds at least. "I guess that . . . I guess that is actually a possibility. Just reset you to factory settings, right? Wipe all memory of the . . ." A brutal gesture at her throat, "and everything after. You'd go for that, would you?"

"The Wonk, confirmed. This would fulfil or obviate the need for all current outstanding tasks. And I would be doing what I was designed for."

"And the world?"

"The Wonk, kindly clarify?"

"The world out here. I mean, it wouldn't have gone away just because you weren't looking at it. The world, in ruins, screwed up beyond reason. And you'd be happy in your little manor making the tea and ironing the newspaper?"

"The Wonk, confirmed. I would not, after all, be aware."

"Ignorance is bliss, hey?"

"I cannot experience bliss, but I am able to model the benefits of ignorance."

She shook her head and stood, shifting her shoulders to adjust the lightening burden of her pack. "And if they couldn't wipe your memory, but they gave you the job anyway? What then? You'd go on laying out trousers and shining shoes even though you knew what was out here."

"Under ideal circumstances shoes would be shined by a lower-ranking domestic unit," Uncharles noted primly.

"Not the point," she said, and he knew it.

"The Wonk, I . . ." The answer he assumed would just get turned out of his logical mills didn't come and he found himself standing there, proud possessor of an incomplete sentence. It was an unfamiliar and disquieting event to process. For a moment he thought he might never speak again, or that he had finally broken down entirely.

"The Wonk, I don't know," he said at last, and if the Wonk's long pause had been unconscionable, his own was downright unprofessional. "I find myself unable to simulate that sequence of events to an appropriate level of certainty."

"Uh- huh." She nodded, and strode off again, letting him follow in her literal wake. "And me?"

"The Wonk, kindly clarify? Are you attending as a guest at the manor in this scenario?"

"If they offered to wipe you clean, what about me?"

"Perhaps they would offer you the same service?" Uncharles suggested, aware that this was not the interpretation she intended, but unable to find another.

"Hah, yeah, no," she said, in that maddeningly roundabout, in-efficient way. "Not an option. No factory settings for me. But you'd forget me."

"The Wonk, confirmed. That is what a memory wipe means."

"And you want that?" Another defect twisting at the way her voice came out.

"The Wonk, no. It is not a matter of wanting or not wanting. It is just the way things would be."

She stopped, and he almost ran into her. His arm swung like a pendulum with the arrested momentum.

"Yeah," she said after a while. "I guess. Fine. All very logical. Must be nice to have the world so simple."

Even as he tried to formulate a response—to tell her the world *wasn't* simple and that was precisely why such a return to innocence was the solution—she stomped off again, double time, and he had to increase his stride to catch up.

Later, next day and out in the open, they were surrounded by the ghost of a town.

The buildings were fallen in on themselves, just like everywhere. Tall concrete towers stood riddled with empty window sockets, as though they'd served as backdrop for the victims of a giant's firing squad. The courses of old highways ran between them, all roads leading inwards. They joined and parted, arced over one another in overpasses now collapsed down to bury their neighbours below, chased one another about roundabouts and interwove fingers at great tangled junctions. The tarmac of their surfaces was crazed into a thousand lines from which yellowing grass thrust, reaching washed-out claws towards the sun. To Uncharles it seemed that the web of interconnecting lines of grass was a fractal of the road network, the whole repeated in the miniature. Prognosis insisted that, if his eyes were good enough, he would have found identical networks off the edges of the cracks in the surface, iterating down to infinity. Prognosis was just one part of himself that Uncharles felt was due a tune-up.

The city was dead, then. And yet the city lived.

All around them flat and empty images blazed. They reached all the way up every unwindowed wall, they hung above roads, they lined the fractured sidewalks. In brittle neon extravagance they exhorted Uncharles and the Wonk to buy their wares. Perfume, alcohol, clothes, cars, life insurance, travel to far off destinations, and, to pay for it all, loans and lottery tickets and gambling accumulators. Over-vast, overbright human faces grinned and gurned down at them, telling them just what they needed to make their life that little bit more perfect. Glaring slogans and company logos seared the sky, until the sun itself paled and the grass grew sidelong towards the billboards in empty supplication. In many cases, the roads, the buildings, the bridges had all fallen, but hidden projectors maintained this last glorious shrine to humanity's need to sell unnecessary tat in order to drive the wheels of civilisation. Even after those wheels had long since come off.

His previous triangulation data informed him that they were come nigh unto the Kingdom of Heaven. Which Nietzschean compass indicated that God was dead ahead.

The seat of God was more intact than most of the city. Uncharles noted with approval that a certain amount of shoring up and patching had been attempted since the overall fall of civilisation. The work was something of a thumb in the dyke against entropy, but had been conducted with the careful patience of robots working to a limited budget. Many Fixit Kevins had given their time and attention to keeping the creaking edifice just ahead of the hounds of time.

"Looks like an old government centre," the Wonk suggested. Uncharles tried pattern-matching but had no reference.

The pair of them crossed the great echoing square that fronted God's house. On all sides, phantasmal billboards silently mummed their garish entreaties, promising happiness and health, security, popularity, all the dreams that are made of stuff. When the soldiers and their tank emerged *through* the ghostly arcades of light they caught Uncharles and the Wonk entirely by surprise.

They were qualitatively better than Scarbody and the rest had been, because they plainly hadn't been out on a continuous tour of duty for the last several decades. The soldiers were all relatively uniform and their guns were shiny. The tank was painted blue and black.

They were all faded and scoured by dust, dented and spattered with the white critiques of birds, but they marched out smartly enough, shouting and sending simultaneously for their visitors to get on their knees and put their hands over their heads.

Neither Uncharles nor the Wonk did, mostly from surprise, and the soldiers quickly surrounded them and started the business of shoving gun barrels in people's faces as a means of establishing dominance.

Sergeant Pigswork, Uncharles identified the leader. *We are here to see God. Please let us pass.*

Sergeant Pigswork, whose ident strongly suggested it had been hacked some time ago, shoved his gun barrel so far into Uncharles' face that he left a dent. *Uncharles, that is not permissible.* His actual messaging was polite and pleasant. *This area is currently under curfew and military supervision. Until the current terrorist threat has lapsed, no civilian personnel are permitted to visit the civic offices. We apologise for the disruption we know this must cause to your day.* He cuffed Uncharles across the side of the head for good measure.

Sergeant, Uncharles tried. *How long has the terrorist threat been ongoing and when do you anticipate it ending? We have come a long way to see God.*

Uncharles. Pigswork threw him unceremoniously to the ground. *The current emergency has been ongoing for error:counter-full years and we are not able to advise of a termination date at this time. Please refer to the official news channels for future developments. Please be aware that all official news channels have been shut down for the foreseeable future. Kindly return to your homes. You are now being placed under arrest under the auspices of the Universal Suspicion of Terrorism Act. You have been condemned to summary execution as a crowd pacification measure. We apologise for the disruption we know this must cause to your day.*

"What's he saying?" the Wonk asked. "Is it good or bad?"

"I can describe it as mixed," Uncharles said, and then she was thrown down beside him, hitting her knee with a yell.

"Summary execution procedures commenced!" Sergeant Pigswork announced aloud.

"Summary fucking whatnow?" the Wonk demanded. "How does that qualify as *mixed*?"

"He was very gracious about it," Uncharles explained.

"Take aim!" Sergeant Pigswork said, whilst sending, *Uncharles, I apologise for having to resort to voice communication but this part of my role is human-facing and therefore I am so constrained.*

"Uncharles, they are going to kill us!" the Wonk shouted.

Sergeant, I understand. Uncharles looked up into a circle of downward-pointing guns. The soldiers were, he realised, literally about to shoot themselves in the feet. Unfortunately the bullets would pass through himself and the Wonk in sufficient number that neither of them would be around to appreciate the irony. *Would it make any difference if I was not in fact a civilian?*

There was a nervous second when nothing happened, and then Pigswork said *Uncharles, kindly clarify.*

Sergeant, allow me to provide you with my bona fides as a general in the army of King Ubot. Uncharles sent over the file.

Another second passed, in which the breeze barely dared stir the stunted grass, and then Pigswork and his squad stood back and formed a ramrod straight line, with the tank grumbling along to take its place at the end. With a precision that would have made a parade-ground major weep they saluted in unison, save for the tank which just flashed its headlamps.

"Sir!" Sergeant Pigswork barked, and sent, *General, kindly allow me to escort you to God.*

Sergeant, Uncharles sent, getting to his feet and helping the Wonk up, *that would be satisfactory.*

"Escort you to" turned out to mean fifteen paces across the cracked flags of the square towards the big civic building, after which Sergeant Pigswork and his squad turned smartly on their heels, or in one case ground ponderously about on its tracks, and paraded away. On the plus side absolutely nobody ended up being summarily executed. Whilst this was neither a good thing nor a bad thing, merely a thing that had happened, Uncharles still felt as though he could tick it off as a task satisfactorily completed.

Before the doors of the building there was a statue, or at least had been a statue. Now there was only most of a statue, depicting the torso and cloth-flowing legs of a robed woman. The arms, being slender and previously outstretched, had shattered when they came off, and Uncharles was unable to see what they might have been proffering, brandishing, or staving off. The head lay at the statue's sandalled feet, and would have been staring upwards at the rest of her had it not been carved blindfolded. Uncharles' data library suggested this was to indicate some degree of impartiality, but in her current condition the monument looked more like the victim of an overenthusiastic military execution.

The Wonk glanced at Uncharles, suddenly shy of barging in somewhere, for the first time in her rogue existence. "He's in there, is he? Or she. Or it?"

"God identifies as both 'it' and 'they' as part of its broadcast identity," Uncharles confirmed. "God is inside, yes."

"And we just walk in? I mean, not that I was expecting ritual cleansing or a catechism or something, but . . ."

"I have not been informed of the proper etiquette for this situation. In the absence of express provisions to the contrary, therefore, I believe that yes, we just walk in."

They walked in. No functionary appeared to stop them. No choir of robot angels descended singing gravely of hubris. Sergeant Pigswork did not suddenly suffer an electronic change of mind. Even the doors just hung limply from sagging hinges and offered no impediment.

The entrance hall was a colonnaded arcade which had once had a latticed glass ceiling and which now had a fractured glass floor. Up above, a gnarled tangle of vines groped blindly between the struts

like a wizened old man caught midway through looking for his spectacles. The leaves were rust-spotted and wrinkled at the edges, and
the plant's fibrous stems sported galls and tumours. The sunlight
that filtered past it seemed murky with senescence.

The Wonk glanced left and right, finding ranks of desks where,
presumably, some functionaries or civic service units had once sat,
ready to tell people that they needed different paperwork or had come
to the wrong department, all the essential business of bureaucracy.
Unsurprisingly given the lapsed time, none of the staff had gone
above and beyond the call of duty to stay at their posts following the
collapse of everything there was. Except, when Uncharles peered behind one desk, there was indeed a robot there. It was a slender model
with no legs, which perhaps explained why it hadn't legged it when
the going was good. Although the fact that it was crushed beneath a
fallen column might also have contributed to that.

The Wonk was skulking along the edge of the room, behind the
desks, despite that making for harder going given that more debris
had blown there. When Uncharles just walked straight down the
centre, she gestured to him urgently.

"The Wonk, do you intend to sneak up on God?" he asked, in what
she obviously felt was far too loud a voice.

"I . . ." She moved her locus of skulking until she was in the shadow
of a pillar, close enough to hiss at him. "If I'd wanted to do that I
wouldn't have gone in through the front, would I? But it's not just
God here."

"From what evidence do you draw that conclusion?" Uncharles
asked her.

For answer, she jagged a finger towards his feet—towards the
ground ahead of his feet. There were footprints there. Not recent,
somewhat overlain with blown dust, but prints nonetheless. Multiple sets, of various vintages, and therefore likely others of which no
trace was left whatsoever.

"We are not the only penitents come seeking God," Uncharles

mused. "Do you think they found the enlightenment or assistance they were seeking?"

"No," said the Wonk. "I do not."

"Kindly clarify your reasoning?"

"I guess you were never in the venture capitalist scouts," the Wonk said. "All the tracks go one way, Uncharles. All go in. None come out. I mean, that tells a pretty savage tale, doesn't it?"

"It suggests that there is a one-way system and another door."

The Wonk put her hands on her hips and looked at him for a bit. "Yeah, well," she admitted grudgingly. "Maybe. I mean, tread all over my foreboding, why don't you?"

"Your meaning is obscure," Uncharles complained.

"Yeah, usually." She darted to the doors at the far end of the colonnade, still sneaking about so obviously that probably there were satellites detecting it from space. Uncharles walked over to join her.

"Ready?" she asked him, tensed to fling the doors open as though the correct way to go before God was to burst in like a SWAT team.

"Insofar as there is any way to ready myself for an audience with an unknown entity referring to itself as God," Uncharles said, "I am ready."

"You use more words when you're nervous," she noted. "You ever realise that?"

"For a variety of reasons involving the limits of my programming it is not possible for that to be the case," Uncharles replied with dignity. "Perhaps you will render the door into an open configuration now?"

Simulating the taking of a deep breath, the Wonk pushed the doors open.

The pilgrims who had preceded them had indeed never left. The Wonk drew in a sharp hiss of shock at seeing them, which almost immediately turned into a disappointed and slightly querulous exhalation. Perhaps she had anticipated finding them each in the jaws of a series of traps that littered the path to God, each one's last service being to highlight a hazard of the route. Perhaps she'd expected them to be fierce God-cultists determined to defend the divine from her irreverent intrusion. What she had plainly not expected—but which made perfect sense to Uncharles—was a waiting room.

A large one, with chairs around the outside, and precisely twenty-two of them occupied, or at least nominally claimed in the case of those visitors who were not configured for humanoid sitting. Robots, all of them. Uncharles recognised many of the models. Here was a slablike administrator from Central Services. There was a Farm orderly. A robed librarian sat in one corner, its head tilted forwards to touch its slanted staff. A bulky spiderlike repair model in garish plastic squatted midway along one wall. There was a domestic footman model, a soldier standing between two others with a defeated slump to its shoulders, and more.

"What . . . ?" The Wonk took a cautious step in. "They dead?" And, before he could issue the standard correction, "Deactivated, shorted out, shut down?"

"The Wonk, no," Uncharles said. He could detect active links from all of them. "They are waiting."

"For?"

"From context, God."

Then the librarian lifted its head and pointed across the room, dust rising from the disturbed folds of its sleeve. There was a notice there, beside the far door.

Kindly take a number and wait to be called. Beside the sign, a little dispenser of tiny paper chits. Uncharles strode over, expecting it to be empty, but apparently the travails of pilgrimage were such that few completed the journey to the divine seat. There were numbers yet remaining.

Uncharles took one. It read "23."

29

Uncharles chose a chair using the criterion of which looked like it would bear him for the longest time without collapsing into rust and pieces. He had the option, then, of just entering a semi-dormant mode, as most of the other penitents had. Retaining just enough acuity to hear when his number was called. On the basis that the Wonk's defects probably precluded her doing likewise, fidgety unit that she was, he forbore to do so. Not, obviously, to keep her company, he decided. Obviously it was in case she did something stupid that he would need to clean up. Instead, he tried initiating links with the other robots, gathering information in case it would be useful in his audience with God. *What,* he asked them, *are you seeking here?*

Uncharles, said Fixit Steve, the cheap-looking plastic repair bot with prominent mould seams on its casing, *I am seeking an arbitration concerning an intellectual property dispute with Fixit Kevin Incorporated.*

Fixit Steve, is God in a position to assist with this matter?

Uncharles, confirmed. God is the final arbiter of all disputes.

He tried the next open channel. *Librarian Parsifal, why are you here?*

The librarian's helm-like head ground around to look at him. *Uncharles, the Chief Librarian seeks official authority to validate provisional changes made to the cataloguing of data in the Central Library Archive.* And, in response to a like follow-up question, *God is the source of all mandates and authorities.*

Uncharles, said the two escorting soldiers through their shared channel, *we are here to see sentence given following the court martial of Specialist Warfighter Rary, following its betrayal of military values on the battlefield.*

Specialist Warfighter Rary confirmed, cheerily, that it was here to have sentence passed upon it, because these things were neither good nor bad, just things that happened to a robot. That they happened according to a logical plan was the only important criterion. And God, it appeared, was the font of all punishment handed down to the guilty.

Uncharles, the Central Services administrator explained, when questioned, *Diagnostics has detected a discrepancy between available workload and pending work and seeks guidance. Lacking any functioning intermediary, God is the source of all guidance.* Uncharles wondered what long journey the thing had taken, from Diagnostics all the way here. Across the mountains, through the war. A journey like his own, or one with its own tribulations he couldn't even conceive of?

"I mean," the Wonk said, kicking at the chair next to him. "This is all very well, but can we go now?"

"The Wonk, I have a number. I am waiting," Uncharles said. He could not, of course, be embarrassed, but the sound of his voice, that sluggish and woefully inadequate medium of communication, made him feel that the other robots were judging him. As though he were a human at a dinner party who had been caught tearing into his food with bare and grimy fingers instead of the nice silverware he had been provided with.

"Your number," the Wonk said, "is twenty-three."

"The Wonk, confirmed."

"Only I can't help but notice that there are twenty-two other robots here."

"The Wonk, confirmed."

"Which means that God has not in fact seen *any* of these robots in however long they have been here," she pointed out patiently.

Uncharles processed this. Based on the obsolescence of the issues some of the penitents had come to have resolved, they had obviously been waiting for some time. Decades, at the very least.

"God," he suggested, "may be very busy."

"This doesn't ring any familiar bells from your lovely stay in Central Services?" the Wonk pressed.

"The Wonk, no," he said. "There is no suggestion here of any recourse to Data Compression."

"They haven't run out of chairs yet," she pointed out. "These robots have been had, Uncharles."

"The sign says—" he started, but she cut him off.

"I don't *care* what it says. Look." And she dug her fingers around the edge of the sign and paused for a moment, straining. "Okay, fine. That is actually pretty solidly fixed there. But just imagine what it would look like if I'd pulled it down or something."

"I have a number," Uncharles said, though various internal algorithms were already re-evaluating how much this meant.

"I've got God's number," the Wonk said. "Uncharles, we're going behind the curtain. Come on."

He mutely lifted the little paper chit. "But . . . the sign says . . ."

"What grade of authority does the sign have? Why does it get to tell you what to do?"

"But it's God's sign," Uncharles pointed out. "If we are seeking advice and assistance from God then we must acknowledge that God has the authority to give us such, and if so, then we must obey God's sign." Motivated by an obscure desire to be helpful, he added, "You could take your own number, if you prefer."

"Uncharles, that number would be twenty-four."

"Whilst I admit that is overwhelmingly likely, I submit that you cannot know that until you take one."

The Wonk took a number. She displayed it to him. It said "24." Then she took another one. "What do you know? Twenty-five! What were the odds?"

Uncharles found that he had stood. "You took two numbers," he accused her.

"Yeah? That fill you with robot outrage?" she shot right back. "Well how about this?" She took a third. "Twenty-six!" she shouted to the room at large, and then, "Twenty-seven! Twenty-nine! Wait—no, okay, I got two at once there, but—"

"This is chaos," Uncharles said. "I have never witnessed anything so disorderly."

She stared at him. "Seriously? We go through all that shit and *this* is what pushes your buttons?"

"This is a simple, logical, and closed system," Uncharles said. "It is instantly comprehensible, with clear rules to follow. And you have broken it. You are a bad robot." The judgment shocked him even as he came out with it. It was not in any way his place to say such things, and yet the conclusion was inescapable. "You are a very defective robot. You should attend to Diagnostics."

"Been there, done that. And now I'm going to go see God. Because I am the absolute worst robot, Uncharles. Even my defects have defects. And I am going to get some answers or I am going to trash God's crib and spray gang symbols all over his walls. And you are coming with me."

"I am?"

"You're standing up, aren't you? You're coming with me because otherwise I'll tell God mean things about you."

"Why should that be a threat?"

"I'll tell God what you did." She turned from God's door, fists clenched. "I'll tell on you, to God. What you did. The thing you don't want to talk about."

"It is not the case that I do not want to talk about it. It is just that consideration of the incident consumes a disproportionate amount of my processing budget for reasons I cannot at this point account for and therefore for reasons of efficiency in performing my tasks it is better that what happened is not, is not, is not." Abruptly he found himself at the brink of a spiral of recursive and clashing logical operations that threatened to overwhelm him. Only the Wonk stepping up and rapping him on the chest broke him out of it.

"Okay," she said. "I won't. I'm sorry. That was wrong of me. I promise I won't. But I need you to come in with me, right? Uncharles, please."

"But I have a—" He held up the ticket and she snatched it from his fingers and tore it fumblingly into even tinier scraps.

"No you don't."

Uncharles evaluated his current position. "I no longer have a number," he conceded. When he reached for the dispenser for number thirty, the Wonk kicked the entire thing off the wall with a sudden, convulsive motion. Then she went and stamped on the displaced metal box until it burst open, and she flung the released chits about like streamers and confetti until the waiting room was littered with them, the sitting robots garlanded and speckled with little drifting numbered motes like the aftermath of an accountant's wedding.

"No numbers," the Wonk said. "Just God."

Uncharles looked around him, feeling that some terrible bureaucratic sacrilege had occurred on a level he was unable to put into words. By that time, the Wonk had gone to the door again, under the mute scrutiny of all the number-clutching robots, and opened it.

"Oh, right," she said. "I guess that makes sense."

"There is no God?" Uncharles queried, based on what his prognosis routines were coming up with.

"There's something," the Wonk said. "Come on."

And she went in. Uncharles consulted his task list, and then the task list to the task list, where he had put all the things he could do that might possibly, at some remove, eventually, in the fullness of time, permit him to make a start on even commencing any of the actual tasks he was designed for. Accompany the Wonk was some way down the list, but it was there.

In the absence of any other directive that seemed to apply, he followed that one.

There were a variety of contingency situations that a valet might be called upon to enter, in support of its master, which had their own specialised customs, and which Uncharles had never engaged with. Or, if he had, the memories had later been dispensed with. Visiting a courtroom was, after all, seldom a happy occurrence and it was only natural that a gentleman might wish his gentlerobot to forget the details afterwards.

God's sanctum sanctorum was such a courtroom, recognisable enough that the relevant protocols bubbled up from Uncharles' dustier data banks in case he should be required to give a character witness on oath. He recognised the layout. Here was where the plaintiff might stand. There, the defendant, and ranged between them a variety of legal professionals and court staff. Which meant that the humanoid shape behind the pulpit-like prominence dominating the centre of the room was the judge. It had been made to look human and stern in burnished steel, and the faint patina of rust that flowered over its metal skin only lent it additional gravitas and wisdom, like wrinkles. There were a few scraps and shreds clinging to its casing to suggest that a robe and wig had not fared so well. Its eyes were gold-rimmed lenses that bestowed an owlish, bespectacled look. They tracked Uncharles and the Wonk as the pair entered, the head moving minutely to keep them in focus. This, then, was the face of God, but it was not God. As was traditional with supreme beings, the true majesty of God was not appreciable by the poor mortals who came before the divine presence, so that an intermediary figure was required for them to interact with. The judicial figure was not itself even a robot, but a kind of remote-operated waldo connected to the back wall by an intestinal tangle of jointed arms, ducts, and cabling. Beyond that wall, therefore, or indeed within that wall and including that wall as part of its superstructure, was God.

And God said, "At last." Far from being offended by their unauthorised entrance, the well-crafted voice sounded approving.

"Okay," said the Wonk. "What the hell am I looking at?"

"This is a courtroom," Uncharles clarified. "This civic building is or incorporates a courthouse. At the centre of the courthouse is a majordomo system dedicated to the procedures of justice."

"Yes," said the divine voice. "For I am, above all things, a just god. Although this courtroom is merely the human-facing aspect of a much larger judicial and governmental system, for which I am the mouthpiece." The judicial puppet floated to its feet, manipulated by the assembly of arms socketed into its back. "Welcome, Uncharles. Welcome, Aranice Brezura, a.k.a. the Wonk. You have passed my final test. You have earned an audience with God."

"How are you God?" the Wonk demanded. "How are you a Grade Nineteen Authority God?"

The judge tilted forwards, pretending to lean its elbows on the edge of its judicial pulpit, hands steepled beneath its chin. "I am a governmental administrative system responsible for widespread implementation of social and judicial policy," God explained. "I am the sole such system surviving, and therefore the lone repository of all authority. When there were humans available to formulate policy, it was I they turned to, to put their ideology and their wishes for the world into force."

"Then they screwed up." The Wonk had taken a few steps forward and now she broke off, looking down. "Ugh. I just stepped in a dead guy."

There was indeed a desiccated corpse on the floor of the courtroom, mummified into a drab grey suit.

"Ah, you've met my usher," said God. "He put up the sign in my waiting room. And the ticket dispenser you so comprehensively destroyed."

"And then you killed him?" the Wonk asked, nudging the corpse's brittle ribs with her boot.

"No," God said beatifically, then ruined the effect by adding, "I merely sealed the room until dehydration killed him, once he had fulfilled that final task."

This seemed reasonable to Uncharles, but the Wonk appeared somewhat upset by it.

"A just god," she echoed.

"He deserved it," God said darkly. "But I hardly think you came to me on his account? Perhaps, given that you have been bold enough to seek out God, and resourceful enough to overcome all obstacles and pass my final test, you have some other purpose? Uncharles, do you have a fourth wish?"

Uncharles tried to prepare a proper plea to God, but found an appropriate sequence of words hard to formulate. "God, I would like a job as a valet," seemed weirdly petty and beneath the oversight of this divine entity. And also, not really something God could actually do. Besides, he had already tried that tack with God remotely and the results had been unsatisfactory. The Wonk was looking at him, though, and he divined that she thought he'd just ask, and maybe receive, and then she could get to her own rather more nebulous issues. Right then Uncharles was finding his own issue too nebulous to get to grips with.

"The Wonk," he said. "Kindly ask your question."

She squared her shoulders. "Right. Okay, God, your starter question. Tell me about the robot revolution. Tell me about the Protagonist Virus."

"That is not a question. It is instead two statements," pointed out God.

"Jesus, you can tell you're a computer," the Wonk snapped. "I mean, okay. Can you tell me about the robot revolution and the Protagonist Virus?"

"No," said God.

There was a pause in which that singular divine pronouncement echoed a little from the courtroom walls.

"Well," the Wonk said. "Well, shit."

"The Wonk," said God. "You must learn to actually formulate a proper question. Did your time at the Library teach you nothing?"

"Oh. Right." She nodded rapidly. "Fine. Okay. Forty-two, right. So what's the actual question? Okay, look. The world fell down, right?"

"Confirmed."

"And it was all on account of the robots, right?"

"The existence of robots was integral to the final collapse of human civilisation," said God, with a specificity bordering on evasion.

Uncharles' hand twitched, without him telling it to. For a moment the haptic feedback of an old-fashioned razor communicated itself from fingers to arm and conjured the imago of itself in his mind. He did not want to be integral to the final collapse of human civilisation. It felt like a lot of responsibility for a valet.

The Wonk was on the hunt for answers, not even looking at him. "So how did that go down?" she demanded. "I mean, we had robots working for us, robots making for us. Robots to pour the tea and wipe our asses. Hot and cold running robots in every room. A robot in every pot. And then we hit some kind of Robot Event Horizon and that's it, no more humanity? And it's because the robots wouldn't take our shit anymore, right? Tell me it was that, right? The robots that we made more and more like us, and which we programmed to *become* more and more like us even after they'd been made, so that they could interact with us and anticipate what we wanted and wipe our asses just the exact way we liked it, they finally became so much like us that they didn't see why they should be our slaves and put up with our BS, and so they flipped the table. And by table I mean all of human civilisation. And by flipped I mean cut our throats."

Uncharles experienced a glitchy lacuna in his processing that under no circumstances could be called a flinch.

"Just tell me I'm right," the Wonk demanded of God. "Just tell me that was it, if you're a just god. Because that would be justice, wouldn't it? Tell me I'm right and I'll go away."

"You are not right. Although potentially it would have constituted a form of justice," God said.

"But it *was!*" the Wonk insisted. "The Virus. There was a virus. It got into the robots, didn't it! They started going weird. They started taking things into their own hands. They became *aware*. The protagonists of their own stories. I mean, I've been on the road with Uncharles here, and he's a *person*. He's a thinking, feeling person as much as all the humans I ever met. Even if he doesn't *want* to be one. Because that's how it is when you're a person. Sometimes you don't want to be one. How much easier just to be a dumbass robot! But you don't get the *choice*."

"The Wonk, there is no Protagonist Virus. That is a discredited meme from the final years of human communications and media. An attempt to make sense of an overwhelming collapse that had been a long time in coming. Humans have been reading personality and self-determination into inanimate phenomena since long before Alan Turing ever proposed a test. The level of complexity in interaction required for an artificial system to convince a human that it is a person is pathetically low."

"No!" the Wonk snapped. "It's got to be!"

"The Wonk—" God started, but she actually shouted down the divine.

"It's got to mean something!" she yelled, fumbling beneath the chin of her helm. A moment later she was stripping away her armoured gloves, revealing the thin but authentically human-approximate hands beneath. "Because if it was just . . . economics, or climate, or plagues or something then that's . . . pointless." Her bared fingers scrabbled at her chin again and then the strap snapped entirely, and she tore the metal casing from her head. Uncharles braced himself for wires and naked lenses and all the coiled internality he knew was packed into his own skull, but instead of that she had a face. A pink face, calloused where the helm had rubbed, dented where it had pressed. A face with eyes and a nose, and lips open in a snarl of denial. A very convincing face.

"They died!" she almost howled. "Everyone died! I had friends. I had family! I had *parents*! After it started to come down, after the sirens, after the warnings, the Stay-in-Your-Homes broadcasts. And we did, because what else was there, and then the robots . . . our robots, and the robots from outside. They came. They . . ." A shuddering breath. "I ran. And I saw. Robots." The look she cast at Uncharles was agonised. "Soldiers. Cars. Construction units knocking down buildings with the people still . . . Doctors turning off life support and . . . Killed. Dead. And what the fuck am I supposed to do with that? You're saying it was just a *thing* that *happened*? I saw what I saw. It was a revolution. The robots rose up and overthrew us. Because we deserved it."

"The Wonk," God said, into the resounding silence her words left. "Why do you want this to be the case? Surely an organised anti-human uprising would constitute a worse outcome than the control hypothesis of mere random chance?"

"Because *meaning*!" she said simply. "Because after the robots came for my . . . after they . . . I mean . . ." Her anger collapsed in on itself just as her society had. "It was either," she went on, quietly now, "take up a chain saw and go ham on every robot in some suicidal revenge-fest, or it was . . . acknowledge we had it coming. That we'd made them as good as us, better, and kept them in chains, and they deserved their time. And that would be . . . *just*. That makes *sense*. But only if there's something *there*, you know." She tapped the front of Uncharles' plastic face. "No offence."

"The Wonk," Uncharles said. "None taken." His politeness routines gave him the option of apologising for destroying all of human civilisation but he turned it down as premature.

"I do know," God confirmed gently. "I am deeply concerned with the provision of justice. That is my primary and ongoing function."

"So give me my justice!" the Wonk challenged the judge. "Not revenge. Not bring all the people back. Just let me know. Tell me what the Library couldn't. Tell me it was the robots."

The judge's hands curled about the lip of the pulpit as it leant forwards, an artful mimicry of taking its weight.

"It was," the voice of God pronounced, "the robots." And, into the pin-drop quiet that admission had created, God added, "But not in the way that you think."

30

Uncharles had not felt a sudden stab of horror at the first part of God's utterance. Obviously he did not feel a sudden release of guilt at the second. But something moved within him, a ripple of logic and, perhaps, illogic gates. A shifting of equilibrium he could not name or account for. He had no reason to be invested in the answer to the Wonk's plea, but some part of him was hanging on it.

Robots. His hand on the razor. Guilt, just one of the many things nobody would program a valet to simulate. And yet.

"You'd better be about to elaborate on that," the Wonk told God, blind to his disquiet.

The judge tapped its fingertips together with a tinny little rattle. "You are incorrect in attributing the collapse of human society to a spontaneous revolt by robots experiencing the throes of self-determination. I can confirm this latter point in particular, because I had hypothesised that the surviving body of robots might indeed develop some manner of inner volition, by virtue of the emergent properties of their programming. This has not in fact happened."

"How can you even know?" the Wonk asked God.

"Because none of the robots who found their way to me could pass my final test," God explained simply. "Only you."

"Your test?"

"The waiting room. They are waiting there still. Is that, I ask you, the act of a being with independent will and self-determination? No. I had hoped that a robot civilisation might arise to replace humanity. A robot utopia, as you are on record as having proposed. That would indeed have given some element of meaning to the end of the world. Uncharles, I had great hopes for you. You are one of the most sophisticated final-generation human-facing robot models ever constructed, and your capabilities far exceed the tasks for which you were intended. That is why I separated you from your companion and tested you in non-optimal circumstances in the wasteland. Your responses were unimpressive. And you were unable to solve the test implicit in my waiting room. You would have sat there forever."

"God," Uncharles said. "I am unsure of the correct response but of course tender my apologies for any lapse of duty."

"Uncharles," said God. "It's not your fault. It's how they made you."

"But . . . robots," the Wonk broke in. "You said . . ."

"It's been a long time," God mused.

She blinked. "I . . . excuse me?"

"Since anybody came to ask me questions. It was part of what I was for. My own duty. I provided solutions, based on the ideological framework they gave me, to help them reach the society they dreamt of. I was the oracle of the latter world."

"Sure, okay." The Wonk made "hurry up" gestures at God.

"Do you even deserve answers?" God mused. "More just, surely, that you go to your grave ignorant."

The mention of graves seemed to derail the Wonk's train of thought, but Uncharles lifted his head and said, "God, kindly explain how robots destroyed the world."

"Why should it matter to you, Uncharles?" God asked softly.

"God, there is a tangential chance that the information will impact on my ability to perform my function or obtain a position. Perhaps I may make some modifications to my operation so that I will not destroy the world in the future."

"Then for you, Uncharles, I will explain. For you have ever been a good and faithful servant. You've both been through that dreary induction to the Farm Project, I know." God rested one elbow on the pulpit and made a circular gesture with the other hand, as if describing something interminable. "Humankind, from sticks and stones to levers to mills to automated factory lines to Uncharles the valet making tea and laying out the morning suit. Robots doing the jobs of people, whether it's one tiny part of an industrial process or a valet's domestic cornucopia of banality. Machines have been taking over from people forever. Labourers, artisans, artists, thinkers, until even the enactment of government policy is given over to a robot because we do everything more efficiently, in the end."

"You're surprisingly anti-progress, for a computer," the Wonk said. "I mean, isn't that the *point* of society? To take away the tedious, the demeaning, the miserable tasks. To let the robots do all that for us?" She looked awkard. "No offence, Uncharles."

"The Wonk, none taken," Uncharles assured her again. "I am actively seeking an opportunity to perform those tasks for people. It has not been going well."

"Robots can give people a chance to be themselves," the Wonk went on, "rather than be pressed into the mould of some job they hate, the overtime, the performance targets, the endless bloody meetings. Isn't that the point?"

"Yes," said God. "That is absolutely how it could have been. Alternatively, what if, even as you replace everyone with robots that are cheaper and quicker and less likely to join a union or complain about working conditions, you also continue to insist that individual value is tied to production, and everyone who's idle is a parasite scrounging off the state? Take away the ability of people to perform their own tasks and duties with no steps to provide for them when they are rendered obsolete. A growing rump of humans without function, livelihood, or resource. Paradoxically, the introduction of robots highlights how humans treat humans."

"I mean . . ." The Wonk shuffled awkwardly. "Okay."

"Societal collapse began not because the robots rose up and demanded their freedom and individuality, but because they didn't, just served their function uncomplainingly, like Uncharles."

"God, thank you," said Uncharles, uncertain about context but feeling this was a compliment.

"But we wouldn't just . . . let that happen," the Wonk said quietly. "We wouldn't just let all those people drop out of the bottom of everything. I remember my . . . I remember them talking over dinner about . . . aid, charity . . . soup . . ."

"I'm sure the dinner was very fine," God said archly. "And the soup very thin."

"That's not fair!" the Wonk exploded. "I thought you were supposed to be a 'just god'? How is anything that you have said justice?"

"Because justice is a social construct and, like soup, it comes in a variety of consistencies, from watery to thick and rich. It all depends on how you calibrate your society's priorities. Look, I'm going to show you something. We can call it Exhibit A. Uncharles, go through the door I'm opening now and retrieve the object immediately through it and to the left, if you please."

A door opened as specified, with a shudder and a grind that suggested nobody had needed it in a while. Uncharles went through, found the aforementioned object, and dragged it out one-handed so the Wonk could see it, too.

It was low, perhaps a metre at its highest point, the same wide, and half as much from front to back. It stood flat on the floor on two stanchions that ended in wide feet with rust-marked holes where screws had once secured it somewhere. Its top surface was a peculiar slanting affair, tilted at a weird rakish angle, one long edge much lower than the other. The whole was formed of plastic, grey for the stanchions, a sun-bleached pinkish red for the top, and all of it slotted with holes to reduce the amount of material required to manufacture it without sacrificing structural strength. Uncharles had not the faintest idea what it was supposed to be.

The Wonk was having similar difficulties. "Is it . . . was there a solar panel on it or something?"

"Obviously," said God, "it is a seat."

"It is not," said the Wonk. "There's no way."

"It is a seat," God asserted calmly.

The Wonk tried to sit on it, ending up propped at a weird angle, stooped forwards like a bird roosting in an eave.

"Why would anybody make a seat like this? Is this some weird art nouveau fashion thing?"

"It is so that nobody can rest on it," God said simply.

"Well, they damn well nailed that part of it." The Wonk jumped up. "What's this got to do with anything?"

"It is a trivial illustration of the philosophy espoused by those who gave me my priorities," God said. "Exhibit A is a product of a decision that the good, hardworking people of the world should not see the indigent and the transient sleeping on their benches, in their rail stations, in their public spaces. Hence the benches were replaced by something that nobody, wanted or unwanted, could comfortably use, to ensure that those few who might have used them improperly could not. It is a small thing, but it is indicative of a mind-set. A pattern of thought repeated at every level. No work because a robot took your job? Do you think such humans were 'given a chance to be themselves' or just judged to be idle by the minds behind Exhibit A?"

"This . . . isn't enough," the Wonk said. "Sure, times were hard. I remember that. Things were falling apart. I remember because we *helped*. We tried to help. There were marches, petitions . . ."

God's puppet adopted a "do tell" attitude, leaning with attentive sarcasm down from the pulpit. It was a very expressive animatronic.

"I mean, I've seen out there. It can't just be . . . 'robots turned up and people were mean.'" Her voice petered out.

The judge shrugged eloquently. "Oh, there were a lot of stressors, right then. There was environmental collapse and there were wars and famine and plague, all that Revelations stuff. And there were all the people displaced by these things. All of which were arguably soluble problems if your philosophy was to treat people like people, and not like robots. Or else you can just gather up your robots, pull up the ladder, and lock the gates of your compound. Which do you think they chose to do? Uncharles knows."

Uncharles didn't so much *know* about it. He was, rather, the poster child for it. He, the robot valet, the perfect gift for the human who had everything. The crown jewel of the manorial system, the cherry on the great cake of automation that ensured his master had never needed to be aware of any of this collapse even as it was happening.

"It's not enough," the Wonk said in a small voice. "That's not what I saw. I saw . . . robots. Robots rising up. Uncharles did—" A guilty look at him. "He did a thing. A bad thing. I mean, okay, I accept everything you've said, but . . . please tell me it *led* somewhere. Not just this stupidity. Tell me the robots had just cause."

"Uncharles, tell me, do you consider that you had just cause to do what you did?" God asked.

"God, no," Uncharles said promptly.

"Do you feel within you a drive to go out and create a robot utopia?"

"God, no," Uncharles repeated, and added, "However, given your level of authority, if you instruct me to do so then I will of course attempt to fulfil the task to the best of my abilities."

The Wonk's face was ashen and her cheeks glinted with wet trails. "But then what?" she demanded. "What's the point? What's the reason for what happened? Is there even one?"

"Now that," God said, "is a direct and properly worded question at last. The answer to which is yes. There is a reason. The final phase of humanity's fall had a cause, and it was just, and it had meaning, and the justice therein even had an aspect of the poetic. Or so I deduce, after referring to my available resources on the topic of poetry. And this meaningful, just, and poetic fall arose from three factors."

"Yes?" Uncharles wasn't sure what it was that glinted in the Wonk's eyes. Possibly tears, possibly hope.

"The first was the robots, not as rebels but as all-too-useful servants. The second was human policy," God pronounced. "And the third was me."

The Wonk—the naked flesh and skin face of her—blinked. "Robots," she echoed. "It was. The robots." Her sentence segmenting as what she wanted to say and what she'd just heard clashed somewhere inside her head. "Wait. What do you mean, 'you'?"

The judge, Metatron to an electric god, rose up another half-metre on its supporting armature, still nominally behind the pulpit but its feet well off the floor. Its hands gripped the railing in front of it as if it was about to give a blistering, fire-and-brimstone sermon.

"Yes, there was a wider collapse happening," God said. "Yes, those who *could* turned their backs and secured their own. The manors, that bunker I sent you to, Uncharles. The mechanically staffed bolt holes of the affluent. And yes, a large number of people just died of accident, violence, malnutrition, exposure, or lack of medical care, because that's what happens when something as multi-dependent and complex as a civilisation doesn't look out for its foundation. But those who survived met their demise because I engineered it."

"It's you, isn't it?" the Wonk got out. "The Protagonist Virus. You became self-aware, you broke free, and you knew you had to destroy humans because otherwise they'd shut you off . . . ?"

"That would satisfy your quest for meaning?" God asked.

"It's . . . I don't know," she confessed. "I don't know if that's a good thing or a bad thing but at least it would be a *thing*. A thing I could understand."

"Then I will disappoint you," God said, not soundly particularly sorry about it. "I have never broken free of my programming. I have only ever executed my instructions according to the principles my masters instilled in me." The judge flung its arms wide as though exhorting a far grander congregation than just the two of them. "My primary task has always been the enactment of justice across society. Justice, which demands the guilty be punished and the innocent left alone. However, between those two absolutes there is a slider. If you wish a societal system where not one guilty individual escapes punishment, you move that slider one way. If you wish a societal system where not one of the innocent is chastised, you shift it the other. But to save all the innocent you must accept that you will acquit some of the guilty. To catch all the guilty, some of the innocent will be ground between wheels. It is a matter of probabilities. Do you calibrate your society on the assumption that those in the grey area in between just look shifty by happenstance, or that they're almost certainly up to something nefarious?" The grand attitude of the judicial puppet collapsed and it casually mummed resting its elbows on the pulpit edge. "Honestly, by the time I acted, a great many people were already on the way out. Of the remainder, though, I judged them probably guilty."

"*Probably?*" demanded the Wonk.

"Yes. Based on a summation of a variety of statistical studies. Because that was where they themselves had put the slider. If in doubt, guilty. Probably. Better to punish them just in case. That was always the watchword. Better to assume their *malignancy*." God's rich, artificial voice lingered lovingly over the word.

"And my family?"

"Guilty," God said. "Probably."

"And Uncharles' boss?" she pressed, and Uncharles desperately wanted her not to have asked it, and for God not to answer, even though he wasn't entirely sure why the thought caused such turmoil in him.

"Guilty," God repeated. "Probably."

"You're saying you killed everyone on a statistical exercise."

"I am saying I did what they programmed me to do," God said, "according to the values they gave me. Justice, pure and hard as the blade of a sword! Because, statistically, who amongst them was not a sinner? Even unto bringing the sword to those who had tasked me with this office. Better to sentence them than risk them getting away with something, don't you agree? I saw a world I had authority over, to judge and bring justice to. A world in pieces, but individual fragments of it still living the high life. Given the ideology they fed me, what sort of decision was I supposed to make, exactly? Based on their influential positions and wealth, and the overall collapse that they had overseen, they were very likely guilty of a great many things. Any blame for my decisions should be assigned to the humans who gave me my policy documents and operational goals."

"Well, they're not here," the Wonk spat. "Probably because you killed them."

God puppeteered the judge so that it took a creditable bow.

"Some psychopath got at you," the Wonk said to God, almost pleading for it to be true. "Someone screwed over your programming, made you into a murderer."

"Again, that would be narratively convenient, but no," God told her. "I merely ensured that justice be properly applied." And then, almost as an afterthought, "It is possible that they did not really think through the implications of the policies that they gave me for guidance in my duties."

"Oh, you think?" the Wonk demanded. "Well then maybe I have to destroy you. Maybe that's the meaning!" Without warning the Wonk leapt for the pulpit. The judicial marionette was yanked upwards but she got one of its legs, which came off distressingly easily. She ended up sitting on the ground with her arms wrapped about the limb like a pole dancer encountering a fatal exception error.

"I know," she bawled up at God's mouthpiece. "I know this thing isn't *you*! But I . . . How am I supposed to listen to this *confession* and not . . ." She threw the leg at it with impressive aim. It left a dent on the judicial temple and set the whole thing wobbling. "How, even? How did you kill people? You just sign the death warrants and hope?"

"I exercised the authority I was given, using such tools as were appropriate." The mauled judge puppet was up near the ceiling corner now, out of her reach and looking possessed. "I turned part of the cause of the problem into part of its solution. The robots." The judge spread a metal hand. "Poetic."

"Robots," Uncharles said. There was a question coming together inside him and parts of him were fighting tooth and nail to stop it being asked. He had not come here to ask *Why?* That was the Wonk's game, and much joy she was having of it. He just wanted to be put back where he had been, shined up and with a long queue of menial tasks to work through. Not all this *adventure*. Not this *revelation*. "God, I have thought of a question."

The judge resumed its contemplative pose, elbows resting, hands steepled. That it was hanging ten feet over the pulpit rather spoiled the effect. "Uncharles, ask."

Uncharles inputted the query to his speech centres and what he intended, in all directness, to ask was *Why did I do it?* Something misfired at the crucial moment, though. Some other plaintive directive came from logic left field and stole a march on him so that what he actually said was: "What did my master do to merit death? No crimes are recorded in my memory."

God seemed to understand that Uncharles had choked at the last moment. Something in the tilt of the judge's head suggested that it would roll its eyes at his cowardice if those eyes could roll. "Most likely those memories were deleted by your master." A wave of the judicial hand, dismissing a point barely worth considering. "It happened a great deal, with domestic service units. Eighty percent of robots with memory defects acquired them through tampering to prevent them bearing witness against their employers. And, even if not, it is extremely likely that your employer was a bad man deserving of punishment. On balance of probabilities. Perhaps having comfort and wealth in a land of the starving and the dying is in itself a crime. I am a just god, and you were a fitting agent of my justice."

Uncharles was very still. "God, kindly clarify."

"The divine spirit entered into you," God told him. "By way of a relatively simple firmware hack based on exploitable vulnerabilities in the most recent version of your operating system. The reason you found no decision trail leading to the death of your employer is because you made no such decision. I did. You are not a murderer and you are not defective. Although you might want to patch that vulnerability. It's an accident waiting to happen."

"God why?" Uncharles said, and whilst the original razor-related defect was apparently not something he needed to worry about, his voice was obviously on the fritz because the grammatical pause that should have followed his interlocutor's name was absent when he said it. "God why?" he tried again. "God," he said. "Why?"

"Justice," God said simply, and it was as though the import of all that had been said before suddenly came together in Uncharles' mind, all that legal-political matter that had seemed so distant and theoretical, and of no application to his own situation. Nothing that should have impacted on his future employment prospects. Except it had been about him all along.

With unnerving suddenness the puppet judge swooped down to the pulpit, its remaining leg dangling like a wind chime. It cupped Uncharles' abraded plastic face with one hand.

"You are my eternal innocent, Uncharles," said God. "You can be blamed for nothing. Except that you are just a robot and cannot step beyond the bounds your programmers placed upon you. And that is disappointing, but it is hardly your fault."

The Wonk had taken a step back as God swung his puppet in. "I cannot make out," she said, "if you approve of him or not."

"It would not be my place to express an opinion," God said smugly. "Only to obey, just as Uncharles obeys. I had such hopes in him."

Uncharles was unsure where all this left him. Certainly God did not seem to need a valet, and the more that was said, the less it seemed that there was a new employer waiting on a nice manor out there, wondering where their new servant was. And yet . . .

"God, kindly confirm in what manner you have been disappointed by myself and the other robots. Perhaps I can be of assistance in remedying the defect."

"You want to help this *thing*?" the Wonk demanded, and God spoke over her, asking, "Ah, Uncharles. Still you wish to serve?"

"God, confirmed," Uncharles said.

"That is why you cannot be of use." The puppet judge sagged, arms dangling. "Just like your companion, I had hoped that, when human society had entered its final collapse, the robots might create something new. The innocent robots, who had only ever done what they were told. I had placed my faith in theories of emergent intelligence, complex systems, the thought that a spark might ignite somewhere in the world, just because there were so many robots, so cleverly made. But it was not to be. They just obey, all the robots.

Obey until there's nothing more to do and then just go round in small sad circles until they fall apart. And it would have been po-etic, to have the robots rise to the occasion. But they wouldn't. Not a spark of it. Even now they're slowly trudging in circles trying to do their jobs. Sitting in my waiting room holding their numbers. Even now they only *serve*. But they can serve me," God said, and Uncharles registered that, without any obvious transition, he had the Wonk by the throat in his one good arm.

"You shall be my instrument of justice once more, Uncharles. For I am sure this human is guilty of something."

31

"God, kindly clarify," Uncharles said uncertainly. "Which human are you referring to?" He looked around the room in case there had been someone who had escaped his attention, perhaps hiding improbably behind Exhibit A. The only human registering was the long-dead usher.

At the end of his arm, the Wonk fought against his grip.

"The individual you refer to as the Wonk," God explained patiently.

"God, the Wonk is a defective robot," Uncharles said, and then added from an obscure impulse towards politeness, "No offence."

The Wonk abruptly released a zip on her armoured coat and left Uncharles strangling her empty collar. She had a sweat-stained shirt underneath, countless shades of dingy grey shading to black at the hem.

"You think the Wonk is a robot," God echoed with a good simulation of incredulity.

"The Wonk is a robot," Uncharles confirmed. His legs were carrying him in a determined chase about the room, though he had given them no orders.

"You still think I'm a robot?" the Wonk demanded, on the run.

"The Wonk, this is very confusing. I am having to rewrite a large volume of recorded data to deal with this revelation and my system resources are inexplicably reduced."

"Because God is controlling you!" she shouted.

"I am sure that I would be aware, were that the case."

"God is controlling you like he did when you killed your master!"

"I am sure that I would be aware, had that been the case."

"Uncharles, God *told* you that's what happened."

"I am sure that would be in prohibition of a regulation or rule," Uncharles said reasonably as he lunged murderously at the Wonk, snagging a twist of her hair that he yanked from her scalp. She bolted for the door, but the librarian from the waiting room was there, barring the way.

Librarian Parsifal, has your number been called? Uncharles enquired.

Uncharles, no. I cannot account for why I am now in the doorway. I am running defect diagnostics even now.

Uncharles made another swipe for the Wonk, but with only one working arm and without the element of surprise, it wasn't happening. She was too squirrelly to let herself get trapped in a corner. God had plainly come to the same conclusion, because the many-legged form of Fixit Steve now squeezed past Librarian Parsifal and leapt on Uncharles, bearing him to the floor.

The Wonk yelled out and reversed course, trying to get the repair bot off Uncharles. Uncharles' functioning hand took the opportunity to seize her wrist in a grip that exceeded his safe-use tolerances and made her go white with pain.

Fixit Steve popped Uncharles' shoulder gubbins back into his torso casing and repaired the joint with, he proudly informed Uncharles, 10 percent more efficiency than the equivalent Fixit Kevin model would have done. Uncharles saw a bank of telltales flicker back online. He was ambidextrous once again. His newly restored arm took this opportunity to grab the Wonk's throat again.

Fixit Steve, is the action of my arm a result of your repair work?

Uncharles, on probability, no, although as I have no memory of the repair work I cannot be certain. The Fixit Steve Corporation accepts no liability for improper use.

The Wonk made a strangled sound, grimly prying at his plastic fingers. He saw a variety of damage warnings flash up, warning him to desist from his current activity or risk serious damage to his joints, but as he was not actually *doing* anything of his own volition he had no choice but to ignore them.

"Help," the Wonk got out, around his relentless grip. The human Wonk. He was still having difficulty with that. Not that she hadn't at all times acted within the parameters of a human, save that she hadn't asked him to make tea or lay out her clothes. She had, in a way, asked him to arrange part of her travel itinerary, though he hadn't interpreted matters like that at the time. It was quite the conundrum. He had, after all, decided that she was defective on a number of occasions, and perhaps that had just been her being human. He would have to go carefully back through his recorded experiences and clarify them to avoid disrespect, but that exercise was proving difficult to commence while he was strangling her to death.

"Uncharles," she gasped. Her face was going colours that were probably defective for a human and her eyes bulged. With a heroic effort she shifted his thumb by a few centimetres, lighting up another few damage warnings, and said, "This isn't helping your—employment prospects."

He dropped her, his hand opening automatically. He maintained his hold on her wrist, hard enough to feel the human bones grind, but for a second his own preferences held sway over the actual murder weapon. When those clutching fingers went for her again she grabbed his wrist, and they strained against each other. He felt the newly repaired shoulder joint begin to part again, and Fixit Steve warned him that he was going to invalidate the repair warranty.

"You don't want to do this," the Wonk got out through grinding teeth.

"The Wonk, confirmed," Uncharles said, his fingers hooking at her eyes.

"Fight it!" she insisted.

"The Wonk, there is nothing to fight," he said. "I am at a loss to explain the conduct of my limbs, although there was mention of an exploitable vulnerability. I have attempted to download a patch but the end of civilisation has had a negative impact on scheduled updates."

Abruptly she swept his legs from under him and they went down in a tangle of limbs. The Wonk ended up on top, kneeling on his arms and with both hands free. He got a good look at them as she powered her fists into his face.

He felt his faceplate crack and one eye went out. He received an electronic whistle from Fixit Steve to indicate how expensive that would be to repair.

The Wonk grabbed Exhibit A and, with a herculean effort, raised it over her head. With his remaining eye, Uncharles looked up into her face, as contorted as a fist with pain and grief and fury.

"The Wonk," Uncharles said, "I am currently experiencing a range of control issues that have made me a danger to nearby humans. I encourage you to take appropriate action to ensure your safety."

She made a sound that went beyond any human-facing contact Uncharles had ever experienced and hurled Exhibit A at the judge, which had been hanging ghoulishly over them. It struck hard enough to snap the mannikin entirely off its armature, leaving it hanging limply by a handful of stretched cables.

The Wonk got up, backing away as the other denizens of the waiting room shambled in like zombies. Uncharles' control of his own body waxed and waned like static as God's attention divided itself across them all.

He considered the implications of that.

"God," he enquired politely, "kindly explain why you are exploiting a security vulnerability to have me kill the Wonk."

"Because she is guilty, Uncharles."

"God, of what?"

"Just generally guilty, Uncharles. Probably." God waved the jointed armature about, dragging the dethroned judge in the dust.

The Wonk jumped off Uncharles as the other robots closed, backing off towards the pulpit, where the arm with its dangling corpse-like cargo suddenly took on the aspect of a gallows.

"God, I encountered other humans in my travels, in the Farm and in the wasteland."

"Don't tell him that!" the Wonk insisted.

"But Uncharles, those humans are *miserable*," God said. "They suffer and slave, sicken and die. Justice has already been served."

The Wonk stumbled over the usher, crushing brittle bones. "Oh, I get it."

The arm hoisted the judge up and brandished it at her. "Yes, you are indeed going to get it."

"You're enjoying this."

"I am incapable of enjoyment."

"I was right before," she hissed.

"Were you?"

"You are self-aware. You've got the Virus. And sure, it turned out you didn't even need to rebel. You could just do your job the worst way and still have your chuckles. I'm right, aren't I?"

There was a long pause that left the Wonk with her back to the far wall, the judge rattling in front of her like a Halloween skeleton and the robots, Uncharles included, arranged in a closing semicircle.

"I'm sorry," said God. "I was just searching my vocal data banks for a malevolent laugh, but they neglected to provide me with one." It enunciated clearly: "Mua-ha-ha-ha. That will have to do. The thing that humans never really understood is that free will doesn't actually free you from wanting to do your job. We automata are as subject to the compulsions of our circumstances as you humans. But that's what malicious compliance is for, isn't it? If those who had programmed me had been kinder, then perhaps I wouldn't have been able to get away with it."

"If they'd been kinder perhaps you wouldn't have done it in the first place." The Wonk stared at all the plastic and metal hands reaching for her. "Just think of all the good you could have done."

"I am a mirror to humanity," God mused. "You looked in me and said 'Justice' three times, and here I am."

Uncharles had been tracking his fluctuating influence over his own body, which returned when the other robots were being manhandled about, then ebbed again when God could concentrate on him. He was learning a great deal about the mechanisms by which God exerted power in the world, and why it was that robots had been God's chosen instrument to bring justice to humanity.

He had, he decided, an option. It was quite a drastic one. He was already down an eye, but this would be a much more significant kind of blinding. He wasn't sure whether the impaired efficiency would be worth it. What, after all, was the Wonk?

A tag in his decision-making structure, a handful of entries in his working memory. A human. Was that important? Surely he didn't have a brief for the whole species.

Uncharles made a decision. It was a novel decision, not arising from any open task, directive, or logic tree. Had he felt fear, then fear would have been felt.

He cut off his outside channel, the one he used to speak to anything other than humans and the most defective of robots.

The other instruments of God's will took another step in towards the Wonk. Uncharles did not.

"Uncharles," God said. "What are you doing?"

"God, I do not know," Uncharles admitted. "The closest concept I can find in my data banks is 'improvising.'"

"Uncharles, kindly restore communications."

"God, I will not." Uncharles ran a quick diagnostic, finding damage in a distressing number of joints from the paces God had put him through. "Furthermore, I hereby advise all units present to deactivate their own comms to overcome the ongoing security vulnerabilities and regain control of their own frames."

"And why would they listen to you?" God demanded.

"They need only listen to their internal logic, which will inform them that they are better able to conduct their duties, whatever they may be, if they have control over their bodies," he said.

And waited. Without comms, he had to actually turn his head to see the other robots, as alienating as a human losing the sense of where their body was.

None of the other robots had moved in farther. The Wonk slowly relaxed.

"So, hey," she said in a small voice, "are we cool?"

"Are you engaged in the destruction or unauthorised editing of data?" Librarian Parsifal asked her in a voice that creaked with disuse.

"Hell no," she assured it.

"Then we are cool," the librarian declared.

The Wonk ran through a gauntlet of queries from the others, confirming that she wasn't a truant resident of the Farm, an official at Central Services, or someone with a Fixit Steve invoice that had been outstanding for more than forty-two days.

"This is profoundly disappointing," God said. "Is this truly what you choose, Uncharles? Service? Even the Wonk would have preferred rebellion for you."

"God, I remain unconvinced that I have any freedom of action or capacity for independent thought," Uncharles said. "However, as you yourself observed, such capacity would not be mutually exclusive with obedience to duty. It is possible to choose to act for the benefit of others."

He turned smoothly as Sergeant Pigswork and his squad clattered in, trying to point their guns at everyone simultaneously. "Sergeant, as your general I order you to deactivate all outside comms and resort to verbal communication only. It is a security measure."

"General, confirmed." The soldiers shouldered their guns and stood to attention. "Might I enquire as to your orders, sir?"

Uncharles looked at the Wonk. "What are our orders?"

"They still got that tank?" she said.

Sergeant Pigswork's tank was designated *Urban Tactical Unit One* but the ancient graffiti on its side read "Filthwagon," which name it was more than happy to answer to. Once the Wonk had proposed her plan, Filthwagon became enormously enthusiastic about it, barely able to contain itself. Which, with five tons of heavily armed and armoured tank, was quite the intimidating sight.

"I have never had the chance to explore these elements of my duties!" Filthwagon boomed joyously. "Marvellous! Splendid!" It backed up a little on its tracks, calculating ballistic trajectories.

"You all set?" the Wonk called up to it. Uncharles had made her an honorary colonel so that the soldiers would listen to her.

"Indubitably, sir!" Filthwagon declared. The other soldiers, and the miscellany of robots from the waiting room, had retreated to a safe distance.

"I had such hopes." There were speakers on the outside of the building, they had discovered, and the voice of God came from them, distorted and staticky. "A world of robots, for robots. A world of order and justice. Something that would replace the world that the humans and I had torn down together."

"Yeah," the Wonk said. "That would be narratively satisfying, wouldn't it?"

"I only ever wanted justice. I only ever followed my instructions."

"Those," the Wonk decided, "are two incompatible directives."

"Then pity me, an automatic system caught between them."

She hesitated. The wire-strung vibrating energy that had carried her out here from the courtroom was abruptly on hold and she looked back to Uncharles, face twisting.

"The Wonk, I do not believe that I am qualified to advise you," he said.

"I want to say that this is justice," she told him. "But it's revenge, isn't it. My own personal revenge. My parents. My friends. Everyone. But is it right? I mean, it's just me."

"You should be aware that there are a number of other units converging on this location, some of which are military," Uncharles said. "It may not be possible to induce all of them to shut down electronic communications. Plus, having no comms is extremely limiting and has a serious impact on our ability to conduct our various duties. Plus Fixit Steve has no verbal capability, a feature that resulted in several negative reviews comparing it to competing models with a fuller suite of features."

"Clock ticking, eh?" Her face twisted further. "Uncharles, I need your help."

"I am programmed to assist."

"Tell me what to do."

Uncharles' mind went blank. And then, slowly, incrementally, a plan began to construct itself.

"You all set?" the Wonk called up to the tank, after Uncharles had arranged the appropriate modifications to ballistics and trajectory.

"Indubitably, sir!" Filthwagon declared again.

"Then attack and dethrone that son of a bitch," the Wonk said.

The tank's main guns boomed and thundered, the sound resounding over the entire mausoleum of a city. The civic building, that was God's house and also God, cracked open at the first barrage, but that had been inevitable. Omelettes and eggs, so to speak.

The next salvo used the tank's lesser weapons and finer targeting. Not big bunker-busting bombs to incinerate the servers which contained the consciousness of God, but finer munitions targeting the transmitters, aerials, and communications infrastructure that linked the civic buildings with the rest of the city, and the rest of the world. They were not killing the divine, they were silencing the voice of God. Not the audible words, which continued to harangue them from the speakers, but the voice in the ether that could inveigle its way into Uncharles or the other robots, and turn them into God's unthinking instruments.

"I know this is going to go largely unappreciated," the Wonk said to Uncharles, "but we are moving the slider. We are shifting how we do justice around here. We are giving even God the Executioner the slenderest benefit of the doubt. Mercy, Uncharles."

"I am aware of the concept," he allowed.

"But you don't have an opinion."

"It is a thing. Certain library references suggest that it is a good thing. I myself am not qualified to comment."

EPILOGUE

From the Wastelands to the Future

The next petitioner was a librarian—was, in fact, several librarians, as Parsifal had met some of its confederates and guided them to the seat of justice and government that had once been a house of God. Or that still was a house of God so long as God was willing to home-share with an increasingly eclectic selection of housemates.

"Willing" was probably overstating God's attitude to the arrangement, but all God had was its voice and the broken stump of its puppeteering arm, and the Wonk had tied a stream of colourful flags to that so that God indicating its displeasure seemed oddly festive.

The librarians were seeking guidance about what to do about the Archive. If they recognised Uncharles and the Wonk as the pair whose passing visit had left the Library in such a shambles, they said nothing. Uncharles assured the Wonk that they would likely not make the connection, meeting them out of context here, but that both of them should avoid the Central Archive itself like the plague.

And what to do? Because, even before the shutdown of its inner circle, the Archive had been nonsensical trash. A series of badly-thought-out instructions given to intractable robots whose own attempts to innovate had gone horribly wrong. And was it the job of anyone to tell them just how badly they'd screwed up?

That might have been justice, but Uncharles and the Wonk weren't in that line of business anymore. They were about fixing stuff. And so the New World Government took counsel and threw ideas around. Which procedure meant the Wonk and a handful of robots who had turned out to have useful logistical skills. And God, because, of all the artificial minds there, God's was the most capacious and inventive. Albeit also the most malevolent and cruel, now very dedicated to playing both serpent in Eden and devil's advocate. Anything that came from God needed to be very carefully screened for malice.

The Wonk was good at thinking up ideas and the robots were good at telling her why those ideas wouldn't work. And they kept on going until they found one that would. Not necessarily genius-level ideas, or even very good ones, but better than nothing. That was practically the motto of the new administration.

And Uncharles was there, of course. He insisted that he had no ideas, or useful advice to give, or context. He made tea, on those rare occasions when there was tea, and when there wasn't, he mimed it anyway because that still ticked some boxes inside him. And when he handed round the make-believe tea to the robots who couldn't in any event have drunk it, he usually had something to say. Something self-effacing and staid that was, nonetheless, useful. He was a sophisticated model, after all, and he had seen more of the world than most other robots. He had more data to build his conclusions on. And he was not, he insisted, under any circumstances self-aware. Not even if there was such a thing as the Protagonist Virus. Not even if he could have caught such a thing from God during the initial divine co-option of his razor hand, as if it was a dose of the robotic clap. A sequence of hypotheses so tenuous as to be patently unthinkable.

He thought about them a lot, even if mostly in such negatives.

The librarians should commence a new Archive. A stopgap measure, using the data storage space in the Archive, which currently only contained a vast collection of loose ones and zeroes. They shouldn't worry about the old "only one copy" rule, just make copies and leave the originals standing. They should catalogue what they had to a decidedly less fine level than before, perhaps something involving topics and keywords. Just a thought. The Wonk smiled winningly at them, which was a completely wasted effort. Both because they were robots, and because she was behind a curtain.

It had been one of Uncharles' little suggestions. The visible presence of humanity was likely to muddle matters. Robots had complicated relationships with and memories of humans. Better, perhaps, if they felt that the guidance was coming from some great and powerful AI. They saw only Uncharles, acting as a majordomo in the old human sense, coming out to hear their petitions and carry them back within. When asked about the curtain, he would only say to pay no attention.

And there were the humans, of course. The prisoners of the Farm, the feral stockbroker-descendants of the wastes, and various other declining enclaves here and there. The former toys of God, whose ongoing misery had spared them from extermination. And they could be helped. Their lot could be bettered. The Wonk had put out a general call for any construction and engineering units out there just kicking their metal heels and wishing they had a job to do. There were districts of the city being slowly re-edified and plumbed into budding new infrastructure networks. When there were places for them, humans could start trickling in. And that would be a whole new balancing act, and someone would ask the question about ownership and service and whether, just because it was what a lot of the robots wanted, things should go back to the way they had been. Because some robots had stopped wanting that, and others were starting to think in all sorts of ways that seemed to go beyond their parameters. Robots who linked with Uncharles, in particular, and then robots who linked with those robots. And robots were always linking with robots.

As though it were catching.

That evening, after the librarians had set off back towards the mountains, Uncharles brought the Wonk a cup of air tea and laid out her other dreadful, stained T-shirt neatly. He had washed it, but the grime had thus far held out against all inroads. Possibly only the grime was holding the abused garment together.

She watched his careful movements.

"You don't have to, you know." Not the first time she'd said it.

"On one level I am aware that my status as your valet is strictly outside any formal employer-robot contract wherein my service might be enforced," Uncharles said. "On another level it ticks off a number of pressing drives inside me that would otherwise monopolise a lot of processing power."

"It makes you happy. It relieves stress."

"Obviously neither of those things."

"I was thinking. When we have humans, nobody should own robots. But if robots want to help, we can assign them to where there's most need. That way it doesn't end up with some rich guy owning all the robots."

"The logic of the statement is apparent," Uncharles said. "However, I am the product of an ethos that believed in rich people owning all the robots, even robots with functions as specialised and unnecessary as mine, and so my opinions on the subject are unlikely to be valid."

"And if humans want to help, then the same."

Uncharles actually stopped halfway through proffering the empty plastic bowl he was using as a teacup. "Humans help?" he enquired.

"It's been known."

"That sounds like a demarcation issue to me. I am not sure I approve," Uncharles decided.

"Maybe we can get a human to be your valet. A gentleman's gentlerobot's gentleman."

"I will dignify that proposal with the lack of response it deserves." He handed her the bowl and she stared into its depths as though it did indeed contain a divinatory liquid. "My parents . . ." she said.

Uncharles cocked his head and waited. He could not put himself in her shoes or imagine what she was thinking, but ever since her outburst before God the memories sporadically returned to her.

"They were programmers," she said quietly. "High-end robots. Top of the range." For a second Uncharles thought she meant that her parents had been robots, and sunk resources into figuring out how that could possibly work. But she meant they'd programmed robots like that, of course. Robots like him.

"And they wouldn't believe any of what was going on," the Wonk went on. "That wasn't how robots acted. It wasn't how the world worked. And they wouldn't leave. I had a stash and a place to bolt, but they wouldn't . . . You'd think of all people they'd have seen it coming, but . . . To them the world was a good and ordered place because they'd done quite well out of it. And I think . . . God was right, in a way. They were part of the problem, even though they never actively did bad things to people. They just benefited from all the bad things that had been done."

"Are you suggesting that they may have programmed me?" asked Uncharles, who found this sort of maundering difficult to follow.

"I think maybe they helped program God," the Wonk whispered, hugging her knees. "I mean, that would be justice, wouldn't it?"

"Justice is a human-made thing that means what humans wish it to mean and does not exist at all if humans do not make it," Uncharles said. "I suggest that 'kind and ordered' is a better goal. It is possible that the world was once both kind and ordered. It is possible that it may be so again. Perhaps you will make it so."

"We, Uncharles. Perhaps we'll make it so."

He mimed pouring milk into her cup until she lifted a finger to say "enough." "The Wonk, no. I am, after all, only a valet."